CAPITOL OFFENSE

Barbara Mikulski and
Marylouise Oates

A SIGNET BOOK

SIGNET
Published by the Penguin Group
Penguin Books USA Inc., 375 Hudson Street,
New York, New York 10014, U.S.A.
Penguin Books Ltd, 27 Wrights Lane,
London W8 5TZ, England
Penguin Books Australia Ltd, Ringwood,
Victoria, Australia
Penguin Books Canada Ltd, 10 Alcorn Avenue,
Toronto, Ontario, Canada M4V 3B2
Penguin Books (N.Z.) Ltd, 182–190 Wairau Road,
Auckland 10, New Zealand

Penguin Books Ltd, Registered Offices:
Harmondsworth, Middlesex, England

Published by Signet, an imprint of Dutton Signet,
a division of Penguin Books USA Inc.
Previously published in a Dutton edition.

First Signet Printing, August, 1997
10 9 8 7 6 5 4 3 2 1

 REGISTERED TRADEMARK—MARCA REGISTRADA

Printed in the United States of America

PUBLISHER'S NOTE
This is a work of fiction. Names, characters, places, and incidents either are
the product of the authors' imaginations or are used fictitiously, and any
resemblance to actual persons, living or dead, events, or locales is entirely
coincidental.

BOOKS ARE AVAILABLE AT QUANTITY DISCOUNTS WHEN USED TO PROMOTE
PRODUCTS OR SERVICES. FOR INFORMATION PLEASE WRITE TO PREMIUM
MARKETING DIVISION, PENGUIN BOOKS USA INC., 375 HUDSON STREET, NEW
YORK, NEW YORK 10014.

SPECIAL TO THE *INQUIRER*

HARRISBURG, PA—State Public Health Director Eleanor Gorzack will be named by Gov. William Hartag to the U.S. Senate, sources close to the governor said Sunday.

The governor was scheduled to announce his choice at a news conference Monday at noon in his office here. Gorzack will join him at the announcement.

Gorzack takes over the Senate seat occupied for more than 19 years by the late Sen. Michael Gannon. Gannon had completed only the first year of his third six-year term in the Senate when he died suddenly at a polka marathon two weeks ago. Although a veteran of state government service, Gorzack is a relative newcomer to politics, having never run for elective office.

Her reputation as a tough-spirited public official was established when Gorzack used her position as head of the state department of health to combat fraud in wide-ranging cases involving seniors and generic drugs. She has been honored by dozens of senior-citizen organizations and public-health groups for her work.

Pennsylvania state law mandates that the special election to fill out the remainder of Sen. Gannon's term be held at the next statewide election, in November.

In the past, law suits have been brought challenging the Pennsylvania appointment procedure, but its legality has been upheld at the appeals court level. One element that has been questioned in the courts is the absence of a primary election as the method to select the candidates for the Senate seat. Instead, at nominating conventions scheduled by each of the parties, state party chairs will choose their respective candidates for the November election.

"The real pros will slug it out between now and the nominating conventions. I don't think that Gorzack will be among the contenders," one party source said.

Another party insider was even more to the point.

"Norie's a great public official, but she's just keeping the Senate seat warm," a former state party chairman said, refusing to allow his name to be used in this story. "The heavy hitters will go in the back rooms, decide just which one of several viable candidates they all agree on, announce their selection at the party convention—and that's who will be the candidate in the special election."

Many political insiders believe that the nominee will be none other than Governor Hartag himself. Pennsylvania law limits the governorship to two terms, and Hartag is serving his second one.

Trained as a nurse, Gorzack received her B.S. from Mount St. Agnes College in Baltimore. She received an M.P.H. and a D.Sc. from the University of North Carolina, Chapel Hill. She was raised in the Oxford Circle section of Northeast Philadelphia.

Gorzack is the wife of an MIA, Marine pilot Capt. John Joseph Gorzack, reported missing in action over North Vietnam.

☆☆☆ **1** ☆☆☆

IF I START BY SAYING THAT I HAD A FUNNY FEELING THAT very first day on Capitol Hill, then I'll sound like my mother's friend Jeanne Callaghan, who, if pushed, would tell you she had a really bad dream the night before Pearl Harbor.

I'm not the kind of person who sees a black cloud inside every silver lining, and about the only hunches I get are what to order for lunch. My foreboding feeling that day certainly had nothing to do with my getting the chance to be a U.S. senator. This is not an offer that comes around very often, and even though it was my governor and not the citizens of my state who picked me, a senator is a senator is a senator.

Anyway, I wrote my squeamishness off to stage fright. The Capitol could make anyone jittery. Massive halls and expansive rooms stretched out before me, all extravagantly done up, lavishly filled with marble and paintings, bursting with history and a sense of the immediate and the important—and people everywhere. Real, live people—unlike the legislative halls of just about every other country, rank-and-file citizens are everywhere on Capitol Hill. There are metal detectors at all the doors, staffed by uniformed security people, but anybody, just anybody, can go through the Capitol, sit in the galleries of the House and the Senate, visit his lawmaker's office, and check on how his elected officials are running the country. It is, as the vice president told me that day, "the people's house."

No wonder I had stage fright. I didn't have much practice chatting it up with vice presidents, but here I was—giving it my best shot.

"The brocade is beautiful. The curtains. The whole Senate. The Senate thing. The Senate Chamber." I sounded like someone from the Home Shopping Network. "Terrific. It makes the state senate back home look like a coffee shop."

It *was* splendid, the Senate Chamber rising around us in gilded majesty, plush and expensive, the perfect movie set for the politicking and the speechmaking. Between C-Span and old Jimmy Stewart movies, it wasn't hard to conjure up the Senate's two-hundred-year history, legislative giants debating the big questions.

I ran my hand over the side of a well-worn desk. In the House of Representatives, the "lower chamber," there was no assigned seating and members of Congress sat wherever they could, or stood in front to use one of the microphones. But here, in the Senate, everyone got his or her own desk—mine being on the extreme left of the well, the down-in-front area where senators cast their votes.

"The chamber looks a lot bigger on TV," I continued. The veep just smiled at my chatter. Obviously, part of a vice president's job was putting up with people talking nonsense at him at various formal occasions. On my part, I'd spent a lengthy time in government service avoiding starchy occasions like the one we were now headed to, this one featuring me. The way Thanksgiving features the turkey.

Random thoughts bounced through my head as I searched for a conversational tack. I imagined telling the veep that *he* looked bigger on television. I thought of asking him what a vice president does. Or of waving my mother down from the balcony and letting her give him a little talk about what she heard on the radio last night.

When my dad died four years ago, my mother lost her best source of information and conversation. Since then, she'd given up sleeping and taken up round-the-clock radio monitoring. News, soaps, bizarre late-night talk shows, or drive-time call-in radio shows with psycho-chatting solutions—it was all equally credible grist for her opinions, beliefs, and constant chatter. She could tell the veep a thing or two—about marital relations, foreign affairs, the flat tax, or the beneficial use of megavitamins and how the medical establishment was keeping America in the dark.

The vice president, unaware of my deranged thoughts, was overcompensating for his lack of height with towering charm. With Yankee efficiency, he held my elbow and guided me down the steps to the Senate well. This was home turf to the veep, who had served several terms here until the nomination of a boyish presidential candidate raised the need for a more seasoned personage as the other half of the ticket. Many observers said that the victory of his ticket came as a complete surprise to the veep, but that he was serving out his term with practiced good nature.

Ancient rules held here. One limited the Senate floor to senators and staff on official business. The balcony above was crowded for the swearing-in with my family—my mother, my brother Joe and sister-in-law Suzie, my three nephews, and several dozen friends, all strung out behind the brass guardrail. Along with some staff and a couple of teenagers in blue blazers whom I took to be pages, they constituted the entire audience, except for the obligatory attendees in the press gallery.

The vice president whipped a Bible out of seemingly nowhere, then, apparently on cue, a handful of senior senators magically materialized, giving silent approval to the ceremony.

It wasn't complicated—a couple of sentences from the veep, a few words of reply, and, in a lot less time than I would have imagined, Eleanor Kurek Gorzack was a U.S. senator, the junior senator from the Commonwealth of Pennsylvania.

"I'm so very sorry that your husband is tragically

absent on this happy day, my dear," the vice president finished up, giving me a paternal pat on the arm. He had caught me off guard, and that's when Jack's absence always hurt the most.

"Me too. I wish he were here," I managed. I twisted the miniature Naval Academy ring I always wear on my right hand. For a while, after Jack first disappeared in Vietnam, I tried to break the habit of playing with the ring—until I decided that it made me feel closer to my husband.

Applause from my family in the balcony broke through my sadness. I looked up to see my mother waving a small American flag. I felt light-headed, like a teenager whose breath is taken away by an inexperienced first kiss—it was a wonderful feeling.

"Let's go. Let's move along."

Not such a wonderful feeling, hearing that nasty and nasal voice in my left ear. Milton Gant, administrative assistant to the late Senator Gannon, was a guy who carried his résumé on his sleeve. Yale Law School, J.D.; Colgate College, B.A.; a decade of experience on the Hill—and an attitude to match. Gant was Senator Gannon's unplanned legacy to me, an overly ripe preppy now apparently too ready to be my AA and take charge of my entire life.

"We're going to go down to the Old Senate Chamber, Senator Gorzack, and there we will reenact the swearing-in," Gant continued in his deep whisper. For reasons known only to Milton, he seemed compelled to overenunciate his words and speak only in simple sentences, like Mr. Rogers. "Your family can be with you and we will do some pictures."

"And cut and paste?" I mumbled. Gant missed my reply, too busy organizing the vice president to join us in the reenactment. The veep discreetly tucked his Bible under his arm and was ready for the road, his one quick gesture summing up years of ceremonial experience.

Milton shot a few scoutmaster-style signals at two young women in the balcony, one of whom stood and announced that "the Gorzack group" was moving on.

"I don't understand, Milton," I tried, following him up the aisle to the back of the chamber. "Why not take photos here? Why *pose* a swearing-in ceremony when I've just had a real, actual swearing-in?"

Barely swinging around to face me, Milton was clear and concise.

"It's Senate rules, *Senator* Gorzack," he said. "*We* just follow the rules. Only people doing business are allowed on the Senate floor. Senators and Senate employees when needed. No exceptions. But then, the people in Pennsylvania, your constituents, would like to see what they think your swearing-in looked like, so you and the veep and your mom will all stand together and we'll get some nice photos. With a Bible. Okay?"

"Are we going to say these photos were the actual swearing-in?" I asked, only half joking. "Sounds like a problem for truth in advertising to me."

"Senator, you need all the advertisements you can get."

I nodded. I didn't like Milton one damn bit.

Especially when he was right. Everybody loved the picture-taking. The veep's presence was augmented by the late arrival of a man whom Milton, back in my ear again, identified as Senator Garrett Baxter, chairman of the Appropriations Committee, chairman of the subcommittee on defense appropriations, and a member of the Armed Services Committee.

I knew that. Only a hermit or a person without cable TV would not know Garrett Baxter. He had a lot of style and an enormous puff of wavy white hair; he was smooth, like an aging movie star who has wound up on an afternoon soap. With a grandiose sweep of his hand, the senator welcomed everyone to Capitol Hill, then launched into a short, colorful history of the room where we stood.

"My God, Kathleen," I whispered to my dear friend Kathleen Burns, a former member of the Sisters of the Holy Child, once a community activist, and now the head of Philly's United Way. "Senator Baxter's really something. He's just what a senator should look like."

"Heck, Norie. Catch on," Kathleen countered. "*You're* what a senator should look and sound like."

I felt myself blush. Leave it to a former nun to manage such a verbal logistical feat—complimenting me while pointing out my political incorrectness.

Senator Baxter finished his little talk and came over to introduce himself. We did more pictures and were just wrapping up when a half-dozen Viet vets, all wearing fatigues, arrived with a lot of cheering and clapping.

"Hey, Norie," one said, sweeping me up in an un-senatorial-style bear hug. "Now we know we've got another real friend on the Hill."

I expected Baxter to back off from the noise and confusion. But instead he went down the ragged line and introduced himself, then listened politely as each gave his name in return. More pictures, these with the vets, along with Baxter, the veep, and an odd assortment of various people. It was pretty confusing, and Milton kept introducing me to various guests he'd invited.

Vietnam—and Jack—seemed to be a big part of the day. Baxter was asking each of the vets where he had served, and one pleasant-faced man in a pinstripe suit shook my hand, announcing, "I always like to be part of the crowd when it's guys I might have known in Nam." It was hurried and mostly happy, and my memories of the day are random mental snapshots of crowds of smiling faces.

Finally, Baxter and the veep made a formal goodbye and a jumble of congratulations and people's faces separated me from the vets and further conversation. One yelled to me that they'd all be by my office to visit, "real soon."

At the last minute, I remembered a truly important photo that had to be shot. I yelled at Kathleen across the crowd: "You're the community organizer. Get the Gang." That's what I call it when I get together with my three closest advisers—we're the Gang of Four. There's Kathleen, and Marco Solari, who runs the political arm of the unions in Pennsylvania, and George Taylor, who I always say is a great guy despite being a hundredth-generation WASP and a high-tech businessman to boot.

Years ago, when I got my first top-level job in public health, Kathleen, Marco, and George helped me figure out how to reach their individual constituencies on public health issues. The trio then evolved into my unofficial advisory committee, giving advice on everything from mounting a statewide infant-immunization campaign to dealing with a somewhat nasty editorial writer for the *Pittsburgh Press*. Each of us is pretty potent on his or her own, but combined we're like those kiddie superheroes, the Power Rangers—put us together and we zoom up to monster force.

"Well, she's here, Norie's really here," Kathleen announced as we lined up for a slightly rowdy shot. "You're expected to get the entire country in order— by nine tomorrow morning."

"I'm here. But now what do I do?"

"Just watch out for yourself," Marco said, putting his arm around my shoulders. "There are about two hundred people back in Pennsylvania who didn't get this appointment—and they're all gunning for you."

"Great, Marco. That warning should relax me." I hugged him. "But, seriously, you three are great. I couldn't ask for better friends."

"You'll need them here, dear," Kathleen said, her smile belying her words. "These Washington waters are filled with sharks."

☆☆☆ 2 ☆☆☆

"THE 'REGULAR' SENATORS ARE GOING TO EAT ME ALIVE."

"Give 'em heartburn. Anyway, you're not irregular. You're just a woman."

"Around here, that's fairly irregular."

I was headed down some major hallway on Capitol Hill along with Nancy Jackson, probably the most perfect assistant since Della Street signed on with Perry Mason—skilled as a secretary, well read, well groomed, and well intentioned. For years I had counted on her advice for everything from policy to prose to perking up my wardrobe and reminding me when my almost natural blond hair needed a little sun-streaking. Nancy's tall, with olive skin and dark brown hair that turns under. She loves to exercise and will probably have firm upper arms when she's seventy-two.

We were making our way through what I now knew was Statuary Hall—not hard to remember, since there are large statues of famous people, mostly famous men, each one representing a state in the union. Most have joined the ranks of the relatively obscure. It shows the danger of freezing fleeting fame in stone.

This massive room was the original chamber for the House of Representatives, as we heard over and over from the tour-group guides, when they weren't busy explaining the trick acoustics that allowed one clever member to overhear the opposition and plan brilliant counterattacks.

" 'Not irregular. Just a woman.' Well, that puts my entire career in perspective." I sounded cranky, almost ungrateful. Our just-finished tour of the Capitol by the deputy assistant to the architect of the Capitol was super-deluxe—but I couldn't figure out why we had taken it.

"I don't need to know about molding and statues," I vented. "I need to know where to go, and what to do when I get there. We should have gone through the mail. There were piles and piles of it on the reception desk when I left."

"There is some system for sorting and handling your mail," Nancy offered, "although I can't get the details. Milton keeps everything top-secret. He told me letters about your appointment are running eight to one. Isn't that great?"

"Great about the eight. But how about the one? Why does one in nine people not want me to be a senator?"

I realized I was twisting my ring. Mail should not be turning me into a tortured soul.

"One of the young staffers who handles mail, Amy Walker, told me that most of the negative stuff is about your being a woman."

"Why does this not come as a surprise? And I'm spending my time touring!"

"Senator—that's what I'm going to call you all the time, so you don't forget. Senator Gorzack! We should have remembered from high school. Nobody learns anything on a tour. What you really need is a tutor, a coach."

"Somebody, anybody, besides Milton. He's so uptight—it's like he went to law school twice."

"He's a pistol, isn't he?" Nancy agreed. "I hope not all the single men in Washington are as uptight as Milton."

"Arrogant." I hate men-bashing, but Milton's attitude seemed to call for it. "He makes me feel dumb. Even the tour made me feel dumb. Like when the guide said, 'Some people are so naive they believe that every senator and member has an office right in the Capitol.' Well, that's what I thought."

"Me too. Want to get a sandwich? I think I remember the way back to the Senate Coffee Shop."

I begged off. I had to hurry to make a meeting in the Russell Office Building, and then head to my office—the *one* office I had. The big guns—the leadership, the committee heads—wound up with several offices, including fancy suites in the Capitol itself. Each of them, along with every other member, also had an office with another fancy room for themselves and more rooms crammed with staff taking care of the state and working on issues—foreign affairs, agriculture, judiciary, education. Those were spread between three Senate Office Buildings—Russell, Dirksen, and Hart.

My office was in Hart, named for the late Michigan senator Philip Hart. My personal office was impressive—an oversized room with heavy-duty paneling looming over a severe mahogany desk. Outside, the rest of the "office" was a maze of cubicles, with staffers I didn't yet know plugging away. Pennsylvania was a big state, so I got a big staff—another fact I had learned this week.

I got on the elevator and noticed a sign warning that only senators would be permitted to ride during a call for a vote. I smiled and nodded at the young woman operator, who gave me a perfunctory nod back. I was tempted to introduce myself, but decided to avoid complications.

Getting off on the bottom floor, I walked a few yards to the escalator, then rode down to the overlit brilliance of the subway platform.

The Senate subway looks like a Disneyland ride. The cars to Hart and Dirksen resemble some futuristic monorail, the passengers enclosed in plastic and metal, while, for some reason unknown to me, the cars to Russell are open. All the cars carry about a dozen passengers, constantly shuttling back and forth, underground, between the Capitol and the office buildings.

A handful of people were waiting on the platform for Russell. One woman introduced herself, saying she had been born in Pennsylvania and she thought it was terrific for her home state to have a woman senator.

"Even if you're only appointed," she added.

"It's much more difficult that way, you know," I found myself saying, flashing back the best *appointed* smile I could marshal. I'd have to watch myself. I was getting touchy. Even the compliments made me feel like a second-class citizen. Make that a second-class senator. I hadn't expected a razzle-dazzle welcome, but, aside from a quick hello from a couple of colleagues, I had arrived as a senator—and nobody, except my mother and my constituents, seemed to know anything about it.

The Russell subway pulled in, and about half the waiting passengers got on. I sat by myself at the back of the car, and searched in my purse for the card with the room number of my meeting. The subway started.

It was at that precise moment that all hell broke loose.

A man shouted, "Norie, Norie!" pushing his way to the front of the platform. That image, that sound, stayed clear in my head. I had looked up just in time to catch a glimpse of him, a middle-aged guy in wrinkled fatigues, forcing his way through the remaining people on the platform, shouting my name.

The nightmare scene could be measured in seconds. It seemed eternal. Somewhere I shouted, "Let me out!"

"No! No!" The woman sitting in front of me

grabbed my jacket and tried to keep me in my seat. I shook her loose. The subway driver hit the brakes.

A powerful yet broken leap put the man in the air, his body a puppet with the strings snapped. I jumped up and turned, leaning toward him, reaching across a space that we could not close, across the emptiness that happens between life and death. People screamed.

The man in the fatigues drifted for an interminable moment, then crumpled, like a piece of paper, crashed onto the tracks beside the platform. My own body jerked in some mute sympathy for the man's shuddering descent.

"Let me out! I'm a nurse," I yelled. More hands reached out to block me, but I jumped down out of the car and onto the tracks. My ankle almost caught on one of the steel bars, but I managed to sprint the half-dozen yards back to the platform.

"I'm a nurse. Get out of the way," I said. "Stretch him out. Help me out," I shouted at a Capitol policeman who had jumped off the platform and was standing between me and the fallen man.

"The paramedics are coming," the policeman tried to explain.

"We can't wait. I'm going for it." I listened for the sound of breath, but heard nothing. I ripped off the man's worn army-issue shirt and started systematically pounding his chest.

"Stand back. Give her room." The cop cleared a circle around me and the fallen man. There was no response, but I kept up the steady pounding, trying to get that heartbeat back.

All I could see was the man, all I could hear was the silence that came from his body.

So I never noticed the TV crew, on its way to Dirksen, that came down the escalator and found this scene. I learned later that the cameraman started taping as soon as he caught sight of me bent over the man lying across the tracks. That was the shot that ran on the evening news: a woman identified as Senator Norie Gorzack trying to bring back the life of a man who then was identified only as a Vietnam veteran.

Everything in me focused on that poor crumpled man. Two minutes, three minutes, it must be four minutes, and still no response.

"Senator Gorzack." I felt a hand on my shoulder. "Senator Gorzack. Let me take over. I'm a paramedic." A fellow in a white uniform knelt down beside me and joined me in the rhythm until he could take over without a pause. I stayed in place, watching the paramedic work, hoping that maybe, somehow his hand would have a magic touch and that the crumpled man in his wrinkled fatigues would start to breathe again.

But both the paramedic and I knew it was hopeless. The man was dead.

One of the Capitol policemen helped me to my feet and started to boost me up on the platform. I shook off his help. Reaching down, I pried loose the paper from the dead man's hand, the scrap he had waved at me with such urgency.

I looked at the piece of paper. It was too sad, too pathetic.

"What is it, Senator?" the policeman asked after we had both clambered back up on the platform.

"Nothing. It's simply nothing." I handed the paper to him. He stared at it in disbelief, turning it over to see if it was anything more than it appeared.

I started toward the escalator. I needed to get out of the subway, out of the building, outside, and then walk back to my office, wherever it turned out to be.

"No," I said, more to myself than to the policeman. "It's nothing, just the story of my swearing-in from this morning's paper. Just a piece of newspaper. Not much to die for at all."

☆☆☆ **3** ☆☆☆

MILTON GANT WALKED JUST A LITTLE TOO FAST.

Not so fast that he left me totally behind. Just fast enough that I had to run a few steps every minute or so to keep up.

I was sure he did it on purpose. It drove me crazy.

But no way was I going to give my AA the satisfaction of asking him to slow down.

"Okay, Milton," I tried, skipping after him, aiming my voice toward the back of his head where his thinning hair drooped over his collar. "How do you think it went? How'd I do?"

We were clip-clopping down the steps of the Capitol, headed back to Hart. Stretched out before us, stark and threadbare after winter frosts, was the grassy area known as the Triangle, separating the Capitol from the trio of Senate Office Buildings. The cold air cut through my coat. Washington weather was deceitful, the bright sunlight on the pristine white buildings implying a warmth which was not there.

I was chilled, exhausted after a long night in which I could not stay asleep. I'd watched the TV news, seen the story and the tape of my attempt to revive the veteran. The scariest footage was the scene I couldn't stop running in my head—the man floating up off the platform, the man who now had a name, Jonathan Browning, known to his friends as Jake. Nancy had talked to someone over at Veterans Administration and been told they'd tracked down a sister in Colorado. She wasn't much help, since Jake had done little to keep up family connections.

"You did swell." Milton managed a slight smile over his shoulder. "You were featured on all the local news shows in Philly and two out of three in Pittsburgh. I don't know why, but we can't crack Channel 4."

"You don't understand. I'm not talking about that poor vet," I said. "I'm talking today. My vote!"

"Great!" Milton's cranky monotone voice was as icy as the air. He sounded like a hard-boiled TV detective. "You voted great. You shouted out your aye with a lot of spirit. Maybe even spunk. Hey, relax. You didn't do anything to embarrass either one of us."

"Milton." I stopped suddenly, waiting, forcing him to about-face and retrace several steps. "You *are* a bummer. It was a thrill to cast my first vote. I'm here, trying to do the right thing for the country, for my state. I thought about my vote, and I was excited to vote aye."

He had to stop to answer me.

"Look, Senator Gorzack, enough with the patriotism. The majority leader would shoot you in the knee if you voted no on a routine motion to proceed to an appropriations bill. Don't get too thrilled."

"Okay, I'm working on my cynicism. Anything else?" I started back down the steps at a good pace, hoping to build up a little lead.

"Yes, you head right back to the office." Milton turned and went back up the steps, tossing his words over his shoulder. "I forgot. I have to ask Charlie Green something. I'll be in the sergeant at arms' office."

Fine by me. I could find my way the one block to Hart without any difficulty, I thought.

But I'd gone only a short distance when someone started shouting at me. The sound of my own name rattled me, jerking me back to the dead man's shouts. This time, however, it was a woman in a soft, obviously designer suit, waving a microphone and followed by a camera crew. I never think of buying anything "taupe" until I see someone dressed like this reporter.

"Senator, hi. Diane Wong." She paused a moment so I could nod that I recognized her and, when I did, she continued, "CNN. Do you mind coming back up the steps, letting me ask you a couple of questions?"

I shrugged and tried for sophistication. It all seemed routine enough. I was a senator. It was Capitol Hill.

She was a reporter. Of course she would want to talk to me.

"I'd like to get your reaction, Senator Gorzack, as the wife of an MIA, to the proposed formation of a Select Committee on Missing in Action and Prisoners of War." Diane Wong had magically wiped away her dazzling smile and replaced it with a serious grimace.

No problem, I thought. Home free. This was the stuff I knew about—not that there's much factual information on finding MIAs, just a lot of detail on how they were lost and what's been done up until now.

"My reaction is delighted. Terrific. A committee working on the fate of the MIAs, a concerted effort to really answer the questions that still remain, after all these years—heck, that would be wonderful."

"And would you be interested in serving on such a committee?"

"You bet I would. After all, I've got real experience—more than any other senator—and I've got a personal stake in finally getting some answers on what happened."

Ms. Wong thanked me and walked away. I couldn't help admire her urbane style. Just a generation away, but the midthirties career women certainly seemed sure of themselves. I did feel a little antsy about the "select" committee title. That's the kind of bureaucratic stuff that Milton or the tour guide or someone should have filled me in on. But I knew that Milton's lock on procedural information was another way for him to run the show, another way to keep me off balance.

Milton seemed pretty off-balance himself when, a couple hours later, he burst into my private office.

"Well, you've killed your chances," he announced, slamming the heavy door behind him and, for once, not speaking in the dreaded monotone. "Not that your chances were very good. But, just maybe, we might have swung you a spot on the select committee. No way now. You ruined it."

"I don't understand, Milton. How did I ruin anything?"

"You don't get it, Senator," he said. "The Senate runs by a committee system. Seniority means everything. Here you go, announcing that you want this plum appointment. Why did you say you were interested?" Milton threw himself on the Senate-issue brown leather sofa like a cranky child. "You should have steered clear of that barracuda Wong."

"You didn't tell me. About Diane Wong. About committees. About plums. If the committee is about MIAs, it's about something I know about. And that's what I said to that reporter."

"The more you talk to the press, the less your colleagues will talk to you, especially the leader." Milton petulantly stuck his feet up on my coffee table. He was agitated, and sweat glistened of his forehead. "You remember him. The majority leader. Runs your side of the aisle in the Senate. Elected by your colleagues."

"Milton, I know about majority leaders." I started

out from behind my desk. His tone was getting to me, not to mention his feet on the table. "I know about government. I know about how things work. I just didn't think I had to clear everything—" An annoying buzzing sound cut me off.

"Hear that?" Milton stared at me. "That's means you've got seven and a half minutes left to cast your vote. Remember what we went over this morning."

I couldn't remember one fact about the arcane system of bells that sounded like buzzers and, along with a system of signal lights, warned senators of an impending vote or called for a quorum. But the vote did give me a momentary reprieve from Milton. I tried to sweep past his slouched form with as much dignity as I could locate. Right outside the door, Nancy waited, with a three-by-five index card.

"Your afternoon appointments and your schedule for tomorrow," she said, handing it to me.

"Follow your schedule. Follow the bells. You'll finally figure out what to do," Milton yelled after me.

That was too much. I came back through the doorway, pulled myself up to my full five feet four inches, and walked menacingly toward him—*my* senior staffer.

"I know what to do, Milton," I said, each word enunciated. "I might not know exactly how this place works, or what each bell means, but somebody who works for me—like you—can teach me that. As for the rest of this job, I'll follow my instincts. And if you want to work for me, you'll follow my lead. And one other thing. Keep your feet off my coffee table."

I turned and stomped out of the office, praying to myself as I marched down the hall that I had turned the right way and was indeed heading toward the elevators.

My apartment was on the seventh floor of a high-security building just six blocks from the Capitol. It was tiny—a small living room, a bedroom barely big enough for me and the twin beds, a bath, and, amazingly, an eat-in kitchen roomy enough for a table and chairs. Although there were apartments above my floor, the building had setbacks, so my kitchen even had the swank addition of a skylight. The staff members who had found the apartment assured me that it was safe and very handy, since right next door was Bice, a trendy but extremely senatorial hangout.

That's how little the staff knew about me.

I loved eating out, but the idea of night after night in restaurants—very much the habit in Harrisburg, and, obviously, in D.C.—just turned me off. My public health career had left me no time for true culinary creativity. Instead, I cooked simple dinners, heart-smart, although I was addicted to reading gourmet magazines and cookbooks, loving the intricacies of recipes that began, "Two days before the dinner . . ."

The phone was ringing just as I came in the door that night, lugging a bag with the makings of a pasta supper. I dropped the groceries on the floor and rushed to answer it.

"Hello?"

Nothing. I helloed a couple more times, and, after silence, there was the click of a hang-up.

I hate hang-ups. I especially hate the credit-card solicitors, the phony police and firemen fund-raisers, the people who insist on calling right at dinnertime—and who frequently hang up if a woman answers the phone. I had just read about a system the phone company had installed to deal with nuisance callers. I punched in "star 69"—the phone company's caller ID service—and waited while I heard a phone ringing.

A man at the other end answered.

"Hello," I started. An ear-piercing noise streamed out of the phone. It sounded like a fax, but if it was a fax, why did someone answer it first?

I unpacked my groceries and peeled and split a few cloves of garlic. It's a must to get the little green stringy thing out of the middle, or there will be a metallic taste. I put on water to boil, and along with the garlic, I began to sauté some broccoli. I was going to have to get myself to the Eastern Market on the other side of the Capitol if I was going to have fresh vegetables. Maybe I would invite Milton over for a little pasta. Maybe we needed a couple of glasses of red wine and some down time. I had to do something to make this working relationship work.

I set a place at the table, then went over to pick up the pile of newspapers I'd dumped on the sofa when I walked into the apartment.

That's when I noticed the envelope beside the front door. I wasn't sure if it had been there when I had come in a few minutes earlier.

It was a lovely eggshell-colored envelope, heavy, the kind people use for wedding invitations and birth announcements. "Mrs. John Gorzack" was written in calligraphy on the front, and I was excited about maybe getting invited to my first Washington event.

Inside, it was more calligraphy, but not so pretty.

I'd gotten hate mail before. I knew people in public office always did. When you had some kind of power over other people's lives, some of them, a very few of them, just couldn't stand it. Letters came to me, when I was in state government, warning me that God would strike me dead if I didn't stop doing one thing or another. Hate-mail writers think they've got sole rights to the God and hell-and-damnation franchise.

Yes, I'd gotten hate mail before. But it was nothing like this.

With beautiful circles and flourishes that streamed across the page, the writer laid out in vivid and grotesque detail what would happen to me if I ran for election in November. Women who "misbehaved," who took men's jobs, "would be taken to task." My "egg head" would be "popped off its stunted body." My husband wasn't around "to get me in line. Other men would do the job."

It wasn't pretty. It turned my stomach and it made me scared.

Not just the language, but the letter, here, in my apartment, my high-security, man-at-the-desk-and-door building. Someone had been right outside my door, in the hallway, perhaps when I walked from the elevator to my apartment. Tomorrow, I'd have to do something about this—talk to the building manager, get a new lock on my door.

But not tonight.

I wasn't hungry. I turned off the pots and pans and went into the bedroom. I put on a flannel nightgown and climbed under the covers.

4

THE PRIDE OF WYOMING, SENATOR PHIL FOX, THE Silver Wrangler, greeted me at the door of his private office, swinging it open like one of those blond models on the quiz shows, showing off the world's biggest refrigerators.

"I guess you never expected to see anything like this on Capitol Hill," he proclaimed with an expansive wave of his hand.

"Never. Not in my wildest dreams," I ventured, telling the total truth. A sight like Fox's office would be a surprise anywhere, anytime anyone came on it, a true original.

The room did look a little like a leftover set from a B western, or maybe the super-deluxe Paul Bunyan suite at an overpriced dude ranch. But it was more, so much more, more of everything.

There were cowboy prints and statues of Western wildlife—dozens of buffalo, cows, fragile desert animals poking their heads out from what had to be sagebrush. Footstools crafted to look like saddles sidled up to oversized sofas covered in Navajo blankets. Between the sofas rested what was obviously the *pièce de résistance*—a chair completely made up of the horns of departed animals.

One crisis got averted when Fox pointed me not to the horn chair but toward the sofa. I sat down, wriggled back against the pillows, and was starting to relax when my eye caught the decorative touch over the bookcases. There, hanging, glass eyes bulging, were at least a dozen heads of some animals that had once happily roamed Senator Fox's home state. I was tempted to ask which were the antelopes and which the deer, but I restrained myself.

"I keep my more official mementoes in my public office. The photographs with presidents, visiting chiefs of state. Constituents like to see that their senator has achieved a mark of international and national recognition. I'm just finishing up my second term in the Senate. I served in the House, five terms, before that."

He paused. He wanted me to acknowledge his importance.

"The people of Wyoming are lucky to have you here." I got right into it.

"No, no. I'm the lucky one. Get a chance to serve my country, my state, my senate. Lucky because I get to work with fine, upstanding, patriotic people. Like yourself."

I nodded. I've never been good at the political thing where one person tells another what great Americans they both are. I'd just like to assume that everybody in government cares about the U.S. of A. and start out from there.

"Now, Norie, I've been a little remiss in my duties as majority leader." Fox grinned, but the friendliness did not stretch from his smile to his eyes. And it was his eyes that scared me. Like he was looking through a rifle sight, and I was the deer caught in the headlights. Or maybe the antelope.

"I understand how busy you are, Senator." I had thought he'd be quicker at making time to meet a new senator from his party.

"Call me Phil, Norie. We're all working for the same goals, here on the majority side of the aisle. Like a trail team driving a herd down to Kansas City."

I resisted looking at a particularly sad painting of a steer. I promised myself never to eat beef again. I had a funny feeling I was heading toward the same fate as the steer.

"I'm ready to sign on. Ready to—" a minor pause and I went right along—"ready to follow your wagon and blaze a new trail." Not bad, since I had seen a lot of *Bonanza* and could probably have called him Pa if it were required.

"I like a team player, Norie."

"I'm that, Senator. Phil! I was a strong member of the governor's team back in Pennsylvania. I want to do my best to work hard here." I sounded sincere, even to my own ears. "So I guess I'm ready to find out about my committee assignments."

The majority leader picked up what looked like a jump rope and, with a quick flip of his wrists, turned it into a noose, which he began to twirl in little circles on the floor beside his horned chair. Fox, I decided, either had been born a hundred years too late or else had been gifted with an overabundance of testosterone.

"You seem real interested in committees," he finally offered.

"Interested in getting to work," I managed. Now both of us were talking like John Wayne.

"I saw you on TV talking about the Select Committee on MIAs. Watched you nominate yourself on a pretty tough job, a pretty big job for a new girl on the block. I mean, woman on the block."

Woman! Thank goodness. Fox saw himself as a feminist. I was safe.

"I know how tough the MIA issue is," I countered, still half distracted because the sofa was so deep that my feet were dangling above the floor. "I've been dealing with the MIA issue myself for twenty years. So I *would* like to be on the select committee. And I would also like to know what my committee assignments are."

"Now that's a lot of 'liking' for one afternoon. And I'd *like* to tell you. But I haven't got all the answers."

Of course he had all the answers. That much I'd learned in my few days on the Hill. As majority leader, Fox controlled everything from committee assignments to office assignments to deciding which senator's fund-raisers he would attend and thus "assign" them extra money. He could put me where he wanted me. I decided to hang tough.

"I talked to Governor Hartag and to some of my friends back in the state. They think Senator Gannon's committee assignments are just what Pennsylvania needs." I sounded businesslike—amazing, since I seemed to be losing my battle with the overstuffed sofa. "Armed Services, Labor and Human Resources, and Veterans' Affairs. These are great committees for my state."

"Not just for your state. For any state," Fox said, still twirling his rope. "They're great vote-getting, great fund-raising committees."

"I agree with your analysis, Phil, and my advisers—in business and labor—" I watched as that description caused Fox's head to snap up—"my advisers back in the state say it's also good for me to be connected with men's issues, male stuff, so I don't get typed as a bleeding heart." I'd repeated almost exactly what Marco, Mr. Labor, and George, Mr. Business, had told me.

"It's good for any senator to be tied into the issues that touch men's souls." The leader stood abruptly and headed for the door. He did not turn back.

Using an exotic hip-swinging motion, I extracted myself from the sofa and followed after him. He turned on his cowboy-boot heel and faced down at me. "Now if you were given those committees, just what special role do you see for yourself on Armed

Services or on Labor and Human Resources? And what subcommittee would you be interested in if you got on Veterans' Affairs?"

He got me. Bull's-eye. Shot down. Bang. One dead deer. Phil Fox had another trophy to add to his wall. The devil was in the details, and I was as innocent as Bambi. I'd broken one of my cardinal rules—know how it works and you can work it.

I knew nothing about individual subcommittees— what they were, which ones to ask for, or even, embarrassingly, what the actual committees specifically did. I was speeding down some bureaucratic interstate, and all I could see were off-ramps. My audience with the all-powerful Phil, my chance, was ended before I thought it had started.

"Don't rush to answer," Fox chortled, all Papa Bear charm again, pointedly holding open the door to the hall. "If you don't know exactly what you want, let me decide, go with what I think is best for you. What I'm targeting right now is Gov Affairs and Agriculture. Important committees. Frequently undervalued."

Undervalued? That I understood. It translated as committees with no power or prestige.

"Phil, I've got no idea what Gov Affairs is or does. I can guess about Agriculture. But I do know that the only big crop in Pennsylvania is unemployment." Score a small point for Bambi.

"Don't worry. I'm taking good care of you." He continued his herding operation, opening the door a little wider, glancing at his watch.

"Well, what about the select committee?" I stood in

the doorway, refusing to move until he answered. "That's where I've got special interests and experience."

"Impossible," Fox responded, after a momentary pause while he waved at a tour group passing outside. "There are senators with long experience in foreign affairs and in military affairs, and with seniority. Seniority counts."

"Senator Fox," I countered, "I've got seniority on the issue of MIAs, years and years and years. This is a select committee. Why can't you select me?"

"This is not the time nor the place for this discussion, Norie," Fox said, correctly, since he had herded me out in the hallway. "Let me lay out one problem. You've been an MIA wife for what, twenty years or more? It's *too* close to you. You might be too emotional to deal with this issue. Too hard on you. Simply out of the question."

5

TOURISTS PUSHED AND SHOVED AND I STOOD OUTSIDE Fox's office, feeling like a lost child in a mall. Damn. I did feel emotional and a little Alice-in-Wonderland. Did I go right or left, up or down?

"Lost?" A cultured voice floated by my left shoulder, Cheshire-cat style. "Felt that way a hundred times here, especially after dealing with Senator Foxy. That 'howdy' of his sure does say it all."

I turned, and walked directly into the enveloping arms of a very tall woman. The luxurious scent of what I thought was Chanel No. 5. If anyone is ever going to kidnap me, he could knock me out with a couple of whiffs.

As I shook my head to clear it, I looked up into the elegant, sculptured face of a steel-gray-haired woman who looked, as the magazine ads promised, great for whatever age she happened to be.

"Hilda! Senator Mendelssohn. Oh, it's you."

"It usually is. Drop the 'Senator.' 'Hilda' is perfect. So glad to run into you. You're settling in? So sorry I missed the swearing-in. But I've been out in Ohio. My state. Foxy made me the head of the DSCC. Do you know how much I travel? It's wreaking havoc with my schedule. Did you love the chair?"

I lost count of which questions I had answered and which remained suspended between us. The DSCC—I thought maybe that was the committee that raised campaign money for Senate Democrats. But before I had a chance to sort out the questions, Hilda was steering me down the corridor.

"The majority leader—and his chair—give new meaning to the word 'macho,' " I managed as she sped me along. "He's not happy that I want to be on the Select MIA Committee."

"He's not happy about much." She paused for a minute, seemingly intent on straightening the pin on the lapel of her simple black suit. I'd been looking for a suit like that since I was seventeen years old and *Glamour* magazine said the perfect little black suit brought instant sophistication.

I stood there, waiting, until Hilda finally nodded her head at some unasked question.

"Come on," she said. "I've got enough time. We'll head upstairs to the Senate Women's Lounge. You been there? Well, it used to be the Senate Wives'

Lounge, but they were always very kind and let the women senators share it."

As we made our way down the corridor, dozens of tourists tried to stop Hilda for a question or a chat. She was easily identifiable—close to six feet tall, beautiful, and, for a long while, one of only two woman senators. That made her as well known as a soap star. Her style in dealing with her fans was admirable and obviously well practiced. She didn't cut anyone off, she just kept moving—smiling, nodding, and making her way through the clusters of tourists.

"The Senate Wives' Lounge? Don't you, ah, don't we, the women senators, have our own lounge?" I asked as we raced up the stairs.

"No," Hilda said crisply. "We have a *powder room* off the Senate floor. 'Powder room' is what a mind as euphemistically damaged as Foxy's would call two stalls and one sink. And can you understand we were all thrilled to get that?"

The lounge was yellow and beige and as cozy as a room with fourteen-foot-high ceilings could feel. I crashed on a sofa and poured out my story, feeling my face redden when I admitted my naive expectations— that I thought Fox would recognize my skills and expertise and make the committee assignments based on those factors.

"My dear, expertise has nothing to do with anything in the seniority system," Hilda explained. She was hunting through the various compartments of a large handbag that I could identify as a Prada by the triangle label on the front. I wasn't sure what a Prada was, but I was sure it was expensive.

"Get your book. Write down these dates. These are the DSCC and national committee briefings for candidates in the November elections. You'd better get started."

Everything Hilda said carried weight. I couldn't figure out if it was her careful enunciation or the way she held her head, but she managed to underline with importance any information she imparted, even about writing down meetings in my appointment book.

"Anyway, as far as committees are concerned, you are not filling out a job application. And if you were, let me assure you that the U.S. Senate has never been an equal-opportunity employer. Women are new here. But the system is old, and the interfacing can be interesting."

"Give me a clue to how the committees work."

"The most important thing to remember is that the chairs of the committees are the chieftains of the Senate." Hilda said it as a matter of fact, while popping her massive daybook back in her purse. But nobody else had taken the time to impart that "important" piece of information to me. "They determine policy. Whatever committees you wind up on, the chairs will expect you to acknowledge their position. And they will want you to do the ordinary chores of a freshman senator, with a big grin on your face."

I put on what I thought was my best freshman smile.

"You know what you need? A copy of the *Almanac*

of American Politics. Michael Barone's book. Has pictures. Tells you who is on what committee and what they like or dislike. Your instincts *are* right. You do need a big committee assignment. Your late predecessor had plums."

I had a hunch she was going to give me some bad news. I wasn't wrong.

"You're not in a place to ask for anything much. Nobody in our party knows if you're going to be the candidate when the election is held for the remainder of Gannon's term."

"If the governor wants the nomination. *If* he wants someone else to run . . ."

"So there's just a lot of ifs. It may seem unfair, but Foxy, as the leader, has a lot of senators to keep happy and the responsibility to help each one of them get reelected. He's not sure, nor am I—"

"Nor am I," I interjected.

"And there's the matter of this dead veteran. It's not a great way to begin. Very messy, really. Especially since it happened on the Senate side of the Capitol."

"Well, dammit, Hilda, I didn't kill the man. He jumped off the subway platform, after me."

"Norie, I know that. And so does everyone else. But we're the Senate. And we don't like that kind of unexpected excitement. It just puts another element into the mix of who you are—and what you're going to get. And if you're going to be the party's candidate for the special election."

She'd finished and obviously wanted me to respond.

"Governor Hartag hasn't really made a decision. The leaders of the state party are split among several candidates. The governor appointed me, it's true, because I didn't fall into any of the camps."

"You're everybody's choice. And nobody's choice."

I nodded. Hilda had no problem coming right to the point.

"How about enemies? Everybody with another choice must have been mad it was you. Maybe one of those enemies has something to do with that dead man?"

"Hilda!" I almost told her about my fancy hate mail, but her next thought distracted me.

"Why not? You have to have some connection to that dead man. We don't have people just dying around here."

"How about Senator Gannon?"

"Didn't he go home to polka and pass away?"

We both laughed at the macabre thought.

"Okay. Back to committees." Hilda started to pace and recite. "Getting placed on committees is like choosing from a menu. You can have a lot of appetizers and side dishes but only one main course."

I nodded. If only Milton could talk like Hilda.

"So senators can only serve on one, let's call it, 'super-committee.' There are four—Finance, Appropriations, Foreign Relations, and Armed Services. All big deals. Then there are 'A' committees. Like Ag, which you might get, or Banking, or Judiciary. In addition to any super-committees, a senator can serve on just two of the A's. Then there are 'B's'—Budget or

Ethics or Veterans' Affairs. Usually a senator can serve on as many of these as he or she wants. Here you usually get something you really want."

"Only I got the blue-plate special." I laughed. "Nothing I really want or need for my state. If I'm going to make this work, I've got to become one of the boys."

"No way, dear." Hilda was adamant. I realized that my newly found friend was as tough as Phil Fox any day—minus a lasso, but plus a compact. "You'll never be one of the boys. And you should never want to be. Look at the Senate as a club with only a hundred members. Be collegial. Be a good sport. But be yourself. Don't try to model yourself after some concept of what a senator is 'supposed' to be."

"So if I'm not one of the boys, but I'm a member of the club . . ."

"You'll be different but important. Not one of the boys, but I'll help you be one of the gang. It's really quite logical."

"Unlike committee assignments, which have nothing to do with logic. But isn't there some logic that as an MIA wife I should be on the select committee?"

"Yes. But it's also logical that half of the Senate should be women, since women are more than half of the population." Hilda jabbed her finger into the air to make her point. "But, logic aside, you've convinced me. You've got a case for the MIA Select Committee. I'll talk to the leader. I'll try to sell you. Maybe we can use the old 'don't we need one woman on the committee and shouldn't it be Norie' routine. You know Baxter? He'll probably head the committee."

"Senator Baxter was gracious at my swearing-in." I waited for Hilda's approval of my assessment.

"Baxter. That pompous stiff."

"He seemed to like me."

" 'Like' is not a Baxter word. Don't get misled by his mint-julep manners. He thinks he owns the whole Senate." Hilda's vehemence surprised me. "Garrett Baxter sees himself as a senator with a capital S. He's used to having his own way, especially here. Relentless. If the Senate is a club, women are merely associate members—tolerated—but, in Baxter's eyes, never senators in the old tradition of the Senate."

"And he seemed like such a nice guy."

☆☆☆ **6** ☆☆☆

THE NEXT MORNING I HAD THE CHANCE TO MEET UP with a roomful of people who thought I had stolen their job.

"Make nice with all the members from your state," Milton had pointed out the night before my first Pennsylvania delegation breakfast. Apparently, both the senators and all the congresspeople—I had to remember to call them "members"—broke bread together at least once a month, regardless of party affiliation.

The advice was so pleasant I thought for a moment that Milton was getting soft, slipping into friendship. But no, he was just setting me up for another worry. "They don't like you. Each member thought he or she was the person the governor should have appointed to fill your Senate seat."

"Come on," I tried, being careful not to jolt Milton back from his friendly stance. "Not everybody in elected office has that much ambition."

"Senator, let me assure you that every single part-time alderman in some backwater town in some doughnut-hole state, every once in a while, late at night, entertains the thought that he too could wind up being the President of the United States. He's lying there picturing himself in the White House Rose Garden—busy reviewing the troops, meeting heads of foreign governments, signing treaties, giving speeches."

It would have been natural for me to tell Milton about my hate letter, my *billet fou* as I thought of it. My letter writer was really upset that I got the appointment, but then again, I didn't want Milton to think I was some kind of a naive weenie.

"Okay, so how do I make them like me, since they all wanted my job?"

"Do what the presidents does—give 'em something. *You're* the senator. They need you. You know Pennsylvania. You know regional issues. Tell 'em you care. Tell 'em they are the most important things on your agenda."

"And they really all want to be president?"

"Except for a couple who want to be appointed to the Supreme Court. That one guy from Chester probably wants to be the pope. So, since you *are* the senator and these members aren't, please make nice."

I did. Ironically, my appearance was made easier by the warm introduction and kind acceptance of the now senior senator from Pennsylvania, Alexander Garrison Smith. Fancy-dancy background and looks that would get him into the House of Lords didn't keep Smith from being a street-smart politician. He wanted to be my ally. He knew Pennsylvania needed all the votes it could muster to get its fair share of government contracts, grants, and general attention—and that means cooperation. He also informally chaired what was fondly known as the "Steel Caucus," an unofficial group that included the senators from our state, Maryland, New Jersey, New York, and Ohio.

Smith spent a good deal of time making sure I talked with each of the members—his party's and mine. I had met most of them casually—at fundraisers and official occasions—over the past several years, but Smith's masterful introductions gave me a little key phrase to hang a connection on each of them: "Here's Clarence Welsh. You know how concerned he is with Pittsburgh redevelopment." Or "Here's Gertrude Shargai. She's been very helpful on health-care issues."

I chatted up each and every one of them. Milton had to be wrong. They all seemed thrilled and happy to be members of the House—except that one guy from Chester.

Nothing in public life, I was finding out, was more exhausting than doing nothing. No wonder everyone hated fund-raising, which translated as standing around and talking to people about what you both thought was important but neither of you really knew each other, and you were each balancing a drink and a bacon-wrapped shrimp and trying not to let the grease run down your chin. Only this wasn't a fund-raiser, it was a delegation breakfast and so the balancing act involved a Danish and a coffee.

By the time I got back from that seemingly eternal get-together I wanted nothing more than a half hour with my Naturalizers off. I'd planned to spend an hour with Nancy's find of the week, something called *The U.S. Senate Handbook.* It was more than how the Senate works. It was how to work the Senate, A to Z. Wouldn't Milton be a surprised young pup to have a senator armed with the senatorial mechanics, the procedural know-how, he kept so carefully to himself?

Curling up on the sofa in my private office, I started in on "procedures for keeping office accounts." I grew up in the days when girls weren't supposed to be good at math, so I've never felt clever, just careful. A diehard checkbook-balance keeper in my personal life, as a state official I prided myself on knowing exactly how much money each section of my department was spending. The devilish details again.

Just as I was beginning to peruse my procedures, Nancy interrupted.

"Leave me alone." I waved her away, and almost meant it. "I need a time-out. I need to know about my paper allowances, my paper clips, my wallpaper options."

"Not just now." She looked too serious. "You have a visitor waiting in the conference room. Lieutenant Thomas Carver, of the Capitol Police."

"Now I handle the parking-pass stuff?"

"I don't think Lieutenant Carver is the parking-pass kind of cop. He's very tall. Very polished. And, I think, very determined." She paused. "A Lou Gossett look-alike."

I slipped my feet back into my red pumps and followed Nancy back to the conference room. Lieutenant Carver seemed to take up half of the room's available space, especially when he leaned over the table to greet me, then dropped back into his chair and picked up his notepad, ready for business. He acted like the host, making me feel like a guest in my own office. I didn't like it. And I liked it less when he started to talk.

"Senator, thanks for your time. This is not a happy visit." He flipped through the notepad, like a teacher giving out a bad grade. "I have the task of informing you that the death you witnessed in the Senate subway was no accident, but that the victim—" he stared at his notes—"one Jake Browning—was murdered. Killed, we think by lethal injection."

"Well, there's no office procedure to cover this." I surprised both of us by the statement and, to regain whatever poise I was supposed to have in this situation, sat down myself.

Carver said nothing, just kept looking at his notes, then up at me.

"Lieutenant, I'm ready to believe what you are telling me. But how do you know it's murder?"

"Well, Browning had a welt on his buttocks the size of an apple. If this crime had happened on a regular city street, with a couple other homicides happening within the same day, maybe Browning wouldn't have gotten as much care and attention. But his murder took place on federal property, so the high-price techies from the FBI moved right in to help. When the forensic people checked him out, seems as though he had about four thousand times as much insulin in his system as anybody would need."

"That would certainly do him in." I couldn't believe I was making small talk about a murder. "Early in my career, I was a nurse, and I know just how much damage a triple or quadruple dose can do."

"For old Jake, this intensive insulin sent him into what you might call a dance of death. Jake's leap up in the air was simply his body bursting, the life being wrenched out of it. Easy, clean, quick. Very sure. Poor Jake. A pinch on his butt and a leap into oblivion. Very clever. A hypodermic syringe is mostly plastic, so it doesn't set off the metal detectors at the entrances to the Capitol."

"Hard to believe."

"I guess it was for Jake, too."

"Do you know why someone would want to kill him? He was just some poor unemployed vet."

"Maybe. Maybe not. But here's a better question, Senator." Carver paused and tapped the notebook against the tabletop, the rat-a-tat-tat like a military march. "Was the needle meant for you?"

"Come on, Lieutenant. Nobody would want to kill me. I don't have any enemies. Except . . ." I tried to lighten it up. "Except some political ones." I thought maybe I should tell him about my poison-pen letter, but that's all this guy would need to suddenly have thugs and gangsters jumping out of the closet. I was more mixed up in all of this than I wanted to be, and giving the lieutenant any loose string would just tie more into his murder scenario.

"Just political enemies," I repeated.

Carver managed what I assumed passed for his smile. "Somebody important was involved in this mess. This murder was very sophisticated, a fairly complicated way to knock off a poor, unemployed vet, requiring a good deal of planning and foresight." He flipped to another page of his notebook and, taking a fountain pen out of his jacket pocket, began to check off items, like a supermarket shopping list.

"First, the killer had the needle with him. Or her. So the killer was following either Jake—or you. And in an attempt to have Jake and you suffer a—what should I call it—a failure to communicate, he snuffs Jake."

"That's nuts. Absolutely crazy. I didn't know Jake."

I was feeling a little impatient with Lieutenant Carver, arriving in my conference room, spinning out wild tales. Absurd. I had enough to handle with Milton and Phil Fox and the members and remembering the bells. I had enough hassles with trying to get committee assignments that wouldn't make me feel like Rebecca of Sunnybrook Farm. And I still hadn't called the manager to find out who was trolling my apartment's hallways, dropping off poisoned valentines.

"Yes, Senator, but Jake knew you. Yelled out your name. Several times. Screamed it out. He knew you."

Carver made no move to end the conversation, just kept tapping, as if he were waiting for me to tell him that I knew Browning.

"My name and my picture have been in the newspapers, Lieutenant. And he was holding the article about my swearing-in. I had a lot of vets up here for the ceremony—but not Jake. A woman becoming a U.S. senator is still an odd enough occurrence to generate a lot of news stories—and I was appointed, not elected, to fill the seat. My husband is an MIA. Browning was a vet. There's another connection." My laundry list of why I couldn't be involved was now longer than Carver's.

"Yes, but the article he had in his hand identified you as Senator Eleanor Gorzack. And the late Jake Browning called out, 'Norie.' Which, I believe, is your nickname." He checked off another item on his list.

I was getting annoyed. I stood up. At least standing I seemed as big as Carver sitting. I was ending this meeting. I walked round the conference table, toward the door. Maybe I'd picked up some of Phil Fox's technique.

"Lieutenant, I am sure you do your job well. That's very clever of you, the nickname stuff. And I am sure that as far as Capitol Hill security and making sure the metal detectors work—I'm sure you're just wonderful. But don't try to tell me about murder. If this were a murder, I'm sure the authorities would be bringing in policemen, experts, who deal with violent crimes every day. They know the kind of cop they need."

"Senator Gorzack, what you say is exactly right."

I nodded, waiting for him to stand up. He didn't move.

"But I *am* the expert. I have been in police work for the past twenty-two years. I left the D.C. Police Department a couple years back, took my 'twenty-and-pension,' so to speak, and came up here to the Hill. I thought it would be a nice, semiretirement kinda place. I did not expect to be climbing over bodies, unless they were environmental nuts chaining themselves to some tree or crazies waving jars around, filled with I don't know what. But as far as murder is concerned, I was with Homicide for eleven years. I'm just the cop *they*, whoever they are, need."

Carver kept my eyes locked with his, willing me to sit back down again. Which I promptly did.

"Well, I apologize, Lieutenant." I tried to be professional. "But I've got no time for this. I've got pressing issues here. Especially the Select Committee on MIAs and POWs. And jobs. And aid to education. And . . . MIAs." I caught myself. "That's my major concern. MIAs."

"I have that as a concern, too, Senator. I spent two delightful years in Vietnam, perfecting my talent with an M-16. But now we're here." Carver stared up at the ceiling, as if he were focusing on the actual crime. "And since we're both concerned about Vietnam, let me tell you what particularly galls me. Poor ole Jake Browning dodged enough bullets to get out of Vietnam and then, on U.S. government property, in the cradle of democracy, he takes a fatal shot. So to speak."

☆☆☆ **7** ☆☆☆

"IT'S ALL THESE SENATORS AND CONGRESSMEN WHO ARE costing me—a lotta money. All I want is a lousy meter. But no, D.C.'s gotta have zones for cabs. Like it was Berlin or something. Whaddaya think, huh?"

I thought we would soon plow into a bus, since he was paying more attention to his diatribe than to his driving.

"What can ya do? Here you are, taking a ten-minute drive, heck, fifteen minutes in the summer. And what are you going to pay, huh?"

My shrug was meant to appear sympathetic in the rearview mirror. Maybe my lack of conversation would keep his eyes on the road.

"Nothing. Nothing. Less than five bucks. An extra buck on heavy traffic. But look. If I drove you to Georgetown, you'd pay the same. You know that. If you got out one block before the zone changed, you'd pay the same. And don't think some people don't do it. Huh. To save a buck or two. If these senators were back home—in New York or Chicago—they couldn't get away with it. But here, these creeps on the Hill won't give us meters in our cabs because it would cost them. Throw them all out, that's what I say."

I was a lot more popular at my breakfast meeting.

In fact, leaving my cab and getting to my meeting was like leaving the streets of Paris during the Revolution and being invited to the last silver-service breakfast. Everybody's manners were just lovely and they were all thrilled to see me.

The two dozen people I was joining for breakfast represented the Washington chapter of Business for Strategic Interest. BSI, from what Milton had told me, was an association of various corporations in the exportable high-tech or military industries.

Not exactly my usual people. But these Star Wars-style lobbyists did try hard to connect with me. Each breakfaster wore a name tag, and as I worked my way around the table for an individualized minute of chat, each pointed out what potent link his particular company had with the Commonwealth of Pennsylvania and graciously welcomed me to the event. Several of the men stressed that they were friends of George Taylor, and that they hoped I would pass on their regards. One of the two women—Bobbi Bernardi, according to her tag—told me that her sister had attended Mount St. Agnes, just a class behind me. I felt warm and cuddled.

One man did make me laugh. He introduced himself as Stewart Conover, "who knows George Taylor and Marco Solari, and I've been to Philadelphia several times. Now will you remember me?"

"I'll try. Is that important?"

"For everybody you've met here, Senator, it's life and death. Or at least this month's fees."

"You don't seem to take it too seriously, Mr. Conover."

"A lot of the stuff people from this group sell—everything from medical lasers to industrial-size bombers—gets sold in the U.S., but, more important, it also gets exported. We've got to have some things that Americans make and sell elsewhere. We can't fix the economy with just McDonald's."

"That's a good line."

"Better than telling you my sister went to Mount St. Agnes," he whispered.

We ate our egg-white omelettes, sitting around a massive round table. There were a lot of questions from them, some passable answers from me. Their major concern, it turned out, was how certain bills that would affect my home state—and their corporations—were faring. Milton had prepared a crib sheet for me, and I did nothing to embarrass myself.

Breakfast was over by ten, and once again, there was a lot of handshaking and pleasant chat. Milton had magically turned up somewhere around the second cup of coffee, and he was quite busy doing his howdies as we wound up.

I had made it to the hallway when I realized my briefcase was still under my chair. When I went back into the room, Milton was standing with one of the fellows and I couldn't help but overhear the end of their conversation.

"So it's ten thousand dollars from the PAC. And we'll put together another hundred thousand from other associations around the country."

Milton took an envelope and slipped it into his suit jacket.

I kept my temper until we were in the cab, but the ride to the Hill was even less pleasant than the one to the breakfast—though this time I was serving up the complaints.

"How dare you use me for a fund-raising event—and not tell me that was what it was?"

"It wasn't. It was a breakfast. And you were lucky to get it. These guys usually only want to deal with people on Armed Forces. Or maybe Finance. I happen to know them from Gannon, and—"

"And you just raffled me off? Is that right?"

"No, Senator. I made one of the best connections you're ever going to have in this town. With American corporations who actually make things in America."

"Right. Bombs and guns and things that go bump in the night."

"What do you think we trade with other countries? America doesn't make much anymore. We don't even protect or patent our technology, so every apartment house in Hong Kong has more high-tech manufacturing than Detroit. Our corporations are worried. There's a lot of concern in Pennsylvania about the fate of the J-2, the rocket launcher."

"Well, that's great. Why should I care about that? The J-2, the B-2, the U-2. Not—"

"No way not. You're a senator. You want jobs. You wanna be reelected—or elected for the first time, in your case. You can't get the government to reopen the Philly Naval Yard. Or the Frankford Arsenal. Those were good jobs. They're gone. Goodbye. But you can play nice with very up-and-up companies—and keep people working in Pennsylvania."

"But I don't like the idea of trading in weapons."

"Foreign aid is a dinky part of the budget—but a big chunk of that small change is chits, markers that countries can cash in for American-made instruments of war. Grow up, Senator, and smell the gunpowder."

"You're all over the papers."

"Good, huh?" I looked around the table, tucked into the corner of the Senate Dining Room, and expected enthusiastic nods from my kitchen cabinet. None were forthcoming. I thought this would be a treat—eating in the dining room reserved for senators and their guests—and that the Gang of Four would be celebrating my celebrity.

No way.

"Good? What's good?" Marco sipped his bowl of Senate Bean Soup and grinned. "The soup is good. The verdict on you is still up in the air."

"I've got editorial support from the *Inquirer* and the *Pittsburgh Press*, both saying I should be on the select committee."

"You've got editorials on every side. Some against your appointment, not just to the committee but to the Senate." George Taylor usually waited until Marco and I had slugged it out, then weighed in with his opinion. "This is not a minor problem."

"You got this guy dropping dead at your feet, and"—Marco raised his hands in a classic gesture probably perfected by Marc Antony—"now you tell us you're involved in a murder case. 'Not good' is the way to describe it."

Marco was convincing. He usually was, after twenty years in the labor movement. He had perfected gruffness to an art. Nobody would guess that he was a *magna* grad of Penn State who met up with labor unions when he was a VISTA volunteer back in the 1960s. "You have this guy chasing you, Norie, then buying the farm. Not too pleasant, kid."

"For example," George interrupted, "we wanted to talk to you about getting a bodyguard. Or maybe you could apply for Secret Service protection."

"Is that why you all trooped down here on a Friday? To save me from people dropping dead on me?" I glanced around the dining room nervously. All I needed was other senators thinking I was a show-boater, interested only in my own importance and publicity.

"A couple days ago I decided to look into private protection for you." George pulled a card out of his jacket pocket. "I talked to somebody I know here, who does private work for major corporations. Very discreet."

"Look," I told the table, "at first I was rattled when this Capitol Hill cop told me about lethal injections. But then, at home last night, I thought about all the new drugs people shoot themselves up with. The poor guy was probably wired on something and, being a vet, saw my picture in the paper . . ." I didn't get to finish my scenario.

"And? *And?* The police are telling you he was murdered? And if he wasn't, what did he do—just decide to drop over to the Senate subway to drop dead? Even I have a problem believing that," Kathleen snipped.

"Look," George said, pushing together the tips of his fingers and looking like some caricature of the businessman he was. From running his successful business, the Pennsylvania-based Taylor Technology Resources, he came at almost any question with a scientist's analysis and a manager's style. "Not every guy with an honorable discharge is a hero. And not every guy still running around wearing fatigues is totally all right in the head."

"And we'd like you to be okay enough to get elected. And reelected," Marco added.

"First, we'll eat." I stood up. I didn't want any rain on my parade, especially since I was wearing my new St. John's knit suit, navy blue with a trim of red. "On to the renowned Senate Seafood Buffet."

I self-righteously chose the shrimp and salad. On the way back to our table, I nodded to Phil Fox and to

Garrett Baxter, both lunching with cloned tables of men who had to be Washington lawyers—dark-blue suits and very flashy ties. Lawyers love ties that belie their stolid states of mind. One of the tie-lie lawyers gave Marco a big wave.

Good! Fox or Baxter wouldn't think me so naive once they knew the identity of my luncheon companions. The political reporters back in Harrisburg would have called the lunch the first meeting of the Elect Norie Committee.

"Have you seen any numbers, seen what all this means to you back home?" Marco was at it as soon as we were back at the table.

"Hold it, Marco," Kathleen Burns interrupted. "I'm much more interested in hearing how Norie's going to handle some of the issues coming up in the next few weeks. Especially these feeding programs."

"And I'm much more concerned about her committee assignments," George finished up.

"A minute, guys. I'd like two bites of food and a chance to be the incumbent for at least part of lunch." I wasn't sure they wanted to hear what I was going to say.

"Okay. Get your strength. Then we need to figure out your best issue." Kathleen was relentless.

"First, committees," George insisted.

"This is cross-purposes. To get an issue," Marco said, "you've gotta get on the right committees. Demand some good assignments. Maybe you need some of my D.C. counterparts to give the majority leader a call."

"He's not budging. It's Ag and Gov Affairs for me. Doesn't sound too promising, does it?"

"Well, Ag does have control over feeding programs, like food stamps. But I just can't see its wider appeal." Even George Taylor couldn't balance out Ag in the plus column. "And, as for Gov Affairs—I just don't see how it affects any voter's life."

"My God, Norie, you have to turn this around. And what the heck is Gov Affairs?" Kathleen turned to look daggers at the majority leader's table. "How dare he?"

"He dares because he's the only game in town. Fox is the leader. That's that. And no," I turned to Marco, "I've got no numbers. I understand the Democratic National Committee has some polling going on in Northeast states, but I don't think it's time to ask how my confrontation over the select committee plays out in the boonies."

"Maybe we should start raising a little money, get a little private polling done back in the state?" George asked. "Some of the people I know with BSI said you did quite well at their breakfast."

"Not now. I'm not going to hold this seat by doing what the polls tell me. Sure, when the election campaign gets started—"

"This means you really want to go for it?" Marco interrupted.

"Yes, I'm pretty sure. I guess. I don't know."

As I expected, this clear-minded statement produced no happy faces around the table.

"I'm figuring it out. I've been to one of Hilda Mendelssohn's DSCC briefings. I'm learning the language and the process. I'm ready, if and when the campaign gets started, to use whatever sophisticated tools I need to get me across to the voters. I'm going to poll, and we'll shape some 'message' stuff on what the polls tell me. I'll hire the best political consultants I can find. But right now, I'm going to try to rely on myself. Me. And you. I guess I'd like to get elected. But I'm not going to spend every minute worrying about how some poll is going to say I'm doing."

"You've made your decision. You just don't know it. You're not going back to the Senate after the November election. You'll be outta work," Marco said definitely.

"Calm down, Marco," Kathleen ordered. "And let's remember," she continued, obviously not following her own advice, "Norie isn't a weenie. She's got a real agenda."

"And I'm going to push my agenda. And not preface every decision with the question 'Is this costing me votes?' "

"Maybe." George dragged out the word to three syllables. "But you could also ask the question 'Who wants this job?' and get almost as many answers as you were losing votes. A lot."

"I'm having dessert if I have to listen to this," I said, waving over the waiter and ordering apple pie. The other three looked at me in horror, but Marco finally decided to join me.

"And I'm keeping the staff, even though Milton Gant is giving me grief."

"Good decision. You couldn't fire anybody until

you found out how he got the job in the first place. Like who's got an important cousin, who's a friend to whomever."

"People get jobs because they worked on campaigns, or have political friends back in the state. Not that they're not qualified, but . . ." I let my voice drag off.

Marco stared at his pie, then motioned the waiter over and asked for vanilla ice cream.

"In for a nickel, in for a dime."

"That's how I feel."

"You want some ice cream?"

"No, no. I feel like I have this shot at doing something. This chance. And if I can't get back for the rest of Gannon's term, well, at least I should do something while I'm here."

After lunch, I walked with them down the Capitol steps. The Washington monument glistened in the sun, and there was a hint, the slightest hint, of spring in the air. We said goodbye, and, at the last moment, with a smile I didn't understand, Marco handed me an envelope. He told me to wait until I was alone to read the contents. I started to ask him about it, but he smiled again and shook his head.

"Where exactly is your apartment?" Kathleen asked, before they walked the two blocks to Union Station and their train back to Philly.

"Just a couple blocks from here, on Pennsylvania around 6th. It's nice and bright, already furnished. And with full security."

"Be careful. Watch yourself," George warned.

"Don't worry," I said. "Nobody fools around with a U.S. senator."

Waving goodbye, I started briskly down the walk toward the Hart Building. It was hard, being away from the three of them. I turned around to look after them, and caught sight of a man in fatigues a couple dozen yards behind me.

I swung my eyes front, crossed the intersection back toward the Senate Office Buildings, and, like a child playing statues, swung around again.

A large truck turned the corner and blocked my view. I waited until it finally pulled onto Constitution Avenue, but the man in fatigues was gone.

8

SATURDAY MORNING I GAVE MYSELF THE LUXURY OF AN early *caffè latte* on the way to work. Sitting in the picture window at the Starbucks coffee shop, enjoying a slow read of the *New York Times* and the coffee smells, I thought Washington was wonderful. I just had to keep my priorities in order and remember the things I wanted to get done.

"You wanna order another *caffè latte*, Senator?" the young waiter yelled at me from behind the counter. "For the road?"

"Yes. Sure. How's the coffee business?" I asked, amazed at his speed with the various handles and tubes on the copper machine.

"You should ask me how the Hill business is, Senator. That's what I do full-time. This is part-time. Saturdays only. Until I pay off my car insurance."

"Tough working two jobs."

"Tough working for the government. It's like that thing John Glenn said, when he was an astronaut, before they shot him out in space." He waited until I shook my head, admitting my ignorance. "Glenn said he was a little nervous sitting on a pile of equipment each piece of which came from the lowest bidder."

I laughed out loud and reached for my wallet. The kid had perked me up. I felt ready for Milton, ready to take him on, ready for—I couldn't help smile at my own joke—ready for "mind-to-hand combat" with Mr. Administrative Assistant Gant.

As I tucked my wallet back into my purse, I came on Marco's envelope. In the after-lunch push at the office, I'd forgotten about it completely. I sat back down at the same window table.

Inside Marco's plain white envelope was a U.S. Senate envelope, bearing my "frank," the copy of my signature that substituted for postage on official mail. Inside that, a short note, signed by me in ink, meant for Marco Solari, thanking him for his good wishes. There were only two problems. The letter was addressed to "Miss Maria Solari." And although it indeed carried my penned signature, I had never seen the letter, nor had I signed it.

The aggravation wired me more than any coffee, and by the time I arrived at the office, I was steaming like the copper espresso machine.

Nancy and Amy Walker were in the conference room, going through piles of constituent mail.

"Great. Just my topic for today. Letter-writing."

"You're not going to be happy," Nancy started. "This is not a happy place. It turns out that we—and I stress the we—do not have an adequate system of handling letters from constituents."

"Some of these letters, Senator," Amy nervously explained, holding up a large pile, "are from last month and the month before. They're mostly requests for specific help or specific information. We get letters about government pensions or Social Security payments or where to look for help about private pension funds. We get lots of other letters complaining about foreign policy or what the guys from the local army base do on a Saturday night."

"So to answer some letters, you must do research, say for a particular constituent problem. But other replies simply state the senator's—I mean my—positions and how I arrived at them?"

"Pretty much. Senator Gannon didn't make constituent problems a big priority for this office. I send out form letters for some correspondence, telling people how to check with Social Security or whatever. And I try to send requests that seem fixable but require individual attention back to the state offices, where they can put a staffer on the problems. But lots of letters . . ." She shrugged.

"Get like a not very specific thank-you-for-your-interest? Just how many of these letters have you sent out over my name?"

"A lot. Remember, you signed the auto-pen machine on your first day. We had a lot of letters congratulating you that came when the governor announced your appointment, and I got those replies out. We had some letters complaining about your appointment"—she looked ashamed to be bringing me bad news—"so I did a letter saying, 'I'm bringing your concerns to the senator,' and signed Milton's name to it."

The auto-pen? Wow. I vaguely recalled using the machine the day of my swearing-in. I should have been more careful, not let the excitement of the day keep me from thinking about what I was doing.

Amy was chattering on about other form letters.

"With Senator Gannon, we had a lot of ways to say 'thanks for your interest.' Or if the person was upset about a vote, we'd send them an 'although we don't agree on this issue, nonetheless' letter. And then there were always the ones that went to people who identify themselves by a group—vets or unions or teachers or seniors or some other special interest—saying that the senator would be talking to the Washington representative. With the auto-pen, I just push a number on the computer, the letter cranks out, and then the auto-pen signs your name."

"And who makes the judgment calls about *how* a letter is treated, whether it's followed up?" I asked. I tapped my fingernails on the conference-room table, but stopped when I realized I was imitating Lieutenant Carver.

Amy said nothing, and I looked up to see Milton standing in the doorway.

"I make the judgment calls on correspondence, Senator. A lot of the letters are people wanting to know where you stand on one issue or another.

Crime. Guns. Peace. Drugs. Europe. Those are *no problema.*"

"But how do you know where I stand, Milton, since I haven't told you yet?" I started to sift through the letters in front of me. When Amy reached out to retrieve a pile, I waved her off.

"Constituent mail has never been a priority in this office," Milton announced.

"I get it. Crank out those letters to folks back home, tell them anything you think they'd like to hear, and then sign my name? Make up my positions, make *me* up as you go along. What a great way to run my office. What a great way to run a government."

I reached in my purse for the Solari letter.

"At least get it right, Milton. If the head of the AFL-CIO political committee sends me a note but doesn't bother to put it on official COPE stationery, at least write him back under his own name."

I tossed the letter across the table at him.

"You want to know what I know about, Milton? It's how the government should run, how a bureaucracy should serve the people. I think you're a pretty sloppy manager, Milton. Who works here? Where's your personnel plan? Who has responsibility to whom? How many letters do we get a week? Just who else handles the responses?"

"The office runs itself. It has for years." Milton's shrug was a little short of nonchalant. "I work on issues, on politics. I leave secretarial jobs to secretaries."

"That ends here. Today." I plopped my pile of letters back on the table. "We're turning off the automatic pilot. Don't worry about doing jobs beneath you. I'm going to run the office."

"You won't have time to run the office and be the senator, Senator," Milton countered.

I wasn't backing off this time.

"Being the senator means that I'm in charge of this office. Working for me means that you help me run it. I'm staying in touch with my constituents."

"A 'people senator,' huh? Well, let me tell you, a good number of the letters that come in go directly to the 'nut basket.' Get me some," he ordered Amy.

Amy looked at me, and I nodded yes. At least she thought I was in charge. With Nancy and me, that made three of us. Amy went to the outer office and returned with several dozen letters.

"Here we go. Here are at least a dozen of your *constituents* who think they are in touch with outer space through speakers in their toaster ovens." Milton spread the letters out in front of me, and I shifted through them. One man was complaining that the government was using high-tension wires that would give his cows hypertension. Another, a woman, claimed that her next-door neighbors were working for "the enemy" and that the FBI was unresponsive to her reports.

But a third letter, on stationery carrying a hand-drawn American flag, caught my eye. It was from a woman in Pittsburgh who believed that the Senate refused to accept the "real dope" on MIAs. The letter urged me to use the "info that public interested citizens get from private patriotic organizations." It was urgent, she wrote, since "these groups can't afford the burden of doing the job and making sure our boys get returned to America, a job the federal government should be doing."

"So?" Milton queried, twisting his pencil like a miniature baton.

"So. Look into this. What does this woman know?" I asked.

"She knows nothing. She's just another person with a talented and sensitive toaster oven." He tried to take the letter back, but I held it out of his reach.

"No way, Milton. I want something done with this. Today. I want this followed up."

"Okay. You're the boss." He gingerly took the letter and carefully, as if he were transporting crystal, passed it over to Amy. "Okay, you heard the senator. Get right on this. Today."

I nodded my approval and motioned Nancy to join me in my own office.

Amy, her blond hair bouncing, followed us out the conference room door and practically raced to her desk.

"She's been on the staff less than a year," Nancy told me, once we'd closed the door. "So Milton hasn't yet had a chance to destroy her initiative. She still thinks she should be doing some good."

"Maybe we've saved her from his Invasion of the Mind Snatchers. Maybe she'll turn out to be a staff member who actually likes the people she's employed to serve."

"Milton would never permit it," Nancy said. "Not in *his* office, he won't."

Lieutenant Carver rang me up early Monday morning.

"I'd like to have a little security talk with you, Senator," was his opener.

"I'm very secure, Lieutenant."

"This is not a joke. Someone has been murdered."

"Lieutenant, I'm an old hand at public health. One sick person doesn't make an epidemic."

"I hope you're right, Senator."

Tragically, I wasn't.

9

THE SECOND LETTER SHOWED UP IN MY IN BASKET.

It looked nothing like the first.

The envelope was government-issue, the kind used for interagency and interoffice mail. I remember glancing at the front, where there were several dozen spaces for names and addresses, so that envelope could be used over and over. And I remember thinking that the envelope was new, since mine was the only name on it: "Sen. Eleanor Gorzack."

Inside, there were several sheets of white Xerox paper, the message written with colorful cut-out letters from magazines. The style of correspondence was different, but the language was the same as the formal note with its calligraphy—maybe even more graphic. This one threatened to cut off my left breast "and expose my bleeding heart."

My crime was taking a man's place in the Senate. "You belong in some man's bed, getting screwed, you slut. You've stolen a job from a man. You will get yours. Men defend this country. You gave up nothing but your no-good husband."

My hands made damp spots on the paper as I laid the pages, five in all, out on the desk. The pasted-on letters marched across the page in neat lines, several words to a page, a variety of colors and sizes.

I had never hated anyone before, but I hated the person who had sent this letter. Sick bastard. Scaring me. Writing about my body. How dare he.

Nancy buzzed me.

"Five minutes, okay? And I'll get a staffer to drive us."

I wondered if I should leave the pages where they were. Maybe moving them destroyed fingerprints or something. But the sight of those crayon-colored letters scared me. So I pushed the pages together and popped them back into the envelope.

Sometimes I thought I'd be late for my own funeral.

"I always think it should be rainy for funerals," Nancy whispered to me. The sun shone brightly down on the corner of lawn where the folding chairs were set.

Keeping my eyes front and center on the looming wall of the Vietnam Veterans Memorial, I ignored her. Since my dad was a liveryman, a professional driver of limos and hearses, I knew funerals *never* were anything you expected.

To me, the memorial was a sacred place. In the years before my Senate appointment, I'd come to it at least a dozen times. Each time, faced with the stark coldness of the marble wall meeting the emotion of the people gathered to pay their respects, well, it was really something.

The Vietnam Memorial is unique, honoring not the military, but the men who made up its ranks. Those who died in Vietnam are classified not by their rank but by the year they died. All soldiers named here are equal in their sacrifice, equal in death. Of course, there is no listing of the MIAs.

During my first visit, years ago, I had found the spot where Jack's name would be inscribed *if* he was dead, if indeed he had died fighting for his country. Sitting here this sunny noontime, waiting for the service for Jake Browning to begin, my eyes searched out the spot, that place I now knew too well.

I felt myself fill up—not at the thought of the particular veteran being remembered that day, but at the fear that I would never know if my Jack was dead or alive.

The service was short, a couple of speeches about Jake, the ex-servicemen focusing on their common bond, their service in Vietnam. There wasn't much to say about someone who had showed up in Washington only a few months before. Jake's body had been shipped back to Denver, to his sister, who declined burial in Arlington National Cemetery. So the speeches were given—and that was that.

Nancy and I had planned on heading right back to

the Hill, but several of the vets asked me to stay for lunch, and I just couldn't refuse.

The area near the memorial has been occupied by groups of veterans, kind of a ragtag encampment—tables and booths where they sell T-shirts or hand out leaflets explaining the effects of Agent Orange or Post-Vietnam Syndrome or simply try to acquaint young people with what Vietnam was all about.

One vet led us past a T-shirt booth to an open spot where a folding table had been set up. Covered with a paper tablecloth with an autumn-leaf motif, the table held two large plastic trays, straight from a supermarket catering department, along with several plastic bowls holding salads. A balding man in a wrinkled army-issue hooded jacket carefully pointed out to me which was the potato salad, which was the cole slaw.

I took a spoonful of each. The man plopped two sandwich halves down beside them, showed me to a folding chair, and ran around the booth to find one for Nancy.

I took a bite of my sandwich, turkey, drowning in lettuce and mayonnaise and stuck together tightly with damp white bread, like the kind that came in your lunchbox when you were little. I had rarely tasted anything better. I managed my thank-yous with my mouth full of sandwich.

"We'd thought we should have like a little reception. You know. Like after a funeral when people come back to the house," one vet said.

"Speaking of coming back to the house—what was

Jake's story?" I tried to sound casual. I knew Carver had probably come around, asking questions, looking at his notebook, but maybe I could find out something they wouldn't tell a cop.

"We don't know very much. Except he told us he'd been around the country a lot. He said he was looking into stuff that happened in Nam. Didn't say why. He was kind of a floater, a loner."

"And did he say anything about why he was trying to talk to me?"

"No, he just said he had something important to tell you. He came by here that morning. Remember, some of us went to your swearing-in the day before." One guy in fatigues with a hat that said "Shark" had taken over the conversation. "We were talking about it. One of the guys had read the piece in the *Post*. Passed it around. And the next thing we know, Jake says he's got to see you. Has something important to tell you. Takes the paper and runs."

"We never got our paper back," one of the more frazzled guys offered. Shark shook his head at him.

I looked around at these dozen men whose chance trip to Vietnam had changed their lives forever. They were my age, or close to it, but I couldn't help thinking of them as "boys," trapped in some painful, irreconcilable time warp. Just as I was.

"Do you think he knew my husband? Do you think that hearing my name he might have remembered something about Jack Gorzack?" It was easy to talk to these guys about Jack. Somehow, MIAs have become shameful to most people. But these boys would understand how I thought about Jack's return every day, several times a day, how my ache had become an old friend.

Shark didn't answer, but just stretched his arms over his head in an elaborate yawn. There was something he didn't want to tell me, I realized. Something that he thought would be too painful, too hard.

"Ah, I don't think it would be your husband, Mrs. Gorzack. Hey, Jake Browning was angry, very mad. He said it was time to set the record straight and he had important information for you."

A hand gripped me on the shoulder, and, startled, I cried out. I looked up to see a baby-faced vet standing over me, a sweet but loony smile spreading across his pink-tinged face.

"It's just Bob Sanders, Mrs. Gorzack," Shark explained. "He doesn't talk. Something happened to his voice in Nam."

Sanders pulled a box up beside my folding chair, and, as Shark and a half-dozen other vets talked, he took my hand and held it. His own hand was remarkably gentle, almost like that of a nurse or a nun.

My car was waiting with a staffer behind the wheel, and after long goodbyes, Nancy and I made our way across the grassy strip to the road. Shark, Sanders, and a couple other vets accompanied us. My only surprise came when Sanders nonchalantly climbed into the front passenger seat, like an honor guard.

"Don't worry about Bob," Shark stuck his head through the window to tell me. "He's a big fan and probably wants to make sure you get back to your office A-OK."

"That's very nice, I'm sure," I said. Nancy shook her head, but I simply turned and looked out the window.

On Capitol Hill, Bob showed no sign of peeling off. Instead, he rushed to open the doors at the Hart Building for us, got held up a minute at the metal detector, but then rushed ahead to get the elevator. When we got off, he preceded us down the hall to my office.

"He knows where the office is," Nancy whispered. "How does he know where the office is, since we barely know where the office is?"

"Maybe he's from Pennsylvania. Maybe he came here to see Gannon."

"That's two big maybes. It's not like we can ask him a lot of questions," Nancy said. "Or at least it's not that we can expect a lot of answers." She managed to give Bob a hopeful nod as we walked past him into the office. He sat down in the waiting area, near the receptionist, and began to read the *New York Times*.

"Don't worry. He'll spend a little time here, we'll give him a cup of coffee and our thanks, and he'll be gone in an hour." His appearance did disturb me a little, but I also knew that people are put off by anyone who cannot speak. I wasn't going to fall victim to that prejudice, and, anyway, how long could he stay?

10

MY HATE MAIL PROVED TO BE A REAL SHOW-STOPPER.

At least for Lieutenant Carver, who sat for a long fifteen minutes across the desk from me, sifting through the five sheets of pasted-on letters that had come to my office, staring at the calligraphic hate note that had been hand-delivered to my apartment.

Wearing surgical gloves, Carver moved the pages back and forth, humming some song that sounded vaguely familiar. He held the pages up to the afternoon light that came through the window behind my desk. He took the note and the pages, went into the outer office, and returned with Xerox copies.

"This is a clever fellow," he said, handing me the Xeroxes. "Maybe you should have mentioned the first note to me when I called you earlier this week."

"I didn't think it was important."

"But you saved the note?"

"I threw it in a kitchen drawer. Anyway, it's frightening how much this letter writer hates women."

"That could be true. Or it could be a woman who hates women. Or a man who wants you to think he hates women. Or just about any other combination you can think of."

"So that's why he—I can call him 'he,' right?—that's why he is clever."

"No. He's clever because he hasn't availed himself of the U.S. Postal Service. He hasn't stuck the necessary and exorbitant postage on either of his missives. Neither of the letters came via the U.S. Mail, so it's a little touchier calling in all the federal resources I'd like to mount."

"Even though I'm a senator?"

"Rules are rules. I do get some needed assistance because this one—the paste-up letter—was delivered to you on federal property and at least was contained in a federal envelope. And I get some assistance because Uncle Sam doesn't want anything happening to his elected officials. But if he'd used the Postal Service . . ."

"Well, if he wanted to scare me, it's working. It's like he's everywhere."

"He's not, but he's clever enough to slip in and out of your life. He got into your high-security building. And into your in basket."

"Nancy doesn't remember putting that envelope in with my other stuff."

"Anybody—a guy in a carpenter's uniform or a

messenger or anybody—could have come into the outside office and just slipped in here."

"What do I do now?"

"As the old song says, 'Do Nothin Till You Hear from Me.' "

Carver left, and I rummaged in my desk drawers until I found a file folder that was unnecessarily holding some papers together. The worse thing about being in a top job, I'd discovered long ago, was that you never got any office supplies—no paper clips, no little yellow sticky pads. Nobody really believed you did any work.

I dumped the papers back in the drawer. I took the Xerox copies and put them in the folder. After a double-check of my calendar, I wrote the two dates I'd received the letters on the outside of the folder.

Then I tried to make categories.

Male. Female. Young. Old. Well-educated. Illiterate. Urban. Rural. I paused. Both times the letters had been delivered right into my hands. No barrier seemed too much for the letter writer. I wrote, "Insider," and put a check beside the word.

Of that much, I was pretty certain.

Sometime after six, Nancy and Milton made a joint appearance in my private office.

"Both of us think," Nancy began, obviously and correctly made uncomfortable by this apparent alliance with Milton, "that Bob has got to go."

"Both of you? Great. Why?" I was happy to let my annoyance show.

"He's creepy. I don't care that he was in Vietnam. You can't go around adopting every damaged person who made it home." Nancy held on to the back of a straight chair, as if she needed ballast.

"And what do you suggest? That I throw Bob out?"

"No," Milton said. "That's why we have the Capitol Police. It's so convenient. *They'll* throw him out."

"Both of you just get off this right now. He's a vet and he's obviously just killing time here."

"Or getting ready to kill one of us," Milton said. "It's not like you haven't had a recent experience with a weird veteran. Who, I may point out, is now dead."

"We don't know that Jake Browning was 'weird.' Anyway, one has nothing to do with the other."

"These guys, these Viet vets, the ones who are still in their fatigues and hanging around D.C., are weird. They're all conspiracy freaks. Somebody should tell them, hey, the war is over."

"Maybe the war's over for you, Milton. But not for a lot of other people. Now let me make this very clear. Bob Sanders is staying right here, in the front office, for as long as he wants. He served his country once—and now he's volunteering to serve again. And if I find out that any of you have messed around with him, I am going to be damn mad." I hit the palm of my hand flat against the desk for emphasis.

"Which might be better than being damn dead," Milton said, heading out. Nancy just shrugged disgustedly and followed him.

Despite my patriotic speech, the sight of an empty waiting room an hour later brought me instant relief.

Bob and his post-Vietnam problems were not something I really wanted to handle. But my comfort evaporated as soon as I walked down the staff corridor, where Bob loomed into sight. He was scrunched in Amy's cubicle, behind her desk, the two of them staring at a computer screen.

"Bob and I are communicating by computer. Isn't that great?" Amy asked.

"Great," I answered. It was going to be another wonderful end to a wonderful day.

Milton did not think it was very great. He was waiting for me when I tried to walk back through the reception area. Obviously, the end of my day had not yet arrived.

"I am not happy about Bob," he told me, sounding almost sincere. "He is crazy and will probably hold you hostage. He belongs in a V.A. hospital ward, not in a Senate office."

"I feel a commitment to these vets. But ..." I paused. Maybe Milton was softened up enough that I could get something done. "Here's a deal. I won't do any of this 'do-gooder' stuff that worries you if, *if*, you get me on the Select Committee on MIAs."

"Come on. Right. I can just pull that off. I just call up the old majority leader and he says all right." Milton waved his arms over his head in a twirling motion, and I knew that he'd spent time with the majority leader.

"No," I answered. "He'd probably say, 'Yep, pardner.' But Milton, you know your way around. You've been here eight years. You know people on other senators' staffs, people on Fox's staff, who will talk to the leader. I'll stop with the spontaneous news conferences. Heck, pardner, I'll even draw the line and let Bob be the only vet who takes up residence in the office. Only help me get that committee slot."

Milton opened the door for me. "This is going to take all my chits. You realize, I'm going to have to cut a lot of deals for this."

"And I appreciate it, Milton. I'm going to be just the kind of senator you want me to be."

Milton managed a smirk. And I grinned back. But not too broadly. I didn't want Milton to realize I'd beaten him. He'd agreed to push for the select committee. I'd managed that concession—and also got to keep Bob Sanders in the office, although that really wasn't what I wanted.

11

A LOT OF ADVICE CAME MY WAY AS THE WEEK MOVED ahead.

First, Hilda gave me a big boost when she called me to report how her "howdy" with Phil Fox had gone.

As I was finding out in my conversations with Hilda, she managed to impart information while making me feel a lot better about my role as a senator. Along that line, she started by reminding me that even a two-term senator, with a graduate degree from the Wharton School, had to make some concessions when dealing with Fox.

"I'm just not a howdy kind of person," she laughed. "But I realize that it's part of Phil Fox's shtick. So I howdy right back. Luckily I avoided the horned chair."

Hilda and Fox were doing a lot of howdying these

days, since she was, as she had told me, head of the Democratic Senate Campaign Committee. Both of the national parties had such a group, headed by a senator, which raised part of the funding needed for their candidates.

Both Hilda and Fox were pretty handy at both raising and making money. Hilda's family had spent three generations cultivating Ohio real estate. On the other hand, as Milton explained to me, Fox was partial to commodities and had made a chunk of his fortune in pork bellies. Like a good number of senators, both Fox and Mendelssohn were millionaires.

Hilda told me that she had started out her conversation with Fox by reminding him that she had not wanted to head up the DSCC, that she was doing it as a favor to him. Fox then offered her the same advice he usually did when a senator said raising campaign money was tough: "Drill where there's oil. Cut where there's timber. Find those friends who need some tax breaks. A little special access goes a long way."

Hilda was quick to remind him—and me, in the telling—that this was not what most voters were looking for in a candidate.

"These days, I told him, 'value' in a senator means 'values.' Spunk. Spirit. Candidates voters can believe in. Somebody with something to say. Like our new Senator Gorzack."

"He must have been thrilled to hear that." I almost added what I was afraid Fox had said in return—that I was a lightweight, an inexperienced do-gooder. But Hilda had warned me not to refer to myself in those terms—not even to her—stressing that there were enough enemies out there willing to be doubly critical of a new woman on the Hill and that no woman should be the first to be critical of herself. So instead I asked:

"So what was his response?"

"To my general statement about you? Or to my suggestion that he place you on the select committee?"

"Either, Hilda. Either or both."

"Well, getting a spot on the select committee is no slamdunk: But I think Foxy has taken your name under consideration. And that's a beginning. We'll have to strategize on getting some other people to advance your cause."

"I wish I had heard your pitch."

"You know, Norie," Hilda said, "I leaned across the buckboard coffee table and I told the leader that I couldn't talk Western. That the only ranch I've ever been to was the Canyon Ranch Spa. That I like my beef corned—lean and on rye. Then I said, 'But I'll tell you something, Leader, that you'll understand—get us moving, or the Senate is going to wind up with a new trail boss. This is no time to circle the wagons.' "

Hilda overwhelmed me.

"I don't know how to thank you."

"Well, just come to the special cattle drive next week, when I'm going to start herding up the big honchos."

"What?"

"That was Foxy talk. What I mean is to come to the fundraiser I'm doing next week. It's a DSCC function, but you'll like the angle. It's for the DSCC Women's Council. All the funds go to women Senate candidates."

"Would that mean me?"

"If you are the official party nominee, you get a cut of the . . . what would Phil call it?"

"The sirloin."

Then Ralph deSantis gave me some political advice.

"I'm having trouble getting you on the phone directly, Senator."

Ralph deSantis, the dean of the Harrisburg press corps, was a whiner. For thirty years Ralph had worked for the number two Harrisburg paper—some critics maintained that Ralph's presence on the staff guaranteed it the number two slot, even if there had been only one paper.

My press secretary, Deborah Orinske, had given me three phone messages from Ralph, all in the past twenty-four hours. Deborah was no novice at Hill press operations. She'd served five years with Gannon, and before that had worked for UPI, first in Trenton and then in Washington.

Her notes all referred to Ralph as "Duca deSantis." I could really get to like Deborah.

"I've got your phone calls, Ralph. But I've been in two committee meetings and was on the floor voting last night, when you first called, until eleven p.m."

"So you're busy, Norie. So's the governor. And so was Senator Gannon. And so is your colleague from Pennsylvania, Senator Smith."

Some people thought Ralph deSantis ran the state—now I knew he thought it too. If I didn't know his power, he was going to tell me, right during this phone call.

I'd buzzed Nancy and, when she came in, handed her a note to rush Deborah in, quietly. As soon as Deborah was in the door, I motioned for her to pick up the receiver beside the sofa. Ralph was rambling on about the governor's power, his friendship with the governor, and just how important it was that I return his calls.

"Ralph, I can promise you it won't happen again. I'll tell Deborah that when you need to reach me, and it's urgent, she should track me down and I'll get right back to you."

"DEB-BOR-RA wouldn't know urgent from passing the time of day . . ."

I looked over at my press secretary, and she shrugged her shoulders, then pantomimed slugging down a drink, over and over again.

Of course. Ralph was loaded. At three in the afternoon. But being drunk didn't make him any less powerful. I'd still have to treat him as though he were the world's most important reporter.

"Anyway, my question is not urgent. At least not for me. But it sure is important for you, Senator. Here's my question: What exactly are your future plans?"

"Today? Tomorrow? Next month?"

"Well, generally the future. You know, people back here are wondering if you plan to make an all-out fight for the Senate. Are you going to tackle some of the big boys if they try to edge you out of the nomination?"

"Ralph, I'm doing the job the governor appointed me to do. If I'm the nominee . . ."

"You gotta lotta work to make yourself known. You need advice, help . . ."

"Ralph, *if* I'm the nominee, the party will be behind me." I decided to push it a little. "I have friends. Supporters. People who really want me to go for it. Important people who have been involved in other campaigns. Who would serve on any committee I would set up. Who would help me to find the best consultants, pollsters, that kind of professional backup. *If* I had the nomination, that is."

"Norie, if you think it's going to be easy getting to be the nominee, you're out in left field. I understand the governor has warned you not to make too big of a splash down there, not to do anything that would hurt a professional who might run for the seat. And, of course, whether he wants it or not, Governor Hartag is getting a lot of pressure to go for the nomination himself. You can understand that, can't you?"

Now I was catching on. Ralph wasn't just calling to chat. Somebody—probably my pal the governor—had set him up to sound me out on my political ambitions, on my loyalty, on what I saw in my future.

I looked over at Deborah. She was wildly shaking her head, drawing her hand across her throat in a "cut-it-off" pantomime.

I was almost ready to do just that. But if other people could use Ralph deSantis, so could I.

"What do you really think about my candidacy, Ralph?"

"Think about your running? Well, you're there. That gives you a kind of funny leg up. *If* you do a good job. If you make an impression, you'll be a strong contender. But that's pretty hard to do by this coming November. Unless you come up with a really strong issue, something that would really show the people here in the state that you know how to operate in Washington."

"Well, I think I'm learning the job as fast as I can. Trying to serve the—"

"Senator, you need to get yourself on that committee. The one on the MIAs. It's a real winner. You think you got a chance?"

DeSantis was amazing. He set up the proposition, questioned it, and then answered his own question. I guessed I could do the same.

"It's looking good, Ralph. Of course, a lot of senators are interested in the committee. But those letters coming in from Pennsylvania—urging Phil Fox to appoint me—they're really a big help. We're all amazed here at my support."

"Are we talking a lot of letters?"

"I'm told from someone close to the process that it's really record-setting just how many letters there are." Deborah was jumping up and down, like a silent-movie cheerleader.

"Well, Senator, filling me in with that kind of

information, now that's the kind of cooperation I appreciate, Senator. Thanks for the story."

I hated to say it, but I knew he was waiting.

"And thank you, Ralph, for such good advice."

"Does that happen a lot?"

"A couple times." Deborah looked uncomfortable. "More than that. When he's drunk, he's worse. Nasty to me."

"Want to have a cup of coffee and talk about it?"

She nodded, and I pointed her to one of the two sofas grouped around a coffee table. I'd had the furniture moved, rearranged, so I didn't feel as if I were holding court.

Nancy always made sure there was a coffee thermos, cups, sugar, and creamer on a tray on my coffee table. It was an old habit from Harrisburg, especially when I was dealing with stuck-in-the-system bureaucrats. Everything was cozy over a nice cup of coffee.

"How bad is deSantis?"

I watched Deborah's reaction. I thought her face showed the strain of trying not to show what she felt.

"Very bad. Threatening. He's got twenty requests for information, for statements, every week. He's not even the Washington correspondent, but he just takes every chance he can to make my life hell. He wants everything. And nothing is ever right."

"Did you ever complain to Senator Gannon?"

"About deSantis? The governor's dearest friend?" She held her coffee cup in both hands and drank it as if her throat were parched. "Once, just once, I brought it up. Had to be five, six years ago, when I first got hired. DeSantis was down here, in D.C., for some newspaper publishers' convention. He came by the office. He asked me out. I said I didn't have nighttime baby-sitters and that my three kids were young."

I waited.

"He said he'd pay for a baby-sitter. That he had a giant expense account. I said I wasn't dating anybody. That I had just separated from my husband and it was all just too fresh."

"Did he let it go at that?"

"No. He picked up a photo of my kids that was on my desk. My husband, the kids' father, is white. My kids are very light-skinned." She bit her lip, but suddenly looked defiant. "DeSantis told me that I just needed an Italian beef injection to clear out my system. I told him I didn't listen to language like that. To please get out of my office. I went to Senator Gannon. I didn't tell him exactly what deSantis said. I was too ashamed. But anyway, he brushed it off. Said, 'Ralph is a great kidder. Great jokester.' "

"And now?"

"Now it's just a constant source of aggravation. I do what my job demands."

"I'm sorry. I'm going to fix this."

"He's too powerful, Senator."

"I'm not going to fight him. I'm going to give him special treatment."

I buzzed Nancy, asked her to get deSantis on the line.

"Ralph. Norie. Been thinking about what you said. Look, I want you to have the most special treatment I can give you. No, no. It's my pleasure. So when you need to reach me, don't hassle with my press operation. Just ring up Nancy." He didn't like that, but he didn't know what to say. "In fact, I'm going to tell Deborah to just forward any calls from you directly to Nancy, so you can come right into my line. No, Ralph, I insist."

I hung up the phone.

"There's more than one way to skin a sexist pig," I told Deborah. "I'm getting better at handling the animals."

"Maybe, Senator," she said, grinning, "that's why they put you on the Agriculture Committee."

12

FOR THE NEXT TWO WEEKS, I COULD BARELY KEEP TRACK of all the advice people wanted to send my way. A few even came up with some actual information. Naturally, not everything I heard made me happy.

On Thursday night the Senate finally wrapped up several twelve-hour days of what was becoming its favorite sport, "dueling amendments." One after another after another amendment was introduced. And one after another after another was voted down. At first, the whole legislative battle was exciting. Then it became exacting. Finally, it reached the exhausting pain-in-the-neck stage.

I stumbled into my apartment long after the dinner hour, once again stopped by yet another graduate student masquerading as the deskman-doorman in my lobby.

"Just checking. Want to keep the security tight." The little automaton was positively smarmy. Probably another political scientist.

Within minutes, though, I'd poured myself a glass of nice Chianti, plopped some diced onions and celery from their plastic bags into a pan with a dash of olive oil, and was happily chunking up a passable eggplant.

I popped the play button on my answering machine and listened to the standard stuff: my mother wondering why the federal government wasn't urging people to become vegetarians, since it would save money in Medicare payments; Kathleen Burns suggesting that I get myself a red blazer or maybe even a pink one, so I could "stand out in that sea of suits"; Lieutenant Carver saying that he could not get me to return phone calls at the office, so he had had the Capitol switchboard put him through to my home and would I please call him back.

I was opening a box of Pomi Italian tomatoes and thinking how impossible it was to find a fresh tomato in Washington, D.C., when I heard the unfamiliar voice put in his two bits.

"Norie, Norie Gorzack. You better watch out, you know. You're treading on dangerous ground. You care about Vietnam. A lot of these bastards . . ."

A piece of my eggplant rolled away. I hit the stop button on the machine, rewound, and listened again.

". . . a lot of these bastards you work with don't want to tell the truth. But guys from Nam, guys from Delta Force, know you're up to the job. And we're ready—ready to take on anybody who gives you any trouble."

I played the recording through two more times, and then went back to my eggplant. I was making my own version of quick caponata, and planned to pour the vegetable mix over some rotelli I was boiling. I covered the sauce, sat down at my kitchen counter, telephoned Kathleen, and told her about my strange phone message.

"Well, with friends like you have, you don't need a lot of enemies. It's pretty weird. I think you should call somebody. That detective you told me about."

"Carver? Why? The man on the phone didn't threaten me. In fact, he said he liked me, wanted to help me."

"It's not what he said. It's that he called you at home."

"Yes?"

"Norie! Your phone's not listed. How did some wacko get your unlisted number?"

I took Kathleen's advice, and called the Capitol switchboard.

"This is Senator Gorzack. Did you put any calls through to me at home tonight?"

There was a pause. Then the operator came back on and told me no. And she was sure, since Lieutenant Carver had instructed them to keep track of any calls through the switchboard to my home number. I asked her to connect me to Lieutenant Carver and said I would wait while she tracked him down.

I turned the burner off under my pasta and, holding

the phone on one shoulder, drained the curly noodles, then flipped them into the pan with the caponata mixture. I grabbed a small can of olives off the shell, sliced a couple, and threw them on top, keeping the heat low. Then I tossed some rough-grated Parmesan on top and covered the pan for maybe thirty seconds, just to soften it up.

"Senator, hold on a sec!" Carver had answered the phone against a background of rock and roll and adolescent voices. "Keep it down! Not you, Senator. The kids. As if three teenagers weren't enough, they all bring their friends home with them. Hold on and I'll pick you up in the kitchen."

Carver's push on his hold button brought on a sudden surge of silence. I sometimes forget how quiet solitude can be.

"Sorry. The kids." The noise was still there, only modulated.

"You have three?"

"Yes, although one will be off to college next September. Addie is going to Emory. The other two, the boys, will probably spend the next ten years trying to finish high school."

"You and your wife must be very proud." My compliment brought an almost imperceptible pause.

"I am. My wife, Senator, is gone."

"I'm so sorry. I know how terrible it is to lose a loved one."

"No, no." Carver almost sounded as if he were laughing. "Not gone as in dead. Gone as in headed out the door about ten years ago, leaving a note that said we were all holding her back from fully developing herself."

Now what was I supposed to say? In my handful of meetings with Carver, I had never thought about him having a family, or being a single parent, or having a sadness of his own.

"But we're not supposed to be talking about me." He took me off the conversational hook. "I called because I can't get you on the phone when you're at work. And I think we've got to stay in touch—both about Jake Browning and about these hate letters."

"I've been trying to figure out if there's any connection. Do you think—"

"I don't think anything. I know that you've been a senator for less than a month and you've got more problems than your whole side of the aisle all put together."

"Speaking of that," I said, trying to sound upbeat, "here's another one. Some other crazy person is trying to communicate with me. This one by telephone. Identified himself as Delta Force. His message was on the machine right after yours. He just offered me some advice and told me he was looking out for me. The strange thing is that my home phone is unlisted."

Now the silence was at the other end of the line. When Carver broke it, his voice was crisp and cold.

"Let me ask you, Senator, to stop answering that phone. Use your machine to screen the calls, and pick up only if it's family or very close friends."

"Okay. If you insist. But it seems really unnecessary."

"I'm not just making conversation, Senator. I'm telling you to keep yourself safe by screening those calls. If someone is crank-calling, then he will quickly realize that he can't tell if you're home or not, because you never, never answer."

"And if I get any more messages like that one?"

"Ring me up. Any hour of the night or day."

I ate my pasta, then went in and got my briefcase. I took out the folders with the letters and wrote down the date, marking beside it, "Delta Force, phone call."

Even Milton brought me some choice tidbits of information.

With Hilda's urging, Fox was sounding out other senators about the importance—or unimportance—of having a woman committee member. And some senators, according to Hilda, were more than supportive of the idea.

Milton got himself busying trying to find out just which senators were supportive and which were leaning. We'd made a deal, Milton and I, for mutual cooperation—but he was going much farther than I had expected, really calling in his chits.

The Hill, I was finding out, was like any other business or bureaucracy—the staff pretty much knew what was going on long before the honchos did. So Milton spent long hours on the phone and over coffee with various administrative assistants, legislative assistants, press secretaries, and committee staffers trying to line up backing for my appointment to the Select Committee on MIAs. He wasn't sure yet who were my real supporters, senators who would go down the line for my appointment—or if there were any such friends. But he had found out who was my enemy.

Seems like somewhere along the way to his chairing the select committee, Garrett Baxter mislaid his Southern gallantry and was now fighting, no holds barred, to keep me off *his* committee.

Once again, Hilda's prediction was right: as soon as I wanted something senatorial, Baxter's friendliness melted away, revealing the hard ground underneath. According to Milton's intelligence, Baxter had told several senators that he would use extraordinary means to block my appointment.

If Baxter thought I was going to roll over and play dead, he was living in the wrong century.

I'd learned my lesson in my first capitulating conversation with Foxy. Be prepared. Know your enemy. Know your agenda. And don't leave the room until you get what you want. If Baxter was my main opposition, so he was also my main target. I'd find out everything I could about him.

On the surface, Baxter's vita was so pristine and patrician that he hardly seemed political. The *Almanac of American Politics*, now handy in my top desk drawer, pointed out that Baxter was the military's main man on Capitol Hill. Bombers, fighters, tracking devices—way-out-in-space high-tech satellites and searchlights—Garrett Baxter voted for them all. He'd just never met a weapons system he didn't like.

A distinguished Korean War hero, Baxter was the

third member of his family to serve in the Senate. A graduate of the Citadel, the "senators' senator," he had geared his public life to protecting legislative procedure and protocol that, at times, only he seemed to remember. The *Almanac* was clear that Baxter's intimate knowledge of the Senate rules gave him inordinate power, able, as one unnamed colleague said, "to kill a piece of legislation in three easy motions to table."

Only thing is, Milton had come across some interesting data on Baxter that might explain how he was glacier-cool on the outside but churning like a volcano underneath. I'd been back in the state for the weekend, and Monday had been so hectic that it was well after dinnertime and I was heading for the elevator when Milton finally caught up to me.

"Just wait a minute. I have to do something. It'll just take a minute and then we'll go down in the elevator together."

I'd cooled my heels, and Milton, true to form, made no attempt to excuse his delay when he reappeared, although his information was more than interesting.

"I talked to that old guy from AP, the one who's been covering the Hill since WWII. Baxter's got some big problem around Vietnam."

"Problem? Did Baxter fight in Vietnam?"

"No. Too old. But neither did his kid. That's the problem. His son, like Baxter, graduated from the Citadel. It was the early 1970s, and the kid just didn't want to go."

"My God, that must have been terrible on Baxter."

"And on the kid. He took his moral stand—he wasn't going to fight in what he saw as an immoral war. The kid resigns his commission. And then, in order not to shame his father or appear a coward, he becomes a noncombat medic. Pretty amazing, huh?"

We got out of the elevator, and Milton offered me a ride to my apartment. I turned him down. I needed the fresh air. He refused to take no for an answer. As we walked toward his parking space, I realized the story wasn't finished.

"So what happened, anyway?" I asked.

"The kid was killed. Served almost the entire year. Then killed. His last month. And to make it even worse, friendly fire."

"And Baxter was left with nothing resolved?"

"To put it mildly. He became more and more of a hawk. If the military wanted something, so did Baxter. His son might not have been a hero, but . . ."

I nodded. I began to understand the complexities of Senator Baxter.

"We've been so jammed today I didn't get to ask you how things went back in the state over the weekend," Milton said, seemingly genuinely interested in what I was about to say.

"The meetings with local party leaders went okay, although I must tell you that the congressman from Chester is getting to be a pain."

"He wanted your job."

"It went well in Pittsburgh. Fred Dexter apparently likes what I'm doing and has reported that back to the county chair."

"Did you take any time for yourself?"

"I'd had an early-Saturday-morning coffee with some friends. And I spent Sunday vegging out at my mother's. And you? Do you ever relax, Milton?"

"I work out. Religiously and regularly. I like to read. I like movies. Sure. I relax. That's how I get so much done. I relax a lot."

Sure, I thought. That's the statement of a relaxed man.

13

LEARNING A LITTLE ABOUT GARRETT BAXTER WAS LIKE having half a chocolate cake sitting in the refrigerator: The more bites you sliced off the edge, the more your appetite got whetted.

Milton's well of information had run dry, so I decided to poke around in Baxter's ideological backyard. I called up Stewart Conover and asked him to dinner.

The plan was for Stewart to come by the office and we'd head out for a quick bite. I thought one of the it-all-tastes-the-same nouveau-Italian-Southwestern places over at Union Station would do just fine—until my leader, Senator Fox, decided to schedule several votes.

"Call up and cancel Mr. Conover," I told Nancy.

"Hey, he's a friend of George Taylor. Or maybe it's

Marco Solari. Whatever. Let me try to work something out."

"You don't need to meddle. It's just a business dinner," I offered.

"I'm just trying to make sure that you meet someone this month besides Bob Sanders." Nancy was relentless on the subject of Bob, who had made himself a fixture in our office. That first morning, after Jake Browning's memorial service, he'd shown up shortly before nine, "ready to work," as he told Amy via her computer screen. And he'd shown up every day since. On the whole, I thought he behaved better than some of my paid staff. He was intent on helping Amy with her projects, and he managed to smile whenever I walked by.

"Well, Mr. Conover had better be either a quick eater or very creative if he plans to fit in dinner with all these votes tonight."

Creative he was. Stewart Conover, complete with the requisite blue pinstripe suit, showed up carrying two of those canvas deck bags with the red handles that get featured in those catalogs from Maine. He'd been waiting outside my private office, and after a hearty handshake, he let me peek inside one bag at stacks of plastic boxes—pasta salad, deli sandwiches, good olives, roasted red peppers, two short baguettes of bread, and a big chunk of Parmesan.

"This is some idea of carryout."

"I don't get asked to dinner by many senators. And I know how heavy the vote schedule is." He waved co-conspiratorially at Nancy. "Do you have your beeper on you?"

I nodded.

"Put on your coat, please." He held open the door with his shoulder. "Okay. Well, follow me."

He led me down the hallway, into the elevator, and outside. It was getting slightly warmer. March was here. Winter had almost ended. The day's tourists were gone, and only an occasional staff member or a Capitol policeman passed us.

"Okay, where are we heading?" I asked. We walked across the Triangle and around the Capitol, and I caught sight of the top of the Washington Monument shooting up from its place on the Mall.

"Bundle up. I've got a big thermos of coffee, but, hey, this is no colder than football weather in Philly. So we are going to pretend its really spring and sit on the back porch—and this is the 'back,' not the 'front,' of the Capitol. And we are going to have a picnic supper. You'll probably make it about eight minutes before you get beeped. But it's only a short walk from our 'table' to the Senate."

It was a little cool, but out of his second canvas bag Stewart produced a red-and-white checkered table-cloth, a couple of stadium blankets, and two pillows. The pillows were a new gadget, he explained, with battery-powered heaters. It made me smile, until I sat on one—and it worked.

Stewart set up the "table." I put my beeper on the cloth in front of me, and, in a kidding game of can-you-top-this, Stewart rummaged in his pockets and produced a small cellular phone, another beeper, and a slim pocket computer.

"I just can't turn a techno-toy down," he said.

I didn't respond. Let Stewart Conover run the conversation for a while, I figured, since I wanted to work Garrett Baxter into the conversation with some degree of casualness—and anyway, I wasn't sure how I would describe this al fresco dinner, even to myself.

"First, I'm going to talk to you about ulterior motives, Senator. And I have a couple of them." He took a piece of the bread and laid a pepper on it, sticking a couple of olives under the shiny red vegetable and taking a bite before he continued. "I have clients. Clients have interests. They pay me to push their agenda. I do a good job. I work hard to get legislation passed that's favorable to their various industries—and to the country's economy."

"I'm sure, Stewart, that any client you have is one that only does the best for America," I laughed.

"Seriously, that's more true than not. I believe in American industry and I believe that we need to create jobs and give the kinds of incentives that allow that industrial success to flourish." He was sounding like a speech. Then he waved a red-checkered napkin around, like a flag. "Not that I don't get paid well. And not that some people up here on the Hill, who support other sides of these same questions, wouldn't assail everything I just said."

"Okay. So you are not St. Francis."

"No. He was worried about feeding birds and animals. I'm concerned about putting bread on working people's tables."

"Me too," I managed, between sips of coffee.

"But I have another agenda."

I took some of the pasta salad and a piece of the bread. I poured some of the coffee into my paper cup. Of course he had another agenda. He was going to tell me right now that he needed such-and-such a piece of legislation brought out of the Agriculture Committee. He probably did chemical and biological warfare on bugs.

"Senator, I want to make sure that you get every break you can. I want to make sure that you succeed."

"That's very nice. Considering that we don't know each other very well. Or that you even know what I stand for."

"Marco Solari has filled me in. A lot. For a long time, I represented one of the major unions here in town—not on all their stuff, but just kind of working out problem areas. So I know Marco—and, through him, I know about you."

"So what you are saying"—I tried to be light—"what you're saying is that you have my best interests at heart."

"Enough to want to see you have an extended stay here. You've got a tight schedule. By the time this special election rolls around in November, you'll have little of the regular support or the stature that most sitting senators have going into an election. Running for reelection to the Senate is a pretty luxurious thing. Senators shop around for the first couple of years of their six-year term, figure out where they want to go, then slowly maneuver themselves into position to get reelected. Not you. It's coming fast down this track."

"That's what my friends tell me."

"But you're a woman. You're going to get some fund-raising punch that way. And, if things work out, you're going to get an issue. You're a natural for the Select Committee on MIAs."

"Maybe you could call up Senator Baxter and tell him your views. He doesn't like mine." I was sorry I had said it as soon as the words were out of my mouth. Criticizing Baxter wasn't a smart way to find out about him.

We were both distracted from what I thought was my faux pas by the arrival at our picnic site of a uniformed Capitol policeman.

"Excuse me, folks, but this is not a . . ." He started, then corrected himself. "Sorry, Senator Gorzack. Thought you were just tourists."

"How about a flavored iced tea?" Stewart offered. But the policeman shook his head and walked away.

"So we were talking about your being a natural for the Select Committee on MIAs."

"A natural?"

"You've got knowledge. It's your issue."

"Baxter doesn't see it that way."

"Baxter wants this issue to go away."

"What?"

"Disappear. Read over his statements on the floor over the past ten years. Look at some of his speeches. I have." Stewart shook his head. "He doesn't want any MIAs. Too messy. Brings attention back to Vietnam."

"And his son?" I offered.

"No. Not his personal defeat. The defeat of the country. America, the loser. It's taken a long time, in Baxter's view, and a lot of Desert Storm, to turn around that unhealthy self-image."

My beeper gave me a ten-minute-to-a-vote-warning. The artificial voice, making the announcement still startled me when I heard it, especially here, coming out of the darkness of the tablecloth.

"You've got a vote. And the batteries on our seat-warming cushions are running down a little."

I started to gather up the paper plates, but Stewart waved away my help.

"I'll do this. You go vote." He contradicted his own offer by stopping his packing. "That's the way I want to help you. I'll do some of the cleanup for your campaign—help you with money, with introductions. And you be the senator."

"Sounds pretty good. Especially good if I get on the committee."

"I'm not promising anything. And I'm sure you've got a lot more connected people than me pulling for you. But I'll put in my two cents wherever I think it'll help."

"That'd be great." I started to stand up. "Thanks for dinner."

"I'll try to be helpful, Senator. I hear a lot of things." His voice drifted off, more said in the nuance than in any words. "It's funny, but the corporate world always knows what's happening, especially corporations with headquarters based overseas, like a couple of my clients. You'd be surprised what stuff I've heard about Southeast Asia. Although, I'm warning you, its nothing that I can verify. That would be up to you—and the committee."

"Do you think the committee will succeed, Stewart?"

"If Baxter lets it. I'm a bad one to ask, Senator. I'm never hopeful about any of this stuff." He popped a pickle into his mouth. "Too good to waste."

"What would make you hopeful?"

"Somebody to stand up to some of the more powerful people up here. Not just Baxter, but others, who think the truth is a fatal disease."

"That's pretty damning. Even for a . . ." I wasn't sure what to call him, but he provided the word.

"For a lobbyist? Don't worry. That's what I am. And it's not a four-letter word. Anyway, I work here because I've got a fatal disease myself. Politics. And sometimes I get to use my influence for something good—get laws governing foreign adoptions improved, benefit packages for vets made bigger. That kind of stuff."

"Sounds like a great job to me," I said, heading up the steps to go and cast my vote against yet another amendment. "Wanna trade?"

My last piece of advice came just the day before Baxter was set to announce the select committee membership. And even though I was blocks from the Hill, the counsel came in a totally appropriate place and from someone I decided was more than appropriate.

I was spending my lunchtime at the Vietnam Memorial. I had been trying to do it one day a week. The walk over, twenty minutes or so to sit there and think about Jack, and then the walk back to the Hill—it made for an oasis of peace, a sanctuary of quiet in days filled with talk and confrontation.

"Senator Gorzack?" The woman standing between me and the shimmering granite wall was trim and tailored, in a crisp khaki trench coat. Her face was pretty, and contradictorily youthful, compared to the mane of white hair that framed it like some New Age halo. She was vaguely familiar, but no name popped into my head.

"Nina. Nina Dexter." She stuck out her hand. Of course, the activist wife of the Neanderthal congressman from Pittsburgh, Fred Dexter. She'd been profiled in just about every Pennsylvania publication, lauded for her commitment to electing women to office.

"Hi. What a surprise. I was just heading back to the Hill."

"Me too. I guess you come here a lot?" She looked pleased at the thought.

"When I can." I hesitated. It was always hard when you met someone at the memorial—like running into an old friend at a doctor's office and being afraid to ask what's wrong.

"Me too. A friend of mine is here. From high school.

In 1968. Tet. Not a pilot or anything like that. A grunt." She seemed to avoid mentioning his name, as though it were too painful.

"I'm sorry." So she was around my age. It was the contradictory hair that confused me.

"Long time ago. We were engaged. Just out of high school. I was back home. Cleveland. Working as a secretary. Just nineteen. What limited horizons I had then."

We walked along the Mall, past the Washington Monument, the Capitol materializing above the trees. We talked, the way women do when they first meet— about their families, their growing up, their friends, their concerns. I always think that men miss the most important parts of learning about each other, since they take such great care to avoid the personal.

As she talked, I wondered why Hilda hadn't mentioned Nina as someone I should get to know. Her work was impressive. For more than ten years, she'd helped women get elected to federal office. Not, she stressed, as part of the effort put on by groups like Emily's List, or the Women's Campaign Fund, which had been instrumental in increasing the number of women officeholders from 1990 on.

No, what she did, Nina explained, was to carefully select just a few women candidates and give them her all.

"I do whatever's necessary. Fund-raising is the most important first step. But I go to those women's districts. I strategize and organize, introduce them around in Washington. And I make sure that they hire women."

It was all volunteer, since "Fred makes enough money for both of us." Details of all those newspaper articles were filling in the gaps. Nina had come to Washington some twenty years before, and gotten a job as a receptionist in a congressman's office. When he was defeated in the great post-Watergate congressional upheaval, his successor kept her on. And then married her. Now Representative Fred Dexter was himself practically a fixture on Capitol Hill, and, although almost thirty years separated their ages, I remembered the *Inquirer* assuring its readers that the Dexters were a singularly successful and happy couple.

"It was wonderful seeing you again, Senator." We'd reached the end of the Mall, and the Capitol rose above us. I reached out and took her in a hug. And was surprised when I felt her tremble.

"I'm sorry, Norie, to get emotional. But you'll never know what your appointment to the Senate meant to me. How deeply it affected me. Can I offer you some advice?"

I nodded eagerly.

"Speak out. Don't listen to what the 'suits' are telling you. People out in the country want to hear the truth, not a lot of political rubbish."

She turned and walked toward the House side of the Hill, striding with an energy I wished I felt.

☆☆☆ **14** ☆☆☆

My mother broke the news to me about the select committee.

"Norie, is that you?" she asked hesitantly, as the day's first light snuck through my blinds. "Are you all right? You sound strange. Muffled."

"Mom, it's the middle of the night. It's like five a.m. Are *you* all right?"

"Well, I had a headache last night. But then I took some of those new, extra-strength—"

"Mom. No. Listen. Are you all right now? Is there any emergency?"

"Not with me. Maybe with you."

"No. I'm looking around my bedroom." I sat up in bed and stuffed the pillows behind my back. "And I can't see any emergency."

"There's going to be one. I didn't sleep well. I've

been up since four and I've been listening to the radio and you won't believe what they said."

"Okay. What."

"You're on the committee. The MIA Committee."

How was I going to explain this.

"Mom, the committee gets announced at ten o'clock this morning. Then we'll know who's on the committee."

"No. The man was very clear. 'Senator Eleanor Gorzack has been named to the committee.' That's what he said."

"Okay, Mom. I'll call you later in the day."

"Hon, it's early. Maybe you should get some sleep."

"You're in. I don't know how I pulled this off, but you're in."

"Milton, it's not announced for another hour. You sound like my mother."

"Your mother? Sometimes I don't understand you, Senator. You're in. You're on. You're it. I can't believe I did this. Right through the hoop. No reaction? You're not happy?"

"I'll be happy when I get the word that I'm on the committee."

"Look, Senator, it's not like God is going to show up here and say, 'Hey, you're on the select committee.' "

"I don't want God to tell me. I want Garrett Baxter to."

"Senator. This is Garrett Baxter. I'll be making my announcement of the committee in the next half hour and I wanted to be the one to inform you that you are a member. The junior member."

"Senator Baxter, I can't tell you how happy I am, how I'm ready to work on this issue, how close it is to—"

"You'll be sent a memo this afternoon on the times and places of the first organizational meetings. I will not need you at the news conference."

"Don't do anything that's not planned. Or Baxter will kill you."

Maybe, someday, I would eventually begin to miss the sound of Milton hissing in my ear. It wouldn't be soon. Milton's concept of communication followed the general conspiracy theories he brought to every aspect of everyday life, like some random Shakespearean minion whose only task is to warn and portend.

But there was no way that he was going to color this morning. *This* morning I wouldn't let his foreboding faze me.

I let him be in charge as we made our way to the Russell Caucus Room. I let him maneuver me down the hall, past seemingly miles of folding tables, all glutted with audio equipment, surrounded by sound crews and associate producers with their walkie-talkies.

"Don't want the senator to be late on her first big committee day." Milton pushed me through the final barrier, the spectators who formed a thick cordon right outside the door.

A blond woman, familiar to me from the nightly

news, waved wildly at Milton and tried to clamber past several people to reach us. Without hesitation, my trusty aide returned the wave, but sped us up, moving us out of reach and into the room.

I'd been a senator for less than two months, but I was learning. As Milton kept telling me, "They can't hit a moving target."

Milton and I were completing our shakedown cruise with a more positive result than I'd ever dreamed possible. The endless face-offs—the go-rounds that left me sure that Milton was a paid agent of the opposition party, the insistent arguments in which *we* debated *my* political future—now were more civil and seemed aimed at getting something accomplished.

The office ran more smoothly—*my* office ran more smoothly. I was learning the ropes, operating more confidently every day, even allowing Milton to push me around occasionally as if I were some slightly shy child. Maybe he knew my mother.

Best of all, my squeaky wheel had gotten greased. I was on the Select Committee on MIAs.

Milton had done his bit. So, obviously, had Hilda. And, I was beginning to realize, so had a lot of other friends. At least that's what my phone messages looked like in the hour after Baxter had announced his committee makeup. Just about everybody was taking a little bit of the credit, including, I was sure, the man who carried out the trash. It seemed that literally hundreds of people had put in a good word with Phil Fox and Baxter—or so they were now saying.

"Rule seven hundred and two." Milton kept up his counsel as we made our way along the back of the committee table, the vast leather chairs rising like cobras with their curved tops. "You know that rule. Right?"

"Remind me."

"Don't kid. It's not hard. Just remember, all the rules are exactly the same. 'Never upstage the chairman.' Let him be the star. Let him be the one to explain how the committee will work, is working. Let Chairman Baxter give out with the interviews and take the bows."

"So, what you are saying is that I shouldn't talk to the press anymore?" I turned so that my back was to the audience. I was tense, and maybe even scared. But I couldn't resist poking Milton's attitude, just a bit. So, with my face away from everyone's but his, I crossed my eyes.

"I promise. No press interviews."

"No. Please, stop that. Senator! I want you to talk to the press. But only when you have something to say. And after you've run it by me first." I shot him a look and he quickly added, "To get my input. My counsel."

I nodded and sat down. My chair swung gently from side to side.

A few feet to the rear of the committee chairs was a row of straight-back chairs for the committee staff—knowledge, experience, advice, all within easy reach of any senator. The TV lights were hot, and I worried that my makeup would start to run in big orange streaks down my face. Then I decided that no one would notice, since the cameras were focused directly on the center chair, where Garrett Lee Baxter would sit.

The Russell Caucus Room was the biggest hearing room on the Senate side of the Capitol. At a short briefing held the day before, a staff member had explained that the room could accommodate slightly more than four hundred observers. From up front, it looked like a lot more. The opening day of the hearings by the Select Committee on Missing in Action and Prisoners of War had turned out the crowds.

This was great theater. There was the whisper heard before the curtain went up on a play destined to be a hit—the confident, impatient breathing of the crowd, and, on every face, the look of success that a theatergoer has, walking down the aisle, a prized ticket stub in hand. On cue, a Senate page distributed to reporters copies of the various opening statements that would be made by committee members.

Up on the dais, several other members of the committee had taken their seats. A folder with their various statements lay on the desk in front of me. The C-Span camera crew and the pool camera, which would feed the networks and CNN, held their stationary positions. Still photographers jockeyed for spots in front, since, Milton had explained to me, they were allowed to shoot only for the hearing's first five minutes. Two pool photographers would shoot for the remainder of the hearing. Reporters were massed around tables at the front of the audience, and a dozen or so seats were reserved for witnesses and their families. The remainder of the four hundred-plus places went on a first-come, first-seated basis.

"Look, it's your debut," Milton whispered, issuing a final warning before escaping offstage. "The first time you're being measured against the big boys. Don't screw up or they'll screw you. They didn't want you on the committee." He absentmindedly patted me on the shoulder. "Remember the S's and you'll do fine—keep it straight, simple, and senatorial."

"Let me add another S. Stupid. That's what I sound like with this statement." I took the two-page text out of my briefcase and put it on top of the folder. "I'm talking like every government bureaucrat I went to when Jack was first declared MIA. I know the rap: 'God and patriotism and country,' although not necessarily in that order."

"So you know the rap," Milton countered. "So stick to it."

There were, magically, still more lights switched on, and a rush of photographers whose impatience heralded the arrival of Senator Baxter. The dozen photographers crouched down in front of the dais trembled like nimble spiders ready to catch their prey in a web of film.

The pops of their flashes and Baxter pounding his gavel started the hearing. His voice was lilting, a tenor in a Technicolor musical.

"Ladies and gentlemen. This hearing of the Select Committee on Missing in Action and Prisoners of War is formally called to order. We have been charged by our colleagues with the following mission: We are here to find the truth."

Like second-grade children following a history lesson, tables of reporters picked up their copies of Baxter's opening statement, and, like a marching band, turned the pages in perfect sync as he read on and on. The prepared statements, which were a constant feature of any opening session of any committee, allowed the print journalists to get each word precisely. Statements also gave TV journalists the chance to tape only the best quotes, knowing them in advance and directing their camera crews to catch the sound bites which carried the most punch.

My own short and quite sad little statement sat in front of me on the table. It seemed to chide me for my lack of courage.

I looked to my left, to the line of senators waiting for their chance to speak. Seating and speaking were decided strictly by seniority, so I would make my statement last, following committee members from both parties, who got the first shots at putting forth their personal twist on the "committee's mission."

I flipped open my folder, and there, on the top of the carefully typed papers, was a sheet of red construction paper, the kind kids use for art projects. There was nothing written on it, merely a pasted-on photograph of me, stuck on crookedly, seemingly afloat on a blood-red sea flooding out from underneath. Drawn around my neck was a noose, also bright red, and a crudely sketched tongue hung out of my mouth. It was ugly and mean.

I closed the folder and looked around. The eyes of my colleagues and the audience were on Baxter. But I knew that one person was watching me, gauging my fear, measuring my response.

I had traveled a long road by myself looking for Jack, waiting for Jack, hoping for Jack.

No piece of hate mail was going to keep me from my love.

I STARTED TO EDIT MY STATEMENT.

First, I changed an adjective, from "unsafe" to "dangerous." Then I switched the order of sentences, drawing small arrows to show their new location. After a few minutes, I gave up. This mush couldn't be helped by some minor editing.

I took a sheet of lined white paper from the pad placed at each committee member's place. On the top of each page was printed "U.S. Senate."

On the page I printed several words, in big block letters. "Personal," I wrote. Then "family," under it "consolation," and, after a short pause, "support" and "answers." Maybe I would stick with my prepared statement. Maybe I wouldn't.

The ranking minority committee member followed Baxter, and after he had read his statement, spotlights were turned off. Other senators read their statements, mostly short, mostly saying how proud they were to be part of this mission.

Their speeches gave me a chance to look at the members of the audience. Nancy was in the third row, and on either side of her were members of the National Yellow Ribbon Society, supporters who were not part of an MIAs immediate family, but who worked hard on the issue.

Milton had given me a list of other key people who had said they would be part of the audience. I recognized the names of nurses from the China Beach Club, who had seen duty in Vietnam, and several members of the National League of MIAs.

One woman kept nodding at me, and when she was sure she had caught my eye, she scribbled something on a piece of paper. I watched as, unexpectedly, she gave up her waited-for seat and walked to the back of the room. Moments later a Senate page dropped her note in front of me. My hands were shaking as I opened it.

It was short and, I was glad to see, it wasn't from my regular correspondent:

"Find them. Please. Find them, Norie. Find them for all of us. We are all counting on you to get at the truth."

Holding the note in my hand, I waited as my colleagues droned on and on. Then the lights were turned on as I was introduced by Baxter. Milton had said that I would "get decent coverage, since you're the MIA wife."

And that's what I was, after all. I sometimes forgot it, in the everyday pressures, in the bustle of my professional life, and here, in the Senate. But I never forgot it in the quiet hours. I was an MIA wife, and so I had certain things to say.

"I am proud to be here, proud because it is a day of so many firsts for me. As the first woman from Pennsylvania to serve in the U.S. Senate, as a wife of an MIA, I am doubly proud to share with my fellow senators the honor of serving on this committee. The work of this committee will rank first in my duties as a member of the Senate.

"This is also my first committee statement, gentlemen, and I hope it won't be my last." There was an embarrassed laugh, and for a moment I felt flustered. But only for a moment.

"I am proud to be a U.S. senator. It is a job I never aspired to. When I was growing up, little girls didn't have the Senate on their list of career goals. I shared the dreams of many women my age—wife, mother, a life in which I would care for my family. And a career, too. Nursing. Another way of caring for people.

"But my dream was taken away. What I thought would be my life is now missing. Taken from me, just as my husband was. Missing, just like Captain John Joseph Gorzack of the United States Marine Corps."

There was a slight stirring among the press, as they put down the copies of my now defunct prepared statement and picked up their notebooks.

"With more than a thousand families, I share a nightmare. We must find out what happened to those men—husbands, brothers, fathers—who proudly went forward to serve our country. We have passed a lifetime without them. And, a lifetime later, we still have no accounting. We are tired of cover-ups, whitewashes, patriotic and patronizing speeches, telling us that a grateful nation will never forget. Don't tell me about remembering. How can I forget Jack Gorzack?"

I paused and, for a second, I felt my speech was over. I'd said what I wanted to, laid out my anger as an MIA wife. Then I looked down and there was a piece of paper with my name on it. And my title. Senator Eleanor Gorzack.

"I sit here, having taken an oath of office, proud to defend the Constitution. But I have other oaths, others promises. Every day, every single morning, I put on the two rings that Jack Gorzack first placed on my hand.

"One ring is a miniature of his own Naval Academy ring. He gave it to me the night he asked me to marry him. The other is, of course, my wedding ring. When we were married we vowed our commitment until death would part us. But every day, when I put on my rings, I ask myself, 'Is Jack alive?' That's what the life of anyone who loved an MIA is like. Questions with no answers. Years passing with no change. A lifetime without the life together that we thought was ours.

"What I have are my rings, some very dear memories, and a telegram that told me my husband was missing. Missing? Let me tell you that Jack Gorzack has never been missing from my life, my thoughts, and my prayers for one minute since the day I met him."

I could see Baxter's hand on the gavel, and for one minute I was afraid that he would silence me, push aside my claims to finally know the truth. I could keep him from doing that.

"I sit here representing the people of Pennsylvania. But I claim another constituency. One that I know too well, and know I must serve. The time has come. Tell us, tell the families, tell the American people the truth about our MIAs and POWs. Let us know what the government knows. Show us what you claim is classified. Until you do, we cannot go on with our lives; we cannot bury our dead."

Pulling myself as high as I could in my chair, I turned to Baxter. "Mr. Chairman, I am looking forward to being a very active member of this select committee."

There was tremendous applause, wave after wave of extraordinary cheering, accentuated by the banging of Baxter's gavel as he vainly tried to restore order.

The tears in my eyes blurred the room, but I looked out and saw the anonymous woman who had written the note standing in the rear, shooting her fist into the air several times, a silent salute.

"This is not a soap opera," Baxter shouted into the microphone. His gavel beat out a message of authority. "This is the United States Senate and we will have order or I will clear this room."

The audience slowly quieted itself.

"We have seven witnesses for this first day," Baxter intoned. "The secretary of state, the secretary of defense, the former head of the Joint Chiefs of Staff . . ."

Outside the hearing room, I was mobbed by camera crews and reporters yelling their questions.

"What do you mean by your statement?" one voice rang out. It was Diane Wong.

"What about cover-ups?" a man shouted into my face, his tape recorder pressed against my cheek.

Part of my brain told me to get away from the press, but the emotions set off by my own speech kept me from understanding the consequences of speaking out in the way I had.

Milton's advice, on playing dodgeball with the press, was somehow forgotten.

"There are reports we must look into," I finally said. "There are sightings and information from international sources that the select committee must investigate. The government . . ."

Milton was suddenly in back of me. I knew because his hand was in a death grip on my elbow, trying hard to pull me away.

"That's it, folks. The senator is needed back in her office." He valiantly tried to stop the questions, which kept popping at me like shots from an automatic weapon.

"Just give us one example. Just one," Diane Wong pressured.

"All right. Here's one." I pulled a Xerox copy of a newspaper clip from my briefcase. "Here's a recent newspaper piece by a Norwegian journalist. He claims that in 1979 he was shown a reeducation camp in Vietnam. He says he was taken by Vietnamese officials to the camp, in the countryside, and he is convinced that at least one of the people he saw there was an American. An American. One of our boys."

Before I knew what hit me, a young man ripped the paper from my hand.

"Senator, this article is in Norwegian. Do you speak Norwegian?"

"No, but a friend of mine assures me that what I am telling you is an accurate translation of what the article says."

Milton was like a crane, pulling me back from the scene of what I was beginning to think was a head-on collision.

"We'll get an authorized translation," he reassured the reporters, finally getting me away from the cameras and the lights. "By tomorrow. I promise."

One reporter tried to stop our escape by blocking me, but I was once again with the program and I stepped on his foot.

"You are something else, Senator," Milton finally hissed when he got me outside the Capitol and hurried me down the steps. "Where the hell did you come up with that Norwegian nonsense? You and I have been talking about your statement for the past forty-eight hours. Never, never once did you say anything to me about any of this nonsense. And while we're at it, why can't you play by the rules?"

I refused to answer him. I was going to protect my source.

The Norwegian article had come out of the blue. Stewart Conover had dropped it by my office late the night before, along with several other articles from non-American newspapers—all specific enough to deserve at least a passing glance by the select committee. Stewart had left it up to me, but had suggested that I *not* release the articles to the press. He thought the best tactic was just to bring them to the attention of the committee. He'd also offered to meet with Milton about the material—but I decided then and there that I didn't need to go through Milton every time I had a thought or an idea or a piece of information.

So here were Milton and I, walking back to Hart, all the hard work of building trust gone, washed away. We walked the distance of several long hallways without another word between us. He was obviously saving his ammunition for the privacy of my office.

"You're dead," he said, pacing in front of the windows. "It's a mess, and you've done it. You've killed your future. What if this stuff isn't true? Do you read Norwegian? Who gave that article to you? This is nutcake stuff. I'm quitting."

"If you've got to go, Milton, here's a copy of the article. At least get a translation of the Norwegian, so you can leave knowing that I'm right."

"Okay, I'll get a translation. But if this is some recipe for Yule grog, I'm out of here."

"If it's a recipe for grog, I'll cook it myself."

He left me alone in the office, and I stood there for a long while, beside my desk, liking the way I felt, liking that I had stood up for what I believed in. Maybe Stewart's articles were written by people who didn't have all the facts—but they were a lot more substantive than the pap I'd been getting over the years churned up by my federal government.

"You've got a phone call." Nancy had come into the office without my hearing her.

"Take a message."

"You've got about a thousand phone calls. We can't field them fast enough. The lines are jammed. Looks like everybody stayed home today and watched TV, and they think you did real good, Senator."

I started to take phone calls, randomly talking to voters, to people Nancy insisted on calling "actual citizens." She was right. They were pleased, thrilled, that I was taking on the bureaucracy that had kept the issue submerged for such a long time. Not many of the callers focused on the Norwegian material. Most kept talking about my opening statement.

And, I had to admit to myself, the few people who did want to talk about the Norwegian article, well, they were dyed-in-the-wool conspiracy buffs. One of them had everything back to Lincoln's assassination being the plot of an international secret society.

It was almost six when Stewart Conover got through.

"You know how to do it, Senator. You know how to hit a home run," he began.

"Maybe I shouldn't have used the Norwegian material," I began. But I didn't get far with my second-guessing.

"Hey, it was what you said about your rings. I know. A lot of women will be touched by that. And a lot of guys, too, will be moved. Me, for instance. A lot of people out there are saying, 'Hey, I wish I had somebody who would care for me like that.' "

"That's very nice of you, Stewart."

"No. Just honest. Like you. We've got to keep this issue alive, Norie. It's the only way we'll ever know. Perhaps the only way we'll ever see any of the guys alive."

Stewart's support felt good, but nothing felt like the calls from the "actual citizens," people who believed that their government could do good.

I had one more salute on my schedule.

As I left the office, I noticed Amy, still hard at work on her report—and, beside her, more faithful than any staffer, Bob.

Sighting me, he jumped to his feet and dramatically snapped his hand to his forehead, standing at attention.

"Hurrah, Senator." Amy squealed and clapped her hands. "You really did it today. And Bob thinks so, too."

"I see Bob's still with us." If I hadn't noticed, there wasn't a day that went by when Nancy wasn't telling me.

"He's so helpful with my report. He really knows

just how to find out things. I can't tell you how wonderful it is, working with an actual Vietnam veteran."

Her naiveté broke through my exhaustion, and I smiled. Bob winked and shot another salute.

By now, I had almost put the latest hate mail out of my mind. I headed home, where the most telling response would be waiting for me, on my answering machine.

"Hi. It's Marco. You're probably real exhausted. Well, that was something. A real bombshell. Tough stuff, but it's exactly the person you are. Great job."

That's one, I thought.

"Norie? Hi. It's Kathleen. That was fabulous, and we are really proud. Is your Milton having a fit or what? And what is this Norwegian stuff, anyway? I didn't exactly understand that part of the story."

Two. A little mixed, but two.

"Norie, this is George Taylor. I think the speech went very well, though I can't imagine Baxter is happy at your having stolen the limelight. I am a little worried about that Norwegian paper thing. We shouldn't be setting up false hopes, or any hopes until the committee does its work."

Always cautious George. Not bad, though, considering he was the kind of guy who I always imagined would like to wear both a belt and suspenders.

I was surprised at the call that wasn't waiting for me. I had thought it would come in the office, or, if not, at home. But no. Hilda hadn't called.

Maybe she thought I had gone too far, pushed myself into the limelight a little too much. Today wasn't a very good example of what she called "being one of the gang."

But I had done what I thought I should do.

Anyway, whatever I had done, there was no going back.

☆☆☆ **16** ☆☆☆

"MOM. DON'T LISTEN TO THAT CRAZY MAN." I WAS
trying, unsuccessfully, to balance both my mother's
conversation and the phone receiver tucked under
my chin.

Mom paid me no mind.

"Everybody listens to *Talk America*. And he's not
nuts when he says what a wonderful patriot you
are. Anyway, Miss Know-it-all, I was stopped by at
least three different people outside church last night,
after the novena, and they all said how terrific you
sounded."

"You're terrific, Mom. Now, please, just write a little
note, explaining how wonderful I am, and send it
off to Senator Baxter. Then everything will be
wonderful."

"What are you talking about?"

"Just make it like the excuse you wrote for me in the fifth grade when I gave Mary Sager the black eye. Only this time I'm starting to feel like I gave myself one."

"Norie, don't be silly. You're grown up. Why would you need a note from your mother?"

Maybe not a note, I thought, whipping some egg whites and a touch of skim milk into a nice frothy blend. Maybe Mom could stand beside me, holding my hand, looking like a sweet little old lady—that would be more the ticket. She could tell Baxter a few things she heard on the radio.

Turning up the flame slightly, I poured the eggs over a mixture of finely minced peppers and mushrooms already warm in the bottom of a small frying pan. The veggies were left over from a pasta two nights before. The egg whites set quickly, and, pushing in the cooked parts from the edge of the pan, in less than two minutes I had an almost-no-cholesterol, protein-rich egg-white omelette.

I stuck a little nonfat sour cream and some hot salsa on the top. It was almost perfect, although I had cheated a little and warmed the veggies in a little butter. I have always been a believer in a little butter.

Anyway, any extra calories I picked up would be run off as soon as Senator Baxter caught sight of me. Which happened a lot sooner than I was hoping.

My chairman caught my eye the instant I entered the Senate Chamber later that morning. He was at his desk, which I had become convinced was substantially larger than any other in the chamber. Or maybe it was just the way he stood behind it, like the captain on a starship.

Casually he waved me over. I made my way between empty desks to his prime location, in the second row. I dreaded a public scolding, loud and embarrassing.

Afterward, I realized that what happened was much worse. Baxter's voice was gentle, as syrupy as some South Carolina praline dessert, but it was directly out of a Tennessee Williams play—all laced with arsenic, lethal and mean.

"It's not the conventional wisdom, but I am from the old school," Baxter began, looking somewhere over my head, like in the direction of Virginia. "Maybe it's unfair, but women just don't have the kind of experience in legislative matters that's called for on the federal level. Certainly not in the United States Senate. But"—he fixed me with a steely glance—"you were here, and I was willing to give you every chance."

I started an answer, but with a twist of his hand Baxter cut me off.

"No excuses. Done is done. What you must realize is that you have made it difficult, much more difficult, for me—and *my* committee—to do our work. You must realize that you are out of your depth. You have never before held elective office. I suppose it was too much to hope that you would watch and you would learn the way business is conducted here. Senators draw attention to an issue—not to themselves."

"I know this issue, Senator. I know about MIAs," I managed before the hand again silenced me. Baxter was like some bishop and I was the sinner, afraid to be sent wailing into the darkness.

"Senator Gorzack, you claim to be concerned with our POW-MIAs. If so, it would serve your interest, that of the Senate, and, indeed, that of the entire nation for you to be more contained in your behavior and speech. Otherwise, your time here, no matter how short it turns out to be, will be most unpleasant."

Before I could defend myself, say one word, anything, Baxter rose from his seat, nodded, and walked into the cloakroom.

I almost followed him, but instead turned and went out the back door. There were a few senators down in the well, and two wrapped in deep conversation at the rear of the chamber. But the balconies were full of schoolkids on class trips, and I felt as if each and every one of them had heard Baxter's reprimand—and I had failed for all of them.

I could feel the heat of the color on my face. Part of my head was still telling me that I'd done the right thing, speaking out, making my opening statement mean something. But another piece of my brain kept insisting that I'd blown it, had my chance and fouled out.

I needed some time alone, to think this all through. But I wasn't going to get it.

Lieutenant Carver was waiting in my private office.

"It doesn't do you much good if I wait outside," he opened. "My presence seems to slow down the whole office. Everywhere I look, the person who happens to be standing in my line of vision gets nervous. Because I'm a cop."

"Or, maybe you're thinking, because he or she did something wrong?"

"Always possible, as we say in the law enforcement business. How's the Senate business, Senator? I thought you did real good yesterday. Thought that speech was very well done."

I realized I was standing in the middle of the room, as if Baxter's scolding had made me skittish to be in my own office, behind my own desk. I sat down on the sofa facing Carver.

"You'll never know just how much that means to me. Especially today. I think I ruffled a few feathers yesterday."

"This place is filled with old birds who—ah, I better not get into that. Anyway, now that we've got you feeling good, let me take some of that good feeling away." Carver spread out on the coffee table copies of my two hate letters. Two of each.

"Wait. I've got another for you." I went over and got the construction-paper letter out of my top drawer. "This showed up in the folder placed in front of me, right at the committee hearings."

Carver focused at the picture of me in my noose as if it were going to talk, going to tell him something. I sat watching him, hoping for the very same result.

"You should have called me right away. That's our deal." He paused. "And it's especially interesting, this threat—it is a threat—coming right to you at the start of the hearings. I'm just trying to link up some facts, trying to make the connection between your hate-mail writer and Jake Browning's killer."

"Why would they be connected?"

"I've found that when two or three strange things happen to someone, there's usually some way to explain why A followed B or B followed C."

"Like there's logic in crime?"

"Logic in the mind of the person who's committing the crime. And consistency. Let's walk through this. Jake Browning wanted to tell you something. No—don't take the inconsequence of the newspaper clip as proof that what he was trying to tell you would be unimportant. He might have had the clip in his hand because he had a hard time remembering names. Or faces. There was a picture of you, right?"

"At my swearing-in. In fact, there were three of them. My mom. Some vets." I shrugged. "It was a slow news day, and I think the Viet vets being up here, kind of cheering me on, made for a nice little story. One in which an elected official was not being indicted or sued."

"So Jake has something to tell you. And he was probably on his way to Hart when he spots you going down to the subway. So the person who was trying to stop Jake—"

"—was following him, seeing where he was going?"

"Wrong. Was following him with the idea of stopping him. Remember, the needle and the insulin are sophisticated and not usual equipment."

"Got it." For the first time, I was getting some understanding of the strange and frightening things happening around me. Sorting things out was good—making it all into neat lists, categorizing it, and, perhaps, getting some control.

"Now a few days after Jake gets killed, you get your first letter. At home. Under the door."

"In my high-security building."

"Which is about as secure as a paper box. I've been by your apartment. There are at least a dozen apartments up for sale. Another dozen, like the one you rented, are vacant and their current owners would like to lease them. There are two sales agents who would take an armed man in a ski mask through the building if they thought he would buy or rent something. No questions asked."

"So somebody got in by saying he was looking for an apartment?"

"Or was delivering something. Or was staying with a friend."

"But," I put in, "wasn't it more difficult, more dangerous, for the person to deliver the letter *in person*? To come into my own apartment building and, in effect, hand it right over to me?"

"Well, yes. So there must have been a good reason for the special delivery—no joke intended—of each piece of mail."

"Well, it does show that the person is right there, in my life, right up in my face. In my apartment. In my office. In my committee. I just figure that the very . . ." I paused. "The very intimacy of the threats is supposed to make them scare me even more."

"That's logical. And consistent. I'll hire you."

"WE LOVE YOU, NORIE."

The sign, actually a large sheet with painted-on green letters and pinned-on sparkly green shamrocks, was stretched between two women, who shouted their greetings as we passed them by.

"I guess this is what they mean by being popular 'outside the Beltway,' huh?" Nancy seemed more delighted with my reception than I was. "I'd like Senator Baxter to spend five minutes in Philly today. I'd like him to hear how these folks believe you're one terrific senator."

A hundred people yelled their hellos as we made our way through the staging area of the St. Patrick's Day parade. Parade marshals were handing out badges to the couple hundred of us deemed VIPs.

"I feel like I've won second prize in a bake-off," I

told Nancy, pinning my badge on a button of my black coat.

"At least no one has given you a green derby," she countered.

It took a while to get the parade organized, even though it would only go the dozen or so blocks down the Benjamin Franklin Parkway to the Cathedral of Sts. Peter and Paul. Winter had made a return appearance, and the several dozen of us in the staging area kept up the little two-step stomp that somehow we all believed kept us warmer. The noise made it impossible to talk, especially with bagpipes randomly sounding off. Hands reached out to grab mine, and maybe it was just my imagination, but the people's warm feelings seemed to penetrate even my thick wool gloves.

Governor Hartag hurried across the street toward me, his emerald-green muffler flapping in his own breeze. His arrival meant the parade marshal could start us off, once a little order was established, but since his plan called for elected officials to lead off, he was having trouble getting anyone's attention.

"My voice is gone from screaming," the governor croaked at me, still managing to be heard above the noise. "I spent last night with the Friendly Sons of St. Patrick in Pittsburgh. Wonderful event. And do you know who we were talking about?"

I shook my head. I knew after several years in the governor's cabinet that he didn't want those rhetorical questions answered.

"You, Norie. You. I was with a big fan of yours.

Nina Dexter. Fred doesn't look too well, but then, he's two years younger than St. Peter. Nina? She'd be a big help on any election effort."

I nodded. I didn't want to detour this conversation away from a path I was liking very much.

"She's a good ally. And she seems pleased as punch that you're the senator. Amazing how pleased she was."

"The job is very exciting," I told Hartag, not too pleased at his use of "amazing." But I was getting much more political and stayed noncommittal and nonconfrontational. Milton kept reminding me that Hartag still could make himself the Senate nominee. If that happened, "Senator Gorzack—a wonderful choice" would become "Senator Hartag—a time for a change."

So, with both of us probably more than a little wary of each other, my governor and I walked the parade route, side by side, down to the speakers' stand in front of the cathedral. The day was sunny through the cold, the crowd large and boisterous, and I caught their feeling. Dozens of people called out to me every few steps.

"You get our boys home, Norie," one elderly man shouted. "And don't let those bastards in Washington scare you off."

"Bring our boys home. Bring our boys home." The chant came from a circle of young women who probably didn't even remember the war. I had a passing thought that maybe the select committee was setting up too many expectations, but this was no time to worry about governing with care. This was politics.

By the time I'd reached the platform, I was heady with my own success. I'd seen at least a dozen signs praising me, and whenever I marched into view, cheers went up from the crowd.

No wonder some people got a little out of touch, I thought. Hey, imagine being the president, or even a presidential candidate. Everywhere you go hundreds, thousands, tens of thousands of people, cheering you, loving you, wanting you. Hard to keep from getting a very large head, then hard to understand when suddenly that love was turned off.

The elected officials were the designated parade reviewers, so we lined up on the platform and smiled and waved as the parade passed us by—dozens and dozens of Irish societies, Catholic school bands, and several groups of what I was now sure was the world's largest contingent of bagpipers.

"I thought bagpipes were Scottish," I questioned a man standing beside me, resplendent in a green satin coat.

"That's what the Scots would like you to think." He snorted at my ignorance. Lost that vote.

At the end of the actual parade, marchers and audience melded into one, gathering for the speakers' program, which I hoped would be short.

I found my folding seat at the front row, as the governor became both emcee and speaker, promising a "very limited set of introductions." He led off with my name, and the crowd starting cheering and kept on going, forcing the band from Monsignor Bonner High School to launch into "Stars and Stripes Forever" to keep up with the enthusiasm. Giving up on introductions, the governor tried to start his speech, pointing out that his maternal grandmother came from County Kerry. The crowd wanted none of it, and started chanting "Norie, Norie, Norie."

It was no fluke that Governor Hartag had never lost an election in thirty years of trying. He knew how to run to the front of where the people were leading. He motioned to me, and I bounded up to the podium.

Never one to miss a good photo opportunity, the governor took my arm and tried to raise it above his head, like a referee indicating a winner. Sadly, he forgot that he stood almost a foot taller than I, and his upward jerking motion stretched me out.

"So what's a nice Polish-American senator supposed to say?" I shouted in the direction of the microphone, finally managing to regain both my feet and my breath.

"Tell them to bring our boys home," several people shouted.

The crowd took up the chant, and we stood there, grinning, "both Senator Gorzack and Governor Hartag," as the *Philadelphia Daily News* reported the next morning, "taking *her* bows."

This was something. In D.C., I was always fighting for my place, always battling that my voice would be heard. Here—well, here, they just couldn't wait. I stretched on my tiptoes and grabbed the microphone.

"Hi. I'm Senator Eleanor Gorzack, and I'm *your*

senator. You bet I'll fight for the truth. I'll fight for you. I want to fight for those men as hard as they fought for us."

The crowd roared.

"I'll work every day to bring jobs back to Pennsylvania. That's it. Bring back the boys. Bring back the jobs. Bring back America."

The governor rushed forward to raise my arm again, but I was too quick for him and instead raised both my hands above my head in a prizefighter's solitary gesture.

This felt good. This was what it was like to win.

While I was having the political moment of my lifetime, Nancy was standing at the back of the platform. She'd gone there, she admitted later, in an attempt to help me make a quick getaway, "before I realized the parade was going to be in your honor, and not St. Patrick's."

So it was just by chance, she told me later, as we were driving to my mother's house, "that I was standing beside the two guys with the green derbies."

"Nancy, there was almost no one *without* a green derby. It's the costume of the day."

I looked out the window at the houses along Roosevelt Boulevard, the first tentative spring bulbs making their debut despite the chill. I missed the everyday things that the Senate left me no time for—helping my mother in her garden on the weekend, or reading the seed catalogs and at least thinking about planting things.

"Don't distract me, Senator." Nancy sounded truly irritated. "So the crowd was shouting and you and the governor were waving and one of the guys keeps shaking his head. Like he's really disgusted."

"With his derby, right?" I asked her. Nancy is very easy to tease.

"Well, you can laugh. But this is what the one guy said: 'This is not what we had in mind for the little lady.' And then the other one answered, 'We'd better just keep an eye on this, hadn't we? This one could be getting too big for her britches.' "

"Who were these guys, anyway?" I asked, suddenly taking Nancy a lot more seriously.

"I don't know," Nancy said, sounding more than distraught. "I just remember their derbies."

☆☆☆ **18** ☆☆☆

THE COOKIES WERE GREEN AND SHAPED LIKE SHAM-rocks, but I was assured by Ruth Slater, coordinator of senior programs in South Philadelphia, that the event that Sunday night celebrated the feast of St. Joseph.

"Almost everyone in the neighborhood is Italian, Senator. And today, March 19th, is the feast day of St. Joseph." Ruth waved her arm expansively around Amerigo Vespucci Hall. "If you're wondering, my maiden name was Rapallo."

"And the trouble, Senator Gorzack, if I can interrupt," said an elderly woman, plucking at my sleeve, "the trouble is that the Irish always take the Sunday. *Their* saint's day is the 17th. Which was Friday. But they have connections, and they always get the Sunday for their parade."

I nodded to her as she went on and on about the

politics of feast days. She looked almost old enough to remember St. Patrick personally—but only if he had been Italian.

"It's a real insecurity, you see." She was waving her fork, between bits of a cream-filled Italian cake which held center stage on the dessert table. The shamrock cookies, I had been told several times, were a symbol forced on Italian-Americans, since "the Marcucci bakery only bakes shamrocks the week of St. Patrick's."

"We try to center all our senior-citizen events around holidays, Senator," Ruth said, trying to get my attention away from the ethnic feuds still festering in older neighborhoods. "The ladies love holidays. And there are, after all, mostly ladies at senior events, since we girls manage to outlive the boys time and time again."

I know I made some strange sound, as if I had taken in a gasp of air too fast. The bubbly Ruth had no idea what a tender nerve she had touched. I was always surprised that no matter how well people knew my story, knew that I was the wife of an MIA, they just never incorporated it into their everyday chatter. Vietnam was long ago and far away and somehow it, and Jack, got forgotten.

Maybe that sudden sadness prompted me to stay late at the party. Or maybe it just felt homey, sitting in a parish hall and hearing people chatter. But I sat on one of the folding chairs and drank cups of cardboard decaf coffee and watched as the ladies danced with each other and chatted. I wished I had brought my mother along.

"Hello. Mrs. Senator Gorzack. Hello. I'm a voter. I'm Linda Vespucci. But, hey, no relation to the famous one. But I'm Italian, too."

Whatever Mrs. Vespucci was, it was undeniably unique. Her immense smile was her best feature, but it was overshadowed by her overwhelming hair, a really quite breathtaking deep, brilliant red. Not orange or strawberry blond, but red. Like Mrs. Vespucci's lipstick. And her purse and her shoes. And the large red carved horn hanging from the gold chain around her neck, peeking out from still more chains suspending other objects of worship and admiration—a crucifix, a gold American flag, several medals.

"I'm signing up right now, Mrs. Senator Gorzack, to help you. I had six boys in the service. Two in Vietnam. The first one he came back. The second one didn't. So even though I know my Robert is dead, I still know what you're feeling, huh?"

"And I know, I think, what you feel, Mrs. Vespucci. Want to sit down?" I slid my purse off the folding chair beside me, and Linda made quick use of the space. Once seated, though, she ignored polite chatter and began to dig in her purse.

"I want you to have these, Mrs. Senator," she said, thrusting a bundle of brightly colored pamphlets into my hand. "I want this information to get out. Let people know. Let the government do something, and not just shoot off its mouth. Find your guy. Whatta ya think?"

It was hard to respond to a question like that. This was the down side of having people love you, I was figuring out. Everybody who knew you thought you knew him or her. I couldn't imagine what it was like for someone like a Kennedy—millions of people wanting to know every intimate detail of your private life, assuming that because they voted for you they had that right.

"So do you think much about your husband, huh? You think he's being held somewhere? A jail in one of those jungles maybe? Or, you know, those Orientals. They've got that brainwashing stuff. I remember it from World War II."

There was no stopping Mrs. Vespucci, no telling what she might say next. If I had been at my best, maybe I could have just shrugged it off and sat there. I didn't want to do anything that would make her small in front of her friends and neighbors, so I took the easy way out, nodding, trying to locate Ruth, to see if a raised eyebrow could rescue me from the over-whelming Mrs. Vespucci.

"We keep sending people to funny countries, but it takes some heroes to get the real story, to send guys in to find out about our boys. Now we got the real story."

Another nod from me and more desperate, furtive looks for help.

"Take these with you. Read 'em all. I think you'll like it, hon. It's your kind of group. Get the record straight."

* * *

A taxi picked me up at my mother's shortly after seven the next morning. Every minute of my day was now run according to the little three-by-five cards that Nancy would stick in my bag every night.

My bag, singular? I now resembled a high-class shopping-bag lady. I had my suitcase, my briefcase, one or two canvas bags with briefing papers, correspondence, legislation—stuff, lots of stuff, that I was supposed to go over in the car, on the train, in bed at night before I fell asleep, and, if someone could figure out how to do it, in my dreams.

"I'm seeing more of you on the TV than in real life," my mother complained, hugging me a little more tightly than she used to. I sometimes forgot that she was truly getting old, that she couldn't hold back the years with heard-on-the-radio advice.

"You could come to Washington, Mom. I'd love to have you." The taxi driver had taken my bags. "We've got radio down there. Lots of talk shows. I've got cable at the apartment. Washington's great."

"Thanks, but I've been there already this year. Remember? Your swearing-in. Maybe when it gets warmer, then maybe a couple of the girls and I will head down." She stood on the steps, waving to me, as the cab drove away.

Nancy met me at the state office, and we had a couple hours for coffee and just conversation with staff people. We caught the 10 A.M. Metroliner to D.C., our bags taking up the two seats in front of us.

We self-righteously announced our intentions to get right down to work. But first a quick second look at the newspapers' St. Patrick's Day coverage, and a laugh about my stealing the show from the governor. Then, searching for my notes for the Gov Affairs meeting, I came on the papers pressed on me by the unforgettable Linda Vespucci.

There were four separate brochures, all carrying an American flag and a logo that said YANKS on the front page. They were slick, crammed with pictures, and each eight pages long. And they were, I knew from my days in state government, expensive, printed on the kind of heavy glossy paper that I never got to use for my immunization or flu shot brochures. Each looked like a very thin magazine. Whoever was running YANKS (Your America Needs Knowledge Society) was doing an amazingly professional job, a lot more sophisticated than they would need to capture Mrs. Vespucci's attention. I decided the YANKS people were pros at promotion.

Each of four leaflets had a front-page headline— "Our Boys Are Dying" or "America Turns Its Face Away"—and a different color scheme. But the message inside was the same in all four brochures: MIAs were still being held in Vietnam and Laos; the American government was refusing to help find or rescue them; YANKS had the inside dope.

Mrs. Vespucci had written me a short note on pale pink stationery.

"Dear Mrs. Senator Gorzack," the note read. "I'm not giving you everything you get when you become part of the YANKS network. Read this. And then I'm sure you'll want more. If you do want more, just ask. Your friend, Linda V."

I hoped I had handled her with enough gentleness last night. I explained to Nancy, who'd skipped Vespucci Hall, the details of my meeting with Mrs. V. Then I handed her the brochures.

"What do you think? Before you answer, let me say that I don't want to become a Milton, I don't want to classify every out-of-the-norm constituent as a nutcake."

"Don't worry. You can't turn into Milton. You, Senator, have not gone to law school." She leafed quickly through the pages. "This just seems like another super-patriotic group to me. I'll just pass all the stuff along to Amy. I've never seen anybody work harder on a project. She's gunning for your job, Senator."

"I like initiative."

"Amy's got it. She's covered a lot of bases—sending out faxes to offices back in the state, and to federal agencies, about MIA information or mailings. She's drowning in information."

I added to the flood, dropping Mrs. V's papers in Amy's inbox as soon as I got to the office. Her cubicle was out of the way of the path I regularly traveled between my private office and the hallway to the elevator. So the size and scope of her research operation came as quite a shock, even with Nancy's description.

Around her, on the floor of the back office, were several large file boxes, each stuffed with folders and piles of paper, following some esoteric categorizing system that required the use of multicolored paper clips and various sizes and shades of Post-its.

In the middle of the seeming mess, Bob Sanders sprawled, carefully pasting labels on folders. He stood up, pointed to his empty box of file folders, and headed out, I presumed toward the supply cabinet. I wasn't sure where we kept our office supplies, but Bob certainly seemed to know.

"I didn't realize this was such a big job," I offered. "Is the end in sight?"

"Well, I'm not quite ready to finish up my report, Senator. It's just really amazing how much information Bob and I have found."

Somehow Bob's continued presence in the office had been lost in the shuffle of the past week's excitement. I was beginning to feel a little squeamish about him myself, although I didn't want to find myself in Milton's category.

"Amy, are you sure you're all right with Bob? He's not giving you any trouble or anything?"

"Oh, Senator, no. He's a very sweet guy. And he's really being very helpful. He knows so much about Vietnam, MIAs, and that stuff. He's saved me dozens of hours by figuring out a filing system, and now he's helping me get all the stuff into folders. I just want to be sure to do a good job. And do it quickly, so you're ready for the next committee meeting."

"The next select committee meeting is Thursday, but Baxter's office called and said you'd have an executive session on Wednesday."

It had been a long day.

Nancy sat on a sofa facing me on a sofa, and our stocking feet almost met on the coffee table between us. I wiggled my toes.

"I know I complain about Milton putting his feet on the table, but we, at least, take off our shoes."

"Milton is bitching about everything these days, especially since the Norwegian newspaper account turned out to be just what you said it was."

"Milton never lets the truth get in the way of his beliefs. I half wonder what I could do to get Milton really crazy."

"Please. He's already crazy about Amy spending so much time on the MIA groups memo. Ya, ya, ya. He feels this is all a wasted effort. Amy should be doing real research, not following up crazy letters. Ya, ya, ya."

"I thought you and Milton were getting along, that the whole office was smoothing out."

"I thought so, too. But the past few days, Milton has been mighty cranky." Nancy got up to get herself a Diet Coke, and after I vehemently nodded my head she brought me one back from the little refrigerator tucked into a cabinet.

"Here's to Milton," I said, raising my soda. "He can jump in a lake. He gives a nickel and takes away a dime. He doesn't worry about constituent mail. He thinks looking into constituent problems is a nonpriority. What does Milton think these people elected us for? Rather, elected the rest of the senators and got me in the bargain."

"Well, I don't want to defend him," Nancy began, as she began to do just that. "But Milton thinks elected officials should be debating the 'big questions.' He hates what he calls the 'rinky-dink' aspect of government, taking care of people's little worries."

"Milton is wrong. The citizens *are* the rinky-dink aspect, all right. And they *are* the government." I took a big gulp of my Diet Coke and wondered when Nancy and Milton were having these deep philosophical conversations.

"Did you get connected with Senator Mendelssohn?" she asked, consulting her list.

"Yes—thanks for tracking her down. I was a little worried that maybe she thought I went too far with my opening statement. But no . . ." I wasn't *sure* Hilda felt comfortable with what I had done, but she hadn't offered any criticism. "Anyway, she gave me some good advice for prioritizing. Don't let all my energy go into the select committee. Don't neglect the work of the Senate. Everything is important. Show up at my other committees, and don't keep other senators waiting for me."

"She's really been a friend." Nancy shuffled through some papers. "By the way, this is my second reminder—she and the other women senators want to be sure to have a lunch with you in the next week or so."

Hilda was great. Here she was with another invite. I had to get that scheduled.

"Now what about Ag?" Nancy asked.

"Oh, God. Ag makes me gag. Last week it was an hour, in executive session, about crop insurance."

"This is certainly fodder for election," Nancy said, laughing at her own joke.

"Moo. Please. No sarcasm. I've had it with Milton with the cracks. But Ag does deal with food stamps and school lunch, so it should be right up my public-interest alley."

☆ ☆ ☆ **19** ☆ ☆ ☆

"I DON'T CARE WHAT MILTON SAYS," THE VOICE SANG IN a rock-and-roll singsong. "My report is done. Yes. My report is done."

"And I'm really proud of you. Your report is done." My singing left a lot to be desired, but Amy Walker seemed to love it.

"Senator, great! Hey, please don't tell Milton about the song. But, hey, I've got the report right here." She waved a bunch of papers at me. "Just give me a minute and I'll print out another copy. I'm so sorry I didn't have it ready for your executive committee meeting today, but tomorrow is a committee hearing day, and we can go over everything right now."

No one can make you feel more tired than a youthful, exuberant, under-twenty-five staffer. The day was done, and here she was, bouncy with enthusiasm. I had put long hours in at the executive session of the select committee—where we hassled out problems behind closed doors and away from the press and public. Not really *we*, since I was keeping myself out of firing range of Senator Baxter's big guns.

"I think we'll have to go over this tomorrow," I said. "I've got time after lunch."

"But, Senator, don't you want to read it now? Take a copy along tonight?" Amy asked, waiting for me to show some real interest.

"Sure, Senator, bring the report." Stewart appeared from behind a filing cabinet. "You can read it to me over dinner."

"Stewart, I'm so sorry. I've kept you waiting. These days never end."

"I'm fine. I chatted with Amy, and I've read the *Washington Post* twice. Come on. Let's eat." He started back toward the reception room.

Amy's face clouded over as I turned to follow him. For one moment, I almost took Stewart at his teasing word and took the report along to dinner.

"My calendar is fairly clear tomorrow afternoon. I know I can't get anything else on the agenda for the hearing tomorrow. So it can hold. Okay?" I walked around the desk and put my arm around her shoulder. Young people cared so much. "In fact, I'll check with Nancy. I don't think I have a lunch, and we could have sandwiches in my office. We'll discuss the report and you can then have until next week to answer any questions I might have."

Stewart held the door to the outside hall open for

me and, inadvertently, for Bob, who was coming in carrying takeout. I didn't get my usual big smile from Bob, but then maybe he, too, was peeved that I wasn't hanging around to appreciate their collaborative work.

"You're really something. You've made the office available to Viet vets, to the families of MIAs. It's terrific." Stewart was bouncy himself as we walked down the hall.

"Yes, but Bob was a little stranger than usual tonight. Maybe it's overwork. He's been volunteering with Amy, helping on the report."

"He's probably just hungry. I get weird and wired when I'm hungry. Like now."

"We can take care of that."

Outside, spring was coming in full force, and I was glad of the chance to walk the few blocks to the Monocle and have some easy conversation. Stewart was just that—easy and no pressure. Yards from the Capitol, my beeper popped my happy mood when it went off signaling a vote.

"You go vote," Stewart said. "I'll get a table and order drinks." I walked back to the Capitol, and he headed toward the restaurant.

Twenty minutes later, when I joined him, he had settled into a booth and had already scoped out every table in this restaurant whose proximity to the Capitol had made it a watering hole for the famous. He was better than a sports announcer, giving the political play-by-play as he lined up the teams and the players, discreetly pointing out which lobbyist was dining with which senator.

"That's Barry over there. Used to be with Hill and Knowlton, then he set up his own shop. He's with your colleague from North Carolina. No surprise, since both of them are very interested in cigarettes. There's Phil Fox, just back from casting his vote. At his table are a couple of guys from his private stable of lobbyists."

My head swung around at Stewart's tone.

"Don't look surprised, Norie. Phil is very interested in the commodities market. At least one of his fellow diners represents some of the biggest stock firms. Nothing that could be construed as a conflict of interest. Especially since Phil makes no secret of how he gets some good information. All up-and-up, he insists."

"This is amazing," I said. "I guess if you could chart it out, you could predict what legislation is coming up with what sponsor?"

"No. I think it's much more insidious than that. It's not what happens behind closed doors. It's just the fact that certain people get behind the door—and others don't."

"So what buys access?"

"Hey, not just one thing. Friendship. A lot of the best influence peddlers are former congressmen themselves. They get hired by a lobbying firm, or a law firm, because of government experience and also because they're seen as 'rainmakers.' They bring in the business."

"But there can't be that many ex-congressmen. Who are the other lobbyists?"

"Well, first, these days there *are* more and more ex-congressmen. Whether they want to be or not. Then there are people who worked for years for one or another of the national parties. Lawyers with a particular expertise—natural gas, or foreign affairs, or banking. Or, in many cases, people who worked on the Hill—as staff directors or AAs—and now work off the Hill, still providing information, only with a slightly different bent."

"And so everything gets skewed toward the lobbyists' side?" I tried to get my questions out between bites of a Caesar salad.

"Now that's a little too cynical. And, of course, you're talking about me when you talk about people who lobby, who try to get things done—their way. Hey, here I am one of those evil lobbyists, and yet here I am having dinner with a senator."

He was right. I didn't know how to answer his own accusation.

"I don't even know who your clients are."

"Nobody you're ever going to meet on the Ag Committee. As you know, I have some international businessmen as clients, but on the whole, it's companies that want to make sure their retooling gets fully written off and that their taxes don't go up."

"Do you like it? Does it seem . . ." The words I was coming up with to end that sentence weren't pleasant.

"Meaningful? Is lobbying meaningful? Is it important? Is it good? It's legit. It pays the bills. And sometimes, like with the Norwegian newspaper piece, I can use my connections to get the right things done."

The waiter came and brought us crab cakes and poured us each a second glass of the nice Pinot Grigio Stewart had picked out.

"In a funny way, that's how I saw myself when I was a state official." I was enjoying dinner, comfortable enough to actually be honest about how my "job" was working out. "An advocate for the people's interests: pressuring, cajoling, wheedling stuff out of 'them,' the legislature. Now I'm one of 'them.' "

"So here in D.C., isn't it just a bigger gameboard and bigger prizes?" he asked.

"No. It's different. Back in the state, I had the credentials to head up the public health department. But here, if you're a 'girl,' you're in trouble. Ditto if you're appointed. But the girl problem is the crucial setback."

I realized as soon as I had said the words how flirty, even provocative, they sounded. Stewart put me so much at ease and still kept me off base. I had spent years having dinner with men, discussing issues, legislation, programs. But this was different, and I was out of practice. Out of practice on purpose.

The wine was good, and the crab cakes delicious. No other votes pulled me back to the Senate, and we sat for a long while over decaf. Following Senate rules about "gifts from lobbyists," we split the bill and I paid for my own meal.

After dinner, we stood outside the restaurant, making small talk about the coming of spring. Since we were both taking cabs, I thought we'd share one.

But Stewart put me in a cab by myself, to take me the few blocks to my apartment.

"It's way past eleven," he said, opening the door. "And it would be all over town tomorrow that you and I left the Monocle together. You would be drunk on champagne and I would be doing a tango. That's how Washington works."

He gave me a friendly handshake and a thank-you.

My apartment seemed quiet after the bustle of the restaurant and the spirited conversation of dinner. I walked into my bedroom, sat on the edge of the bed, and looked at the picture of Jack I always keep on my night table.

"What do you think, Jack?" I asked the photo. Jack looked so wonderfully young, so gloriously healthy in the picture. He was wearing a denim work shirt and his face was tan. We'd spent a week at the Jersey shore, and I remembered taking the photograph, remembered the actual instant as he laughed. We were very happy.

"I must say I found Stewart quite charming," I said, keeping up my one-way conversation. I was quite good at it, after years of practice. "I felt a little relieved when he didn't escort me back to my dorm. I'm not sure why. Out of practice, I guess. But I think Stewart could help me—you know, become a real senator, on my own."

Jack smiled at me, and I felt foolish. Not for talking to the photo, which I always did. But a little shy that I was a U.S. senator. I had grown older and worked hard—and my husband was still the young guy in the photograph.

"Would you recognize me, sweetie?" I asked him. "Would you, could you, recognize me at all? I was young and so innocent. I had no ambitions, except for us. Now I worry about my career and my election. And my hair is getting gray and my blond streaks come from a bottle."

I picked up the photo and wondered what he would see if he could look back. When he left for the war, we had been as young as Amy Walker. "It's been such a long time. I think you'd like the person I've grown up to be, the person I've become 'on my own.' But, dear, I've missed you so very much."

I was careful not to let my tears spill on the picture. I told myself that I had to stop this daydreaming so late at night, and went to bed.

"AMY WALKER IS DEAD. I HAVE TO TALK TO YOU."

Lieutenant Carver stood in the doorway of my apartment, polite, waiting to be invited in.

"Amy dead? The car?" I wasn't making sense, even to myself. "She had that long ride down past Alexandria. I know Nancy told me how far out she lived. It's so expensive to be in the District, especially for young people. Was it the car? Do you know if it happened late? She was still working when I left for dinner last night."

It was shortly before six in the morning. What I'd thought was the alarm had awakened me minutes before. I hit the snooze button several times, then realized it was the phone, the man at the desk asking if I would allow a policeman to come up to my apartment.

I waved Carver inside. Told him I was going to make coffee and motioned him to sit down at the kitchen table. I wanted to cry, but couldn't, as if I had just come out of a dream, only this was *into* a dream. If the alarm would go off, everything would be okay.

Carver looked too large for my tiny kitchen table, like some daddy visiting the kindergarten. He waited silently until we were facing each other across the table, coffee in front of us.

"She was killed late last night. Walking between Hart and the parking lot. She was right near the day-care center. A guard-dog unit on regular patrol found the body shortly after eleven. I've been working on it since midnight."

"Killed? She was murdered? No. It's a mistake. Tell me . . ." I couldn't even get the question out. "How could this happen? I was with her, right before I went to dinner . . ."

I was with her, all right. Brushing off her work. Refusing to take the time to read her report. And now she was dead.

"Amy worked until just about ten p.m. Her friend from down the hall"—he looked at his notes— "Marla, no, Carla Conti from Senator Pudney's office, well, she came by about nine-thirty and wanted to know if Amy wanted to go out for a beer. Amy told her she still had to run the spell-check on her work and then print it out. She told Carla how important the report was. She didn't want it to have any dumb mistakes."

"Was Bob with her?" I asked. Maybe Milton had

been right all along. Maybe Bob was a psycho. What had I done, with my know-it-all attitude, putting that young woman in truly mortal danger?

"Bob the veteran? Yes. At least when Carla saw her. But the guard says she left alone. The guard at the door remembers that clearly. Because she came back a minute after leaving. She told the guard she'd forgotten the magnetic card that opens the gate at her apartment's underground garage. She was very funny about it, the guard said, saying her roommate had promised to kill her if she had to go down and let her in again. So she went back up to the office and came down in a couple minutes and said good night. And left again."

"But Amy was by herself both times?"

"Going up. And coming down. That was a little after ten p.m. The last person to see her alive was the guard as she headed out to her car. The last person, that is, except the murderer."

"Does the guard remember Bob? What time Bob left?"

"No. The guard probably wouldn't remember Amy, except she made her about-face."

"And then what happened?"

Carver played with his coffee cup, jiggling it in the saucer like some balancing game.

"This isn't nice. But you've got to hear it." He took a gulp of coffee, and I somehow realized that he didn't like this part very much either. "So Amy walked to her car, to her lot, which was near the Capitol Hill day-care center. She was close to the lot. The murderer gets hold of her bag. One of those bags with the gold chains."

I knew what he meant. The fake Chanel bags. The street vendors sold them. All the young women on the Hill had them.

"The murderer gets the bag. He rips it off her shoulder, in one quick movement. He was fast, since there are no obvious marks on her jacket. Or there is a chance it's someone she knows and she hands him the bag."

Carver paused again. His coffee cup was empty. I got up and poured both of us refills.

"When we get there, it looks like an assault, or even rape, with Amy's clothes ripped off, her pantyhose pulled down around her ankles. The lab will take a day. That will let us know if there's the presence of sperm or violent entry. Then, of course, there would also be the question of whether the rape took place before or after the death."

Carver looked solid, but his words kept spinning around, like the steam from the coffee. I must have looked confused, because he stared at me for a minute and then asked me if I felt okay.

"I'm fine. It's not something I'm used to. But I'm okay. Go on." I knew about death. I'd grown up in a house where funerals were discussed every night over dinner. But murder was something very different.

"The actual murder was very professional. The murderer took the chain, put it around her neck—"

"And strangled her? Oh my God." Carver's description had been so clipped, so precise, that I could see the tragedy with my own eyes. I shook my head, and the movement somehow loosed tears that started to run down my cheeks. Carver looked around the kitchen, located a box of tissues, got up, and handed it to me.

"No. Not strangled." He was seated across from me again. "The chain was strong, and the killer made it tight. He broke her neck. It probably took less than ten seconds."

That made me cry again, that tiny moment in time, that ten seconds in which Amy Walker stopped being Amy Walker.

"There were marks on her face. Punches, probably. Or at least we were supposed to think that. But the bruises were too pale and too concentrated. I think there's a chance the killer struck her *after* she was dead."

"It's evil."

"Murder always is." He looked over my shoulder at my refrigerator, stared as if he had suddenly noticed something hiding there, between the magnets and assorted odds and ends I keep clipped there.

"Please keep going."

"Okay. Sorry. I got distracted. Sorry. It also could be a robbery. At least it was supposed to look like one. The stuff from her bag and her canvas carryall was all over the ground. Maybe the killer took something that we don't know about. Her skirt was torn, but again, there's a problem with that, too."

"I don't understand."

"When she was killed, or punched, whichever came

first, she fell to the ground. It rained all day yesterday, until about dinnertime, and the area near the parking lot was very muddy. She had on a long skirt, almost to her ankles. Her skirt had a lot of dirt on it. But on her legs, where the skirt was torn, where the pantyhose had been ripped, there was no dirt, only tiny pieces of leaves. Her body was found trapped in some box hedges where the killer threw it. So I'm figuring he tore the skirt and pulled down her panties, but he didn't let the body touch the ground again—just threw it in the bushes. So I'm thinking he probably didn't rape her."

"And when exactly do you think all this happened, Lieutenant?"

"Had to be shortly after ten p.m. There would be nowhere for her to go between leaving Hart and getting to the spot where she was killed."

"I was finishing dinner a block away."

"By yourself?"

"No. With a man I know. Stewart Conover. A friend. At the Monocle."

"Did you walk over to the restaurant with Mr. Conover?"

"No. I started to. From my office in Hart. But then my beeper went off and I had to double back, to the Capitol for a vote."

"So you walked there, all by yourself. All alone. And what time did you get to the restaurant?"

"I don't know. Like eight forty-five. There were people on the street. People in the Triangle."

"Did you notice anything strange or different on the way over?"

"No. I got to the restaurant. Sat down. Do I need an alibi? I never left the table once I sat down. And Mr. Conover can swear to that."

"Come on, Senator." Carver looked annoyed. "I'm worried about your safety. I just want everything to check out. We want to get this guy, quick. This was a sophisticated murder, and this is one nasty dude, Senator. Professional, too. Just like with Jake Browning. Imagine, using the gold-plated chain on her handbag, you know? Who makes the bags? I mean the ones the cheap ones are copies from, with the chain and the C's on the front."

"Chanel. I know the bag. We don't have to be going over and over these things, do we, Lieutenant?"

"Some things, Senator, just don't go away. And I'm going to say this to you again—*you* have got to be more careful."

"Lieutenant, I *am* going to be more careful."

"Now, I've talked to your AA," he started, taking a notebook out of his jacket pocket. "Mr. Gant and I got together about four a.m. And he is concerned about this veteran who's been hanging around your office, Bob . . . ?"

"Bob Sanders, Lieutenant. I know Milton is concerned. He's been complaining ever since Bob came into the office. He's just volunteering. People volunteer all over the Hill. Interns. Seniors. Wives."

"Well, we're going to want to talk to him. Gant had no idea where to reach him."

"I don't either, but the men at the Vietnam Memorial know him. Someone will know how to reach him."

Carver started his tap-tap-tap on the table, perhaps impatient at his own inability to come up with an instant solution.

"The sudden snapping of Miss Walker's neck was clean and professional. No struggle. If I'm right—and the ripped skirt and the torn panties are just window-dressing—then it was very, very fast. Think about it. Young women are more on the alert today. Would she, even at gunpoint, even if she had handed over her purse, would Amy have just stood there and let the assailant put the chain around her neck? No way. It was either somebody she knew—a person who offered to hold her bag, maybe to give her something, and that person could have whipped the chain around her neck—or somebody so skilled . . ."

"Somebody who knew about killing people? Like somebody who was in Vietnam? Come on, Lieutenant. Bob Sanders was some grunt, a nobody."

"If he was a nobody, why was he in your office? Was he a friend of Amy's?"

"No. He was a friend of that man who was killed. Jake Browning."

"Why didn't anybody tell me that before? Why didn't I ever see him?"

"Because, Lieutenant, you come immediately into my private office. And because Amy's cubicle is off the beaten path. Anyway, I don't believe it could be Bob."

"Senator, you've got people dropping dead around you like flies. I've got ninety-nine other senators up on that Hill, and nobody, no one, no way, is piling up bodies the way you are."

"I don't think this is a time to be funny, Lieutenant."

"I don't think there's a better time, ma'am."

"So I met Bob at Jake's memorial service."

"And that was enough for you to let him work in your office?"

"Volunteer! He wasn't on the payroll. Anyway, we didn't ask him a lot of questions before we let him fight for our country."

"Senator, I appreciate your patriotism. And I more than appreciate how close you feel to anyone who fought in Vietnam. But some vets, a few Viet vets, didn't come back the nice kids we sent over there. A few, only a few, just couldn't leave Vietnam behind. I just read about some guys in Northern California roaming the hills, living off the land. What about all these so-called superpatriots who join the militia? They've become people involved in different lives with different rules."

"So what are you saying? That the person who killed Jake Browning and now Amy Walker has to be a vet?"

"No, I'm asking you what else could the connection be *besides* Vietnam."

"Jake was killed trying to tell me something. And Amy was killed . . ." I hesitated. "She was also trying to tell me something. She'd done her report. Tomorrow. I mean today. Thursday. Today we were sup-

posed to go over Amy's report on the MIA groups. I
didn't think of it as anything that important. Just constituents writing us about MIAs and MIA groups.
Telling us how great some of these groups are. Or else
telling us that these same groups are real dogs. Or
both."

"And Amy's been dealing with this?"

"With Bob. And she finished it last night. Bob
helped her with it. That's sounds crazy, I know, but he
sat beside her and knew what she was writing. And I
was so unfeeling, so uncaring. I didn't even take the
time last night to take a copy of her report."

"We can fix that."

"How?"

"We simply go to your office right now. And get
ourselves a copy of the report and have a little read."

☆☆☆ **21** ☆☆☆

FINDING AMY WALKER'S REPORT WAS EASIER SAID than done.

For more than an hour, Carver and I searched the office. We tore Amy's cubicle apart, combing through the dozens of file folders set up in boxes all around her desk. Something struck me as wrong about the folders, but I couldn't put my finger on it.

Anyway, there was no trace of a report.

The arrival of the staff, starting at eight, meant Carver and I needed to deal with the hard business at hand—telling people about Amy's murder. Searching the files the past hour had taken the edge off me. I remembered as a kid arguing with my father about how funerals were too complicated, and his contention that it was good for people to be distracted by the details until they had a little time to heal.

I stood at the reception area and greeted the staffers as they arrived, telling them that Amy was dead and sending them into my private office. A few of the younger ones started to cry. They were her friends and knew her best. Mabel Lawrence, the older woman who filled in at reception, said she would make coffee for everyone. She obviously knew my father's theory of death and distraction.

So did Carver, who delegated Nancy to start a search through Amy's computer directory.

By now, Bob was the only one who hadn't shown up. After a couple minutes with Milton, Carver put out an all-points bulletin on the vet. Then he and I went into my office, joined by three Capitol Police officers, all women.

"These three officers and I are going to try to talk with each and every one of you this morning," Carver told the assembled staff. "We're going to take over the conference room and the mailing room and Mr. Gant's office. We'll keep our interviews as short as possible. Those of you who knew Amy best are going to have to spend the longest time with us. But even if you only had a hello-and-goodbye kind of relationship, you might know something that you don't even know you know. So be patient, please."

"I'd like to make this a short day, Lieutenant." Milton made the request from the back of the room. I hadn't seen him come in. He looked more disheveled than usual, actually unshaven.

The Lieutenant shook his head.

"I can't promise that, Mr. Gant. Everyone is going to

stay here today until we get through what we need to get through. I don't want to disrupt the business of the office, and everybody can go ahead and work on whatever you work on here. But"—Carver held up his hand like a crossing guard forbidding children to enter an intersection—"if you think this is hard on you, think about Amy."

Carver had called Amy's parents in the middle of the night to break the tragic news. I called them as soon as my meeting with the staff ended.

"She really loved working for you, Senator Gorzack," Mrs. Walker managed. "Loved doing her special important work for you, on her MIA report. She was so proud."

I called the press office and asked Deborah to take on helping with the details. But Milton, always doing the unexpected, insisted that he be allowed to help, too, showing more traces of humanity than I thought possible. He took it upon himself to call her parents back, then talked to the funeral home, working out the details with the police of when the autopsy would be finished and when the body of Amy Walker could make the short trip home to Gettysburg.

Poor, young Amy Walker—so very proud. And I had simply walked away from her work, pushed it aside, given it no importance. I felt that I was somehow to blame for her death, especially now that Carver was convincing me that the report was of total importance in finding her killer.

"If her report had nothing to do with her death, then it would still be here, Senator," he insisted.

"But it's not," Nancy announced, having finished two hours of picking through the computer files. She'd gotten a young staffer from the mailroom who knew Amy's password to go into her directory. Nothing remotely concerned with MIAs had turned up.

"I give up. And there's no hard copy, even though we knew she printed out pages last night. Nothing is in Amy's directory. I used the executive override and we surfed through everyone else's directory—just in case it somehow got stored in the wrong basket. Not a trace of MIA information."

"How about a floppy disk, a backup? Wouldn't Amy have protected all the time she invested in this and made a backup copy?" I asked. I am not a whiz at traveling the information highway, but anyone who stuck various-colored labels on file folders was too organized not to make a protection copy.

Wait a minute. Now I knew what was wrong.

"Look, Lieutenant, somebody's been through these file boxes." I picked up a handful of the folders. "Look at the labels and look at the paper clips."

"Yes. I'm looking."

"Well, somebody's switched the contents of the file folders. Either switched the papers between folders or actually brought in phony files. Because these weren't the files that were here yesterday."

"Okay, Senator. I give up. How do you know this?"

"Because the papers inside a lot of the folders have different-colored paper clips from the color tabs on the labels."

"That's good. Tell me more." He was nodding his head steadily.

"Amy had everything color-coordinated. She was totally methodical and organized. Even if I didn't remember it, why would someone have five—count 'em, five—colors of labels, and five, not six but five, colors of paper clips? It was all supposed to be interrelated."

"Would anybody else have noticed this?"

"No one. Except Bob. She had him organizing the folders. In fact, she told me he'd helped her work out a system. Now . . ." I picked up a couple of the files and flipped them open. "Here's a file that has nothing but press releases from the Department of Defense. They're all sorted with red clips. But they are in a blue-label folder, marked 'Significant Information.' There's no way a press release would be significant. And besides, it's the wrong color."

"So we can't trust the files in folders and we can't find the report. Okay, what about a backup disk?"

"Here's her disk file." Nancy handed me a long plastic box. "Everything's labeled. And I don't see anything that would be relevant—'Report' or 'MIA' or 'Vietnam.' "

"It's just all gone. Disappeared."

Nina Dexter showed up with lunch just before noon. Two deliverymen were with her, carrying three trays of thick deli sandwiches, plastic tubs of potato salad and cole slaw, and waxed-paper packages of pickles and peppers.

"I heard about your young staff person," she told me, sticking her head into my private office. "I always think you should bring food when there's a death in the family. And we are all one big family, really. Come on and eat something."

The sandwiches were exactly the right thing. The staff, who had gone from my early-morning announcement back to their individual cubicles, then one by one into their police questioning, and then back to their desks again, were once again brought together. We all crowded into the conference room, where I split a corned beef on rye with Deborah.

"We've had more than two hundred press calls this morning, all about Amy. Senator Mendelssohn's press aide is coming down this afternoon to give me a hand. Some of the requests are really maddening." I thought she was going to say something more, but she turned away.

"What's maddening? What's the matter, Deborah?"

"I don't want to get you more depressed, Senator. But here it is. I just spent fifteen minutes dealing with some TV show that wants to do a piece on the 'Gorzack Curse.' Like wherever you go, death follows."

"Great. Now I'm a jinx."

Nina leaned between us, armed with a plate heaped with pickles and spicy round peppers.

"Jinx? What nonsense. It's what always happens to women. No women on board ship, or the ship will go down. Mermaids calling men to their deaths. I hate all this anti-women nonsense."

"I hate it, too, Nina. But it's getting a little close to home."

People were in and out of the office all afternoon.

Stewart came by right after lunch, saying he'd heard about Amy on the radio, and offering his help. He and Nina Dexter, who was now cleaning up the conference room despite my pleas not to, nodded and said hello. But there was obviously no friendship between these two political activists.

He was gone in a few minutes, so I took the chance and asked Nina how she knew Stewart.

"Here's how I don't know him. I don't know him for getting money for women candidates. Just not on his agenda. He can raise a lot of money, but not for us."

"Funny—he's offered to help me out, but I've never followed up."

"Norie." Nina took me by the arm. "You just don't know how hard it is for women candidates. You've never been through an election. A primary election, in which you see your friends line up against you. A general election, in which every intimate detail of your personal life gets dragged through the papers. A campaign where women are held to different standards from men."

I was amazed at her vehemence. Her husband, Fred, had sailed through election after election—and I said so.

"I'm not talking about Fred. I'm talking about a woman candidate. Any woman. Who comes under scrutiny for her hairstyle, and her clothes, and whether or not she wears a scarf around her neck, and if she spends enough time with her kids and why doesn't she have kids anyway? Just get ready. It's a lot harder than you can imagine."

Carver had taken over a corner of my private office, setting up a desklike arrangement on a coffee table, busily printing words on sheets of yellow legal paper.

"So, no report. Okay. So what do we have? Let's start at the beginning. Let's go back to Jake Browning."

"Lieutenant, what does he have to do with this?" I was really angry, afraid that Carver was using this tragedy to prove some point, but I couldn't figure out what.

"Well, he's dead. Amy Walker's dead. How's that for a connection?"

"Okay, so back to Jake." I could doubt but not fight his logic. I didn't have the energy.

"You never met him, right?" Carver looked down at his papers and tapped his pencil on the table. I wondered if he knew he did that all the time. "But Browning was a vet and the guys down at the memorial knew him, if only for a short time. I assumed, and the guys at the memorial agreed, that Bob and Jake had become close in that same short time. The VA tells me that Browning was one heck of a soldier, mucho decorations. Big war record and a lot of changes of addresses since he was discharged. Jake was a loner, but he picked up with Bob."

"And I met Bob at the memorial service for Jake," I added, probably to keep Carver happy that I was tying that noose he wanted to put around poor Bob's neck.

"Here's what Jake had in his hand when he was killed." He slid a Xerox copy of the newspaper clip across the table to me. Two pictures were at the top of the story, both from my swearing-in—one of me with my mother, the vice president, and Senator Baxter, the other an unposed shot as a vet hugged me and the crowd looked on. A third picture, a head shot of me, was at the bottom of the page.

"My God." I pulled the photo closer. "This one vet off to the side looks like Bob Sanders. Maybe not. Maybe I'm just seeing things."

"It's hard to tell, because newspapers print with a dot system and this is a copy. I'll call the *Post* and get a glossy copy of the photo."

"And, of course, here's my good friend Senator Garrett Lee Baxter." I kept staring at the paper. "He'd like to see me dead, at least politically. And Milton Gant. I didn't realize that Milton was in a photo with me. And my—"

"Stop, please, Senator Gorzack." Carver was using the voice I bet he used with the kids at home. "You've got to work on this with me. Two people are dead. And we've got no reason to believe that you're not next on the list."

"Come on, Lieutenant. I'm not going down that

road. It's all some terrible coincidence." I said that quickly, but my mind wasn't making any such chancy leap of faith. Both times I had been within striking distance of the killer. Both times someone connected with Vietnam had died. "No one would want to kill me. Look, we're dealing up here on the Hill with strong feelings about important issues. But my political enemies are not the kind of people who run around killing off the opposition."

"When it comes to murder, Senator, the rules change. I always believe that murder requires a little bit of craziness." Carver sat back and put his hands behind his head. "Not enough craziness that a murderer would be found insane. No, judging someone competent does not exclude that person's possessing a deranged sense of importance, of urgency."

"And you think that some political issue could result in people being killed?"

"We've had Oklahoma City. We've had dozens of bombings and even murders at abortion clinics over the past several years. It's not a new tactic. Look at the 1950s and 1960s in the South. More bombings, more killings. These are people who don't like what the government is doing, so they decide they are important enough—or hooked up directly to a greater sense of good—that they can just do the right thing themselves. Wipe out the sinners. Cleanse the country."

"But who could feel that strongly about me?" I stopped for a second, then answered my own question. "There's Senator Baxter. He does want to keep control of the MIA issue." The thought just slipped out.

"Hold on," Carver said. "Senator Gorzack, I'm going to assume that you just never said what you said. You are talking about a U.S. senator. Some people are protected by virtue of their office and reputation. As a member of the Capitol Police, one of my major jobs is investigating threats against members of Congress or their families. But until you or someone else shows me different, Senator Baxter is one of those I'm protecting, not investigating."

"You're right, Lieutenant. Let's go on." I tried to backtrack from my Baxter accusation.

"Now we've got two murders. Two. And three letters. Also one phone call. There are three possible solutions. One—that none of them has anything to do with the others. Two—that the murders are connected, but the hate mail isn't. Three—that it's all one nice criminal package."

I went and got a yellow pad and started to make categories. "I don't think the letters and the murders are connected."

"That's an interesting theory," Carver answered. "Got anything to back it up?"

"The letters want me to pay attention. To scare me off. Off what I'm not sure."

"Don't you think the murders are *scary*?"

"The murders are terrifying, tragic. The letters are childish. I didn't think that when I got the first one, or the second, but there's a show-off quality to the letters. It's like some kid in a schoolyard saying, 'Hey, I can swing on the high bar.' The letters are like Halloween terror."

"They are also very amateur."

"They seem pretty professional when they show up regularly in your life. I can tell you that."

"No, not amateur in their delivery, or even their existence." Carver picked up a copy of the first threat, the calligraphic one. "Amateur in that the person writing the letter wants to seem a lot less educated than he or she really is. Look at this word, 'Gotcha.' Now, someone without much education might say 'gotcha,' but only someone who's fairly well educated will know how to spell a slang phrase like that."

"And what does all this mean?" I asked hopefully.

"That we've got a long way to go and we've got to find Amy's report."

The phone rang.

A squad of police had spent the day at the Vietnam Memorial.

No one had seen Bob Sanders. No one knew where he lived or where he might be. At least that's what the veterans were saying.

☆☆☆ **22** ☆☆☆

AMY'S REPORT SHOWED UP—BUT NOT FOR ANOTHER twenty-four hours.

Mabel Lawrence found the report. She was printing out expense accounts and came along an unnamed file, carrying only a date—the date of Amy's murder. She told Nancy, who punched it up on her computer. Milton and I gathered around to read it off the screen.

The office was at a standstill. I'd talked several times with her parents back in Gettysburg, with her sisters and her brother in Pittsburgh. Her pals from the Hill kept dropping by. Nancy came into my office at one point, sobbing, telling me that dozens of bouquets had been left at the spot behind the Capitol where Amy had been killed.

I had such hope for Amy's report. But as Nancy scrolled down the screen and I scanned through it, the report appeared to hold no key. Amy had been so excited, had worked so hard on the report, but, as often happened with younger people in their first jobs, an enormous investment in time seemed to produce no real results.

I was disappointed, and I knew how frustrated Carver would be. Now where would we look for some kind of key to understanding what had happened?

"Print it out," Milton ordered over Nancy's shoulder.

"Why don't you do just that, Milton?" Nancy swung around, looking a lot crankier than I'd ever seen her. "You just go right ahead and do it."

"I can't. And you know that. Because I don't do computer stuff."

"Fine. Then because you need my help to carry out your job, I'm delighted to be of service." She punched a few keys, then pointed to the laser printer at the far end of the room. "But don't you mean you *won't* do computer stuff, that you think doing computer stuff is beneath you?"

Milton sheepishly escaped to the printer and waited as four pages came out, one by one. He glanced over the pages, then, as if he were carrying a live grenade, gingerly made his way back to where I was standing and waved me into my own office.

"Amy Walker's report," Milton said, dropping it on my desk. "Nothing. There's nothing. She found out nothing. She was killed for nothing. Or else the report had nothing to do with it. You and Lieutenant Carver have made us all crazy for twenty-four hours—and there's nothing. Simply nothing."

He slouched, his hands thrust defiantly in his pockets. I reread the same words that had disappointed me on the screen. I finished, went back to the first page, turned to the fourth and final page, then looked up at my AA.

"This is not Amy's report." It was an idea, just a guess, but as soon as I said it, any doubts faded. "Amy never wrote this."

"Dammit, Senator. You're beginning to sound like one of the talking-through-my-toaster people. It *is* her report. It was in the computer."

"No way it's hers." I picked up my pen and started to mark up the copy as I pointed out the problems. "I've spent years talking with young people who don't understand the war. People like Amy, who were babies when the war ended. There's a world of difference between their experience and mine, and a different way of talking and writing about Vietnam."

"What do you mean?"

I motioned him to read over my shoulder. "No twenty-four-year-old woman would write about the Vietnam War using the language in this memo. Look at this. 'Our time in Vietnam . . .' Whose time? She wasn't born until the early 1970s."

Milton stared at the page, and I could see him mentally building up ammunition. "Amy immersed herself in Vietnam. She did nothing for weeks but read about the war. She stayed in the office. She worked on weekends. Nothing but Vietnam and MIAs."

"Okay. That's a soft but an acceptable explanation. Now answer this one: Did Amy go to military school? This reads as if she did. The terminology—all this stuff with the technical titles of various grades of soldiers—nobody but an experienced military man knows this. There are some categories here I sure haven't heard of. Somebody a lot more familiar with the way the military works than Amy—or you or me—wrote this report."

"Okay. Great. Well, Bob was helping her. You know. Bob the Killer. Mr. Vietnam-Screwed-up-Experience. So maybe that's why it sounds so professional."

Still no Bob. I was furious at myself for ever bringing him into the office, but I wasn't going to let Milton cash in on my own insecurity about this.

"Milton, you have an answer for everything. I don't think you're right, but if you are, there are still things wrong with this report. First of all, it's too short. Secondly, something I know about is missing. There's no mention of the material from Linda Vespucci."

"Some woman you met? Some woman with her own toaster oven?"

"Yes." I wasn't going to defend Mrs. V on the toaster-oven charge. She was probably directly in touch with General Patton via her many gold chains. But it wasn't Mrs. V. It was her material. There was no mention of it. And I knew from Carver's and my rummaging through the files, the brochures themselves were gone. "I particularly asked Amy to include the material that the woman gave me. And Amy was efficient."

"So, what are you going to do? Call the FBI and report her report missing?" Milton was still slouched angrily in front of me, looking much more upset than the missing report should have left him. I wondered just how close he and Amy had been.

"No. I'm going to call Lieutenant Carver. And tell him that I think whoever murdered Amy stuck this phony report in our computer."

"This does not make me happy."

Carver had reestablished his outpost on my sofa and was popping M&M's into his mouth. I watched as he went through almost an entire bag, the big movie-size bag, and then started in on another.

"How do you eat all the time and never gain any weight?" I asked.

"I exercise."

Of course, I thought. What else?

"This is worrisome," he finally said, between M&M's. "You're right. No young woman, unless she's a grad of Green Beret school, would use this language. If I didn't know better, and if I didn't know where this report was supposed to come from, it would read an awful lot like somebody in the spook business to me."

I walked over to Carver and held out my palm, keeping it cupped so as to hold the most M&M's possible.

"You keep bringing me better and better news." I picked the three yellow M&M's out of my palm. I always tried to eat by color. "Now I'm supposed to be afraid of some international spy. I can see it now. Hey, all you high-paid secret agents—let's just track down the ex-nurse from Philadelphia.' "

"Are you joking because you think it's funny? Or are you joking because you're getting scared?" Carver sat back on the sofa and waited, patiently it seemed, for me to answer him. I took my time.

I walked back to my desk and sat for a while, swinging my chair to the right and the left.

"I'm scared. I'm absolutely terrified," I finally said. "I can't believe I'm playing around in this world."

Carver dumped a pile of M&M's onto his notebook and carried it to the desk.

"Here. The green ones are the best for a bad case of nerves."

"Nerves? Yes. But I'm furious. How dare somebody invade my life? This is not supposed to happen here in the United States. Jake Browning was some poor vet. Amy Walker never hurt anybody." I paused. Incongruously I added, "I also don't like someone breaking into my computer system."

"What's your schedule for the weekend, Senator?"

"I'm going to Philadelphia on the five p.m. Metroliner. I've scheduled Saturday office hours this weekend. And then I've got two drop-bys and a dinner for women members of the assembly and state senate, along with some possible women candidates."

"Terrific. Philadelphia is a great town. I'll meet you on the train."

"You're not worried about my safety, are you, Lieutenant?"

"No, Senator. I've just got an unstoppable yen for a Philly cheese steak. With onions."

"I just love that girl, that Amy Walker. That's the first thing I gotta tell you, Mrs. Senator Gorzack."

It turned out that Linda Vespucci was my 11:00 a.m. appointment. Obviously, she hadn't read the morning papers. They probably weren't esoteric enough. Before her, the Saturday morning "meet the senator" hours had been uneventful. After the obligatory condolences, representatives of several business groups had huffed and puffed and tried to get me to see how pending legislation shouldn't apply to smaller manufacturers. And a pleasant woman, about my own age, stopped by to thank me for my office's help in finding out what had happened to her Small Business Administration loan.

Unknown to me, Mrs. V had gotten herself on the schedule and swept into my office like Liz Taylor coming down the Nile. Her hair today was overshadowed by a kimono-style coat in violent violet, with a large green dragon swirling from the back to the front.

"It's a wonderful outfit, Mrs. V," I said, as much as to explain my stare as to catch myself before I said anything about Amy's death.

"It's spring, ya know. And I always try to perk up a little for the season. Not like the old days, when we'd all have a new outfit for Easter Sunday. Girls with those little straw hats and boys with a new suit. Ya never see a boy in a suit no more."

"That's true. Very true. But then people weren't so, ah, creative, like with your kimono."

"Thanks. So, how are we coming with the other stuff I told Amy on the MIAs?"

Before I answered, I had someone outside who'd have a few more questions.

"Mrs. V, you just sit here a minute. I want to bring in another U.S. government official, somebody who works directly for the federal government. He needs to talk to you."

In a minute I was introducing Carver. I didn't point out his actual occupation. This was Philadelphia, and in Philly, a cop was a cop was a cop.

"I thought this was a special time just for the two of us to talk, Mrs. Senator Gorzack," Linda said, sounding a little cranky. "This is my time to tell you all this stuff about the YANKS so you can begin to really be in the know. I told Amy I was signing up to see you and I wanted plenty of time to go through my stuff. Did you bring along the papers I gave you?"

I tried to be gentle. I put my hand on Mrs. V's shoulder.

"Mrs. Vespucci, Amy Walker has been killed. Murdered." The elderly woman stiffened under my touch. "Lieutenant Carver here is in charge of the federal investigation."

Her reaction was swift and strong. Fat tears ran down her face, staining the front of her kimono.

Suddenly, the red hair and the bright-colored clothes couldn't hide the truth. This was a very old lady.

"So sad," she finally managed. "And with no husband or kids to mourn her. That's what's sad about going so young. Alone."

"Not so alone, Mrs. Vespucci." I sat down on the sofa, facing her. "She has parents. Sisters. A brother. I'm her friend. You're her friend."

"What about her work? She was on to some important stuff."

Carver pulled a chair beside me, putting himself into Mrs. V's vision.

"I know a lot about her work," he said. "I was in Vietnam myself. Did a two-year tour there."

Mrs. Vespucci looked even sadder.

"That was a long time ago. You've been in the service a long time and you're still just a lieutenant? I'm so sorry."

I had to smile.

"The lieutenant's in a special branch of government work now. In his unit, lieutenant is really high up." Mrs. V smiled, happy to be dealing with what she would call "top-level guys," not to mention the allure of a secret ranking system.

"Now we're all concerned about Amy's work." Carver moved the conversation back on track. I listened and realized how careful he was to draw no connection between Amy's murder and her report. "We want to make sure that her work goes on, even though this terrible thing has happened. And so I'm helping Senator Gorzack finish up Amy's report. She'd want to have her job well done."

"So you need to tell us everything you told her," I said. "We need to know about YANKS and about what you and Amy discussed on the phone."

I watched Mrs. V carefully. I believed then, and believe now, that if I had blinked, I would have sworn that someone had switched people. The change in her demeanor, her whole physical being, was extraordinary. Welcome to the wonderful world of conspiracy freaks, I thought. Here's how a nice elderly housewife turns herself into a raging super-patriotic paranoid.

"My own personal take on this, well, is that the United Nations is one real bad group, keeping secret the information on MIAs, all part of the International Communist Conspiracy—which isn't really gone. It's just hiding. Like underground. And then there's the Rockefellers and the Trilateral Commission."

"The Trilateral Commission? Mrs. Vespucci, what does that have to do with anything?" The Trilateral Commission, long a target of conspiracy theories, brought together business and political leaders from the United States, Europe, and Japan. The Rockefellers and the Trilateral Commission? It was the improbable secret from the toaster ovens. Mrs. V. cleared her throat, and then explained, or at least gave what she regarded as an explanation.

"You don't understand. They're into everything. I'm not really sure what that Trilateral Commission does, but it's at the center of the mess. Not that it was what Amy and I discussed. We were talking about MIAs. About jungle prisons. Like I told you."

"Did you get all the information from YANKS, Mrs. Vespucci? I know that the stuff you gave me was from YANKS, but was the stuff you sent Amy also from them?"

"And what is YANKS?" Carver interrupted.

"The YANKS are the good guys. I get my twice-a-month magazine. It's really like a parish bulletin. That's what I gave you, Senator." Patriotic talk really perked up Mrs. V.

I nodded.

"And I know Amy had talked to at least one other lady who knew the real stuff, because she had a couple of copies of some other YANKS stuff. The lady had written a letter about it."

"So do you get anything else from YANKS?" Carver asked.

"Not for free, I don't. I subscribe to several different 'services,' and, hey, no offense, but I hope that Amy didn't lose my big file. It had a lot of good stuff. A lot of details. Secret missions into Vietnam to find MIAs, and what's really going on down there in D.C. I hope she didn't lose it, because I sent her a lot of what I had gotten. It was a big pile."

CARVER STUCK TO ME LIKE CHEESE ON A PHILLY STEAK
sandwich.

"This isn't necessary, you know," I insisted after he
had come to both my drop-bys and was now walking
me through the lobby of the Bellevue Stratford Hotel.
"Anyway, you won't like this. It's the chicken-dinner
circuit, this one for women candidates. It could run
very late. You get these feminists at a dinner, with a
little Chablis, and you just have no idea how long it
will take. Anyway, don't you need to get home?"

"I have a room at the Holiday Inn about three miles
from your mother's house. Where I will drop you after
this dinner. Then I will turn in myself. You go to your
chicken dinner," he said, walking me to the ballroom
door. "I'm going to find the Palm Restaurant and have
a very good meal on Uncle Sam."

We separated, but I was alone for only a moment. As soon as I went through the ballroom door, I was mobbed. The official count of women who held major elected offices in Pennsylvania, anything from state assembly to city council to county district attorney, was upward of four hundred. It looked like they'd all shown up for dinner, along with hundreds of supporters and potential check-writers.

My host for the evening, Kathleen Burns, was waiting for me at the check-in table.

"Watch out. Everybody wants you to speak at her fund-raising dinner. Make sure you're making contacts and not just commitments."

I nodded. I was making no commitments to anyone, except already elected women. Hilda had warned me to avoid primary fights, especially ones in which a woman challenged a male incumbent who was good on all the women's issues. "We can't keep telling men to support women's stuff or we'll run against them—then, after they support women's stuff, we run against them. Bad politics," Hilda had explained.

So I did a lot of handshaking and chatting and told the women already holding office that I'd love to hear from them in Washington. Across the room I noticed Nina Dexter, who could have gotten the Miss Congeniality Award for the evening. Every potential or first-time-out candidate was in line to be her new best friend. And why not? She had a reputation for putting her energies behind emerging women candidates as well as translating her support into credibility that turned into checks. She deserved attention.

Nina and I met up as we worked the tables during dessert and walked arm in arm, like old friends, to the back of the ballroom for a private conversation.

"How can I thank you?" I asked. Her showing up with lunch the day after Amy's murder was, I hoped, the beginning of a friendship. "Nina, sandwiches never did so much to pick up one office's spirits."

"My pleasure. Now, has anything turned up? Any news? Any clues to the murderer? Any suspects? I understand the cops are looking for that vet you had helping out. Too bad."

"No. No news. Nothing concrete." Certainly no news of Bob Sanders, but I pushed the thought and the guilt to the back of my mind.

"It worries me, Norie. I'm always worried about women in public office. All of you are such targets. The men just get to be elected, advance, do their jobs."

Not really true, I thought, but I let it go. I was getting the picture that Nina didn't take well to opinions that differed from hers.

"Except for these murders—did I really say that? But honestly, except for these murders, I love being a senator. I'm working hard. I'm getting ready for the election. I hope I'll be able to talk to you about it soon and ask for your help."

Her head twisted around with such suddenness that her white hair flew out like a shampoo commercial, all billowy like a cloud. Her words were not so fluffy.

"Are you kidding? I'm happy to see you, to talk to you. To be friendly when you have a problem in the office. But I'm not going to raise you money or help in your campaign. It's not what I'm about. It's not my priority. I'm into supporting first-time women candidates who otherwise couldn't get elected." She had a tough stare. No wonder people wrote her checks.

"Nina, I'm sorry." I stumbled over the words. "I obviously didn't understand. This is my first election."

"Well, I'm explaining it. I work for women who really need the help. Where *I* really make a difference. You're going to have no problems raising money. That just goes along with being the incumbent senator. I've got to direct my energies toward women who deserve to win but who don't have the resources." She put her arm around me in a hug that contradicted her words. "You understand, don't you, Norie? You just don't need that basic kind of help."

I nodded and smiled and said how good it was to see her and thanked her again for the sandwiches. I watched her walk away and felt a deep sense of failure—or frustration. Obviously I hadn't passed some kind of a litmus test—and I had no idea what it could be.

There wasn't a politician in the state who didn't know that I needed all the fund-raising help I could muster. And nobody had a reputation for fund-raising like Nina Dexter, who was very definitely not on board.

Nobody was happy about my rushing back to Washington Sunday morning.

Kathleen and I had a fast nightcap with Carver

before he drove me home. Her line was that she thought I had moved to Eastern Europe, since she never saw me, and hoped I liked my dacha on the Black Sea.

Governor Hartag tracked me down early in the morning at my mother's to tell me that he was unhappy about the story in the Harrisburg papers about some woman being killed in my office. His take was that my association with random crimes wasn't doing me any political good.

My mother was unhappy "since I have a daughter who can't come home at a decent hour and then can't stay for a cup of coffee after mass." She promised to come down to D.C. and stay for a while "as soon as it gets a little warmer."

Carver and I made the noon Metroliner and spent the ride back reading the papers and drinking coffee. He did the *New York Times* crossword puzzle in ink. I was impressed.

Nancy met us at the office. She'd already spread out the contents of the file boxes and was doing her own reorganization.

"I'm glad we're with a cop," I told her, looking around at the mess that covered Amy's cubicle and spread out into the hallway for several feet. "Somebody might come in and think we're trying to rob the place."

"I think somebody already did. I've looked through everything for anything that says YANKS. Nothing."

"Could somebody just have walked out of here, the

night she was murdered, carrying the files? This is a government office building. There *is* security."

"Senator, we've got people stealing the plans for our antiterrorist defenses. You're talking about some papers." Carver shook his head at my naiveté. "People walk in and out of this building carrying everything except refrigerators. And nobody would stop them if they tried that. Our security on the doors of the Senate Office Buildings is to keep bad stuff from coming in. There's no way to ensure that good stuff isn't going out." Carver was a little testy.

"So it could be anybody—a cleaning lady, another staff person, a messenger."

"Anybody. And it didn't have to be the night she was killed. It could have been the next day. We searched through the files for her report. I can't remember every piece of paper we looked at. I should have locked up all the files as soon as you and I couldn't find the report."

"Don't blame yourself," I answered. "Everything just seems to be a problem."

"Of course, you know," Carver pointed out with a straight face, "many things are potential problems since I have no M&M's. And all you have in this office are those sugarless things, filled with chemicals and additives. It makes me very unhappy."

"I can help," Nancy said, climbing out over the files, then returning from her desk with a large bag of M&M's, which she waved at Carver. "Here's a backup bag. I file them under 'emergency supplies.' But you get them only if you'll help look once again for the missing floppy disk. I'm convinced there's one. There is no way that a girl as organized as Amy didn't make a backup floppy."

Carver took the candies with a deep bow, but something Nancy said had given me an idea.

"Maybe her backup is right here, in her disk box, and we just don't have the right name for it," I wondered half aloud. I sat down at her terminal and slipped in a floppy. "Maybe we don't know Amy's categories. Everybody labels differently. Like you filing candy under 'emergency.' For example, in my checkbook, I've always noted tax-deductible business expenses by putting the letters T-T-T. That stands for 'Take that, taxman.'"

Both Carver and Nancy looked at me with something between pity and disgust, but I started popping in those floppies. It took seventeen disks until the screen lit up with the "From AMY WALKER" that titled the report.

"Scoreboard," I yelled and printed out three copies.

The report was a rough but heavily documented piece, twenty pages long, with quotes from dozens of sources, including various YANKS newsletters.

Amy had written her report in a crisp, subjective style, carefully pointing up the emotion-laden vocabulary common in the printed material that she quoted.

"I don't want to seem cynical, but what is this nonsense about 'humanitarian missions' and 'platoons of private patriots searching out Americans hidden in the jungles of Southeast Asia'?" Nancy read off the lines in a stilted voice. "'Repatriated into brain-washed zombies, these survivors of North Vietnamese hatred are scratching out their lives.' If this is what YANKS and these other groups are selling America, I'm amazed anybody's buying. It all sounds goofy to me."

"Yes, but you're not supposed to be reading this. You're too knowledgeable about the issue. So are all the MIA families and their friends. This stuff is aimed at people who want to 'do something about MIAs,' but don't know very much about them," I said.

"Some things in the YANKS quotes seem real enough," Carver offered.

There were descriptions of present-day village life, photographs of YANKS humanitarians and Asians described as "current heroes of democracy," careful quotes from three presidents and a dozen senators saying nothing more than that they wished that any MIAs were back on American soil. Put together, with the right kind of exploitative headlines and with statements from "sources," the material made its own kind of reality.

"But, wow, listen to this," Nancy shouted, reading from her copy. "Amy had the original letter from the nut box, with the woman praising what turned out to be YANKS. A recent convert. And Amy got more info from Linda, through you and directly from Mrs. V. But Amy on her own tracked down at least a dozen complaints from people who previously had given money to the YANKS Network. Three complaints came from our state offices and one had come in here. But she got another four letters from the offices of our members of the House. And several more complaints from Pennsylvanians had been filed with the U.S. Post Office."

"The letters seem to zero in on two points," Carver said. "This man, for example, complains that he gave money to the YANKS Network, hundreds of dollars, then found out that his money did not go, as he was promised, to MIA families, but that the 'help to MIA families' meant these so-called humanitarian missions into Southeast Asia."

"YANKS must be constantly changing its hooks, its pitch for money. Two years ago, when the first letters of complaint were written, YANKS must have been pushing direct aid to MIA families," I added.

"The more recent complaints are totally different. Two say YANKS is violating the law by not revealing that it is a religious group. This woman is asking that someone look into its tax-exempt status," Carver said, shaking his head. "Boy, as you read all this, it becomes a heavy indictment. It wouldn't have made the YANKS people very happy."

"You mean Amy might have put herself directly in danger by finding out so much about YANKS?" Once again the guilt bubbled to the front of my head. I had so blithely asked her to get herself immersed in something that could have led directly to her murder. "But how would anybody know that she was putting this all together? It started out as a follow-up to just one letter—from that lady in Pittsburgh—and she liked YANKS."

"Would she have called the YANKS offices? Asked them to send her material?" Nancy asked.

"I don't think so. But who knows?" Carver asked, looking directly at me.

"Okay. One person who knew was Bob Sanders. But anybody Amy contacted in writing her report also was in the know. Even Mrs. V, who could have innocently told someone involved with YANKS how interested Amy had become." My words sounded strained, even to my ears.

Amy had done a terrific job on the report.

She had even located the publisher of YANKS, by back-tracking on the bulk postage number and searching out the Postal Service complaints.

"YANKS and the YANKS Network turn out to be the sole property of a Florida TV evangelist, the Reverend Larry Joe Wiggins. Whee-ew. Look at what Amy lists as Wiggins's committee of 'Freedom-Fighting Friends.' Look at all these famous names. Both political parties, and more than a handful of officeholders. A lot more." Nancy shook her head in disbelief.

I looked at my own copy of the report. "Leading off one list of Wiggins's prominent supporters is Senator Garrett Baxter, chair of the Senate Intelligence Committee. And of the Select Committee on MIAs. Isn't that cozy? My friend Senator Baxter."

Carver didn't answer for a moment, so I rephrased my question: "It is cozy, isn't it?"

"Senator, I just don't know," Carver finally responded, only each word seemed hard pressed to follow the one before. "Are you asking if it may be possible that Senator Baxter is involved with an organization that has some questionable business dealings? That looks like an affirmative. Here's his name. But if you're asking if that affirmative implies a lot more, that answer is likely not."

"You seem very determined, Lieutenant, to cut off any questions on Baxter's motives—and his actions. His name *is* on the list." I was not happy about Carver's attitude.

"Heck, these guys up here on the Hill lend their names to almost any group and cause they can. It's a simple political rule. Causes have people who believe in them. And people who believe are people who vote. I learned that on National Public Radio," Carver countered.

"But Amy's report does have something to do with her death," I insisted. "That's for sure. Somebody didn't want us to read the real report. So that somebody destroyed it, he or she thought, and substituted a fake report. Somebody also took the files with all the YANKS material. But now we have the real report and we can use it to track down the original documents."

"Who knows how much we can put together quickly?"

"Or how long it will take." I shot a glance at Carver. "Or how long it will take before we figure out how involved Senator Baxter is with YANKS."

"Should I check if the good Senator Baxter is sneaking into your computer?" Carver started to gather up his copy of the report in what I took as a dismissive gesture.

"Don't give me that, Lieutenant. Nobody is very worried about anybody breaking into a senator's computer system. I'm sure this one barely has a technological lock on it. But let's go back, the way you like to do. I'm not exaggerating a senator's involvement. How about the newspaper clipping, the one that Jake had in his hand when he was killed? Randall Baxter was in one of those photographs."

"That's irrelevant. Yes, there's some link between Amy's report and her attack. I'm with you on that. But I'm not heading down the path where you're questioning the motives of a U.S. senator. That, Senator, is not my job."

"Amy did her job, Lieutenant. And while we're talking about jobs, the last page of her report urges me to investigate YANKS. So now that's part of my job."

☆☆☆ **24** ☆☆☆

CARVER LEFT, AN UNHAPPY MAN. HIS SHOULDERS WERE stooped, and despite his infusion of M&M's, he looked tired.

Nancy and I left the building together about a half hour later. I told her what Carver had said about Hill security—good stuff could get out, but guards had to keep the bad stuff from getting in.

The metal detectors at the entrance to every Hill building were installed in 1982, I said, repeating what Carver had told me. Until that time, everyone—senators, representatives, staff, tourists—simply walked in and out. Then it became known that before he shot Ronald Reagan, John Hinckley had brought a gun into a senator's office—and the metal detectors went up. One random criminal act, and everyone is a suspect.

"I think you have to be careful about this 'suspect'

thing," Nancy said as we walked toward Pennsylvania Avenue. I was heading to the Vietnam Veterans Memorial for a quick late-afternoon visit. She was on her way to Georgetown for a dinner date, but had decided that since it was so early, she'd take the thirty-block walk for exercise. "You could get a little carried away. Get paranoid. Say things you regretted afterward. It would be easy, with all the pressure on you. So you have to be careful."

"You mean about Baxter?" I couldn't believe that she just didn't want to jump on his case.

"I mean about everything. It's not strange. What could prepare anybody to deal with two murders? Nothing. And it's easy to then blame *everything* on a person responsible for some of your trouble."

"You *do* mean Baxter."

"Okay. Baxter is a pain in the neck. But that doesn't mean that he is responsible for any of this evil stuff. You can't say that someone is a major crook because he steals paper clips." Nancy was always practical.

"But someone who is a major crook would steal the major stuff and the paper clips too, right?" I was mad at myself for just not backing off, but I felt that my crisis support system—Carver and now Nancy—was just leaving me in the lurch.

Nancy shrugged, and for a couple more blocks we chatted about nothings, until I peeled off to go to the memorial and she headed to Georgetown.

The memorial was crowded. I found myself looking around for Nina Dexter, and hoping that I wouldn't see her. Our talk at the Bellevue had left a bad taste.

I'd have to tell Hilda about my conversation with her. Hilda *did* seem more distant since I had made my speech at the select committee hearing. Hilda was, after all, part of the Senate establishment. She was close enough to Fox, and maybe to Baxter, to be influential in getting me on the committee. Or, maybe I had cost her too many chits. Maybe Nancy was right, and, like some cranky child, I thought everyone was on the other side.

The memorial would pick up my spirits. The crowds were obviously a sign that the first waves of D.C.'s spring flood of tourists had hit the shores, and dozens of people crowded in front of me on the walk down to the center of the wall. The memorial looked actually "pretty" in the late-afternoon sun. Every season seemed to bring a different feel to the wall— stern or inviting or soaring or intimate. Or maybe it was just the feelings people brought with them to this special place.

A park ranger was helping an elderly man make a copy of a name, holding a piece of thin tracing paper stretched across the stone. The man rubbed back and forth with a pencil. It was ironic, really. It was a thousand years since knights went off on Crusades, came back, died, and were buried with their bronze likenesses on their tombs—effigies that young American tourists now rub off as souvenirs. It still went on, nations offering up monuments to their lost young men. It still went on, this mourning for heroes, this dispute about the wars that made them.

I went directly to a nearby bench. I really needed to

be alone, and not spend time with the vets who were memorial regulars.

Now, I told myself, now I have to figure out what I'm all about. I've got to get myself focused and ready to get through these committee hearings and not explode.

I sat there a long time, chatting in my head with Jack, doing a mental list of what I wanted the select committee to do, how I was going to proceed and keep my anger at Baxter under control.

The time left me peaceful. I had thought no deep thoughts, but I had figured out a plan.

I started to walk back to my apartment. I turned in the fading light to look back at the memorial. A man in a crisp army uniform, maybe a captain, walked into my line of vision, following in my path.

As I watched the officer he waved, but stopped where he was.

He looked familiar, but I couldn't place him. I waved back, turned, and kept heading home.

Afterward, I often wondered what would have happened if I had turned back, walked up to that officer—and recognized him. But that pretty spring evening, my mind was preoccupied, and it never occurred to me who that man in the uniform was.

"Senator."

"Senator."

"Senator."

The sounds of the members of the select committee

greeting each other Monday afternoon at the start of this particular week's executive session.

Many senators delayed their return to D.C. until Monday nights, since votes and debates were usually scheduled for Tuesday, Wednesday, and Thursday. But the committee's public hearing this week had been set for Tuesday, and since Baxter insisted that all committee members meet in executive session before each public session, here we all were.

The executive sessions were supposedly a time to agree on the order of witnesses for the next day's hearing and to discuss the progress of staff and research work. I thought of Baxter's insistence on weekly executive sessions as the "Norie rule," enabling him to do as much as he could to keep his committee on his track—not mine.

Baxter and the committee's chief of staff did this little back-and-forth routine. It reminded me of those segments on late-night talk shows when the host asks the movie star what he's been doing lately. As if they both didn't know.

This day the run-through about scheduled witnesses took about half an hour, the questions back and forth between other committee members took up another half hour. I tried to follow my battle plan— saying as little as possible, nodding my head in obvious agreement at anything I considered remotely intelligent. Assuming our work was completed, I began to gather up my papers.

"Please, Senator Gorzack," Baxter intoned, "don't you have any witnesses you want to add?"

"No, Senator. I think everything is just fine." I flashed my biggest brownie smile. He was putting me on the spot, and, nervously, I thought how I could really shake him up. Yes, I could say, ah, how about your henchman, that fake radio evangelist.

"Umm, just fine." Baxter kept trying to get to me. "But could it be more than 'fine'? Could we not begin to bring in a few surprise witnesses, to keep the public interest at a peak? I remember that first day just how much the media loved the nonscheduled aspect of your opening statement."

"I think the public is already more than interested in our work."

"But maybe we need to include some additional witnesses. Perhaps some foreign opinions would be helpful. Like, perhaps, some Norwegians. What do you think about that, Senator? Or some Norwegian journalists? They seem to have a better idea of what is happening than any of us."

I sat there, biting my lip. Several other committee members, in what I realized later was a show of support for me, stood and gathered up their papers, reinforcing the idea that the meeting was over. But Baxter just sat, staring at me.

"Can't think of anybody, Senator Gorzack?"

"We could call some ministers," I blurted out. So much for my tactical plan.

"A prime minister? Now that is interesting, Senator Gorzack. From what country?" Baxter could make his questions twice as long, pulling out on his drawl at every syllable.

"No. Not a *prime* minister. A second-rate minister. A radio preacher," I continued. In for a nickel, in for a dime. Next I'd be telling Phil Fox how bad his toupee was. "How about that? You, Senator Baxter, have a lot of constituents who listen to the radio, don't you?"

Baxter looked confused, an actor caught without a script. Now it was Baxter's chief of staff who was wiggling around, trying to get this conversation ended. But I took the moment to press what I hoped was my advantage. I dug in my briefcase for Amy's report.

"Here is an interesting statement on MIAs, Senator. And it's not even in Norwegian. It was put together right here. On Capitol Hill. By a member of my staff."

I slid the report across the table to him. It stopped a couple of inches short of his reach, and for a second I thought he would just let the report sit there, until it died or shriveled up.

"It seems there's a lot of information about MIAs being circulated by a radio preacher, a Reverend Larry Joe Wiggins, who is based in Florida. He seems to know what's going on. He claims to have a direct line into Southeast Asia—and he's collecting a lot of money from people to advance his work."

"Please, Senator Gorzack." Baxter looked actually flustered. "Let's stay on track. I was only joking about the Norwegians." He was ready to give in. But his style of condescension was something far worse than if he had fought with me. Baxter was making light of me, shrugging off my concerns. And discrediting Amy Walker's report without even a second glance.

"But this man, this Reverend Wiggins, seems a lot

more authoritative than the Norwegians, Senator Baxter." I wasn't going to let him wiggle away. "This man Wiggins claims to know what happened with the MIAs. He says he's sending 'humanitarian heroes' into Southeast Asian jungles to find brainwashed Americans."

"Waste of time. This is a fellow with absolutely no credentials." Baxter stood up.

"He's got a very good credential as far as I am concerned, Senator. He's got you."

Baxter leaned on the table and turned slowly. His big guns were pointed right at my future.

"Senator Gorzack, this committee does not have the time to deal with members of the lunatic fringe. Now, if I can adjourn this session . . ."

"But he *does* have you, Senator Baxter."

"Come on. What do you mean?"

"Just turn to page ten. You're listed as a member of his Freedom-Fighting Friends. I don't have the actual newsletters that held this list—"

"Well, Senator, is this another sighting?"

"Senator Baxter," I practically shouted. "Give me, sir, the same respect I have given you."

The table grew very quiet.

"This is a rough draft of a report that was prepared by my staffer Amy Walker, who was murdered last week. We cannot find her raw information. But if she wrote that you were signed on to support Reverend Wiggins, then, Senator Baxter, you were signed on to support him."

Baxter looked at the report. Finally he looked up at

me and around at the rest of the committee. Nobody was standing now.

"This is nothing. I see the names of several other senators listed here. I'm sure this is just some cause we have all lent our names to."

"Then you are saying, Senator, that Reverend Wiggins *is* a good cause?"

"I might not agree with every point of his analysis, and I don't remember exactly how I joined his committee. But obviously this is a man of God, trying to live out the gospel, do good works."

"Then why hide Reverend Wiggins's good words under a basket—that is, if he is not, as you put it, 'a member of the lunatic fringe'? Let all America see what a patriotic American looks like. Let Reverend Wiggins testify. He's got sightings, secret information. He knows something about MIAs."

We went back and forth, trading barbs, each of us occasionally scoring a direct hit.

Baxter was brilliant, but I was tenacious. Several times he tried to end what was now a seesaw argument, but I refused. His decades in the Senate had made him almost attack-proof, his style honed to a splinter sharpness. What Hilda had called Baxter's mint-julep manners managed to mask, but did not dilute, his bitterness.

"Senator, your white hat has a little dust on it," I finally cut him off. "You put your name behind this guy. Now I think you should put him out front—in front of this committee."

✩✩✩ 25 ✩✩✩

THE WEEK HAD BEEN TOUGH. AFTER MY FACE-OFF WITH
Baxter about the good Reverend Wiggins, the hearings
before the select committee were lengthy but uneventful. My work on Ag was tedious. Then everything was put in perspective by Amy's funeral,
delayed by the autopsy.

Milton drove Nancy and me to Gettysburg for the
services Friday. We used my car, since his, he said,
didn't have the correct inspection sticker and he was
afraid that if it broke down he'd get walloped with a
big ticket.

The trip took about an hour and a half, the interstate
getting us out in farm country just forty minutes from
the Hill. The three of us didn't talk much, although
Milton started to explain about Amy's growing up.

"It was just your typical Norman Rockwell family.

Wonderful mom. Sweet dad. Three kids. And then, when they were in high school, along came Amy. They treated her like a treasure from the first day."

He finished his short speech, and fell silent for the rest of the ride. When we got to the church, it was Milton who made sure that we met the folks, the brothers and sisters. Milton even knew the names of Amy's nieces and nephews. And at the brunch at the Walkers' after the burial, Milton announced that he was staying with them for the rest of the day—and that he'd rent a car to drive back to Washington. Nancy and I gave a couple of the younger staffers a lift back to D.C., so it wasn't until two days later, when we were alone in the car again, that we had a chance to compare notes. We were headed to Annapolis so I could participate in my first Naval Academy Board of Visitors meeting.

Or, as Milton had told me about my appointment, "a real coup."

I was a little more ambivalent. The appointment had actually come at the end of my first month in the Senate, but with the tragedy and excitement reeling around me, it hadn't been a major priority.

At first, I hadn't even been sure whether to take the appointment.

I hadn't been back to the academy since the summer of Jack's graduation and our wedding. Back then, those few square miles in Annapolis, Maryland, were the center of my universe. My own graduation, from Mount St. Agnes, had been held in late May. Jack's came at the beginning of June. And a few days after he got his diploma and his commission, we were married.

So this was a homecoming, but after a long time away. The academy was the past; my work in the Senate was the present and the future. I wasn't sure that I wanted to mix the two, but I had thought it through, thanks to Hilda, who had given a heads-up on Foxy's decision.

"This is a very nice plum for you, Norie," she had said. "I'm not calling to take credit for the appointment. Had nothing to do with it. Really. Foxy mentioned it. That's all. But you might want some time to think about it—what with Jack and everything."

I did want to think about it. I wasn't quite sure what was expected of me. And I wasn't sure of what feelings I would have.

Hilda and Nancy were two of the few people here who even gave my missing husband a name—"Jack." I probably contributed to other people's cautiousness in talking about Jack, since, except for my statement at the select committee, I very rarely mentioned him publicly.

It was selfish, in a way. I had had so little time with him, so relatively few days and weeks to store away as memories, that to take them out, put them on display, made them somehow less precious.

When Fox approached me and brought up the appointment, though, I *had* made up my mind. I told him that I was taking the job because I thought that the Board of Visitors needed people who loved the academy—and I was first in line.

Admiral Matthew Monroe had invited me to be his and his wife Becky's guest at Buchanan House the night before my first board meeting. I brought Nancy along for company. I had an easy excuse, that I wanted a top staff member to be familiar with the academy. But what I really wanted was moral support.

"So that was strange, that Milton knew the family so well, huh?" Nancy began as soon as we figured out the way out of D.C. and onto Route 50. "Milton's not from Gettysburg, is he? I can't remember the two of them being very friendly in the office. Maybe he's a friend of the family and helped her get the job?"

I didn't answer any of her questions, just kept watching the road. Nancy had her lap piled with folders that I was sure she would soon start to open. I knew staff usually drove senators, but I loved my red Taurus and I loved driving on highways. Anyway, traffic was light and it was keeping my mind off the academy.

"Well, this will be a real break." Nancy doesn't give up on conversations easily. "It is a break, right?"

"I think so. I'm a little anxious. I don't know how this is going to hit me. As time goes on, it's not the sad memories that hurt the hardest. Hearing the news about Jack's being missing in action, that used to be the worst memory. But now, some memory about a happy time will just come out of left field and hurt the most. And the academy was filled with happy times and happy memories."

"I think this Board of Visitors thing is just perfect for you," Nancy offered.

"Okay. Just what I need. More memories."

"I think you're just too touchy. . . ."

"When Jack was at the academy, we didn't even know they had a board of visitors. The academy . . ." I paused. "Here's your first lesson. If you ever hear someone say 'the Naval Academy,' you know he's never gone there, worked there, or loved there. To family, it's simply 'the academy.' "

"Well, it's a good appointment. Work, too. I'm going to run through this briefing material. Talk about data overkill. Although I found 'Purpose' pretty interesting. There's an extra copy along with your task force assignments in your briefcase."

"I'm a captive audience. Read to me. I know you're dying to."

"This *is* interesting. Listen to what the 'objective and scope of activity' is. You're supposed to inquire into the state of morale and discipline, the curriculum, instruction, physical equipment, fiscal affairs, academic methods, and other matters relating to the Naval Academy. Then, within sixty days of your annual meeting, you submit your findings and recommendations to the president."

"Pretty big job. I don't know about the rest of the board, but I'm going to take it seriously. I've been so caught up in the select committee, I had no idea. I'd better thank the leader with enthusiasm when I see him this week. Hilda would be disappointed at my 'lack of civility,' my lack of appreciation. Now what are my task force assignments?"

"Right here. After 'Purpose.' " Nancy spent a long time finding just the right paragraph. And no wonder.

"Nancy! You're telling me I'm on something called the 'Task Force on Gender Equality'? Give me a break. What am I? The gender cop?"

"I was afraid you'd say that. I know how much you hate anything that pigeonholes you on women's stuff." She waited to see if I was going to explode. I didn't. "But this task force got put together a couple years ago, right after that terrible sexual harassment scandal where a young woman was handcuffed to a latrine."

"So it's a response. What has it done?"

"Look in your papers tonight. You'll see some interim reports from the navy. They say they've made improvements."

Before I could quiz Nancy any further, I was interrupted by the sign pointing the way to "Rowe Boulevard—State House and U.S. Naval Academy."

Following directions I knew by heart, I drove us by the Navy-Marine Corps Stadium. An old, forgotten habit kicked in and I strained to see the fall football schedule.

My throat was suddenly very dry. This return was really rattling me. I turned on College Avenue. "Dear Mother of God," I said in a quick silent prayer. "Help me get through this. I can't do it alone."

I stopped for a light, and the roller-coaster of my feelings continued. "Hey, look," I almost shouted.

"That's the Flower Box Shop. That's where Jack got all my corsages. Navy guys call from all over the world to order their flowers here. It's where we bought our wedding flowers."

"This is hard, dear," Nancy said.

"Hard! It's breaking my heart. But I wouldn't miss it for the world."

We were met at the gate by our uniformed escort, Commander Victoria Duncan. She was, as the old hands used to say, "strictly navy." No reticence here.

"Your husband was class of 1960 . . . ?"

I started to fill in the blanks. Told about Jack's pilot training. His war record. His being reported missing.

"I've stayed in touch with a good number of fellows from his class, both those who stayed in and those who left the navy. Matt Monroe, *Admiral* Monroe, was two years behind my husband at the academy."

At Commander Duncan's suggestion, we were walking the long way across campus to Buchanan House, "which, you know, Senator, is named for Franklin Buchanan, the first superintendent and the commander of the *Merrimac*." She glanced at Nancy and added: "The Confederate ironclad that fought the *Monitor* in the first battle of modern naval warfare."

Yes, I thought, strictly navy. I slowed slightly as we passed the Navy Chapel, but turned down an offer to stop in. "No, not today. And don't worry, I'm just getting my sea legs. It's been a long time since I've been here."

"A lot has changed."

"You, Commander Duncan, are a prime example. You don't look much like the commanders I used to see here."

"And you, Senator, don't look like a lot of the senators who come visiting." Vickie Duncan flashed a broad grin. "My plebe summer was '76. I'm a member of the class of 1980, the first to include women. Just eight-one of us, out of twelve hundred plebes. It might have been the Bicentennial summer, but here you would have thought it was the new American Revolution." She laughed, but I knew it couldn't have been a very fun time.

"Numbers do make a difference. I see it, I *feel* it, in the Senate all the time. There are just six women there, out of a hundred."

"Sounds like we have better odds, ma'am."

"The only odds for a woman when I was young, Commander, were the odds of getting a date after one of the academy dances, or—and I came up a winner here—marrying one of those handsome cadets."

Unconsciously, we slowed our pace, and I told the story of coming down to Annapolis that Saturday of my sophomore year, for a social.

"We called the dances 'mixers.' It was a fall day, with no football game, so the place was crowded with jocks. The girls—we called ourselves 'girls' then—huddled in small groups, trying to look cool, making small talk. That Saturday I was standing talking with Barbara O'Toole, a genius pre-med who passed for a cheerleader. This great-looking mid came toward us, and I was sure he was heading for Barbie the

Beautiful, but no, he asked me to dance. We hit it right off. Kept dancing and talking. Jack and I loved to talk. I still talk to him in my head."

"It's the hardest thing, I think, Senator. I think it's the thing most people in the military fear most—leaving their families behind, leaving them with no idea of what happened to their loved one in the service. Maybe your committee will answer some of those questions."

"I hope so. I've tried to keep some hope alive, all these years. Now my hope is all directed to finding out the truth."

"So I find myself still talking to Jack in my head."

Dinner was finished, and Matt and Becky had moved Nancy and me to the comfortable family room of Buchanan House. Early in the evening, titles had been dropped and we talked more about our personal pasts than the Board of Visitors meeting the next morning.

"You served in Vietnam, Matt. How do you feel about the select committee, about what Senator Baxter and the rest of us are trying to do?"

Garrett Baxter and I—just one happy committee with the same objectives. But I knew better than to wash any dirty Senate laundry in front of a military man, no matter how supportive he seemed. Anyway, knowing how Baxter was tied into the higher echelons of all the services, I wasn't going to say anything that would reflect badly on him—or on me.

"I've been back, Norie. Back to Southeast Asia. I

went two years ago as part of a special group of military to meet with officials there, trying to get them to 'pick up the pace' of turning up evidence on MIAs. That was the phrase the State Department fellow kept using."

"Did you go into Vietnam?"

"Yes, and into Laos. Efforts there have been a lot tougher. The situation in Laos during the war was very different from Vietnam. The Laotian army, if army is what it could be called, lived in caves and off of the land, constantly on the move. Downed planes— and the potential captives they would have provided—were avoided. First, prisoners would have slowed down the Laotians' movements. Second, their fear of attack by rescue choppers kept them many times from even approaching the planes."

"Are we going to get answers, Matt?" I asked the question I was supposed to be answering.

"Some." He had a funny habit of nodding his head in agreement before he spoke, as if underlining the correctness of what he was saying. "We brought in Lao-Americans as part of my mission, and their presence on the team seemed to help. Certainly by the time I was there, the recoveries were being documented. Several ID cards. Bone fragments. Teeth. Pieces of flight suits."

His wife jammed an elbow into his side, and the admiral stopped. "Sorry, Norie."

"No, I'm quite okay about any such discussions. For every bone fragment, every piece of paper or tooth or scrap of uniform, we get closer to answering the questions, and the prayers, of at least one more family."

"I'll tell you what's frustrating," Monroe offered. "You need eyewitnesses. You need people who lived near where prisoners supposedly were housed. You need people who remember seeing Americans—who can remember how many and where and even when. And every year there are just fewer and fewer eyewitnesses. They're getting old. They're dying off."

"And the young people? What were the young people like?" No matter what I insisted, I *did* want to move this conversation to more impersonal topics.

"We didn't get to talk to many of them in Laos. But in Vietnam, I guess a lot of them are like a lot of young Americans. They just want to get on with their lives. Look at our kids, here. They've seen a movie about Vietnam. They might know somebody—an uncle, maybe even a father—who served there. But Vietnam means nothing to them."

"Except maybe someplace to someday go on vacation?"

"That's right, Norie. Who can believe it?"

☆☆☆ **26** ☆☆☆

"It's been just two weeks since Amy was killed. It seems like such a long, long time."

Carver was ruminating over a cup of coffee. For a tall, handsome man, he could look downright homey when he started chatting it up. It probably made him more able to do his cop job, and less threatening to the people he was questioning.

He had stopped by unannounced, and I took the visit as a peace offering. It was now clear to me that everything Lieutenant Carver did had a purpose.

"No sign of Bob Sanders, huh?" Carver asked. "Didn't call? Didn't write?"

"Nope. You know Bob. Not a sound. Not even a letter."

"Well, that does beat all." Carver had propped his coffee on the arm of the sofa and was starting to work on the large cut-glass bowl of M&M's that was waiting just for him on the coffee table. "I'm so glad the sweets have been upped in quality. Although I was trying to acquire a taste for those little sugarless things. Very New Age. Or kind of like when you're a kid and have a favorite cough syrup."

"What have you found out about Bob?"

"No luck there. No luck anywhere. Bad news is I can't find him now—and I can't locate his past. He's been and gone without a trace. Where there should be stuff about ole Bob, there's nothing."

"Doesn't the VA have something on him? I'm sure he was on some kind of disability or at least insurance."

"Nothing at all shows up in records at the Pentagon or the VA. Of course, as a vet myself, I know somebody could just fall through the bureaucratic cracks."

"That's what our mail keeps saying. People complaining that the government loses them. We know where they are when it's tax time. But when it's time for Uncle Sam to give out money . . ."

We both laughed.

"Of course," Carver said, acting even more folksy, "if a real honest-and-true senator made a request for information, it would get much better attention than a query from some old cop. Somehow everyone in government responds better to the people who vote on the budget."

It was my responsibility. I had brought Bob into the conversation, just as I had brought him into the office. I was guilty, but more and more, as I thought about both murders, I was less convinced of Bob's guilt. I knew Carver had drawn almost indelible lines connecting Bob to both Amy's and Jake's death, but I didn't agree with all of his reasoning.

"Sure. I'll get Nancy to call over the first thing tomorrow morning. But you must know something or you wouldn't be so sure there was information to find." I didn't want Carver going down any investigative paths without me. I wanted to help figure this out, help to end the questions hanging over me.

"I know what some other vets at the memorial have told me about Bob, and it's not very nice. They're afraid Bob's gone to ground—and they think he's had the training to be able to pull it off." Carver went over and refilled his coffee cup. I felt he was giving himself time, to make sure his story was straight. "Now, none of them know if Bob was exactly who he 'said' he was. He couldn't talk, and you don't have a big conversation with pen and paper. But, over time, he 'told' several of them that he had been involved with a failed POW rescue raid into North Vietnam."

"Did any such raid happen?"

"The vets said they'd always heard about such tries. So had I when I was in Vietnam and from old army buddies when I got back. So Bob identified himself as one of the soldiers who went in. Nobody questioned him much. First, because he had to write down his answers. Second, and more important, he let on that the raid cost him his voice. Then there's the natural reluctance of anybody who's been in Vietnam to question anyone else about his time there."

"Can't we check out Bob's story?"

"Not without his army records." Carver looked at his notes before he continued. "The raid is a likely story, since we know such actions took place. Here are the details that the guys at the memorial could piece together, but remember, some stuff they might be ascribing to Bob could have come in a story from somebody else."

With clipped precision, Carver laid out Bob's story:

"A dozen-plus men from Special Forces went into the North, in two helicopters so there would be extra space to ferry out the dozen prisoners held at this one location. The way Bob told it, the information the rescuers had was wrong. Either they were set up, or the North Vietnamese had decided on a whim to guard this particular place with a lotta Cong. The rescuers got cut off. They fought hard. But they were forced back, forced to take off with no POWs."

"And Bob's voice? Why can't he talk?"

"Who knows? A bullet. Fear. Could be psychological *or* physical. Can't know until we find his VA records. Maybe he just doesn't have much to say."

"Every time I hear about a raid, every time I hear about an actual contact with a POW, I always wonder if the prisoner was Jack."

Carver seemed not to hear me.

"If what the other vets say about Bob is true," Carver explained, a catch in his voice, "then he is a well-trained killing machine. He would sure know how to kill—quietly, efficiently, and without any remorse. The guys at the memorial told me one other thing about Bob. He's been hanging out at the memorial for more than a year and spent a lot of time in the Library of Congress. Jake showed up, they became friends. Then Jake told the guys that Bob was a big help to him."

"So Bob was friendly and helpful to Jake. And then to Amy. And now they're both dead. Why would he kill the people he liked, people who liked him?"

"People get their minds twisted around ideas or beliefs," Carver said. "This time, maybe Bob's after the good guys."

"That would be very sad."

"For you, Senator. Because if someone is a Vietnam vet, *you* are the biggest good guy around."

I tried to raise Nancy on the intercom, but got no response. So I buzzed Milton and asked him to fire a request over to the VA, asking for Bob Sanders's records.

Seconds later, Milton was at my door, as amazingly angry as I'd ever seen him. He came straight at me, only my desk providing any protection from the turbulence of his emotions. He put his hands on the edge of the desk and leaned toward me, like some street thug on the side of an old Chevrolet.

"You just have no sense, do you, Senator?" He kept his face bent to my level. "This bastard Sanders killed Amy and we're trying to locate his service record? I guess so we can help him plead temporary insanity at the trial. Or maybe he's not getting his disability pension for being a crazy."

"I don't think that's an appropriate way to talk to a U.S. senator, sir," Carver said, coming up behind Milton. He put his hand on Milton's shoulder, apparently applying enough pressure to separate him from my desk.

"But if she hadn't let Bob in the office, Amy would still be alive." Milton obviously hadn't realized Carver was still in the office. I watched as his anger turned almost to tears. "She did it. She let Sanders in and he killed Amy."

"I understand what he feels," I told Carver as I walked around from the back of the desk and sat in one of the wingback chairs. Carver directed the now shaking Milton to the other.

"You seem to be taking all this very personally, Milton," Carver said, standing above him. "Now why don't you just level with us about why you're so very upset."

"She was a kid. Just a kid. A nice kid."

I waited for Milton to add something else before I put into words a question. I already thought I knew the answer.

"How well did you know Amy?" I finally asked, remembering Milton at the funeral, introducing us around, telling me about Amy's parents.

"Don't make it sound nasty, Senator. I knew her. She worked for me. And if you hadn't made this the homeless veterans' center, Amy would still be here."

"Milton, answer the senator's question. How well did you know her?" If Carver hadn't made the Milton-Amy connection on his own, that wasn't going to stop him from following it up. He pulled out his notebook. "Okay, you don't have to answer that particular question. Just tell me when your affair with Amy began and when it ended. And who ended it."

Milton didn't break down until Carver brought up the question of pregnancy.

Carver took his time getting to it.

First he concentrated on the "dating"—the off-again, on-again affair that had been happening since before she came to work in Senator Gannon's office.

"I met her at one of those career-day things. She had worked on a couple campaigns. So what? I dated her. At first, I kept it under wraps because of the difference in our ages. Then when I became her boss, that was touchy, too." His voice seemed to drift off as he searched for the next thought.

"But you *were* dating, right, Milton? Surely you took her to small dinner parties with friends, out with people you knew for a couple of drinks?" Carver asked.

Milton was flustered. "I didn't see her that regularly. But I hated to give it up. Give *her* up."

Carver kept on, asking his questions, slowly taking all the puff and pomp out of Milton. Milton obviously liked Amy, maybe even loved her—but the same innocence and naiveté that he found so attractive made her an unsuitable escort in Washington, where cleverness and quips counted for more than quality.

"It just wouldn't have worked, see. Her golly-gee-whiz kind of stuff. Can you imagine her at some event with big givers or people from the White House? All excited and squeaky. Can you imagine that, huh?"

"You certainly couldn't, could you, Milton?"

It took him off guard, and it was only the setup.

"So, with no big future, did you get a little rattled when Amy told you she might be pregnant?"

"No. Yes. I don't know. She wasn't, anyway. I thought she was on the pill."

"What about condoms? Aren't you the kind of smart guy who would protect himself?"

Again, the fluster, this time almost embarrassment.

"It was safe. She hadn't done it with anyone else."

"So she comes to you. And she tells you she might be pregnant. And what do you do?" Carver held his pencil out toward Milton like a lance. Here he was, the defending knight of law and order, and Milton was the enemy.

"I did nothing. I got mad. Very mad. I screamed and yelled at her. For not being more careful. And then I stopped seeing her. I told her she really made me mad and I wouldn't date her anymore."

"And when was that?"

"Right before Senator Gannon died. Right before Christmas."

"Nice. So you break up with her before Christmas. And then what happens?"

"Nothing. We don't date anymore. And then she's killed."

"Was she angry that you dropped her?"

"No."

"Did she ask you to go out again?"

"No."

"And how angry did you get when you went to her, asked her to go out again? And she said no, that she wasn't right for you and she knew it? How angry were you when she turned you down?"

"I was angry, all right, but not enough to kill her. I couldn't kill her. I couldn't."

☆☆☆ **27** ☆☆☆

I WAS READY FOR MORE BOMBSHELLS WHEN MILTON came into my office later that day and said he had a few things he needed to discuss.

I thought he might want to talk about Amy, about her murder, but instead it was all routine—schedule, legislation, state offices—with Milton seemingly recovered enough to be pushing his usual to-the-barricades opinions on everything. He was still playing offensive, but now he was acting as if we were on the same team. Then he asked: "Carver thinks I had something to do with her death, doesn't he?"

"I don't know what Carver thinks. I hardly know what I think."

I did know I didn't want to have this discussion until I talked privately to Carver and found out what he had dug up after his chat with Milton.

"And you think . . ."

"I think I should be more organized in thinking about all of this." I was determined to get Milton back to some unemotional ground.

"About Amy's report?"

"Yes, in the sense that I can't get over the casual way a senator or member of Congress would just hand over his or her name, lend it to some organization or cause. Look at the names of the senators who have linked themselves up with this radio crazy, Reverend Wiggins. It doesn't matter how basically honest and hardworking they are, the connection just looks funny."

"You have to measure minor 'funny-looking' instances against their longtime records."

"Longtime shouldn't count for everything," I argued. "Because Garrett Lee Baxter is a longtime member of the Senate club, we're not supposed to give him a funny look, what my mother would call 'an up-and-down'? We're not supposed to be asking him questions? He tells us he's a patriot, so we have to agree—he's a patriot."

"I agree. It's pretty messy, Norie," Milton said. "Is it okay if I call you Norie?" Milton was looking less and less like a lawyer to me.

"Sure. And I'll call you Mr. Gant. No, it's fine. Really."

Milton got up and looked in my under-counter refrigerator.

"I've got better stuff in my private fridge," he said, left for the moment, and returned with two Sam

Adams beers, some generous slabs of cheese, a box of
Carr's biscuits, two ripe pears, and the wire basket
filled with Snyder's pretzels that was kept in the
reception area.

"Cheese? Beers? You have your own refrigerator?
Milton, what else do you have stashed away?" Maybe
Milton had some redeeming qualities.

"Four jars of Petrossian caviar and about eight
pounds of Hershey bars. Only I never eat sweets. And
only one beer." Milton sounded almost too definite
about his dietary habits, but it was of no pressing
interest.

"If there's some sinister reason Baxter and Wiggins
are buddies," I asked him between bites of pretzel and
cheese, "what could it be?"

"Anything. The world is a U.S. senator's oyster, and
there are a lot of pearls for somebody who's crooked
and wants to fish around a little. Look around the Hill.
Who do you see up here, pushing the narrowest
agenda? A herd of former elected officials or cabinet
members, that's who. But don't call them lobbyists.
They've got fancy titles. Government affairs special-
ists. Public affairs vice presidents."

Milton took a long drag on his Sam Adams.

"They've got access everywhere, so they float
around the Hill, dragging clients and their special
interests after them. Maybe the voters retired these
guys, but they've come up with a lucrative way to
handle their spare time. Whatever they call themselves, they're lobbyists. Either registered or 'informal.' They 'represent' foreign governments.

They're always bringing by some guy wrapped in a sheet or in a uniform that looks like he bought it at Sunny Surplus. And what do these friends of democracy want? They want us to supply them with Stingers. Chemicals. Weapons. And we don't ask the right questions. We don't ask about human rights. Or whether they still have fingernail pullers. We just say, 'Well, any friend of former Senator Poobah is a friend of the U.S. of A.' "

"Do I know these guys?"

"No. Maybe. I mostly try to keep that kind of crap out of this office. I'm guilty too. I push anything America makes—guns or butter—because that kind of business makes jobs. You get on the right committees—like your predecessor Senator Gannon on Armed Services—the foreign governments or their friends will be fighting to give you a helping hand. Just remember"—Milton snapped to attention—"the international Communist threat is dead everywhere around the world—except in our military assistance programs and in certain offices on Capitol Hill."

"Was Gannon really tied in to these types?"

"Gannon was as good as he could be. He didn't need their help in any big way. He was such a fixture that he, and the opposition, assumed he'd be winning reelection until . . ."

"Until the polka ended? But how would this affect Baxter on the MIA issue?" I knew that everything Milton was saying was pure supposition, but I didn't want to stop his train of thought, as it seemed to be reaching a station.

"Baxter and you and the select committee have got to clean up some messy stuff in Southeast Asia before countries there can apply for all the help they hope the U.S. will give them. Your job, the select committee's job, is a public relations job as well as real policy. You've got to convince the American people that there are at least some possible allies among all those former enemies. Back in a second."

He returned in less than a minute with more pretzels and a handful of Hershey bars, which he piled in front of me before he continued:

"So suppose Baxter and Wiggins like one particular group in Vietnam, one political faction. It wouldn't be the first time in our history when an Asian country got a big friend on Capitol Hill—and then got a big political hand up back home. Look at the support the Diems got in Vietnam because they had Cardinal Spellman and Henry Luce. Look at Madame Chiang Kai-shek and how she convinced the rest of the world that Taiwan was really China and China was really nothing."

"And once this political group was in power?"

"Sky's the limit. Guns. Nuclear proliferation. These guys want it all. Of course, it could be as simple as Baxter wanting to do something on the international rice market. Or, since it's Southeast Asia, it could always be drugs. Or guns. Or both."

"Too much, Milton. I can't believe that Baxter would have friends who were real crooks."

"Every administration, the president appoints high-ranking types. We see them being sworn in. Next time their pictures are in the papers, they're going in to the grand jury or the special prosecutor." He spread some cheese on a pretzel. "Now, there is an easy way to find out just who Senator Baxter's friends are and what their businesses might be."

"I'm listening."

"I'll check his Federal Election Committee report. It's a public document, so everyone has access to who gives how much money to what candidate. The official procedure is that I would make a public request. Only I know a guy at the FEC, so he could handle it and nobody would know we were looking at Baxter's contributors."

"Milton," I said, "this could be the beginning of a beautiful . . ."

I paused.

He filled in: ". . . friendship?"

I shook my head. "I was thinking more in the line of 'working relationship.' "

I had a good number of friends these days. Like the gravelly voiced nightcrawler who kept turning up on my answering machine.

"Senator. Don't back down. Delta Force is counting on you. Bring our boys back."

Great. It didn't feel like home anymore without a message from my secret admirer. At least I knew who my phone pal represented, since a staff member on the select committee had filled me in.

"Delta Force is one of several slightly fringe groups, made up of Vietnam vets who go a little further, are a little more committed, than just about anybody else. For them, the war really never ended. It just got bigger. They're mostly legit, but they are really far out."

"As in crazy?"

"Well, paranoid. Terrified that the government is trying to hoodwink its citizens. They're organized around MIAs. But they've also targeted international trade agreements, the UN, multinational corporations. They haven't joined the militias—yet!"

"Are there any good guys?" I had asked her.

"Sure there are," she said. "But they're all obsessed."

But why should I be afraid of a phone message, anyway, I thought.

I switched the machine back on.

"Don't back down, Senator. We are watching you. Protecting you. Be alert. Remember, Amy Walker was killed because she wasn't careful. Take care of yourself. Don't wind up dead like Amy."

My hands were shaking so hard I couldn't turn off the machine a second time. It made a strange whirring sound.

I took a couple of deep breaths and sat down at the kitchen table.

Amy wasn't dead because she wasn't careful.

Amy was dead because of me.

I had sent her on her search. I had asked her to look into the underside of the world of veterans and MIAs, the small, dark, and frightening piece of terrain where the war still raged. This was a world where people fought for years about scratched-out symbols that some reconnaissance plane happened to notice in 1976. This was a place where army intelligence was kept from the CIA, information was hidden from the American people—and the government betrayed its soldiers. That was the world I had sent her to explore.

Then I sent along Bob Sanders as her friend and guide.

Suddenly, the worst thought came into my head, and although I had had a lot of practice, this time I couldn't turn it off. If only I had talked to her that night, I told myself. If only I had taken that report.

I put my head in my hands and cried, and the soft whirring of the answering machine that had nothing more to say kept time in the background.

28

I WAS PRESIDING OVER THE SENATE OF THE UNITED States of America, and I didn't like it one single bit.

Although the Vice President of the United States held the constitutionally decreed title of president of the Senate—meaning he at least got to be president of something—he had, over two hundred years, acquired other tasks and duties. So senators from the majority party, especially those with less seniority, took turns filling in as presiding officer, and today was another of my two-hour stints.

I hated the chair, the gigantic one, on the rostrum, where the president of the Senate ruled and gaveled the chamber to order. My feet did not touch the floor. I felt like one of those eighth-graders who got to play mayor-for-a-day.

On a more serious note, legislative grandeur was

like ice skating—it looked easy and smooth, until you tried to do it. But presiding over the Senate was a real chore, tedious and time-consuming, with a lot of slippery procedural places.

Most senators knew the rules. They had done their apprenticeship in either the House or a state legislature. To me, *Robert's Rules of Order* and the parliamentary system could have been written in medieval English—and frequently read as though they were. The parliamentarian was at my beck and call, but I still got antsy.

It didn't help that after one particularly lengthy debate, with motions and calls for a quorum, Baxter came charging down the aisle and up the steps, right to my side.

He made a sweeping hand gesture, and for a moment I foolishly thought he wanted me to clear out, that he was so annoyed at my performance he was claiming the chair for himself. Then I realized that he wanted me to cover the microphone with my hand.

"I've subpoenaed him," he said.

I nodded, having no idea what he was talking about.

"He'll testify next Tuesday. And he'll answer whatever questions you, *and I*, care to put to him."

Without waiting for my reply, Baxter left me and strode through the Senate chamber and out the rear door.

"Wiggins!" The name popped into my head with such force I almost blurted it out. I couldn't believe it. The Reverend Larry Joe Wiggins before the select committee. Not bad, I told myself. Not bad at all.

* * *

Larry Joe Wiggins was smooth, plump, and pampered, like somebody's pet pig. He came without an attorney or an aide, although I noted several spectators wearing big yellow buttons that read "YANKS." He brought no folders, no briefcases crammed with papers, but instead plunked down an oversized and well-worn copy of what I had to assume was the Bible.

Wiggins greeted the committee as though he were a heavenly maître d', as though the hearing room were his church or his radio studio, and he wanted the senators to feel very much at home.

Delighted to be testifying, as he told us over and over in his opening statement, Wiggins could hardly control himself. He wiggled and bowed and, if it can be done sitting down, he pranced. His voice was made for radio. Wiggins sounded like one of the deejays on the stations that play big-band music, his voice carrying a touch of sweet and slightly sexy sophistication. I could just imagine him saying, "And now, for our good friends in Chicago, here's 'Stairway to the Stars.' "

Theatrics aside, his opening statement was about as noncommittal as a commercial for pet food. Wiggins acknowledged that he had "concerns about MIAs," that he wanted to "activate American citizens," but from his tone and his actual words, he sure wasn't suggesting any direct action.

He might have come forewarned, but he was soon to be disarmed. By none other than Garrett Baxter, our chairman, who set Wiggins up. It was classic, Baxter pointing out that since Wiggins had put him on the YANKS honorary committee, "this was a conversation between friends."

"Thank you, Senator. You are among the ranks of those patriotic Americans who are leading us to answers about our boys who are missing in action. We all have a lot of questions. Serious questions. But we also have confidence in the large number of elected officials, like yourself, who will ask the questions—and get the answers."

"I've got some questions, Reverend. First, about what you see as your mission, your ministry, your call to serve the people of America."

Wiggins wasn't ready for that slider.

"My ministry? I'm concerned with the teachings of the Lord. And spreading His word. Helping people find the truth."

"Now is that 'truth' with a capital T or is that just your ordinary kind of . . ." Baxter let his voice drift off, but it was Wiggins who was at sea. "Never mind, Reverend. That was a little esoteric, wasn't it? And we're just concerned with the cold, hard truth. And the facts. So what is your basis for being empowered to know the truth?"

"I am a minister of Christ, Jesus, and He is the Way, the Truth, and the Light. And the Truth shall set ye free."

"In a spiritual sense, yes, indeed. I would echo that. But you're trying to free what you claim are hundreds of Americans. I believe in the power of prayer and in the divine inspiration of scripture, but I sure don't believe that the Bible has given you any hidden messages about the fate of these boys."

"I'm concerned about the weakening of America's spirit, of its conscience. We are God's chosen people, as were the Israelites. And we must follow God's law."

Baxter leaned close to the microphone and hissed out his response: "The last time I looked, Reverend, the laws of God were the same ones given to the Israelites as they were wandering in that desert. And, if I may be so bold as to talk to a man of God about the law of God, the last time I looked, the seventh commandment still instructed us to tell the truth."

Silence hung between the senator and the preacher. Baxter sat back in his chair for a moment, then leaned forward. Gosh, I thought, he sure does know how to do it.

"Who has empowered you to advance these theories of yours about the fate of American soldiers—with so little justification? Who has told you to make up stories out of whole cloth? Smidgens of truth burdened down with these enormous lies! Now I have some very detailed questions, sir, and you will have to answer them. One by one."

As Baxter was speaking, two aides came in the side door, carrying two large portable file boxes. A third deposited a tab-indexed loose-leaf folder in front of Baxter.

"I have asked the ranking member if we may disregard our usual procedure of taking turns and keeping our questions to a set time minimum. I told him that I had become extremely familiar with your organization—via your publications and also from some material supplied to me by other branches of our federal government. The ranking member agreed. So let's get started, Reverend. For the record, your publications refer to so-called secret information. What do you know and how do you know it? Could you please lay it out."

Wiggins was starting to resemble a pig product. Fried bacon. Barbecued pork.

One by one, Baxter listed a dozen instances where Wiggins had said MIAs had been sighted. He probed, he pushed, he seemingly left Wiggins as stranded as the preacher kept insisting the POWS were.

"Now, I'm going to return to this area of questioning." Baxter seemed to know more about Wiggins's claims than Wiggins did. He must have had every Senate staff member under his control working on this for the past two weeks.

"Now let's focus a little on some of your earlier publications. From two years ago, from three years ago."

"Senator Baxter, my group has been reorganized, and even though I realize that through the malfeasance of one of my former money managers—in whom I foolishly misplaced my trust—well, from his malfeasance, money set to go to the families of MIAs has been—"

"Wait! Hold up a minute, Reverend. Do you mean you were infiltrated by someone who diverted the cash? My, my. Well, we'll go back to that. We have a lot of time. But now you've worried me. Your recent publications say you're collecting a lot of money for what you call overseas humanitarian relief. Who's watching the till, guarding the cash? What particular humans get those supplies? Who makes the arrangements?"

"Senator, this is the kind of question I came here ready, willing, and able to answer. Of course, I have been advised that I cannot speak on this particular issue. I cannot give you the details of our work. I must protect some of our underground Freedom Fighters. If the story gets out, their lives will be in danger."

Wiggins managed a smile. He thought he was back on safe ground, and he seemed pleased.

Baxter was not.

"Reverend Wiggins, you *are* going to give a great many details. You are going to start today. You *will* talk to this committee."

"Sir, Senator Baxter. I do not think that you understand what is happening in Southeast Asia. I think the Congress has been kept in the dark for all these many years. You have been given false information."

"But you're here, Reverend. And we're hanging on your every word, anxious to hear your information. Why are you not forthcoming?"

Wiggins kept on wiggling, and Baxter kept on pursuing him.

He refused to answer Baxter's questions as to whether he himself had ever been in Vietnam. He refused to say if his Freedom Fighters were armed with U.S. weaponry. He refused to explain how he recruited his Freedom Fighters, and whether they were Americans or Asians.

I had thought from the early part of the testimony that Wiggins was a goner. But now, as Baxter battled Wiggins on "humanitarian relief," I was amazed, first at Baxter's ability to get him in his sights, and then at Wiggins's talent for getting away.

Time and time again, Wiggins returned to his plea that the senators were in the dark because they had no firsthand experience in Southeast Asia.

"You might question my information, Senator, on various sightings. But, Senator, I question you. You are here, thousands and thousands of miles away. I am getting direct information from people on the ground, brave men and women who know what the taste of victory will be to these tragically imprisoned Americans. Your information is being filtered through bureaucracies guaranteed to lie and slant and protect those in power."

"Being there is what matters, is that right, Reverend?"

"Being there is half the battle, Senator."

"You know, Reverend, for the first time—no offense—I find a great deal of truth in what you are saying. Not in the answers to our questions, mind you, but in the simple concept that what we don't know we just don't know."

"Thank you, Senator Baxter. That's why we have experts there, in Southeast Asia, sending us the news, the truth."

"And this is all with private money, correct, Reverend?"

"Yes, indeed. We rely on the grace and giving of our supporters."

"Well, Reverend Wiggins, I don't think international policy is the job of a churchman, no matter how dedicated. And I don't think you or your so-called Freedom Fighters should be bouncing around Southeast Asia, perhaps doing work contrary to what the U.S. government has decided on as our course of action. So—and this will come as a surprise to my fellow committee members, but I am sure they will agree it is the only way—the entire select committee will go to Vietnam during the upcoming Congressional recess. And we will see for ourselves what the story is."

"That's very good of you, Senator Baxter."

"And perhaps bad for you, Reverend Wiggins. Since we are exchanging information"—Baxter's smile was as deadly as his hissing whisper—"I want you to know that I took it upon myself to invite several representatives from various government agencies here today—to hear the truth."

"Thank you, sir. I knew you were a good man. And I know that the CIA, and the Defense Department—"

"Oh, no, Reverend Wiggins. Not representatives from *those* branches of government. I invited officials from the Internal Revenue Service, the Postal Service, and the Federal Communications Commission. Each and every one of them is, I believe, terribly interested in what-all you-all are doing, messing around over there in Southeast Asia. Witness dismissed."

29

"YOU MIGHT NOT LIKE IT, NORIE, BUT YOU'RE GOING TO have to thank Garrett Baxter for this trip."

Stewart Conover and I were having a Diet Coke break early in the evening in my office and he was annoying me. I didn't want to hear what a great job my buddy Baxter had done. The elation I had felt when Baxter announced our trip to Vietnam had more than faded.

Not about the trip. Stewart was right. It was an amazing opportunity. But my thrill at seeing Baxter put Wiggins in his place was now tempered by some of the information Milton was uncovering. Milton was still in the preliminary investigative stages, but he assured me that Baxter's list of contributors, when finally assembled, would hold some surprises.

With the long hours of the Senate and trying to get

organized for the CODEL—another bureaucratese term, this one translating as Congressional delegation—I was short on sleep and long on meals that were either eaten standing up or centered around crunchy chocolate things. I hadn't cooked in weeks. Even tonight, when I was supposed to have dinner with Stewart, I had to cancel out. We were leaving in a few days, and I hadn't figured out what to pack.

"Baxter was great. He's a great showman." I didn't want to go too far, but I thought Stewart would understand. "I just don't know if he's sincere."

"About what?"

"I wouldn't say this publicly, but I believe that Baxter could be involved in some kind of dirty business in Vietnam."

"God, Norie." Stewart managed those two words before choking on his Coke. It took him a moment to recover. "Here's a U.S. senator and he takes this guy Wiggins apart on nationwide TV, and you think he's maybe a bad dude."

"Maybe he's sincere. Maybe his sincerity is a smoke screen. For spies and I don't know what else." Even to me that line sounded dumb.

"Norie, Baxter isn't just a U.S. senator. He's a decorated war hero. You're off track, Senator. And it's important—for you, for your career, for the whole country—that you stay on your issue. The major emphasis of your time and work has got to be MIAs. Not any cloak-and-dagger stuff."

"Milton is looking into some of Baxter's dealings. Maybe this attack on Wiggins was just to cover up. Maybe Baxter is really involved. Milton said that anytime you're dealing in Southeast Asia it's guns and drugs and—"

"Norie, you should hear yourself. Catch on to Milton. A while back he was screaming at you about the Norwegian journalist material. Now he's decided to tell you about guns and drugs. Doesn't it seem obvious to you what Milton's about, what he's trying to do about your relationship with Baxter?"

"No. I don't see anything sinister. I think Milton and I are building a better relationship."

"Sounds like Milton is setting you up for one big sandbag. As a member of the select committee, you stand a pretty good chance to be involved with finding out what really happened to MIAs. Once you do, you're a shoo-in for election. Maybe that kind of success is not in Milton's playbook. Maybe Milton has his own candidate for that Senate seat."

"Stewart, that's all very well and good. But I've got real questions. Two people are dead, one of them was working on the MIA report—"

"Leave the cops-and-robbers stuff to the cops, Norie. You could be solving the biggest mystery this country has ever faced. You could help us all come to closure on one of the saddest chapters in America's history."

"I guess you're right, Stewart. But I don't like Baxter, and I have this strange feeling that somehow it's all tied together."

* * *

For the first time, Carver looked happy without a handful of M&M's.

"I've got a little bad news first," he started, "but maybe it's bad news of a delaying, not a definite, character. We can't tie Reverend Wiggins to anything about Amy's murder. He was in Florida. On the radio. Selling God and patriotism."

"And he couldn't be recorded or anything?" I asked.

"He's got hundreds of witnesses. Now, after we actually track down the person who carried out the deed, perhaps a link can be made back to Wiggins. But—"

"And the good news? Please."

"Are people pleased that you are their senator?"

"This is the good part? Okay, one or two. Yes. Sure. I think so. I'm told whatever slapdash public polls exist say voters see me in a 'favorable' light. Are you thinking about giving up your police career to run against me?"

"Who did you knock out?"

"Nobody." That wasn't right. "Everybody." According to Milton, just about everybody who holds elective office thought the seat was his for the asking."

"I want you to think. Long and hard. I want you to come up with as long a list as you can of political types who wanted your job. Or who don't want you here."

"Any other requirements to make the cut? And am I allowed to know what this is all about?"

"This," Carver said, rummaging around in the

pockets of his raincoat, "is about high-class, intensive, superlative police work. And a little bit of luck."

He pulled out his notebook.

"I had the files at home with me last night. Xeroxes of all your letters. I had been looking at them before I went to bed, and by mistake I left them on the kitchen table. Addie, my wonderful oldest child, worked last summer for a party planner. I'm not sure what that means, but it was a paying job and she brought home great leftover desserts."

Carver, usually so direct, had me mystified. Where was he going?

"Addie did a lot of different stuff around big events, especially weddings, which there are a lot of during the early summer months."

I was smiling. I was nodding. I had no idea what he was talking about. But it was a pleasant break in an otherwise terribly rushed day.

"So she's trying to make conversation today, before she tells me she's late and will need a note for school. And she begins telling me just how much computers have changed the wedding business."

"Computer dating?" True, I wanted to know more about Carver's personal life, but not like this. It was too confusing.

"Not computer dating, Senator. Computer invitations. Used to be you had to have some little old lady who knew how to do the fancy writing that goes on invitations. But now there is a font that you put in your regular computer—or printer or something— and you can make stuff come out the same way. The only difference is that the computer makes it more perfect—every 's' is the same, every 't' is crossed the same way."

"And my invitation . . . ?"

"Addie noticed a Xerox of the envelope on the top of my papers. To quote her, 'Who do you know who has a calligraphy font?'—which, of course, is my question to you."

"I have no idea. I don't think I know people in the wedding business. Wait a minute." I buzzed Nancy and then Deborah. "Bring in every invitation I've received since I got here. Everything. Especially the invitations to fund-raisers."

"Senator, I don't think you have any idea what 'everything' means." Nancy's voice had a wee touch of irritation. She was as tied up in the preparations for this trip as I was, only she had to stay home.

"Everything." I released the button and looked up at Carver. "Weddings are not the only time you get a fancy invitation. When somebody wants you to write a check and asks you to a political or a charity event, some of the invites are pretty posh. I get handfuls every day. It's like professional courtesy or something. Especially from the members from my state. They like having a senator do a drop-by."

"So if you figure out who doesn't like you . . ."

"And they have the calligraphy font . . ."

"We still don't have anything definite."

Carver could be such a killjoy.

* * *

Milton looked as if he were going to burst his three-piece suit.

"This will, in sixties parlance, blow your mind."

"Milton, I was a nurse. I wasn't a hippie."

"Neither are the folks who gave money to Senator Baxter."

"What does that have to do with anything?"

"A lot. My friend at the Federal Elections Commission printed out the complete list of people who gave last year to Baxter's campaign. And guess what? An extraordinary number of his contributors came from Florida. Reverend Wiggins's home turf."

"Isn't that a big jump? Florida is a big state."

"Well, we'd have to check it out."

"Maybe we should be getting me ready to go to Vietnam and just lay off the Baxter stuff until the trip is over. You can leave a copy with me and keep one for yourself, and we'll look into it when I get back."

"Sure. If that's what you want. Sorry to trouble you."

Milton gave me a noncommittal shrug and strolled out the door.

I pulled out of my briefcase one of my two, as I now thought of them, "crime" files. One was labeled "YANKS," the other "Letters." I found that just the mundane process of keeping the files, writing things down, allowed me to still feel in control as people were murdered around me and I was the target of an intensive hate campaign.

I stared at the calligraphy on my first hate note. What an odd choice of medium, I thought. So perfectly done. Obviously the hate-mail writer had very nice manners.

The Vesper Club was what the Union League could never be—a meeting place for the powers in Philadelphia who made it on their own, who were not born Protestant, rich, or well-bred.

So it was natural that the Vesper was the favorite gathering place for politicos of every variety of multi-ethnic persuasion. The food was the kind once known as "cuisine," favorites like Crab Meat au Gratin, Jumbo Shrimp Cocktail, and Roast Beef au Jus. A rowing club out on the Schuylkill River carried the same name, but the sports at this Vesper were eating and drinking

George Taylor had the money, the position, and the background to be a member of the Union League. Which was why, I told him once, he contrarily insisted on belonging to the Vesper Club. He was hosting the Gang of Four this evening, less than two weeks before I headed off to Southeast Asia.

"I thought you needed some all-American food before the trip," he said.

"Great. I'll have the Linguine with Clams and the Veal Marsala." We all laughed, and George ordered two bottles of a great Italian red, a Tiganello. He'd sent his car to pick us all up, so Martin, his driver waiting outside, was the designated driver.

"So give us some inside stuff. Like who do you see, who are your friends? We want details." Kathleen was such a political junkie.

"Do you mean am I happy and do I have a partner

for the recess line? Yes. As far as my friends, Hilda, Senator Mendelssohn, is my friend. I can't think of another colleague who'd fall into that group. Although a lot fewer of them seem like enemies."

"And things are going better with the staff?"

I nodded at Marco.

"So if you're not busy with all your new friends and you're not having such a fun time, why aren't you seeing the important people from the state?" Marco asked, playing with a stalk of celery in a finger grip that reminded the others that he had once been a heavy smoker.

"The guys from the western part of the state, the Steel Caucus, have called me, but I haven't had time to go out to dinner with them. I should schedule better. And I should try to see more of the senior senator."

"You're right. And you also need to be in touch with the other people from the state who are trying to get things done. You need them—and they need you."

"Well, I had such a turn-off from Nina Dexter, Fred Dexter's wife. She helps out women candidates, and I thought she would give me a hand with some fund-raising, but she told me that I was just too important for her to care. In other words . . ."

"Maybe she felt you didn't deal with her properly. I mean . . ." Kathleen paused. "Even with us you describe her as 'Fred Dexter's wife.' I know she does a lot of networking and fund-raising for women candidates, so she doesn't need that kind of description."

Kathleen can be a little overly touchy on some of the feminist accouterment.

"Anyway, I feel I'm accomplishing a lot. I'm getting things done."

"Not for Pennsylvania," Marco countered.

"What do you mean?"

"Now, we're the people who love you, and we don't have the feeling that you're taking care of the state. How do you think total strangers see you?"

"Marco, I'm being the best senator I can be. I go to my committee hearings, I don't miss a vote. You two . . ." I looked at Kathy and then at George. "You don't agree with him, do you?"

"Well," George said, "I had a meeting with a staff member from the Commerce Department who told me that business just wasn't a priority in your office. That it wasn't like the days of the late, great Senator Gannon. That you were on a crusade to solve the mystery of Vietnam and everything else was irrelevant."

"You said I needed an issue." This was so unfair. "I've got one. MIAs. And now you're telling me that I don't give enough time to the Commerce Department?"

"You need both, Norie. An issue and the regular-senator stuff. You need to bring the state some business—bridges, contracts, a lot of the stuff that the federal government ladles out."

George picked up Marco's refrain. "Now you don't have any seniority, but you do have the president. Pull and push the White House staff. Get some perks. Get the president here in the state, for Pete's sake. Try to get more of the piecework for the Defense Department sent out to those small factories outside of Chester."

"Wow. You guys beat all. I've got urgent, life-threatening questions and you're telling me I've got to concentrate on getting a bigger pork barrel for Pennsylvania?"

"Yes," George Taylor finally said. "That's a ticket you have to punch to get elected. Be a hero—but never forget that your job is Pennsylvania jobs."

The jumble of the days before we left was as confusing as the piles of work that kept growing on my desk.

I *did* listen to the Gang of Four. I came back from that dinner and made sure that I connected with Senator Smith, with the House members from my state, and with the unions, the seniors, and anybody else I could think about.

I brought the staff together and I reminded them— as much as I had been reminded—that I and they were supposedly taking care of the people of Pennsylvania.

And I made sure I went out to dinner with Hilda and the other women senators.

What a dope I had been—thinking that I could do all this myself. No wonder I had seemed presumptuous to Nina Dexter. I'd have to try again.

"It's a mistake a lot of women make," Hilda told me when I called her up, personally, to set up dinner. "We need to be in touch. It's what that overused word 'networking' is all about. But we've got our hang-ups. It's just generations and generations of staying home, by ourselves, taking care of the cave."

"So we'll have this dinner. I'm really glad."

"Glad is not the word. You'll be thankful and grateful, especially when you hear Senator Vanessa Morris do her imitations of Phil Fox. We let her do it, even though she's from the other party, because she's got such a gift at twirling her napkin just like a lasso."

I laughed at the thought.

"And, Norie," Hilda added, "I want you to know personally that we're all cheering you on for your CODEL."

"I'm really excited, Hilda."

"Only problem is . . ." She paused melodramatically.

"Yes? Yes?"

"I hear there's just no good shopping."

"You didn't have to stay here tonight. Maybe you should be in Washington, in case the president or somebody calls."

"Mom, I wanted to be here, with you, tonight. I'm leaving in less than forty-eight hours."

"How long is the plane ride?"

"Forever. First we go to Hawaii . . ."

"That'll be nice. You could get a little time in the sun, but you must remember to wear your hat."

"Mom, I'm going to be at CINCPAC headquarters. The commander in chief of our forces in the Pacific. For briefings. Then we fly on to Guam. We cross the international dateline, and lose a day."

"I've never understood that dateline thing."

"Me neither. But we get the day back on the way home. Guam is just to refuel. Then we go to Bangkok.

We meet with lots of government types who investigate MIAs. More briefings."

"Sounds like hard work."

"The schedule for this whole enterprise looks like one of those lesson books the nuns used to keep. An hour for this, a half hour for that. Then finally we get to Hanoi. We meet with the Vietnamese who have been investigating MIAs. We then go to Saigon. I mean Ho Chi Minh City. We meet with more people there. We're set for Laos. Lots of MIAs were last seen in Laos, but the investigations there are pretty confused."

"And you go all the way on the same plane? Is it the one the president travels on, Air Force One?"

I didn't bother explaining that technically Air Force One was whatever plane the president was on. The special 747 he usually flew in was, I knew, the plane my mother meant.

"Mom, this plane is from the air force's VIP fleet. But, no, only the president gets to use Air Force One. It goes with the job. But we're going in a big plane, because we've got so many staff and press along. I think, it's the one the secretary of state uses."

"I hear there's a bed on the president's plane. Do you think you'll get a chance to sleep in the bed? You could ask, you know. You're the only woman senator on the trip."

"Mom, I know you, and I know you're just building up this story to tell the ladies."

"Norie! Don't be silly. Now how big is this plane, anyway?"

☆☆☆ **30** ☆☆☆

TRAVEL IS NOT MY FORTE. IT'S JUST TOO FINAL. I MAKE jokes, but, face it, you get on a plane and there's just no changing your mind.

Even the packing puts me in a panic. What to wear is always simple for the guys—a blazer, shirts, khakis, and gray flannel pants. And then suits after you arrive. *Voilà!* Mr. Classic. I, on the other hand, when faced with deciding what I should be putting on three mornings later, in a city that's hundreds of thousands of miles away, lose it.

Over the years, I had developed a practiced and predictable pattern for trip preparation. The night before I left, I would put everything I owned in various bundles on my bed and bedroom floor. I'd then sift through the piles, moving combinations from one to another, until, finally, exhausted, I would take the least offensive bunch, roll the various pieces into tight cloth sausages, and stuff them all into my suitcase.

But this trip was too important. So, with advice from Hilda and prodding from Kathleen, I organized myself well in advance and arrived at Andrews Air Force Base with one well-thought-out suitcase, a garment bag, and a big canvas tote for my briefing papers. Hilda had stressed how long the flight to Asia was, and how long it felt, so I was wearing one of those Speedo cotton dress-up sweat suits, navy blue, with a red-white-and-blue scarf. Also my Reeboks. Practical and patriotic.

I was as well planned, well packed, well inoculated, and well briefed as any first-time-around senator could be. All the pretrip excitement—the dinners with friends, the doctor visits, the visa applications, the rush—had kept me from thinking about the actual destination.

Then came a moment, as I left the Hart Senate Office Building and walked the few steps to the car waiting in the circle, when it really hit me. What the trip was all about. What waited at the end. I was going to Jack, to where Jack was lost. And maybe, just one chance in a million, maybe he'd be found.

It took my breath away.

Andrews is just a short ride outside of Washington, and it's the departure point for almost all CODELs. Deborah was driving me. She'd been to Andrews several times with Senator Gannon and knew the drill;

she entered the gate, immediately turned left, and presented credentials to a smartly dressed air force sergeant.

We got okayed, and drove on to the VIP lounge, a small building off to the side. Out of the car, then another ID verification as I checked my luggage with two airmen and waved Deborah goodbye.

"Big security today, Senator," the younger man told me. "You guys, I mean you senators, are heading to Vietnam. But we've also got the president going down to Texas, so it's a double alert."

"Will I see the president in the lounge?" I asked.

"No, ma'am. The president goes directly to the plane. Air Force One. *His* plane," the younger one explained, a little too forcefully, like a Boy Scout giving an old lady directions on crossing the street.

"Wait a minute. Don't lead the senator wrong," the sergeant interrupted, picking up the tinge in the young man's tone. "Senator, to kinda quote the immortal words of President Lyndon Johnson when a young airman asked if LBJ was going to *his* helicopter, 'Son, they are *all* my helicopters.' These are all the president's planes. So my young friend here was incorrect."

I grinned. It is wonderful how people in their forties stick together.

I bounded with all the energy I could muster up a short flight of stairs and into the lounge. At the right was a high bar. Behind it staff were serving coffee, soft drinks, bagels, and doughnuts. Hanging directly beside the bar was a recent artistic addition that Hilda had urged me not to miss. How could I? It jumped out to greet me—a collage of portraits of service-women, all wearing the headgear symbolic of various air force jobs.

"I know it's meant to be nice," Hilda had cautioned. "But do they always have to show women in *hats*?"

With the hat exception, the lounge was a monument to masculinity, the once exclusive masculinity of the armed services, with large leather sofas and dozens of pictures of air force men and the planes they flew. The only other feminine thing I could locate was the one-stall women's bathroom, complete with a basket holding toiletries and hair spray—obviously for use if your hat messed up your "do."

I freshened up, returned to the lounge to chat with one or two colleagues, then followed Baxter and the others on the five-minute walk to the plane.

At the bottom of the steps, another sergeant re-checked my credentials and sent me on board. A steward directed me to the back of the plane, past the staff room, and finally to a large conference room. It didn't look like the inside of any plane I'd ever seen, but rather like one of those make-believe train lounges in a 1940 movie.

Large sofas ran along the sides of the plane, flanked by chairs and fronted with tables. We were a large group. In addition to our committee members, there were State Department staffers, select committee sup-port people, CIA and Department of Defense experts on Southeast Asia, and Lao-Americans and Vietamese-Americans who were veterans of other meetings on the MIA question. I was the exception. The official party, except for me, were all men.

En route briefings would be held on everything from the major battles of the Vietnam War to the suspected locations of former POW camps to Southeast Asia's cultural traditions to Vietnam's current economic situation. We were handed large bundles of material—some prepared by government agencies, others from the Carnegie Foundation or from the School of Advanced International Studies at Johns Hopkins.

The plane, a VC137BC, the military version of a 747, was reconfigured so that it would serve as our office, hotel, and briefing room as well as transportation. There was an air force crew—men and women, I noticed thankfully—who served as stewards.

And—this really surprised me—a doctor, Joseph Kelly, from a small town outside Pittsburgh. "I'm authorized to do gallbladders, but not open-heart surgery," he explained. "When a big CODEL is traveling to a truly underdeveloped country, or to a place where the United States hasn't maintained diplomatic relations, there's always an M.D. along." He'd brought complete copies of the medical records of everyone on board, in addition to a sizable supply of Type O blood—the universal donor.

Seven print reporters were on the flight, along with four television crews. I needed no introduction to some of them, including the ubiquitous Diane Wong.

We'd been in the air less than an hour when she just happened to sit beside me in the briefing room. One of the State Department experts was discussing the diplomatic history of the war years, part of the non-classified information that would be gone through en route and that the press was welcome to sit in on.

For me, this was old stuff. In the years right after Jack was declared MIA, I had read everything available on Vietnam's culture, history, or politics, as if by finding out about the country I could understand, or at least accept, what had happened to my husband.

"Kind of boring, huh?" Wong whispered conspiratorially.

"Only if you didn't know it already," I countered.

"I'd love to get the chance to know you better, Senator. And I thought this flight was a perfect way to begin."

"I don't think the schedule allows it. This briefing is set to go on another half hour. Then a late lunch, then the military guys take over. That's for the CODEL and staff only. But I know all of what's being covered now, so let's grab a cup of coffee."

She lobbed me one of those million-dollar television smiles, and we made our way back to the galley. I was sure Baxter was shooting stares at my back. I swung my head around, caught his eye, and gave him a wink. He looked shocked.

Diane looked happy. I felt happy. She might be clever and relentless, but she had burned me once.

"I'm so glad you're on this trip, Senator," she began. "It always makes me feel so much better when there's a woman in a position of power."

"Not very powerful, not this woman. Just the lowest-ranking committee member."

"But you've got that special link, your husband I mean. And I want to be sure, Senator, that the uniqueness of your story doesn't get lost in the politics."

"I don't understand you, Diane. I think nothing about this trip is political. Senator Baxter seems clear that this is a nonpartisan mission." This time I was in the driver's seat, and I wasn't moving over.

"Maybe I'm not clear. I think it's crucial for people to get a personal look at this story, really empathize with what you are going through. Maybe we could make some time, the first day in Vietnam, after you've seen a little of the country, and you could talk to me— one-to-one—about how you're feeling and the, you know, the—"

"Kind of an exclusive interview about the pain and suffering I'm going through?" Subtlety was a lost art.

"Exactly. The real emotional drama of being in Vietnam." She was so pleased I'd gotten her drift.

"Nope. I don't think so." I *had* understood her. Perfectly. I stood up and mouthed a thank-you to the galley staff.

"But wouldn't it be important for you to tell your story to the American people? To tell what you are feeling, seeing, hoping?"

"Nope. I don't think so. I'm here to do a job. The select committee will make a report when we return."

"But, Senator." Wong was following me back to the briefing room. "What about your husband?"

"Jack came to do a job. That's what I'm doing. My

job." I flashed my big non-TV smile. "But thanks for thinking of me. You're really a nice person. Truly warm and nice. Not at all like your reputation."

I made my way between the tables and pulled a chair up beside Baxter. I gave him a little nudge with my elbow. "She tried to sandbag me," I reported. "But no go. I might be taken for a ride once, but I hope I know not to get on the same roller coaster the second time around."

He nodded approval.

I wanted him to know that nobody was pushing me around on this trip. I was on my way to Jack.

"It's a commonly accepted fact. Without body identification, no family is ever really satisfied."

Baxter barely looked up, but I knew the words were directed at me. We were flying between Hawaii and Guam, and Baxter, Senator Mike Kincaid, and I were working in a small office in front of the conference room. Mike and I were flying backward, Baxter seated across from me.

The compartment was fairly private. The press and most of the military were to the rear of the conference room, where business-class-size seats lined up as on a commercial flight. There was a working space for the press, a tiny, jammed room at the very rear of the plane.

Baxter was busy sorting papers into piles and arranging them on the fold-out table between us. He held one sheet out, reading it as if his glasses were too weak or his arms too short. He repeated himself.

" 'Without body identification, no family is ever really satisfied.' Do you think, Senator Gorzack, that statement is correct?"

I pursed my lips. Baxter just didn't give up.

"Probably. I went to a seminar once, about handling the survivors of large-scale tragedies. Earthquakes. Tornadoes. I guess war qualifies. Anyway, as health professionals we were warned that families just don't want to believe that their loved one is in the building or the fire or the wreck. They want to believe that somehow the person missed the train or went out for a cup of coffee or something."

"And what about you, Senator?" Baxter asked. Obviously, he'd gone to the same school of relentlessness as Diane Wong.

"I'm like everybody else. We all hope. But after a very long time, as with MIAs, I think the common feeling is just wanting to know the truth. I've been looking into the reports of several groups who believe they have the truth. I'm sure many of them are scoundrels." I sorted through the folders crammed into my canvas tote.

"Very good," Baxter allowed. He still hadn't explained to me personally or to the committee how he'd gotten linked up with Wiggins. Instead, the good senator dealt with Wiggins like some character he'd once met at a cocktail party, not like the head of a questionable group that Baxter had supported.

"It appears that as far back as 1987, the Defense Intelligence Agency was warning that several self-styled MIA groups were using questionable fund-raising appeals." I paused and looked up. Baxter was staring right into my face.

"Keep going, Norie. This is the stuff that makes my blood boil." Kincaid was himself a Vietnam vet, from early in the war, and, I thought, a potential ally if I had to take on Baxter again.

"Listen to this: 'The fund-raising appeals offer no proof that prisoners are held, but allude to having secret intelligence of some inside information on POWs. . . . In a few instances so-called "live sightings" are concocted to prove absurd claims . . . none of which have any basis in reality.' Like Reverend Wiggins and his talk of his Freedom Fighters."

"I don't know, Senator," Baxter said, sounding more melodious than ever. "Wiggins is under a lot of scrutiny, and unless he has broken a specific law—tax, communication, postal regulation—he can keep on going. Some patriotic groups, even though they've claimed these 'live sightings,' do good work."

"Wiggins isn't the first scam artist," I countered. "Several groups have existed just to raise money—for themselves. The CIA says that the illegitimate groups have a common fund-raising ploy—they are just on the verge of rescuing POWs. Let me read you this." I grabbed another folder. I had worked late into the night, kept the staff working, to be over-prepared for this trip.

I had disappointed Milton when I refused to look into the Baxter contributor list until this trip was over. Milton wanted me to pursue Baxter. Stewart thought it was a bad idea. But staying away from a confrontation, temporarily, was a strategic decision to keep my priorities straight. I wasn't going to let Amy Walker down, or let her work go in vain. "Here's more nonsense. 'We're close to making contact with an American POW who has been alone since his fellow prisoner died of natural causes less than a year ago. That effort could fail for lack of funds.' Or 'You may wake up tomorrow morning and hear that the first American POW has been rescued. We are that close.' Or how about 'Must raise thirteen thousand six hundred and seventy-one dollars by Friday, October 31, or vital intelligence-gathering missions may have to be stopped.' How dare these people!"

"We have to be cautious," Baxter said, beginning to preach to himself. "The people supporting some of these groups are also involved in real MIA efforts. And those are the people who have kept the issue alive in real and sincere ways. And they've also tried to do their bit for the vets who got home."

Kincaid's antennae must have been working, since he stood up and said he was going to rustle up some coffee and snacks. I was getting tense, ready to take Baxter on about just how much I knew about the feeling of families whose boys didn't come home. But he stopped me, held up his hand like a traffic cop.

"Senator, I want to say one thing. Before we get to Vietnam."

I felt the pressure of Baxter's words and his entire looming presence heavy on my shoulders. I wanted to crawl under the table, anything to avoid the warning that I feared was coming.

"Yes, Senator."

"I hope no matter what happens with our trip, no matter what we eventually find out, I hope your personal quest ends soon. It must be very hard."

I nodded my head yes, but didn't allow myself to answer. It was decent of Baxter to say that. But it could just be another ploy.

☆☆☆ **31** ☆☆☆

FLYING INTO VIETNAM, I CALLED HOME.

It was all so simple, with razzle-dazzle global communication links, all part of the plane's galaxy of high-tech abilities. The system allowed me to hook up with satellites and ring my mother, back in Philly. Of course, as Milton had dutifully reminded me before we left, the U.S. Senate would be billed by the U.S. Air Force for all such personal calls. One State Department expert had promised that it was easier to call D.C. from Hong Kong across the Pacific than from Arlington across the Potomac.

My mother loved it. She kept telling me how thrilled she was, and we had one of those "What time is it there?" conversations.

"I don't believe this international line thing," she opined. "How can you be in a totally different day since you're on the other side of California and I know that California is earlier?"

Somehow I convinced her that this was not the best time for the how-the-world-turns talk, then gave her a few details about the trip and the food and the hotels so she could show off a little with her lady friends.

"I have something so interesting to tell you, Norie," she started. "About Vietnam . . ."

At that point, I changed the topic. Even for the cost of a local call, I just didn't have the patience today to listen to what was being said on the radio.

Technology keeps making these leaps and bounds that would have changed history if they had happened just a few decades earlier. How different life would have been if some grunt or some young ensign could have just rung up home from Saigon twenty-five years ago, not even using the air force's high-tech goodies, but simply dialing one of those international access codes and getting hooked up by someone who spoke English and was working out of Butte, Montana, or Athens, Georgia. What if my Jack could have just dialed direct?

What if he could have called me, every week or every two weeks, instead of those letters that came in fits and spurts and those haphazard phone links with our voices drifting in and out and sounding even farther apart than the war had made us? He must have felt so alone, with the gunfire of this strange country swirling around him.

I felt it, the strangeness. First in Guam and then in Laos, the exotic differences of people, weather, landscape, everything would envelop us, and then we would return to the plane and it would be America—until we once again set down in a different exotic place.

Americans come to Vietnam now in the name of tourism. If I hadn't known better, that's what this plane could be—just a group of happy tourists, all wearing our civvies. Not even the military types were in uniforms, since we were entering countries which we did not diplomatically recognize. But I think it was also true that the absence of uniforms made conversations with present and former North Vietnamese military much easier.

En route from Laos to Vietnam, the captain came back and asked me if I wanted to come up and look out the cockpit window. Not even a question, I told him. Mike Kincaid came along with me, and as we made a quick descent and a fast circle around the city, he pointed out the general location of the Hanoi Hilton, the nickname for the odious Hoa Lo Prison near the capital's downtown. I was numb. I said a prayer.

The Red River rushed up to meet the plane. Mike broke through my sadness by jokingly insisting that the river was named for the color of its water, not the tint of Vietnam's politics. Kincaid could turn a real fact inside out and make it unbelievable.

There was a great spread of rice paddies, coming up on both sides of the airport's runways, and dozens and dozens of people working, bent over, their faces hidden by cone-shaped straw hats. Vietnam, the briefing had continually pointed out, was the world's third-largest exporter of rice.

We had cut through heavy cloud cover, and the overcast weather jolted me. In my mind Vietnam was hot and sunny. It was the first but far from the only time my beliefs and preconceptions about this place were dead wrong.

If you judged things by airports, Hanoi could have been a town in rural Pennsylvania. The Hanoi airport was about as basic as you could get and still land a plane. There wasn't even a fancy control tower.

As I walked down the steps pushed against the plane, I revised my initial impression—yes, this could be an airport in rural Pennsylvania, but during the Depression. It would hit me again and again in Vietnam, but never with the clarity of that first few minutes: Hanoi, and Vietnam, were poor. Dirt poor.

The air force personnel had given out "friendship pins," showing the American flag with the Vietnamese flag. "You wear the pin as a gesture of friendship," the young woman told me.

I smiled, but I put the pin in my pocket. I could not put it on. I could not bring myself to do this simple thing.

We were all loaded onto airport shuttle buses, the same the world over, but the bus didn't stop at the terminal. Instead, it headed down the road to Hanoi. Over and over again, in the rhythm of the thump-thump of the tires on the macadam, I repeated to myself: "I am in Vietnam. I am in Vietnam."

The country passed outside the bus windows—rice paddies, peasants working with hoes, water buffaloes, a large billboard advertising the American Express Card. Our baggage went on to the hotel, and we headed directly to the MIA office.

Hanoi and I shared the same time warp, but in different ways. For both the city and me, it was as if the war had ended yesterday. The city was fairly clean, but it seemed worn out.

Young people were everywhere—walking, or on the ubiquitous motorbikes. Sixty percent of Vietnam's population is under twenty. These young people, except for their straw hats and pith helmets topping off their Western jeans and T-shirts, could have been walking or riding the streets of Los Angeles or Chicago or Philadelphia. And their relatives probably were.

Generations of conflict had taught Hanoi how to make do. Like other Asian countries, shops here were grouped by commodities. One street was for building supplies, another for food, another for clothes. There were stalls in the streets and peddlers, but it was all very organized and utilized.

There was one strip of buildings—baroque, neo-Romantic, as French as New Orleans—layered with the decay of decades. The high first story was crammed with bazaar materials, then came the apartments with clothing drying on the crumbling ornate balconies. Electric wire was strung like Christmas decorations between the buildings and a tilting utility pole. There was no way of knowing if this "temporary" arrangement had been there for a day or for years.

We were heading directly to the Ranch, the home-and-office combination used by the U.S. military and the civilians who make up the Joint Task Force on MIAs—yet another all-male group. I couldn't help wonder if the name, the Ranch, evolved because they felt so herded in here, an oasis in the city.

One thing I was sure of—as soon as we went through the gate and met them, I knew that this was one swell group of people. Civilians and military, all skilled in archival work, practiced in taking oral histories, they did their jobs with the right combination of know-how and dedication.

Lunch was cheese sandwiches and baked beans, and it made me think of that lunch at the Vietnam Memorial following the service for Jake Browning.

Then we began to talk. Or rather, to listen to the experts, as they barraged us with facts. It was all very factual, tough, like the duty they were performing, stark duty, a lot of sacrifice, and, for many military and civilians alike, a return to Vietnam. One by one, they began to discuss their own investigations. One archivist, who spoke fluent Vietnamese, explained how he himself was the basis for several live sightings.

"I go into the field. I'm wearing some mishmash of American clothes and a pith helmet. I'm speaking to Vietnamese. And suddenly there is a missing American who has been sighted."

I remember exactly what he said, because this was the moment when my hope started to fail—not just for

Jack, but for the hundreds and hundreds of other MIAs lost in this faraway country.

Another analyst, who looked too young to be an expert, explained the techniques for uncovering actual witnesses. "We've had many people come forward. The ads in the phone books have been especially successful. Of course, there is the problem of the falsified remains." His voice trailed off, uncomfortable at discussing particulars of his project. "And there is the question of rewards. We're still debating among ourselves the most effective reward. Should we offer money, I mean if people produce actual remains? Or should they be given visas, a special status to leave Vietnam?"

Baxter cleared his throat. "I'd like someone here to discuss the falsified-remains problem."

"Senator. Ah, Senators." It was the young one who spoke up. "Most of the walk-ins we've had, people who show up and claim they know something, well, most of them, like ninety percent, are bogus. One big problem we have is that people show up with animal bones or Vietnamese bones. And then there's the growing hassle brought on by our very presence here—yet another black market. Like during the war. Only this is the production of bogus dog tags. There are a couple places outside of Hanoi where people have like cottage industries and they make the tags."

"Do you have any questions, Senator Gorzack?" Baxter asked out of nowhere.

"Not on this, Senator. But, Colonel, what about live sightings? When someone reliable says he or she has seen an American—and it's not you or anybody connected with the project?" Baxter had thrown down the gauntlet, and I was ready. Stewart had briefed me twice in the weeks before the trip, managing to supply more information about live sightings from international corporate sources.

"Live sightings? We've investigated over a hundred such reports. We've found no camps. It's not just me. It's other Americans, or Europeans, or, early on, Russians who might have been working in the area. We've been through the countryside. We've talked to a lot of people. And we know there are just no prisoner-of-war camps. None. Zip."

"That seems contrary to some reports published in non-American newspapers and journals. Isn't that the kind of news reporting we want to follow up? Isn't that good news?" I just couldn't give up that easily.

"The way I see it, ma'am, is that the bad news is we haven't found anybody. The good news is people have been alerted. They know what we are looking for. And they are coming to us and reporting."

"The bones," the younger analyst interrupted. "When we get bones. First. We make sure they're human. Then we see if they are non-Vietnamese. Size, density. Further identification is based on a whole series of specialties—teeth, placement, archaeology."

"And what do you think is your most effective tool, Colonel, in tracking down remains?" Baxter asked his question, having obviously, in his mind, just wiped out any hope of live sightings.

"The oral history, sir. Retired military, especially

from the officer ranks, are certainly the best. They kept diaries. Crash sights. They pulled the dead out. They noted the time, days, numbers, when they took prisoners. 'Who drove the prisoners? Who saw them last?' One story from the military was that there was a plane crash. They were taking the survivors as prisoners. Then came another air attack. Our guys tried to get away. The Vietnamese shot them. And this one captain recorded it in his diary, with their names."

"Are you moving fast enough in finding these Vietnamese soldiers?" I said, trying to keep myself in the conversation.

"Senator Gorzack, we have to move fast. Little was done before 1988. Vietnam was resistant. And the U.S. was pretty tepid in pursuing information. The joint task force means the Vietnamese military have been helping. When we go out to sites, it's the Vietnamese that fly us out. On Russian helicopters. Of course, we do unilateral investigations as well as joint ones."

"What's been your biggest help, Colonel?" Mike Kincaid asked the question as though he really wanted to know the answer, not as if he was checking to see if the colonel's answer jibed with what we'd been told in Washington. It was a solid kind of technique and I decided to borrow it permanently.

"The biggest help is that these people, the Vietnamese, are searching too, for their own MIAs. Only they're looking for three hundred thousand missing."

"Do we help them in other ways?" Kincaid asked.

"The Vietnam vets back in the States have. Out of respect and also to thank the individual Vietnamese who cooperated, the vets canvassed their own members, asking them if they had any information."

"Did any information come in?"

"Some. It also brought us information on our own MIAs. We must have gotten a couple thousand letters from vets who thought they knew something, remembered something. We went through them all. A few were just out of it, guys who had never really come back from the war. Very sad. Strange stories. Maybe even a couple of them were true. Some other letters seem to have real leads. We're trying to follow them."

We broke up into informal groups to talk more. I made sure I was far away from Baxter. I liked these Americans and I was touched to find them working hard in the face of little hope and in these comfortless surroundings.

They had convinced me of one fact: I could now look at myself in a mirror or meet with the most intense MIA wife and could say and believe that these guys were pulling out all the stops. That they were doing a top-notch job.

On our way to the Joint Document Center, we passed the Hanoi Hilton. It was familiar the way frequently televised places seem familiar—like the White House or the shot of a street that's an opening scene from a popular sitcom. I had watched prisoners being led in and out of the Hanoi Hilton for years. So had the whole world. According to my briefing papers, it was now owned by the Singapore Development Corporation. It was being used temporarily by the

Vietnam Film Institute. Peace and culture had come to Hanoi.

The city was a place of great beauty, with lakes and little parks interrupting the urban landscape. No wonder the French loved it.

Our bus slowed down near a small park and stopped by a statue on the edge of a lake. The three-foot-high statue of an aviator with his arms outstretched, being taken prisoner, had a shockingly familiar face, since it commemorated the capture of John McCain—now my colleague in the Senate.

"He was one of ten Americans shot down that day," Mike explained. "McCain was a real trophy. He had flown a lot of missions, and his father was a high-ranking military man."

The children were playing, the motorbikes were whizzing by, and vendors were hawking postcards. It was a good day to spend in a park.

☆☆☆ **32** ☆☆☆

IT WAS NAGGING AT ME. THAT LINE FROM THE COLONEL
at the Ranch, when he just barely mentioned the letters that had come in from American vets: "For some
the war just never ended." Back home, Lieutenant
Carver had used that same line about Jake Browning.

I asked Mike Kincaid if we could see some of the
letters.

"Sure, Norie. After the appointment with the joint
task force, we'll head back to the Ranch. I hope we
don't get headed off at the pass."

I was so distracted I barely got the joke.

The Archive on U.S. Missing Personnel in the
Vietnam War was under the direction of a joint task
force headed by an old Vietnam hand, Bob deVries,
and his retired Vietnamese counterpart Colonel Binh.
Opened in downtown Hanoi in May 1993, the center

was a combination office and museum. The United States applied a lot of pressure to get the operation going, to make the documents available to our researchers. Now the representatives of both countries pored over the papers together, questioning people and trying to solve technical problems.

Bob deVries had retired from the Marine Corps with the rank of lieutenant colonel, and Colonel Binh had served in what was now called "the infantry in the South," what we used to refer to as the Vietcong. They might have shot at each other.

I was ready for their talk; I was ready for the documentation center. But I was in no way ready for the area outside. Everywhere I looked there were what the schedule had coolly described as "military artifacts." Everywhere.

There was a Russian MiG that had shot down U.S. planes. There was example after example of captured U.S. artillery. And then there were pieces of U.S. aircraft—the wing of a B-52, the blade of a Huey—piled into a grotesque modern sculpture.

There was no way to sort it out—the wreckage or the thoughts that blasted through my head. This could be a piece of Jack's plane, or this. A lot of things, of dead metal, all meaning nothing and everything.

By the time we gathered in the circular Joint Documentation Room, I'd regained my breath but was close to losing my temper. Tables functioning as desks were pushed against the wall, with out-of-date computers and scanners scattered about. Kincaid whispered to me that the whole place was decorated in "modern-day comrade," but I shrugged off his attempts at lightening the situation.

Above the work area were dozens of pictures of American POWs. A large glass case stood over to one side. It was filled with artifacts—badges, insignia, rings—along with dozens of white envelopes.

"And in the envelopes?" I asked Colonel Binh through the interpreter.

"Pictures. Photographs."

"I'd like to see some of them."

I went through dozens of photographs, looking at those great young hopeful, and tragic, American faces. I knew these faces. I had seen faces like this on the buttons MIA wives wear. I had looked through wedding albums and yearbooks, and I knew these faces.

This was not a moment filled with sadness or with any poignant sense. It was too raw to carry any title or label. I was sifting through the ashes of lives that were gone, through the remains of all these lost hopes and dreams.

I knew these faces, and yet I dreaded seeing that one face I truly knew. I prayed I would. I didn't.

Through the interpreter, Colonel Binh continued to explain the procedure. He held his head high, and it was obvious that he regarded this appointment, this work, as a badge of honor. If his country looked shabby and worn, the colonel dispelled that image. He stood ramrod-straight, and his olive-with-red-trim uniform looked as spanking clean as the red star on the peaked hat he had tucked under his arm.

It was another thirty minutes of details—how they

went through the documents; how the review was
conducted; how they had arrived at the number of
1,624 Americans still unaccounted for. Bob deVries
was at Binh's side, occasionally interjecting yet more
details.

The room was stuffy, and when Binh hit a point in
his dialogue where he was focusing on the minutia
surrounding insignia identification, I felt my hands
clench.

"Excuse me, Colonel," I heard myself saying. "The
details on the procedure are very interesting. But what
do you think the eventual outcome of all this paper-
work is going to be?"

I could feel Kincaid stiffen beside me, and the
interpreter blinked nervously, as if on the alert.

"Madame Senator," Binh replied, in heavily ac-
cented English, "you are not the only one who grows
impatient. You are not the only one who has lost
someone."

"I understand that, Colonel, but—"

"Let me interrupt. Let me, if I can, say that I feel for
you, for Americans. But you must feel for us. We are
missing three hundred thousand Vietnamese. Who
weeps for them? Who asks for them? Who knows
enough to say the prayers that a son or daughter
should be saying, a wife or husband?"

I gritted my teeth. I understood his pain, but his job
was to deal with mine—with the American MIAs,
with Jack.

"Does the Madame Senator have time for a personal
story? . . . Good. A young Vietnamese officer is told

one day that the American planes are coming to Hanoi. It is early in the war, and he thinks he can save his wife by sending her to the country. To the house of his mother and his sisters. The air raids come. They are everywhere. His family flees. When the officer finally can get to the village of his mother, it is gone. And they are gone. Nine members. No one ever hears from them again."

I knew what Binh would say next, but it didn't make hearing it any easier.

"Don't you think, Madame Senator, that I would like to know where my wife, my mother, and my sisters are? Don't you think I mourn my wife, that I want to visit their graves?"

Mike and I agreed we'd go back to the Ranch after dinner, but I was beat and needed a break. I skipped the group meal in the Metropole dining room and instead went upstairs, stretched out, turned on CNN, and ordered an Uncle Samburger from room service.

I thought about what Mike had said on the plane out. The old comrades in Vietnam are old men. The young comrades are watching CNN and trying to figure out the West.

Downstairs in this traditional and once again faintly swank hotel there was a dining room filled with businessmen, discussing import taxes and embargoes and finishing up dinner with a cream-filled napoleon and a Cuban cigar. The Chamber of Commerce, according to a small sign in the lobby, met every other

Tuesday for lunch. And the displays at the Joint Archives were towers of destroyed plane parts.

A nap helped restore whatever equilibrium was possible in this place, both frozen in the past and breaking toward a future. I washed my face and changed into the one pair of casual pants I'd brought along, pulled on an oversize cotton sweater, rang up Mike Kincaid, and headed back to the Ranch in the cool evening.

The guys served us up coffee and thick sweetened cream and dragged out the files of letters that vets in America had sent.

I wasn't sure what I was looking for, maybe something from Jake Browning or Bob Sanders. Kincaid was a champ. He took a pile of letters and started to help in the search. After an hour, we knew it was fruitless.

More coffee got poured, and as Kincaid and the fellows talked, I went once again through the letters—some laser-printed on bond stationery, some scribbled on three-ring ruled paper.

It hit me the instant I saw it.

The name. Saunders Bobb. *Saunders Bobb!* No wonder Carver hadn't found him in the Veterans Administration files. We had the name backward!

Reading the letter took away any feeling of satisfaction or exhilaration. It was pure paranoia. I began to think that maybe Carver and Milton and Nancy and everyone else were right. Bob—rather, Saunders Bobb—sure seemed crazy.

The four-page letter was dated almost six months

earlier. It centered on his and his friend Jake's search for Americans who had "betrayed other soldiers, betrayed their friends, and led us into deathtraps throughout the war."

The letter made clear, and the guys at the Ranch agreed, that Saunders Bobb had been on an actual POW raid into North Vietnam.

"Obviously his unit found some POWs, but couldn't get to them. I would figure that they had bad info on how many troops were guarding the prisoners, or on the exact extent of the compound."

Bobb blamed the mission's failure on what he called "turncoat Americans and black market profiteers."

Kincaid and I finished our coffee and, with a copy of Bobb's letter tucked carefully into my purse, headed back to the hotel.

It was a playing field.

If I squinted, and held my eyes close on the field itself, if I blocked out the apartment buildings that ranged around its edges, it looked just like any playing field in my neighborhood.

Kids were playing on it now, some kind of soccer. They looked like all other kids.

Or maybe they were young men. I found it easy to talk to the younger Vietnamese, harder to make conversation with the older men and women. I knew I should stop myself, but I kept obsessively trying to figure out each person's age, then subtracting and trying to calculate how old he or she had been during the war.

With every conversation, I reminded myself what Edwina Nussbaum at the State Department had told me: "These are people of small stature, Senator, and sometimes, inadvertently, we allow ourselves to translate that difference in build, in physique, into a condescending attitude. Do not allow yourself to slip into a paternalistic attitude. These are not children."

"Edwina," I had been quick to respond, "not me. I've dealt with a wide range of immigrant groups working in public health back in Pennsylvania. You obviously think I'm a bit naive. And maybe a bit racist."

"No, Senator, on both counts. It's just that I've been involved in this racket for a long time." Her appearance belied her words. "I speak Thai. I've been to Bangkok some two dozen times. I've been to Vietnam on at least six trips. And I have to remind myself, when surrounded by these petite, fine-boned people, that they are adults, strong, and, in many ways, the victors over our big, brawling America."

It turned out that she was right on target. I'd have to call and tell her when we got home.

No briefing could explain the knockout beauty of the country. Somehow the TV news footage and the films and the pictures that had burned their images into our consciousness—people dying and killing—somehow none of those images showed Vietnam. It was lush and green, rain forests and fields, and when we had flown in the day before, it had been wondrous.

Even here, as I tramped across this playing field, the beauty was breathtaking. Or maybe I was a little short of breath from trying to keep up with Baxter and the other members of the delegation.

Since the end of the war, this field had been identified as a supposed prison, especially during the last months of the war. Not the field itself, but tunnels and shelters dug under it. We were here with government officials who planned to prove to us that this place, at least, had housed no Americans.

There were four—no, five—entrances to the underground, all strategically located near the apartment buildings that ringed the field. Baxter and the Vietnamese official started down the stairs of one of them. I followed, as did two other senators.

It was dark and dank inside, and smelled like nothing I could quite remember.

"There are no doorframes," a Vietnamese official announced. His English was almost perfect American, but he was under thirty. I wondered where he had picked up his command of the language. "No doorframes, no doors, and no hardware—which all indicate that there was no way to close off any of the tunnels that come to this point."

We walked in and out of the various doorways, Baxter and I venturing far back into one tunnel. The ceilings were low, maybe five feet high. Even I had to bend over. I shuddered, thinking of the tunnels like this where Americans had been held. Maybe not here, not under this playing field, but somewhere in this country where children now played, under fields, Americans had been imprisoned and then buried.

Not all of the prisoners, I corrected myself. Not all

of the Americans had to be buried. Some *could* still be held. I was not giving up my dream that easily.

Saddened and silent, senators, Vietnamese officials, and their respective staffs walked the few blocks to the next supposed holding location. Again, a series of tunnels, this time built along the side of what was now a paved four-lane road. An aqueduct of some kind ran between the tunnel entrance and the highway.

"Here . . ." The staff person was pointing again to the tunnel openings. "Here we have evidence of doors. This location could, on that basis, be construed as a possible holding area. But," he said, walking the few feet into the tunnel and coming out again, "there is no evidence of any POW habitation. No graffiti, no sign of longtime residence."

I ran my hand along the damp walls. As I tried to stand up, my hair brushed the ceiling. I thought of Jack, tall and straight and very strong. I kept running my hand, back and forth, along the wall and tried to read the history of the place through my touch.

☆☆☆ **33** ☆☆☆

THE INVITATION WAS PRESENTED AT THE START OF OUR third day in Hanoi.

A young woman approached me at breakfast. The crispness of her white linen suit was the first thing that struck me, especially since my own white shirt had melted in the humidity and heat minutes after I put it on. In a formal, old-fashioned manner, the young woman presented me with a white envelope with only my name written on it. Inside was a handwritten invitation, asking me to break off from the regular schedule and visit a nearby school that had once housed many war orphans.

"But I don't want to go to the orphanage. Not if it's the 'woman's thing to do,' " I complained to Baxter. As soon as the invitation had been placed in my hands, I had rushed it by him, hopeful that he would see it as some kind of publicity ploy.

"Don't give me that feminist claptrap. Just go. Build some goodwill." Baxter and the other committee members headed off to meet in a more formal way with government officials, and I couldn't help but be suspicious that something would happen behind my back as I was off doing the woman's thing.

The woman in the white suit accompanied me, pointing out various buildings and sites. Her English was more than fluent, but it carried a heavy flavoring of French. The destination—the school, she called it and made it sound like *l'ecole*—had originally been for the children of National Liberation Front fighters killed in the war.

"Some of our very best soldiers were women. So many children left behind. Now, those children are grown up. Peace is here. And yet other children suffer the sadness of losing their parents."

At the entrance to the orphanage grounds, we hesitated for a moment, watching the children play.

"You wonder how those war orphans fared, don't you? Alone. In a country torn with war. Bombs raining down." The war seemed near to me, and for the first time I understood the pain of the "enemy."

"I don't wonder, Senator Gorzack," the woman replied. "I know. I came to this place in 1969. I know it well. I grew up here. And before I went to study English in"—she hesitated—"in Europe, this was the only home I ever knew."

An elderly man walked onto the playground and was greeted with instant silence. The children, grave and serious, lined up to be, I assumed, reviewed or inspected. But a few slow steps down the row was all the man wanted. He held his hands in front of him, and clapped once. Shouts and yells followed, and for a moment I wondered if the man would be pushed over in the excitement. But the children joyfully touched him, receiving in return a pat on the head, a squeeze on the shoulder. Once thus acknowledged, they went quickly back to their play.

"The doctor. That's who wanted you here today," the young woman said. She led me to a side building and showed me into a clean, sparse office, bookshelves lined with volumes in French and English, novels and biographies and shelf upon shelf crammed with books about Vietnam.

"Welcome, Mrs. Gorzack." The doctor was suddenly beside me, and the fragility that worried me as I watched him with the children seemed to be overcome by the strength of his persona. He motioned me to a chair. The young woman, who had disappeared for a moment, returned with cold drinks.

"I am very happy to have you here today, in my place," the doctor started. I recognized the young woman's unique accent in the old man's speech. "I have been here for almost forty years. Before we talk, let me tell you about my life a little. I already know about yours."

He held up a worn copy of *Time* magazine, the

edition which carried the story about my opening speech at the select committee.

"I went to Paris to be educated in the 1930s. I was half through my medical schooling when World War II broke out, and I was evacuated, with some other Indochinese, to England. I was permitted to finish medical school, and then, at the end of the war, I was put into service, helping to read out data maps of the area and other such tasks."

He took a long sip of his juice, and I followed his example.

"I returned here, first to work in an army hospital that was in this place. And then, after the war of liberation against the French, to first treat civilians and then, again, as the war between parts of my country grew more deadly, to treat Vietnamese soldiers. Those from both sides, at least when we had the supplies."

The orphanage, he explained, had been built near the hospital, and at the end of the war the hospital, "old and out of date like me," had been torn down. "So there is not too much to see here. But when I learned that you were coming here, to my country, I had to have you visit this place. I had to see you."

"You are very kind, Doctor. And I am happy to get this opportunity to take back to the United States images of the way things are now."

"Mrs. Gorzack, I am not someone trying to indoctrinate you. No. I had a great confusion about your visit. But also a great relief."

I smiled and waited. So did he. The silence spoke

loudly, put the words in my head that I was afraid to speak out loud. But the doctor left me no alternative.

"Doctor, do you know something about my husband? Do you have information about Captain Gorzack, Captain Jack Gorzack?"

The doctor nodded gently before he spoke, and my head moved up and down with his, signaling my agreement and acceptance of what was to come.

"Senator, I know you brought personal questions to Vietnam with you. And I have an answer. But I wanted to give you the answer privately, not in front of the whole world."

The doctor opened the drawer of his desk and pulled out a box.

"Now, I am old. I am not afraid of this government. Or of the government before. Or of whatever government comes after. There was a time, after all those years I was operating the hospital, a time that I feared having to answer questions before a tribunal, an American tribunal, a Vietnamese tribunal. Some court, somewhere. I was afraid of accusations of war crimes. Which I did not commit. But all these fears brought a younger man's silence. Now I am liberated by the courage of old age."

Opening the box, he turned it over and dumped a jumble of dog tags on his desk. From the muddle of chains and tags, four shiny rings dropped on the metal desk. One rolled toward me, making a clicking sound, a train rushing down a track.

I sat, unable to reach out and pick up the ring. The

doctor seemed not to notice my hesitation and concentrated on pulling one of the dog tags from the pile.

"I think this is your husband's," he said, placing it carefully on the desk in front of me.

I touched the metal with my finger, moving it slightly closer to me, then allowing my hand to reach out and pick up the tag. I held it firmly in my clenched hand, and with the other reached out for the ring. Funny, I thought, look—my fingers are shaking. I wonder if I'll be able to hold on to the ring and not drop it.

I turned it around. The class crest matched the one on my miniature. I looked inside. There was a name engraved: "John J. Gorzack."

"My husband's ring. My Jack's ring," I said. I could feel the tears rolling down my face, watch them as they silently dropped on the dented desktop.

"I'm sorry, but you have come with a question, and I have a piece of the answer." The doctor reached over and gently touched my hand. I tried to talk, but words didn't come and sobs were all I could manage.

It took me several minutes to stop crying. The doctor passed me a tissue from a bright white box. It was rough against my skin, and somewhere in my head I realized just how poor this country was, with its own broken memories and its tissues that felt like wrapping paper.

"A *piece* of my answer?" I managed. "But you must tell me about Jack. When did he come here? Did he talk to you? Was he shot? Was he injured in a crash?"

"Mrs. Gorzack." The doctor's voice was gentle. "I

can tell you no more. I have shown you what I know. These tags. These rings. I could lie to you. I could tell you stories, but they would not be true. The deaths were a long time ago."

"Nothing more? No memories of my husband?"

"I know that all the Americans died quickly. We did not have many. Only this handful." The doctor placed his hand over the tags and chains. "Two Americans came without tags. I cannot even tell you if your husband was conscious when he was brought to the hospital. There is a grave, one grave for all the Americans. They are buried in the corner of the schoolyard, near the swings."

The car taking me back to the hotel bumped its way along crowded, noisy streets. I saw nothing, heard nothing. I was far away.

I was in MacDonough Hall. With Jack.

It was May and Jack was finishing his junior, his second-class, year, and he was going to get his ring.

MacDonough Hall was the usual site of boxing and fencing competitions. Jack had kidded me, saying the Ring Dance was just another way for a middie to build muscles. "Just pushing around a girl and carrying that big ring," I could hear him joking.

I could see the big cardboard ring, over against the wall, the academy seal on one side, the class crest on the other.

"Come on. We'll stand inside the ring. It's supposed to be good luck or something."

"I feel funny. Can't we just stand here and look at the ring, look at *your* ring?"

"Eleanor Kurek! You are such a scaredy cat. Into the ring with you, my girl."

He held my hand, and then he held me, and he took my hand and he slipped a ring on my finger. It was a miniature of the one he had just been given.

"Do you know what this means, Norie? What it means is I love you."

Other mids were shouting for us to move on, giving Jack a hard time for taking too long inside the ring.

We walked away. I kept squeezing his hand, his arm. I couldn't hug him hard enough.

"You're squashing your corsage! The people at the Flower Box would be so disappointed. I told them I only wanted the very best."

"I'm so happy, Jack."

"Now why would a ring make you so happy?"

I was afraid to answer, but he pulled my face from his chest and made me look into his eyes.

"You know what I want, Norie. I want to marry you."

"Me too. Yes, I mean. Yes. I love you."

He kissed me and kissed me.

"Now we have an important task. As we set out on our life cruise."

I giggled as Jack hurried me across the floor, to where the binnacle held the water collected from the seven seas.

"Now we dip our hands in the waters. It's good luck, m'dear, as we pirates say."

He held my hand, and the two of us felt the waters from everywhere on the globe touch them, together.

We danced all the slow tunes that night. We held each other close.

"One more year. My ring means I'm on my way."

"My ring means we're on *our* way, Jack. We're on our way."

The car slammed on its brakes.

I looked around at the packed streets, hundreds of people, on bicycles, rushing by, hurrying to their homes and their families and their lives.

I turned the big Annapolis ring around and around on my finger, feeling the weight of the gold, the roughness of the engraving.

"We're on our way now, dear. We're on our way home."

☆☆☆ **34** ☆☆☆

I HELD THE PURSE ACROSS MY CHEST, LIKE A CHILD WITH a cherished toy. On my right hand I had Jack's Annapolis ring and his wedding ring. Two other wedding rings and a total of sixteen pairs of dog tags were in the purse, sacred relics all, handed over into my trust.

Baxter was waiting in the hotel lobby. He at first looked almost pleased to see my arrival and started to walk toward me. I startled both of us, running instead toward him. Several reporters, sensing my urgency, yelled questions at me, but I stayed silent. I guess there was no way to hide my face, and that itself was enough indication that something had happened.

Baxter put his arm around me and led me to a side room off the lobby, telling the reporters in no uncer-

tain terms that they were not to bother Senator
Gorzack.

Inside the room, I broke down, then opened my
purse and dumped my treasure of tags and chains and
rings into Baxter's lap, and my story tumbled out, all
jumbled like the chains.

"It's a great sadness, Senator, to lose a loved one,"
he told me. "But you must remember that your husband and all these fine young men died as heroes."

When I looked up at Baxter, I saw his eyes bright
with tears.

"Everyone who went to Vietnam was a hero, Garrett. Every single person."

The next twenty-four-hours were chaotic.

As soon as Baxter and I could get the president on
the line we told him about my meeting, about what I
had been given. Through State Department officials,
the Vietnamese government was told, bringing on a
flood of explanations.

The vice president was dispatched to Vietnam, to
provide an executive branch honor guard for the
remains of the Americans I was bringing back to the
States.

Vietnamese officials set up almost round-the-clock
meetings, promising a full investigation of any other
hospital sites, complaining that if only the old doctor
had told them, this evidence would have been turned
over many years before. U.S. military teams were sent
to the orphanage to observe the excavation.

Through the excitement, I kept a stoic face turned to

the world. I felt unsure of myself. All those years alone, coping, managing, were really all years of waiting, believing, hoping. And now that part of my life was over.

Less than a hundred hours had passed since our arrival in Vietnam, and I was ready to board the plane back home. The vice president, Baxter, and I gathered around a microphone at the bottom of the plane's boarding ramp.

The vice president had been on the ground for less than three hours and was now ready to start the long flight home. He said a few honorific words, then motioned Baxter to take over the microphone.

But instead the committee chair pulled me forward.

"Senator Gorzack," Baxter said, "is carrying home with her the answer to the anxious questions asked by sixteen families for the past two decades."

I showed the rings, the dog tags. In the baggage compartment of the plane were the newly excavated remains of the Americans buried so long ago in that faraway corner of the earth. I kept remembering the sound of the children laughing and playing. I knew that my Jack was far away from that place that was now a playground, but I also felt comforted that in a place of death, life went on.

I stood beside Baxter. For the first time since the Vietnamese doctor told me, I felt I could speak and not cry.

"I have enormous sadness and enormous relief. My husband is dead. I know that. And it causes me great pain. But the knowing of his death also gives me great comfort. I know what happened. I know."

There were hundreds and hundreds of flags.

The president and the first lady met the plane, along with the secretary of defense, the chiefs of staff, and, in the crowd, a dozen or more members of Jack's class.

Parents, wives, children of the returning MIAs were at the foot of the stairs, standing with the president. It was a strange receiving line, as we hugged and kissed and hugged again, all of us so relieved, so grateful, so very sad. My mother was there, along with Nancy and Kathleen. And Milton, who attached himself to me the second I got off the plane and stuck with me every second of the next several days.

Then came the very saddest time, as the president, the chiefs of staff, dozens of officers, and hundreds of enlisted men stood at attention while flag-draped coffins were brought from the rear of the plane. Somewhere, far on the other side of the field, two trumpets played an echoing "America the Beautiful." It would take several days for authorities and experts to authenticate the remains, to designate which bones were attached to which memories.

In Vietnam, I had been alone, even with crowds of senators and officials and government experts. But here I had my family and my friends. My mother kept squeezing my hand, as if to make sure I was really there.

The president took my other hand and led my mother and me back to his car, and, from Andrews, to the White House, where the rest of the families of the MIAs—no, the now-known-to-be-dead servicemen—would gather for a dinner.

I had been to the White House several times, for large meetings with the president, or for formal receptions. I wasn't up for much pomp and circumstance, but the evening turned out to be a very family-feeling reception. The president and the first lady were kind, not trying to pry out any details of my feelings, but offering sympathy and a chance for all of us to begin the formal part of our mourning among friends.

The president first held a short news conference in the Rose Garden, offering his condolences to the families who now knew that their son, their uncle, their father, their brother had been found in the schoolyard grave. He told the reporters that he thought there would be a better time to ask questions of Senator Gorzack, and I nodded my head in agreement.

After dinner, Mom and I went back to my apartment, where an enormous arrangement of flowers overwhelmed the coffee table. They'd been sent by Baxter, along with a lovely note. He must have made the arrangements from the plane.

"Very gallant. Very sweet. I'm really confused. I just thought such bad stuff about him."

"Sometimes," Mom said, holding out a nightgown that she insisted I put on, "good people can do bad things, and bad people can do good things. You have to figure out which category Senator Baxter belongs in."

Maybe it was the air conditioning or just exhaustion, but whatever the cause, I was suddenly cold, so cold that I got into bed and snuggled under the covers.

Mom came to sit beside me, patting my hand, chatting about how tired I must be. For the first time in a long time, she offered no advice or opinions, only her deep motherly love.

"Do you want to see the rings, Mom? I was wearing them, but they were so loose I was afraid they'd just fall off."

"Don't get out of bed. You're exhausted. I'm going to make you tea and toast and then you'll sleep."

"No, I'm not hungry. I want to show you."

I ran to get my purse, came back, and sat on the bed beside my mother, the two of us like schoolgirls. Carefully, reverentially, I took out the handkerchief so tightly wrapped around its treasure. Unwinding it, I held the two rings in the palm of my hand. For a quick second, I thought of the doctor, of his same motion.

"I guess this answers a lot of prayers, Norie."

"I guess it does, Mom. But it sure wasn't the answer I wanted."

MY FACE WAS EVERYWHERE I LOOKED.

The *Newsweek* cover hit the hardest: a color shot of the present-day me, solemn-faced, superimposed beside a black-and-white of Jack at his graduation, now a whole generation ago. The blood-red headline over the photos read: "A Reunion That Brings Tears."

Milton turned out to be just the aide I needed. He stepped in, with previously undiscovered aplomb and grace, to handle the personal details of Jack's memorial service. The only hassle came when Nina Dexter and he collided head to head over what I first thought was my senior aide's insensitivity.

It all happened in the strange limbo period, the seven days between my return from Vietnam and Jack's memorial service. I was keeping a low profile, going into the office just a couple hours a day to go over staff matters and vote.

Nina arrived at my office, carrying pots of coffee and followed by what looked like a deliveryman hauling several white boxes that had to contain pastries. She whipped past the staff and right into my private office.

"I just have so much difficulty getting to you, Norie, that I thought I'd pose as a deliverywoman." Nina purposefully strode over to the far window and plunked down the coffee-pots on the small table there, ordering the man to do the same with his boxes. "I thought a quick coffee klatch would be in order, and as you are the senator, I brought the caffeine and the cookies."

I was touched by her thoughtfulness, but couldn't quite figure out her conversational drift. *I* was the one who should feel rejected. I had asked her for help and been turned down, not the other way around.

"We've got to get going on telling your story, Norie. Yours and Jack's, of course." She leaned across the table and looked directly into my face. I have to admit I was hunting in the top pastry box among dozens of cookies, looking for something very chocolate.

"I think there's been an enormous amount of publicity, really too much." I bit my cookie and took a sip of coffee.

"No. No. This is important. That you utilize this time to tell the people of our state just how all of this happened. How you went to Vietnam. The orphanage. The doctor. Your return with Jack."

It *was* my story, but Nina was telling it as though I should learn the details. She just kept speeding along, talking about the campaign, lecturing me about the state of Pennsylvania and its unique and special voting blocs, shaking her finger at me like a dorm mother.

It was a mesmerizing performance. So it was only when he interrupted her lecture that I realized Milton was standing in the doorway.

"This is confusing, Nina. What are you talking about?" Milton asked, in his usual gentle and round-about way, making no attempt to come and join our klatch.

"Why, Milton Gant. What a surprise! I guess I forgot you decided to stay on." Nina turned and flashed me a kewpie-doll wink. "You must have really convinced him he'd have a future, Norie. Just a couple months ago, he was desperate to bolt this office. Now, Milton"—she whipped that smile back on him—"good for you. Stand by your senator."

"Hey, Nina. It's no secret that Senator Gorzack and I got off to a rocky start." Milton's slouch looked more defiant than ever, and he let the word "Senator" roll off his tongue. "But I've made a commitment to stay. And I'm involved. And I think we've got a pretty good handle on our message. And we've gotten plenty of unplanned coverage on Norie's trip to Vietnam."

"That's what you think, Milton. I'm out and around. I'm talking to voters, women voters, all over the country. And you're not pushing her enough."

"For Pete's sake, Nina, she's been on the cover of every magazine except *Sports Illustrated* and *Playboy*."

"I don't want to hear any of your usual sexist banter, Milton. There's no time for that. There's work to be done."

"That's true, Nina." Someone had to take control, and I was the senator. "You and I need to talk. But I'd scheduled this very time to meet with Milton. And I really need to go over some of the more routine matters."

"I understand. But there's a long campaign ahead, Norie. And you need women's support. And I am the person, not Milton here, who can help put that support together. So why don't we, just the two of us, get together next week?"

I nodded my agreement, and Milton actually managed a civil goodbye.

"How the hell did she get in here?" was his first volley as soon as the door closed behind Nina.

"She's just trying to help."

"Sure. The Wicked Witch of the West. What suddenly puts you on her most-important-to-elect list?"

"I think Nina is trying, was trying, to reach out, to be my friend."

"In other words, you're a lot easier to befriend when you're the top name on the network news."

"Milton, don't cut down every connection I make. And I do need the support of women."

"You'll get it, Norie. You'll get Emily's List, and that means a lot of money. And you'll get the Senate

Democratic Women's Council. And the Women's Campaign Fund. But with Nina, you get a lot more."

"I'll bite. What?"

"With Nina, you get Nina. Anyway, I have more relevant stuff to show you." Milton pulled several pages out of the folder he was carrying. "I made a chart on the computer. Nancy helped me. I'm learning how to do it."

"Great. What's the chart?"

"It's kind of a diagram. It shows how many contributors of Baxter also show up as givers or as board or advisory members to Reverend Wiggins and YANKS." Whatever bad affect Nina might have had on Milton had faded. He was grinning like a cartoon character.

"I'll bite. How many?"

"Nineteen! Can you believe it? So it's not just like Wiggins stole Baxter's name or anything for an honorary committee. Old Wiggins was pumping money right into Baxter's hands."

"Good work, Milton," I managed.

"I'm trying to find out just how the money worked. If we could turn up some kind of a fund-raising letter from Wiggins, asking for contributions for Baxter . . ."

"That would be great."

"I guess that would show who owned the MIA issue."

The bells kept me from getting into what I was afraid would be a knock-down-drag-out fight with Milton. Baxter had been terrific to me, both in Vietnam and since I'd gotten home. Of course, I had problems with his connections to YANKS, but I wanted to handle it my way. I couldn't afford another direct confrontation with a senior senator of his reputation—especially since I'd been gaining his support and respect. Why did Milton want me to take him on? Whose political advantage was that?

And everything, as I had learned, was politics. That's all people in this town cared about, talked about, worried about. What happened to government, to service to country?

I turned down Milton's offer to walk over to the Senate with me. I needed some quiet time, I said, and that was accurate. I was overreacting. There were great public servants here. It was just that for a few moments, I couldn't focus on them. The smoke of back rooms and political wheeling-and-dealing was messing up my vision.

Baxter! His mint-julep manners could sure reel me in. Now, when I was starting to like him, would he turn out to be as scuzzy as I had thought in the first place?

Everybody hated everybody. Everybody used everybody.

Nina was down on Milton. Stewart and Nina were obviously at odds. Garrett Baxter was having Wiggins help him in his fund-raising efforts. And Milton seemed determined to have me face off with Baxter in some high-noon shootout.

No wonder I hadn't made up my mind if I could run for election.

☆☆☆ **36** ☆☆☆

THE SERVICE AT ARLINGTON CEMETERY WAS SHORT and, I thought, truly poignant. That's a word I never used, and I'll probably never use it again.

The president, most members of the Senate, dozens of members of Jack's Annapolis class, and a large contingent of families of MIAs had come to the funeral mass at Holy Trinity Church in Georgetown and were now grouped around my Jack's grave. It was halfway up a hill, within sight of the graves of President Kennedy, Jacqueline Onassis, and Robert Kennedy. I liked this, since my Jack considered John Kennedy a personal hero.

I didn't cry. I had promised myself, and Jack, to cry only in private. There were too many MIA families who still were without the luxury of tears.

After the burial, the president and the first lady left

and people started saying their goodbyes and drifting down the hill. I stood surrounded by several officers who had served as members of the honor guard at our wedding. It seemed so ironic—such a long time between ceremonies, and yet they were so connected, by the flag, and the uniforms, and Jack.

A terrible wave of exhaustion came over me. I searched among the hundreds of faces that suddenly were floating past me in the hot afternoon sun. I wanted to find Milton, hoping to give him a signal to help me get to the car as soon as possible. I couldn't handle much more.

Stewart Conover was suddenly at my side, offering condolences. He squeezed my hand so tightly that my ring, the miniature Annapolis ring, cut into my finger, and I made a little cry of pain. One of Jack's friends, Chris Corrigan, turned at the sound.

Stewart grinned and stuck out his hand. Chris, half reluctantly, returned the gesture. It became a little clumsy when Stewart tried to pat me on the shoulder and Chris's arm got in the way. Stewart graciously backed off, said he would call me in the next few days, and left.

I gave Chris a look that was more a question, and he shrugged and mumbled, "Saigon desk jockey." Of course. The old inner-service prejudices die hard. I was ready to say something about it when I was distracted by the sight of an unexpected face, a friendly face beaming at me across the several yards that separated us.

Dressed in the uniform of an army captain, Bob (as I

was always going to think of him) looked spit-and-polish, fitting right in with this assembly of important people. His trim haircut, his clean-shaven face, his all-American look gave credence to his disguise. He held his finger to his mouth in a "shush" sign and gave me a somewhat goofy wave and salute.

I stared at him, half listening to the conversation around me, leaning on Chris, not quite believing that Bob was here, at Jack's funeral. Then slowly, because I couldn't cry out, I turned my head and searched the crowd for Carver or Milton or Nancy. I was sure Carter would be here. Where was he?

In a few minutes, when Milton came to take me to the car, I looked where Bob had been standing, but he was gone.

"I can stay, you know. I do have a few things waiting in Philadelphia, but if you need me . . ." My mother looked up from her already packed suitcase.

"I know. If I needed you, Mom, I'd tell you. You've been great this past week. Past *two* weeks. You're more than welcome to stay—if you want to spend the week?" My mother and I had been playing this cat-and-mouse, after-you-after-me thing all our lives.

"No. If you don't need me, I'll head back. I've sprung for a Club ticket on the Monday-morning train. If you don't take the fancy Metroliner, but the regular old-fashioned train, it's a little slower. But the first class, where they serve you breakfast, is exactly the same price as the not first class on the Metroliner. So I'm going back that way."

"How did you figure that out?" I asked, laughing.

"Jeanne Callaghan's nephew worked for Amtrak and he told her and she told me." She busied herself picking and choosing from my magazine pile. "Norie, I left you a bunch of material that I want you to look at—mail that came to the house and other stuff—some of it important, I think." She waved vaguely at the kitchen.

I nodded yes to everything, took her to the station, and was the first person in the Senate Dining Room for breakfast. I plopped my newspapers on the seat across from me, ordered fruit and yogurt, and was hunting in my briefcase for a pen to write down a passing thought when Lieutenant Carver showed up. The night before, I had had Milton call him and ask him to meet me here early.

"Lieutenant, thank you for that lovely note. And the muffins. My mother and I loved them."

"They're from a little place out in Bethesda. Been there forever."

"Sit down. I'll buy you breakfast—as long as it's not M&M's."

Carver carefully moved the papers to under his chair and sat down directly across from me.

"You might not want to talk about it, but I thought the service was wonderful."

"I didn't see you. I couldn't find you."

"I didn't want to bother you. You had enough to handle. All those old friends . . ."

"One in particular. That's why I was looking for you. I saw Bob."

"You saw Bob Sanders at the funeral?"

"At the cemetery, to be exact. And we've got his name wrong. It's Saunders Bobb." I spelled it out as I reached in my briefcase and pulled out a Xerox copy of the Bobb letter to the guys at the Ranch. I passed it to Carver, who read it between slow sips of coffee, got to the end, and went back to read it all through again.

"Wonderful. Yep. That sounds like the kind of crazy we've been looking for. And you say you saw him at the Arlington service? How did he get in?"

"He was in a captain's uniform. Very neat and military. He smiled and saluted."

"That's extraordinary. The president and half the Senate and that goofball is standing there with a uniform. I'm amazed he wasn't part of the honor guard. Too bad you couldn't have pointed him out to one of the seven thousand security standing around that day. It might have facilitated our capturing him. Since we have spent a considerable amount of time trying to do just that."

"I'm sorry. I was just trying to tell you—"

"Senator, I'm sorry. I know what all this has been for you. But this character is obviously off-base. And I'm going to give you my lecture. Not just about Bob whatever-his-name-is. I'm not so focused on Bob these days. But I want you to be a little more careful, a little less reckless. I want you to take better care of yourself. And any suspicions of people, any ideas you have about anybody, just call me. Right away. Got it?"

I nodded. There had been one depressing question

that kept popping into my head. I decided to spring it on Carver.

"Why do people kill people?" I asked him.

"It's a little early in the day for this conversation, but, okay—two reasons. Love and hate. They love the person, and feel that the person has betrayed them. Or they hate the person—either for betraying them, or having the power to betray them, or having what they don't have. A kid holding up a liquor store kills so the clerk can't identify him. A woman kills her husband for running around."

"That's it?"

"Every scenario fits into those two general categories. Take our two murders. Somebody would be betrayed by allowing the two people to live. All you gotta do is figure out who gets betrayed—and bingo, you got your murderer."

"So the murderer had to 'know' both Jake Browning and Amy Walker? Heck, can't we just start to figure out who connects with both of them?"

"That's why Bob is such a hot prospect. Someone had to *know* that Jake Browning knew something, that he wanted to tell you something."

"So between the time Jake left the memorial and the time he tried to reach me, he had to talk to someone."

"Right." Carver reached in his pocket and pulled out a pen—not the usual M&M's. "And he had to know that you were on that subway—or else he just ran into you, on his way to see you in your office."

"Okay, but isn't Bob's love and hate, well, 'old'? I

can't believe anybody would be killing someone for something that happened twenty-five years ago."

Carver sat for a long time, playing with his teacup. "That's a good point, Senator," he said. "So what do these people have in common, right now, in the present?"

Without a second's hesitation, I answered: "Me."

"That's exactly the answer I came up with, several weeks back. You weren't buying it then. Maybe it seems more logical now. If so, let me tell you—be careful. And try to think just who really loves you. Or who really hates you."

☆☆☆ **37** ☆☆☆

THE NEXT FEW DAYS I PLAYED CATCH-UP.

I have lists and more lists in my appointment book—lists of thank-yous and phone calls. I have boxes, literally boxes, of notes and letters that people all over America sent me—girls I went to high school with, people Jack knew from Vietnam, his high school football coach, the older brother of a girl I roomed with in nursing school—and people neither of us ever knew.

They sent out their condolences and their love, and somehow that time passed and I started back on my life. Only now I understood that I was starting the next part of my life, the time after Jack, after I knew and accepted that he wasn't coming back.

Kathleen, Marco, and George insisted on coming down on Friday, and took the small back room at Galileo for a private meal.

Nancy was supposed to join us, but at the last minute confessed that a young lawyer who worked with her brother-in-law had asked her out for dinner—and I insisted that she go.

I was tempted to ask Milton to join us, but I still didn't feel quite comfortable including him among my closest friends. He seemed to be trying to cadge an invitation—the dinner was certainly on my schedule—but I pretended that I didn't get his hints. Anyway, I just wanted it to be the Gang of Four.

So I was surprised when I went through the Tuscan-white dining room of Galileo and found Stewart Conover waiting at the entrance to the small private room. Then I figured it out. Of course, Marco Solari had brought him along. That was Stewart's original introduction to me. He'd gotten to be so much a part of my life that I'd forgotten just how we linked up.

"We're just going to take one minute, and ask how the week went, and then, unless you think you have to, I think we should talk about your future," Kathleen announced, after George had made a moving toast about friendship and love and brought tears to my eyes.

I waited while the waiter poured me a second glass of red wine. The room doubled as the wine cellar, and I thought that it would be great fun to have a celebration here—not the quiet, supportive dinner we were having, but a noisy party.

"What I want to talk about is something quite different from what you've got on your agenda." I took a sip of wine. "I want to talk about whether or not I'm going to run for election."

"Norie, are you nuts? Of course you're going to run. You are very, very popular in the state." George sounded almost emotional.

"George, the tragedy that happened to me is very, very popular. And maybe I can become popular too. But I don't know if I want it." The wine was good, musky and deep.

"I thought we were going to talk about the logistics of the campaign," Marco said, pulling a list out of his pocket. "About managers, issues, media. About what your message should be."

"It's an open field. The governor is telling everybody you're the one. Because that's the reality," George added.

"The most important conversation is the one about money." Stewart had spoken up. I had almost forgotten he was there: I was so used to having meals with just the other three. He pressed on: "Pennsylvania is a big state. Not just Philadelphia and Pittsburgh but six separate media markets—seven if you count Wheeling, West Virginia. Very, very expensive."

Stewart was talking to us as though he were the guy from back home and we were all inside-the-Beltway types. Then he reverted to Washington type. "You need a rainmaker, Norie. Somebody able to make the money clouds open up. I'm signing on. The corporate political action committees know you, and they'll be ready to kick in."

"I'm sorry, Stewart. I thought I made myself clear. I want to talk about whether or not I'm going to run. Can I make a difference? What are issues that *I* care about?"

"You can do a lot of good as a U.S. senator any way you want to define good. But you can't get there from here without a lot of money, without ..." George Taylor waved his hand at Stewart, unable for a moment to remember his name. ". . . without Conover and others like him. Without money, no one hears your message, your beliefs, or your hopes."

I looked around the table, and my eyes caught Kathleen's. Surely she would understand that a philosophical discussion was what should be happening. She failed me, too.

"Norie, you can't do good things unless you run—and win," she said. "Maybe you don't want to run. Maybe it's all too much. And that's your choice. I can't imagine how hard all this has been. But right now you've got to know if you're going to run or not. Having a grad-school seminar on good and evil won't make up your mind. You have to know, in your heart."

"No, I don't. Not now." I heard myself yelling, and was suddenly thankful we were in the private room. I guess my outburst showed how shaky I still was, and so for the rest of the dinner the conversation drifted between Pennsylvania politics and general gossip, the stiffness from the argument melting as the evening went on and several rounds of wine were poured.

By the time George's driver was tucking the Gang into the Lincoln Town Car for the ride up I-95, the warmth had been renewed.

"I'll take her home in a cab," Stewart assured Marco. But when the car pulled away, I asked if we could walk the dozen or so blocks to my apartment.

"Stewart, I have something to tell you. I'm a little worried about something you said tonight. In fact, I'm a little uncomfortable about the role you've begun to play in my political life."

"Me? What did I do?"

"Tonight, something you said made me feel that you've talked about me with your corporate clients, somehow, oh, I don't know. I don't even know who all your clients are."

"You think I might be using our friendship for business?"

He did have a way of bringing it down to the bottom line.

I shrugged, an answer and a question.

"Look, it's my job to be friends with senators. That's not to say I haven't been a good friend to you. I do like you. And I'd like to help you get elected. Heck, it's more than that. I care about you personally. It's hard to say more to you than that. You're still in love with Jack."

This was not what I had bargained for. And he again had evaded my question.

"Stewart, I can't have a conversation like this so soon after my husband's memorial service. Why bring this up? And why do you avoid answering questions about your clients? You're constantly quizzing me— about my motives, my life, my plans for the future. I can't get two answers out of you. It's like you work for the CIA or something."

He shrugged and mumbled something about trying to watch out for me. That somehow ended the conversation. We walked down that eerie stretch of Pennsylvania Avenue that was closed in front of the White House and then turned down 14th Street. As we neared my building, I noticed a man in an army uniform walking on the other side of the street. At first it didn't register, but at the light, I stared across.

He made no acknowledgment, but I was sure it was Bob.

I didn't tell Stewart, but I picked up the pace, rushing the last few yards home so I could call Carver.

Just when I thought I'd negotiated a peaceful settlement with Milton Gant, he went and quit.

It was all very civil. We'd had a good week, as I tried to keep in mind what the Gang kept insisting were priorities if I was going to run. Still an "if." And then Milton quit.

He looked pained, pasty again, as he had that day when he broke down over Amy's death. I probably didn't look too good myself, since I wasn't ready for the authentic feeling of regret and loss his decision gave me. I certainly had factored Milton's help into any thinking I was making about running. He was a pain in the neck—but he was becoming *my* pain in the neck.

That night, back in my apartment, I couldn't help thinking of Milton's face as he told me it was time for him to move on. What kind of nonsense was that, anyway? I asked myself. He didn't have any job to go to. Our sandpapery relationship was finally smoothing out, so that we hadn't had a blowup in, well, it had to be weeks. Our only major run-in had been over

Nina Dexter's trying to bigfoot—to use Milton's vocabulary—my campaign.

I checked the clock and decided that ten-fifteen was still early enough to call Nancy. She always knew what was happening in the office, although I tried not to trade too heavily on her insider knowledge. With only a little preamble, I started in on my questions about Milton's resignation. Nancy just listened. I went into my theories of how people who seem diametrically opposed can often work well together, and even pointed to a few encounters she and I had had over the years.

She just listened.

"Nancy, you're not saying anything. Is anything the matter?"

"No."

"Is this a bad time to talk?"

"Yes."

"Sorry. It'll hold until tomorrow."

"Okay."

I don't know what possessed me, or if when I asked it was merely a tease, but I couldn't resist.

"You don't have Milton there by any chance, do you?"

She was so quiet I could hear Linda Ronstadt on the stereo in the background.

"Hey, I'm just kidding," I managed to choke out.

"Well, you should understand that Milton does care about your future." Nancy sounded on the offensive. "Does care about your election. Enough that he would—"

There was a quick explosion of words in the background. Milton, in person, for sure. And then the dull nothing sound as Nancy put her hand over the phone's mouthpiece.

"We shouldn't go into this now," she said as she returned to the conversation, her combativeness replaced by a strained, sad voice.

"Look, if anybody has given Milton any idea that he's not welcome on this staff, that couldn't be further from the truth." And, anyway, I wanted to add, who had enough authority to convince Milton of anything? *That* was a person I wanted to meet.

"You don't have to say anything, Norie. Milton understands. He's a lot more sensitive on this women thing than you might realize. And he knows how important raising money is, especially in your first election."

I was lost. And said so.

"Nancy, unless I've fallen down some rabbit hole, none of this is making sense."

"The money. From the Democratic Senate Campaign Committee. From Senator Mendelssohn. Milton wants you to get as big a piece as you can. He doesn't want to do anything to keep you from getting your share. And if it means leaving—"

"Okay. Let me understand. Milton thinks he needs to leave to make my campaign financially successful and *feminist!*"

"That's exactly right."

"That's a pile of junk. Some of the best feminists I know are men. I don't want to have any separatist campaign. And neither does Hilda Mendelssohn. Where did he get his information?"

Again, the dull sound of a hand blotting out voices.

"He doesn't want to tell you."

"Nancy, it's late. I'm tired. Enough games. Put my AA on the phone. Please." More muffled sounds, this time long enough to give me a second chance to wonder how Milton had wound up at Nancy's. But then I told myself that it wasn't any of my business. Darn.

"Senator."

"Milton. Wonderful to talk to you. Now spill the beans."

"It was all in a confidential memo, a memo that Senator Mendelssohn sent to the majority leader. She makes it very clear that a big piece of your fund-raising base is women. We knew that. But she says you need top women running your staff. Including a woman AA. Women want to see higher-profile women in your office."

"Hilda Mendelssohn is not running my office. I am. You, of all people, know that, Milton."

"I know. I just realized, from the memo, that my staying on would prove a problem in the fund-raising department. And to tell the truth, Norie, I'd like you to get elected."

"How did you get a copy of the memo?"

"I'd rather not say."

"Milton, I'd rather not be having this conversation."

"Okay. This is really hard to tell. It makes me seem so sleazy. Anyway, I found it. At the Hawk and Dove. On a chair. I was waiting for my luncheon appointment and I saw it. It was right beside me. It said 'confidential.' So I picked it up. I just couldn't resist. You know me."

"Milton, someone else obviously knew you, too. You're a conspiracy freak. You only believe things you overhear or have to ferret out. Someone set you up. And you really fell for it."

"But I . . . ah . . . why would you think it was a put-up job? How do you know that Mendelssohn wouldn't have written that memo?"

"Because it's not the way she operates. She wouldn't even bother telling Foxy if her office was flooded with demands about an 'all-woman staff.' No woman who is operating in a mostly male world is going to tell the biggest male around that women want to be separatist. It doesn't follow Hilda's rule— to be a member of the club, even when you're also part of something new."

"I'm lost."

"You should be, Milton. I'll explain Hilda's principle to you sometime in the near future. As far as your unemployment, well—tomorrow's Friday. Take the day off. Take the weekend off. Take Monday off. You looked terrible today. You need a long weekend. Then just find your way back to the office and withdraw your resignation. And, one last thing. It could be worse."

"Like what?"

"Like you didn't decide to release the memo to the press."

☆☆☆ **38** ☆☆☆

THE DOORMAN WAS BLOCKING MY WAY TO THE elevators.

"Fabulous, huh, Senator?" He pranced around his desk, poking at the purple plastic wrapping that was unsuccessfully containing the greenery of one of the largest floral displays ever seen outside a parade. "I believe this is the record-size flowers ever delivered to this building."

He wasn't getting any argument from me. I urged him to leave it at the desk, until the Saturday-morning crew came in, but he insisted on lugging the "record-size flowers" up to my apartment.

"Look, I'll get them tomorrow morning. Who delivers flowers this late at night, anyway?"

But he said the messenger had been persistent, and

now he seemed obsessed, so I gave him the okay to bring up the gift.

It *was* fabulous. He placed it in the center of my coffee table, and then I shooed him back to his post. I had a message on my machine from Carver, saying he'd come up with new information and he'd like to get together over the weekend.

I nodded agreement to the machine as I tried to unwrap the planting. It took me five minutes just to get the plastic wrap off, and then more than a dozen plants tumbled freely in careful disarray from the center of an enormous white basket. I tried to stuff them back into the basket, but then decided that was the "design."

I thoroughly searched through the greenery, but came up minus a greeting card. I figured I'd track down the sender in the a.m., and opted for sweet dreams.

I was dreaming and it wasn't sweet. Somehow my hands had turned into alarm clocks, with burning hot metal, ringing and ringing, and I couldn't turn them off, couldn't stop the racket or the heat.

From the light on my bedside lamp, I could see that my right hand was even more of a nightmare—swollen red, great purple streaks running through rosy and puffy lumps. Good God! The left hand looked as bad. I sat on the edge of the bed, trying, through the pain, to figure out what had hit me.

It looked like an allergic reaction. My travel first-aid kit was still in my carry-on bag, at the bottom of the hall closet. It took everything I could muster to unzip the duffel, find the plastic kit, unlock the safety catch, and find the Atarax. It was a triple-strength antihistamine, in case some foreign fish or fauna played havoc with my immune system.

I was assuming that all of this was some kind of allergic reaction, and I was also fairly sure that it couldn't hurt to try to cool it down. The swelling and pain stopped at my wrists, so it looked like I was wearing grotesque Halloween gloves. I took the pills, then, painfully, I sprayed my hands with some Benadryl lotion. Gosh, did I ache!

My diagnosis was proved correct, since the cure worked—or at least it began to reduce the level of swelling and the color faded slightly. I suddenly remembered what Carver had told me weeks before. I called the Capitol switchboard and said I needed the help of the Capitol Police. I pulled on some sweats and tried to grab my purse, but had to wait until the arrival of two uniformed Capitol policewomen. Out of habit, I checked the kitchen to make sure I hadn't left anything turned on. Somewhere in the back of my head I'd already connected my ghastly hands with my late-night floral gift. But it still stunned me to see the flowers, in a droopy mangle, tumbling out of the basket, and catch a good look at the layers of shiny wet leaves that had held them all in place.

"I'd say poison sumac. That's my guess, although I'm not a specialist."

Dr. Michael George looked too young to be any

kind of a specialist or even any kind of a doctor, although he assured me he was a full-fledged M.D. and was assigned to the Surgeon General's Office.

"I just fill in here, a couple times a year, on weekend nights. The on-call person." My hands were soaking in a basin of some milky liquid he'd whipped up. Carver stood a couple of feet away, shaking his head at every sentence the doctor uttered. "This is a recipe of a cook I knew, in a camp in the Berkshires. Don't get nervous, Senator. That cook had seen a lot more poison sumac in his day than any doctor you or I would know."

Carver had sent an officer, armed with a pair of rubber gloves, back to my apartment. The young woman had reappeared carrying the basket, quite gingerly I thought, encased in a large green trash bag.

The doctor peered inside the bag at the remains. "The person who sent you this present knew what he was doing, all right. The stems have been cut so that the sappy, sticky stuff—that's what we scientists call it—so that the bad stuff was right there, just waiting to get on your hands. Did it feel yucky as you were rooting around?"

"To tell you the truth, Doctor, I was half asleep. I'd had three glasses of wine, a heavy dinner, and a walk home, so I wasn't thinking too straight."

"No major harm done. You're not one of those people who blow up like a balloon and it just takes forever to get them deflated."

"More scientific talk?" I couldn't help asking.

"You know how it is, Senator. We medico-professionals just have to keep up the mumbo-jumbo smoke screen or we'd be shown for the charlatans we are."

By the time Carver and I left the good doctor behind, it was well into Saturday morning.

"The doctor advised you to rest and eat hearty. So I'm going to take you home and cook up some breakfast." He gave me a funny look. "After I send one of the guys out for a little grocery shopping."

The drugs and the soaking took effect, and an hour later, I was—under doctor's orders—chowing down on eggs and ham and home fries. And biscuits with butter. Yum.

"Now that we've got you detoxified, don't you think we should chat a little about how you got zapped?" Carver flipped a plastic bag holding a small envelope across the table at me. "The man downstairs saved this envelope. It's how they keep track of packages they've accepted. They just keep the delivery slip."

"I know *how* I got zapped. You mean who was the zapper, right?" I looked at the block printing on the envelope. It was from a Georgetown florist.

"I tracked the florist down at home while you were getting deflated. He told me that they had a phone order for the gigantic basket, that a messenger picked it up, and that when the basket left their shop, it was minus poison anything."

"Did they know who placed the order? Man or woman?"

"Funny you should ask. It was a 'husky voice.' Very particular about what should be in the basket. How it should be arranged. The messenger came with cash. Pretty clever, huh?"

"Pretty mean. Petty. Like the hate mail."

"Whoever it is, I just want to find him."

"Me too," I said, looking up at Carver and somewhat pleased with myself. "I think we know two things. One, the zapper is not very liberated. And two, I don't think the zapper has anything to do with the deaths of Jake Browning or Amy Walker."

"Whoa. Go back to the not-very-liberated stuff." Carter was slowly spreading spoonfuls of jam on a hot biscuit. That's why there was no need for M&M's at the breakfast. The man could turn anything into a dessert.

"No big mystery," I said. "Second item first. The letter writer and the killer are just too diverse. Not the same people. You don't go around murdering people in sophisticated ways, and then turn around and send them childish nasty letters. Or zap them with poison sumac. It's just not the same person."

"And the lack of liberation?"

"The empty envelope. Mrs. John Gorzack. Not Senator Eleanor Gorzack, which is official rather than personal—and a gift of flowers is personal. Not Ms. Eleanor Gorzack, which is—oh, sort of slipshod. Not Mrs. Eleanor Gorzack, which is awful—just plain wrong, except maybe for a divorcée. Nope. Like my first nasty note, it's addressed to Mrs. John Gorzack. Very proper. Even your daughter said that."

"Of course. You're right. Most people wouldn't give

you any title at all. What do your hate letters call you? *Mrs.* Gorzack, no?"

I pointed at my briefcase across the room, and Carver extracted my files.

"That's right," he said. "Except the note that came to your office in an interoffice envelope was addressed to Senator Eleanor Gorzack—the correct form in that context."

"Yes. The zapper-letter writer obviously has nice manners, nice old-fashioned manners."

"And what does that mean, since you're on such a theoretical streak?" Carver asked.

"People with good manners, who know things like that, are usually from backgrounds where that kind of polish is necessary. Women who've sent out a lot of invitations to social events. Or, in another light, women who've worked as secretaries, and who would always use the proper form of address, as we girls call it."

"Women."

"Just what hit me as I was saying it. Women."

"So the letter writer is not a woman hater . . ."

"But—and I don't know why this doesn't excite me—the letter writer, *she*, is just a Norie Gorzack hater."

"Okay. Puzzle out your theory. What would that mean?"

"Somebody wants to scare me. To kind of *cash in* on the emotional stuff the killer is doing. The killer is keeping people from getting to me. Or from talking to me. From giving me info. *Ms.* Zapper is just plain pissed at me. Excuse my French, but that's the word."

"I would also venture," Carver said, "that the mail has been so obviously antiwoman because it is a clever way for a woman to disguise herself. Of course, they're supposed to be your people. The feminine contingent."

"The other reason it's likely to be a woman." I sped on, trying to hold the thought, "is that a woman could get in and out of my office more easily than a man."

"Come on!"

"No. It happened the other day with Nina Dexter. She came by to see me. Walked right into my office. No one stopped her. All people, especially women in offices, are used to having other women pass by their desks. If a man, especially a man in a suit, wanders by, he'll get some attention. Wow! The suit man could be somebody important."

"So women are sexist too?" Carver laughed, but I know he was taking me seriously.

"We're just not sensitive about this. When I was with the state government, if I called up an office where I wasn't known and identified myself as 'Norie Gorzack,' the receptionist would usually say, 'Hold on, please, Norie,' never Ms. or Mrs. Gorzack. If I called and said it was Dr. Gorzack calling, half the time the receptionist would assume I was the doctor's assistant. If I was a guy, Norman Gorzack, everybody would call me *Mr.* Gorzack. That's for sure."

"So we're looking not just for a killer, but a turncoat woman. And Ms. Turncoat—"

"Ms. Zapper, please!"

"Okay. Ms. Zapper. She is bothering you for what?"

"I'm not sure." Carver was annoyingly insistent, but I kept on my theoretical track. "Ms. Zapper sure doesn't want me to run for election. Not just that—she wants to rattle me, to make me personally on edge. It's weird, Carver. The murders were terrifying and tragic. But the letters kept me rattled for a long time, had me question what I was doing, how I was doing it."

"And now?"

"I just want to find Ms. Zapper. And give her a taste of her own poison. Make that sumac."

Before he left, Carver reviewed what he'd turned up on Bob. The news wasn't very reassuring. They didn't know where he was, but they knew who and where he had been—a Ranger who'd taken every postgraduate course in killing that the army had to offer.

"We know him—but we can't find him," Carver finished up.

"That's funny. I seem to spot him on every street corner. Sometimes he even hangs out with the president."

I didn't have to see his face to know that Carver winced.

☆☆☆ **39** ☆☆☆

By Monday, I was less swollen and more on edge. I'd swallowed my pills and taken it easy, and every time I looked at my hands, I wanted to use them to inflict some kind of bodily harm on Ms. Zapper. I wondered why the rack had gone out of favor.

I'd had breakfast by myself in the Senate Dining Room—back to my old Raisin Bran and fruit—and was walking down the hall when a door opened, seemingly out of nowhere, and I was face to face with Garrett Baxter. He hesitated, then invited me in, with a "Welcome to my hideaway."

Soaring windows covered two walls, and the room looked like something out of a hip design magazine. There were two deep sofas, one leather, one faded chintz, both crowded with pillows in contrasting fabric. A large, low table separated the sofas, and on the table was a tray with a silver coffee service and two cups.

Baxter motioned to one of the sofas, and after I got comfortable, he sat on the other, facing me. I was pretty sure from my comfort that these pieces of furniture were not government-issue, nor was the desk that sat catty-cornered, with the chair turned so that the view would be out the windows.

"This is very pretty, Senator. This room deserves the name 'hideaway.' It must be a wonderful retreat."

"Thank you. My father had this office. And my grandfather, although when he first served, it was his primary office. They ran things at a much more personal level in the Senate in those days."

"That's not to say, Senator, that people aren't just as attentive these days." Baxter seemed to take my remark as political, so I hurried to reassure him. "I thought your note moving, and I will keep it always. But I am most grateful for your care and concern during the trip back."

"I'm just so sorry you had to go through this, Senator," he said, pouring me a cup of coffee.

"It's better to know what happened to Jack than to be worrying about him, wondering if he's okay."

"I think you did magnificently, Norie," he said, using my name as though he had been doing it for years. "You were a credit to the Senate. A real credit. And I think your courage will be a big plus when the special election rolls around in November."

"I've been thinking about all this since we came back from Vietnam. I know now that I like the idea of being a senator, but I'm not sure I've got what it takes for the campaign. You know, being appointed was a pretty easy way in."

"Don't be hard on yourself. You should be starting to concentrate on your campaign staff. If you like, I'll have the team I used—media, grass roots, and pollster—call you up. There's no time to lose."

"That's what everybody is telling me, but I'm still not there. I don't like the idea of the fund-raising, of asking strangers for money. Do you know all the people who give you contributions?"

Baxter laughed at the idea. It didn't seem funny to me.

"I hope I never know *all* my contributors personally. It would mean my base had really shrunk. I get a great deal of money from my state, from people in both parties who like what I do—and the committees I chair. And I get a good deal from citizens outside my state who like what I stand for. I seem to get money from people, and groups, with every known agenda. I get money from a special-interest group that wants to build nuclear power plants. And I also get money from another group that wants plants—only with them it's planting trees."

I looked around the room and tried to decide if I should go on. What had my mother said about good people who do bad and bad people who do good? If I was looking to Mom for strategic advice, I was on thin ice.

"I was just wondering if you had ever noticed how many of Reverend Wiggins's board members are your contributors. Like maybe more than half his board. Not his honorary board, that you and other senators were on, but the real board, which is almost all people from Florida."

Baxter's jaw got tight, and I could see the nerve in his cheek spring out.

"I'm sure there's no correlation," he said too quickly. "Anyway, I've never been to a Florida fund-raiser. Never held a fund-raiser here in Washington aimed at Floridians. It's not my state. I'm not a clear-water, elderly-rights kind of senator."

"Well, I've got the names written down." I pulled my notebook out of my purse and flipped to the right page, all the while trying to assess Baxter's reaction. I hoped I wasn't blowing it. But then I wasn't sure what *it* was. "Ralph Poindexter. Manuel Rivas. Here's the list. There are nineteen of them."

"I'll look into this right away." Baxter took my note-book and ripped out the page on which I'd listed the contributors. "As I say, I don't know the name of everyone who writes me a check. I've been in the Senate a long time, I'm on influential committees, and, I must admit, my stands are well known. But I don't take any money from anyone to move me along or make me change my vote."

I got up.

"And how did you happen to figure out that I was receiving money from the YANKS people? I've never had another senator take such an interest in my contributors."

"Staff work, Senator. One of my staff just happened

to figure out that there were a lot of Wiggins's Freedom-Fighting Friends showing up on your contributor lists." I hoped he wouldn't ask me where the staff had gotten the list in the first place.

"I'll have an answer on this in the next couple days. Maybe some supporter in Florida 'bundled' the checks—put them together without needing me for the fund-raising draw."

I thought that was a little too matter-of-fact.

"Does bundling happen a lot?" I asked.

"Pretty common practice, but the amounts written beside these names are all one thousand dollars. That's the limit, unless I have a primary fight. Which I don't plan on having. Now, I'm going to get right on this, Senator. I'll be in touch the moment I have some hard information at hand. Are you here all week?"

"Right here, Senator. In fact, I'll be here through the weekend. I've got the Mine Workers convention, and also a meeting of health professionals. Two big speeches and a lot of handshaking. If I can shake."

"Senator, your hands—is that an allergic reaction?"

"Yes, Senator," I said, opening the door to the hall. "Somebody reacts quite badly to my being a senator."

Nancy and I worked late that night. My body gets confused signals from antihistamines, so when I have a cold—or with this allergic reaction—I'm wired from drugs that put most people to sleep.

Nancy seemed distracted, so I didn't ask her what I'd been thinking about all week: What *was* Milton doing at her apartment? It wasn't any of my business.

And besides, if she wanted me to know, she would tell me. And anyway, why wasn't she telling me unless it was important enough to keep it a secret?

I was starved for gossip of the sweetheart kind. Also, I was noticing, very physically hungry, too. My refrigerator, as usual, contained nothing but Diet Coke. But I knew who had a stash of goodies nearby.

"I'm going to get us a treat," I announced as I walked past Nancy, across the hall, and into Milton's office. I realized when I crossed the threshold that I had never been inside his office before. He was always in my office, or we were meeting in the conference room, or he was storming down the hall.

It was foreign territory, so it took me a couple of minutes to find his refrigerator, carefully built in so that it looked like a file cabinet. Leave it to Milton to make sure the amenities of his life weren't government-issue.

I popped open the door, visions of caviar in my head.

I felt the gasp come out of me like air out a burst balloon.

There, lined up in a neat little row, were tiny glass bottles, their clear liquid shimmering in the glare from the refrigerator's light bulb.

I knew what they were. Any student nurse could recognize and identify those bottles. They were as standard as the hypodermic syringe that lay on the shelf beside them.

Milton had a stash of insulin in his refrigerator.

☆☆☆ **40** ☆☆☆

I STOPPED AT THE STARBUCKS AROUND THE CORNER
from my apartment and watched as all the young
folks ahead of me ordered up a "tall *caffè latte* skinny
with a double shot" or whatever strange variation of
coffee they were all into that early morning. The
young woman working the various controls was spinning along, keeping everything straight without a
note in sight.

Her memory secret was a lot simpler than I could
have imagined. It was all in the way she turned the
paper cup. Another young woman had explained the
system to me several months before. If the Starbucks
logo was facing her, it translated as, say, a cappuccino.
If it was placed a quarter turn away, it translated as
another drink, maybe a *caffè latte*.

I thought about it as I popped some shaved

chocolate on my *caffè latte*, stuck on the plastic top
with the slit-so-you-could-sip, and got out the door. I
was trying not to think of much else, at least until I
could sit down and work through a lot of information
and ideas.

It was before eight, but the summertime tourists
were already filling in the blanks along the Mall. I
located a favorite spot near the Vietnam Memorial and
idly people-watched, at least until I finished my
coffee. Then I sat in the sunshine and pulled out of my
briefcase what I now thought of as my "annoyance"
file. Inside were copies of the three hate letters I'd
received, notes on my poison sumac floral arrangement, and, finally, the phony Hilda memo that Milton
had sent into the office the day before.

Milton! That had shaken me. But I was clear on one
agenda item—questions about Milton and about the
insulin were on hold until I got this other matter off
my desk and into the hands of Lieutenant Carver.

I had all the ingredients here—all I had to do was
analyze them. I took a piece of paper from a yellow
legal pad and drew several boxes along the left-hand
margin. Beside the first box I wrote: "scare off." Beside
the second I wrote: "insider." The third came more
slowly. Finally I printed: "advantage/influence."

The letters had been to scare me. The poison sumac
the same. Did Ms. Zapper want me out of politics?
That seemed likely, especially since getting Milton to
quit would have dearly cost me—both in expertise on
the Hill and in the election. Ms. Zapper was moving in

and out of my life as if she belonged there, as if she somehow deserved to have this power over me.

I played with my empty Starbucks cup. No matter what concoction people had ordered up this morning, it was still coffee. Coffee was coffee, and, as Carver had told me from the very beginning, crime was crime. He held firm to the conviction that there was a weird consistency to crime, and a discernible method—if only you could pick out the common threads.

So I sat with my yellow legal pad and tried to pick out the similarities between Ms. Zapper's attacks—on my sanity and my security—and my life as a U.S. Senator. I looked again and again at the hate mail and tried to read not just between the lines, but also the lines themselves. If I just thought it out, I could peel the disguise off Ms. Zapper.

I played with the cup and stared off at the memorial, and the connection was there.

Nina Dexter couldn't wait to give me a hand.

"I have to tell you, Norie, I was wondering when you would wise up to Milton Gant and his games."

I'd called Nina as soon as I got into the office, my empty coffee container in my hand. We'd arranged a working dinner, in my office, that same day at 7:30 P.M.

"I don't want to move on any of this without your input. And I want you to begin by giving me some good advice on picking the right AA." I started in along with the salad.

Nina couldn't have been more pleased.

"It's exactly what I told you, right during our first meeting—nothing pleases me more than giving the 'right' women a hand. There's just too many pitfalls, especially for a newcomer like you, Norie."

"I'm thinking back to our conversation at that Philly fund-raiser. You really made me feel you were down on me, Nina. As if I hadn't paid my dues. But now I understand what a very generous soul you are— reaching out to me, a woman, when I was the main reason Fred didn't get this job."

Give her credit, she didn't even blanch. But I knew exactly what I was mixing up. Put in the sugar, whip in those egg whites, and then beat the hell out of the whole mix.

"Fred? For your Senate seat?" Never had "your" sounded stronger. "Norie, you amaze me. First, Fred just loves the House. He loves his committee. Sure, his name was floated for your Senate seat, but Fred never gave the governor the go-ahead on even seriously considering him for the appointment."

"That's not what the governor said." Whip, whip, whip. "I probably talked to him three, maybe four times today, as we tried to compare notes. I talked to a bunch of other people, too. I talked to Senator Mendelssohn—who told me I could quote from our conversation. Nina, you've never been able to raise anywhere near the money you claim for your so-called carefully selected women candidates. You just use their campaigns to give you a power base, a *raison d'être*, here in D.C. You don't get involved with fund-raising for Emily's List or the Women's Campaign Fund or any established group—because you just can't deliver. Today I called some of the candidates you've supported. You've given them promises—and not much else. In fact, you kept them from getting their fair share from the organized women's groups—so you've hurt, not helped."

Nina pulled her icy hair above her head and dropped it down in a wave of frothy annoyance.

"That's absurd. And how dare you make calls about me, Senator? My husband—"

"Let me be clear, Nina. I've spent the whole day on you. I even had the audacity to look up an earlier part of your life. Your 'grunt' boyfriend, so to speak. It wasn't exactly as you'd like to have people believe, back there in Cleveland, was it?"

"Listen here, you bitch. You self-righteous saint. I'll have your ass. I will." In a quick lunge Nina was across the coffee table and towered above me, her face scarlet, her arm moving up, a hammer ready to pound a nail. A warning, and she froze, looking remarkably like the Statue of Liberty in a grammar-school pageant.

"I think, Ms. Dexter, that you should sit down." Carver's voice could frost hot coffee. "Just move on back, to where you were sitting, and just chill out."

She'd frightened me, even though I had known Carver was behind the door, waiting to help me. Nina Dexter scared the living hell out of me. And that's exactly what she had been trying to do.

Making sure she was firmly parked on the sofa, I stood up and walked behind my desk.

"Your fiancé, your, as you called him, 'grunt hero,' wasn't exactly your fiancé when he died, isn't that right?" I glanced at the pages of notes before me, the results of dozens and dozens of phone calls Hilda, Carver, and I had made, back to Cleveland, to florists, to the phone company.

"What right do you have to question me?"

"Wait a minute, Senator. Let me proceed. I have that right." Carver placed himself directly in Nina's line of sight before he flashed the badge that identified him as a member of the Capitol Police. "Ms. Dexter, we believe that you have harassed a member of the United States Senate. We believe that you have delivered correspondence of a threatening nature to this same senator. And we believe that you have endangered the health and well-being of a senator by use of a possibly toxic substance, poison sumac. Do you have anything to say?"

"Get me a lawyer. Call my husband. I'll have your ass on a plate."

"The psychiatrists have the first crack at her," Carver began, pacing behind one of the sofas in my office, popping M&M's. "Her husband is claiming that she's had a mental breakdown, that the burden—let me get this straight—the 'burden of electing women to federal office' was just too much."

"Although—and this is where Senator Mendelssohn was such a help—it's not Nina's first time harassing somebody," I said. It was early the next morning, and I was treating everyone—Hilda, Nancy, Milton,

Carver, Deborah—to breakfast in the Senate Dining Room. I hadn't slept much, waiting for Carver's various phone reports, but it felt good to talk about what Nina had been up to.

"First, we tracked down the name of her former fiancé," Carver continued. "Not hard. We just located Nina's high school, then talked to some teachers there, and some of her classmates."

"The 'fiancé' was a guy, let's call him Joe, who 'lavaliered' her their junior year," I said. Nancy and Milton looked lost, but Hilda, who had been key in digging out Nina's history and who was also of the lavaliered generation, nodded knowingly. "That was the step before you got pinned or got a ring or anything. The fellow gave you a little charm on a chain. Joe gave it to Nina, then broke off with her their senior year. And got involved with someone else. Call her Jean. Got engaged to Jean. Got drafted. Went to Vietnam and got killed."

I took a bite of my muffin and nodded to Carver to pick up the story.

"Nina was not a nice loser. She crazily thought Jean was somehow responsible for Joe's death. No logic, of course, but that's how she felt. Decided to torture Jean. Sent her anonymous letters, claiming that Joe had had affairs, was going to break off their engagement. Sent her a picture of Joe in a beautiful frame—but with a large red X drawn through his face."

"Nina was a lot less sophisticated then," I broke in. "She sent one of the hate letters from the real estate office where she worked. And used the postage meter."

"In three weeks, Nina was identified." Hilda picked up the story. "Her uncle, who was a local big-deal contractor, greased her way out of a court case. But everybody in their neighborhood in Cleveland was familiar with the story. And very anxious to tell us every detail as soon as we prodded their memories."

"So once we looked into Nina's background, it was clear that she was the one who had sent the hate mail and the basket of poison sumac and did the phony memo from Senator Mendelssohn," Carver said.

Milton nodded happily. "But how did you figure out to look at her in the first place?" His question, which would have sounded so innocent a week ago, now carried other, sinister connotations. Was Milton trying to understand the way I thought, the way I figured things out, so that he could avoid detection?

"The credit goes solely to your boss," Carver said. "She put it all together."

"Lieutenant Carver is being overgenerous," I said, trying to appear modest. "I kept trying to pinpoint the personality, to spot a consistent feature that would identify the person we had nicknamed Ms. Zapper. The lieutenant and I had figured out that it was most probably a woman." I paused, savoring my own reasoning powers—and the luck of a coincidence. "We knew it was somebody with a real knowledge of the Hill, and the ability to either duplicate or steal stationery from Senator Mendelssohn's office for the phony memo. But what hit me, right at that instant, was that Ms. Zapper was always *giving* me things—letters, the poison sumac basket, etc. I was thinking about this 'characteristic' of Ms. Zapper's as I was drinking my coffee at the memorial. Hey, *Nina* was always bringing me things—including coffee. The first time I met her, it was at the memorial. And there was something wrong, something off, about the way she behaved."

Milton was shaking his head, I hoped in amazement, fear, and trembling—if he was guilty of much more.

"She didn't tell me her loved one's name. She didn't show me his place on the memorial. It was a strange way to behave."

"And now?" Nancy asked.

"And now, I'm paying the bill and we're all going back to our real lives." Hilda waved for the check and ignored my attempts to pay.

"Ms. Nina Dexter is going to run up one amazing bill herself, between shrinking and lawyering," Carver added.

"Well, she said she was good at raising money for women . . ." I stopped. Nina Dexter was too tragic to joke about.

As we all walked toward the subway to go back to our offices, Carver and I lagged behind.

"Well," Carver said, "we got the person who gave you poison sumac. Now we'd better find the person who's trying to kill you, because that's harder to cure."

"Yep," I managed.

"That's succinct. Is something on your mind, Senator? Something you want to share with your old friend Carver? You seem a little evasive. Are you back to keeping secrets? Have you figured something out?"

"Nope," I announced, setting my course and sealing my fate. "Not a single thing."

☆☆☆ **41** ☆☆☆

OF COURSE, I WAS TELLING THE TRUTH. PARTIALLY.

I didn't have any new information. But I had a plan.

The real work of the Senate had piled up, and I worked longer and longer hours the rest of that week and well into the next, all on substantive, routine issues that make up most of a senator's life—and that never make it into the headlines.

Everyone involved with unmasking Nina and her schemes was pledged to "no comment." But the Hill, I was finding out, was a very small town. No surprise, then, to have Baxter call me to sympathize, and, I thought, to try to ferret out more details. Just a little too interested, it seemed.

When I asked him how his inquiry about his contributor list was going, he promised, "I'm on it. I'll have the information soon. And I think it will be very interesting."

What does that mean? "Interesting" was like "nice," as in "She was a nice girl." Baxter was elusive.

As was Stewart Conover. Absolutely pushy on the phone, grilling me about the methods I had used to unmask Nina. Then, when I gave in and told him that I'd just "figured it out," almost calling me a liar.

Who was good? Who was bad? Like Santa, I was making a list and checking it twice. For sure, there were four men in my life—there's a funny phrase— but four men in my life who were not ringing true. Now either I had surrounded myself with a quartet of rascals or I simply misunderstood innocent activity from fellows who assumed they were on familiar and friendly terms with me.

In the best-case scenario: Baxter was connected to Reverend Wiggins only by circumstance and coincidence; Milton just happened to have a week's supply of insulin in his refrigerator; Bob was a misunderstood veteran who was in the wrong place at the wrong time; and Stewart's quizzing, questions, and queries expressed only his concern.

In the worse case: Baxter and Wiggins were so intertwined in nefarious deeds that only murder could protect them; Milton was so smitten with Amy that he had killed her in a crime of passion; Bob was a homicidal maniac who confused right and wrong, friend and foe. And Stewart? He was so protective of Baxter, so interested in the unmasking of Nina, and, without my realizing it, so involved in many aspects of my

political life. I had been bothered since the day of
Jack's memorial service about the "desk jockey" label
stuck on Stewart. I wondered if the phrase meant
more than I understood.

By five that day, I needed some space. I refused
Nancy and Milton's offer to get a pizza. The memorial
seemed like such a good idea. I stopped on the way for
a hot dog and Diet Coke, spent a couple minutes
making small talk with the guys who kept the twenty-
four-hour vigil, then, in my head, started to discuss
the problem with Jack. Since I'd come back from
Vietnam, I'd felt closer to my husband, to my late
husband. I hated that phrase. To my husband. Closer
than ever.

So who do I have on the maybe most wanted list?
I thought, chewing my hot dog. I should use
Carver's rule. Love or hate. Crime is crime. Look for
consistency.

And, as Carver had insisted to me, I shouldn't leave
anybody out—even though he himself wanted to
leave out all senators. Who would kill for love? Milton
had loved Amy, but Milton couldn't kill her, I was
sure of that. Bob kept coming back on the list in the
top spot. Maybe Bob for something a long time ago.
Sometimes love turns to hate. Bob seemed to care for
Amy. And people said he was real close to Jake
Browning. And Baxter—from his lofty perch, whom
would he hate? Whom did Stewart Conover love? Did
Baxter hate his son so much that he hated other vet-

erans? Stewart had been in Vietnam. Baxter's son had been in Vietnam. Bob and Jake had been in Vietnam.

I waited, finishing up my hot dog, waited for Jack to tell me something. In front of me, the drama that was always the memorial went on, as dozens of people searched for names and then pushed their pencils across pieces of paper to make copies of a particular man's immortality. I walked closer to the wall.

"Do you need to find a name?" a park ranger asked me after I had been just standing there for a while. I looked up and smiled.

"Oh, Senator Gorzack. I'm sorry, I didn't recognize you."

"With my Diet Coke? I'm in disguise."

"But can I help you find a name, Senator?"

"No. I'm not looking for a name, Ranger." I had just figured out what I could do that would make me feel better. "Could I have a piece of paper and a pencil, the kind you give out for tracing?"

In large block letters I printed: "Capt. Jack Gorzack, USMC."

Carefully I tucked the paper between the flowers in a floral piece at the base of the wall.

"You see, Ranger, I wasn't copying a name. I was adding one. Sometimes you can't wait for things to happen. You have to make them happen yourself."

I had a plan. Not the best thought-out plan, and certainly not one that would pass Carver's muster. So I didn't tell him. My plan was to give Baxter, Milton, and Stewart try-outs, let each read for the part of friend or foe. Bob would be cast as the villain only by process of elimination. No way that plan would have gotten Carver's okay.

Milton got the first shot. I couldn't figure if I picked him because I thought he was guilty—or innocent. So I wrote off his starting position to his being the home-grown talent.

"I'm starved. Just starved," I announced to him about seven that night. We were working across from each other, papers spread out on the coffee table in my private office.

"Head home. Get some dinner. Put your feet up." Typical Milton. Tell the boss what to do.

"Too much work. What's in your refrigerator?" I tried to sound casual. "You've usually got something good." I stood up and started toward the door.

"No. Don't bother. You'd never find it anyway." Milton was waving his arms, windmill–style. "I'll check. I've got something."

"No. Let me see the larder." I was headed across the hall, past the conference room, speaking over my shoulder as he stumbled over the coffee table and bumped into the door. "I'm trying to remember if I've ever been in your office, Milton. Have I? Well, it's really quite nice. And where, pray tell, is the fridge?"

"Come on, Senator. I'll get you something. Don't bother yourself. I'll share." Milton rushed ahead to place himself between me and the place in the built-ins where I knew the refrigerator was camouflaged. "Just give me a sec—"

"Where is that refrigerator, Milton?" I started to pull

open drawers and cabinets, working quickly toward the spot I knew housed it. He got there first and planted himself directly in front. "I bet it's built in, hidden away. Let me see if I can find it."

"Really, Senator. We can just stop all this right now. I know you think you're being funny, but I don't think it's funny, and I don't want you messing around with my stuff."

Milton leaned on the refrigerator cabinet and looked menacing. He needn't have bothered.

With one quick chop to his elbow, I half pushed, half shook him off balance. He took three steps backward, and in those few moments, I popped open the refrigerator.

There, as before, was his crystalline stash.

"I don't think this is any of your damn business, Senator." Milton shoved the refrigerator shut and planted his buns right against the door. My clever whack to his elbow was a tactic left over from a two-hour self-defense class, but I could recall no way to move him from his current position.

"What's got you so nervous, Milton? Afraid I'll see your insulin?"

"You snoop! You've been looking around my office. Anyway, it's my business."

"Not when it's used to kill someone."

His hands came up high over my head, and I ducked before he could bring them down with full force. I crouched there, terrified, for maybe a minute, maybe half that time, but no blow came.

When I looked up, Milton was holding his own

head in his hands, sobbing, his tears already staining his blue Oxford-cloth shirt.

"My God, Norie," he sobbed, "you must really hate me."

I didn't answer. I wasn't sure what I was supposed to hate him about. I slowly stood up and half-guided him back to my office.

"Okay, Milton, I think we have to talk."

"It just would ruin me. You see, don't you? People don't look at you the same. They're always ready for you to fall over in a heap. Or take a fit. Or something. So I never told anybody here. Except Amy. She knew because when we spent weekends together I would need to take my insulin."

"Is that what we're talking about—that you're a diabetic?"

"Yes. Yes. I've been one since I was seven. Insulin four times a day. Like clockwork."

"And yet, when Jake Browning was killed with insulin, you never said anything. Never told Carver or me that you were a diabetic."

"Look, it's my business. I never played sports, because the doctor wouldn't give me the written permission. My mother came into my bedroom two or three times every night, checking that I was still breathing. So, a long time ago, I decided not to tell anybody. And when Browning was killed, it didn't seem relevant. I sure as hell didn't kill him, so what was the difference?"

"Milton, it's hard to believe that you didn't see any connection."

"You mean like connect the dots? Give me some credit, Norie. I'm not going to use insulin to kill somebody when I'm the only person around who uses insulin."

"And the night Amy was killed . . ."

"Carver questioned me about it. I had a date. I told Carver that. I spent the evening, the night, with somebody—but I didn't want to make her name public unless I really had to. And he said that was all right."

"And does this woman know you're a diabetic?" Two and two were giving me a big four.

"Yes. Now she does."

"And, knowing all this, does Nancy believe that you've got nothing to do with any of this?"

"Yes. She believes me."

"I hope she's right. Because I believe you too."

☆☆☆ **42** ☆☆☆

MILTON AND I GOT THROUGH THE NEXT DAY LIKE TWO people walking through Bosnia—carefully, so as not to set off any land mines.

I did believe Milton—but his telling his story, and my now knowing it, made our connection a little tender and personal. It would take some days to heal the wound caused by my trickery and his eventual honesty. Those few minutes of confrontation and collapse had cost Milton all his defenses—which was no way to leave another human being, and I was guilty.

I was also unsure about how to proceed with ferreting out Stewart or Baxter. It was bugging me. Why wasn't I clever, like one of those British TV detectives, who always know everything about opera or antiques or puddings or something esoteric? With Milton, I had stumbled on the insulin. But with Stewart and Baxter, I hadn't a clue on how to proceed.

Until the good senator showed me the way.

At three in the afternoon, my phone rang.

"Senator, it's Garrett Baxter. I'm sorry to bother you, but I'm tied up the rest of the day and I'd like to see you as soon as possible. May I stop by your home this evening? It's a little irregular, but I've turned up some information, and I'd like to talk to you privately before doing anything else about it."

"Okay." Did I sound as reticent as I felt? What was Baxter going to do, anyway? Bop me over the head? In my own apartment?

"What time should I expect you?" I asked after too long a hesitation.

"I'm, ah, waiting for some papers. Some names. Someone is supposed to deliver them to me by dinnertime. Would it be permissible to come as late as ten o'clock? We have to talk in private."

So that was a done deal. Which kind of pushed me down the path to figure things out. The senator was behind door number two. Was he a lion—or a lamb?

I needed some protection if I was going to face off with Baxter "privately." And I knew Carver wasn't going to play any games with a U.S. senator. So I figured it out: I'd confront Stewart with my doubts. He'd have to either answer my questions or fold—and I'd turn him in. If he passed, I'd enlist his help. If he failed, I'd cancel my meeting with Baxter.

The pressure was terrific. It even gave me a funny feeling about facing Stewart in private, so I set up our rendezvous in my private office. As usual, Stewart was totally helpful and conciliatory. He'd bounce right over at five o'clock.

There I was, with two hours to be really jittery. So jittery, in fact, that my phone's ringing made me jump.

"Yes, yes," I snapped into the receiver.

"Yes, yes, indeed. It's me. Carver. I picked up some interesting scuttlebutt today, from someone I know at the agency."

"What agency?"

"The CIA, that's what agency. You've got to start to get these things right, since you're running the government." He waited, and I should have laughed, but I wasn't going to fake it. "You all right, Senator? You don't sound like yourself."

I could tell him what had me rattled. He could come over and just be hanging around when I chatted with Stewart. That would make me a lot less nervous. But then I would have to put up with all his nonsense about how I didn't like Baxter. And there was no way that Carver was going to eavesdrop on another member of the U.S. Senate without a lot more cause than I had. I knew that.

"Are you okay?" he asked again.

"Yes. Yes. I'm great. I just need some sleep, and that's just what I'm going to get."

"I do have to see you first thing in the morning, Senator. So I'll catch up with you at breakfast?"

"No. I've got a state delegation meeting. How about ten a.m. in my office?"

"Only if you've still got those M&M's."

* * *

Stewart made the whole thing easy.

"So I've got a few questions to ask you."

"Shoot."

"How did you get yourself so insinuated into my life, my office, my campaign? Who are you, anyway?"

I hadn't planned it that way, but, once said, it seemed right.

"One question at a time. I met you at the Business for Strategic Interest meeting, where I was invited by your office. You called, asked me to have dinner. Drilled me a little about Senator Baxter. You asked for my help—wait, no, I offered my help in getting you on the select committee. Gave you some information that I got through a corporate source, and which you used to great advantage. And went to some meetings with your kitchen cabinet, asked by both George Taylor—whom I know in the high-tech world—and Marco Solari, an old connection. Here today because you asked me."

I was a little embarrassed. Maybe I had just conjured up Stewart's constant presence, constant questions, constant pressure. But maybe I hadn't.

"But why me? Why did you decide to help me? And really, Stewart, no personal talk about boys and girls." I was hanging tough. "Like you've always been really gracious about Jack—and about both of your times in Vietnam. But Chris Corrigan, at the memorial service, called you a desk jockey, and . . ."

He laughed and reached over to Carver's M&M candies.

"Desk jockey? Is that all? I'm surprised he didn't talk about the Five O'clock Follies. Or Spooksville." Stewart shook his head, and his hair fell down on his forehead, like a teenager's. "That's what the real fighters used to call us, stuck back in Saigon, buying information from one group of liars so we could try to peddle it to the news media, another bunch of the same."

"That's the feeling you give me, Stewart. Like you're trying to find out everything about me—ask me too many questions, steer me, push me."

He dumped a handful of M&M's on the table and began to separate them by colors. He didn't answer me, didn't look up until he finished his task, then, with one sweep of his hand, he mixed them up again.

"Looking for a pattern, Norie? I can't give you one. Want to know why I got connected to you? You're a senator. You met me. You called me." He grinned. "Only we both know that's not all there is. I am what I was. I was what I am. I work for high-tech companies. You know that. We have business overseas. You know that. You're a senator. We both know that."

"And . . ."

"And I do work for our Uncle. Not like contract work. But like we-never-let-you-out-of-your-contract work."

"You're telling me you're an agent?"

"No way. I'd be in trouble if I told you that—and a liar besides. Nothing regular. Just on call."

"And what am I supposed to make of that, Stewart?"

"Nothing. Everything. There was info that somebody wanted to get out. Stuff about MIA sightings. I gave it to you. You got it out. There were people who thought Baxter was going to bigfoot the select committee, run it as his own particular fiefdom. You stopped that. I helped get you appointed."

"You're telling me that things that I was involved with, that I cared about, were nothing. You and your, your friends just used me!"

"No. Not at all. Somebody figured out how important you were. To good causes. To doing the right thing." He got up slowly, walked over, and put his hand on my shoulder. "There are a lot of people, left over from Vietnam days, who realized what an important symbol you were. And, more than a symbol, an agent of reconciliation. That didn't do well for some other types, some people who meant harm to you. Mean harm to you. And you had to be watched. Closely."

"Watched?" Now I was mad. "You've been watching me?"

"Not just me. A whole passel of people. In your office. In the Starbucks where you like to have coffee. At the Vietnam Memorial. We've been protecting you all along. Making sure that what happened to Jake Browning, and to Amy Walker, doesn't happen to you."

He walked to my desk and picked up the receiver on my phone.

"Just dial the operator. Ask for the CIA out at Langley. Ask for the director's office. Give them your name and they'll put you through. And they'll tell you that what I'm telling you is true." Stewart grinned again. "Honest and true."

"That you've been hanging around me, feeding me information, getting into my life—because you were told to, by the CIA?"

"Ah, somewhat true. I'm not a professional. Just what you might call a 'pro-am.' The game has changed. In the old days, the agency would infiltrate countries. Now we probe companies. I'm an old hand, called in for an occasional play. No pay, no formal assignment. There are probably hundreds, maybe thousands, of us, who wear the old school tie—and are tied in for the rest of our lives. And, yes, I was supposed to do most of those things to help you, to watch you. But I did a few other things, I got a little too much into my job, because you're you. You are who you are. And that's terrific."

He held the receiver out to me, a silent question.

I answered him with a wave of my hand, and he slowly replaced the phone on the cradle.

"If I ask you something, Stewart, you won't think I'm crazy, will you? Of course you won't. Would you come and sit in my closet this evening?"

"And you think I'm strange? With ideas like that, you could be running foreign policy."

"No. I'm serious. I've got to have a conversation with a well-known senator, and I want someone to listen in. That's what you guys do, right, eavesdrop?"

"Not my line, Norie. I can't step outside of certain

boundaries. Just can't. I went too far with you today. Said too much."

"I just need you to be a witness."

"Let me just say that it's not in my self-interest—either in my professional or my semiprofessional capacity—to be a witness in a conversation between two senators. Not what the lobbying world is all about. And not what my friends at Langley would like."

"I know. And probably you will never have to say or do anything. But I'm scared . . ."

"Then you shouldn't see *this* senator."

"Stewart, I *am* going to see *this* senator. I've found out a lot more about Wiggins and his YANKS people. And I'm going to have this confrontation."

My saying it made it more a reality, even for me. "It's Baxter. You know that. I've confronted him about Wiggins, and he's coming over to see me about it."

"That's heavy. I've told you all along to stay clear of Baxter. But not because he's going to do you any harm. Except in a political sense. Norie, are you sure I can't talk you out of this?"

"No way." I held on.

"All right." Stewart sounded cranky but committed. "It will probably cause me to bankrupt my entire business plus get me in trouble with the other guys. You'll have to give me a job answering mail. But put on the teakettle and I'll come by."

"I don't expect the senator until ten."

"Garrett Baxter, huh? Well, if you have to go after a

senator, he's a big one. Clear out your closet. Here comes the white knight. I'll be there by nine."

The time dragged from when I got home at seven. I didn't even want to cook.

I watched *Wheel of Fortune* and clipped a fantastic recipe for Tiramisu Wedding Cake from *Bon Appétit*. I tried to channel-surf, but I kept getting either sporting events or shopping channels. Where did my mother find all her news?

The phone rang again. My mother.

"I can't stay on for more than a minute," I said, trying to sound calm. "I'm just overloaded with work."

"Well, do me a favor. I've had something for you since before you went to Vietnam, and I left it for you when I was down. I told you before I got on the train. I knew you'd forgotten to look at it when you didn't call me about it. It's in the drawer under your toaster. Do you see that big envelope?"

"Yes." I pulled out a slightly rumpled manila envelope. "What is it?"

"Mail. Stuff that keeps coming to my house. But also some stuff I got for you."

"Mom, I don't have time to do the mail now. I'm under a lot of pressure—"

"But this is about that YANKS thing."

"What thing?"

"YANKS. That group. The one that pink man runs, the man who spoke in front of your committee. The Southern preacher. Well, I belong. I thought I should tell you, in case there's any sort of an investigation or anything."

"What?" I yelled. "You joined YANKS?"

"It was on the TV. It sounded like such a good cause." I could hear her taking a deep breath and letting out a sigh of annoyance. "Don't yell. It was after you got appointed and before I came to Washington and I was doing my coupons and listening. I couldn't sleep. And the man was talking about you and Vietnam and MIAs and I didn't know that he was a preacher or anything. He just sounded patriotic."

"Mom, cut to the chase. YANKS. What about it?"

"Well, I sent money. For information. It sounded very informative. And it was also some kind of a contribution. And then I started getting all this stuff. I didn't read it, because I still don't think that young doctor has my prescription right. I can't get my right eye to focus up close, but with television—"

"The YANKS stuff. Please, Mom."

"I sent in the contribution in my name. So I've been flooded with stuff from YANKS. And I think if you are mad at them, I should tell them to stop sending me things in the mail. Or at least you should look at the stuff and tell me what I should do. Now don't be mad, dear."

"Mom, I'm never mad at you. I'm just tired. Thank you for putting all the stuff together. And I'll call you tomorrow for a long chat."

I hung up the phone and dumped the contents of the stuffed envelope on the kitchen table. Some of the newsletters looked familiar. I'd seen them when Linda Vespucci put them into my hands.

One unfamiliar piece, labeled "For New Recruits," bannered a headline that promised: "Inside Information—What Washington Won't Tell You."

Wiggins was one clever confidence man. Just as Amy Walker's report had pointed out, he was a whiz at changing his pitch. In the past few months he was putting less emphasis on "humanitarian heroes" and much more on "fact-finding missions" and "investigative journalists." I guessed it was easier to explain away tens of thousands of dollars spent on "investigations" than to come up with receipts for food and supplies that had actually reached peasants in Southeast Asia. Not to mention earlier appeals that Amy had found, asking for money for MIA families.

"Wow." The sound of my own voice made me jump. Here was my "sighting," a major article complete with fuzzy pictures similar to the ones in the newspaper that had started my go-round with Baxter. Just wait, I thought, until I show Senator Baxter how YANKS was publicizing the same information he'd laughed off.

Then I got it—the photo was an outrageous theft. Wiggins and his people had just lifted, stolen, my information. I had released the photo after that first hearing of the MIA Select Committee, last spring, and here it was.

I stared at the brochure for a long time. Something was here. Then I went and got my date book out of my briefcase. I flipped to find the time of the first meeting of the select committee. I checked the date against the one printed on the top of the brochure. The YANKS publication was dated a full four months before the date of the hearing—November of last year.

So Wiggins—and probably Baxter—had had the information months before, but I was the only one who made it public. No wonder Stewart's friends needed me. What kind of games was Baxter playing, anyway?

Whatever I found out tonight, I was going to have to move on it fast. I did what I should have done several hours before. I dialed the Capitol Hill switchboard and asked if someone could track down Lieutenant Carver. The operator said that he wasn't on duty, and could she take a message. I hesitated, but only for a moment.

"This is Senator Eleanor Gorzack. I need to talk to Lieutenant Carver sometime this evening. As soon as possible. It's important. In fact, it's urgent. Please track him down and have him call me. I'll wait at home to hear from him."

☆☆☆ **43** ☆☆☆

A MOMENT AFTER I HUNG UP THE PHONE, IT RANG WITH the funny buzz that meant it was the garage intercom.

"I've got my car. Want to buzz me into the garage? There's just nowhere to park on the street tonight."

"Stewart, I'm so glad you're here," I said, although I was beginning to think I wasn't. "I'm piping you aboard."

In a couple minutes, perfect as always, he arrived, lugging a big pot of geraniums, "standard issue for white knights." I took him into the kitchen and poured us both cups of coffee.

"Look at this," I started, waving the YANKS brochure around. "Here's my latest. *Your* information. Stolen by Baxter."

"Has he called you? Changed your meeting? What

is the meeting about, anyway? New information about MIAs?"

Always with the questions, that was Stewart. "No. About YANKS. And money. People who show up as big contributors on the lists of both YANKS—and Senator Garrett Baxter. What do you think about that?"

"How did you get this? The lists, I mean. You might have tipped Baxter off."

"Milton knew somebody at the FEC. There was no formal request. I've just been holding on to it. Waiting. I brought it up to Baxter days ago. Kind of a fair warning. He said he didn't know the people on the list. That he would find out how the money got raised."

"And tonight?"

"He's coming here tonight to tell me something— probably who raised the money. I'm afraid. Especially afraid now that I see that the YANKS people have been picking up on my information. On *your* information, Stewart. Look at this." I handed him the brochure.

"Exactly when is Baxter due?"

"An hour. Forty-five minutes."

"I don't think you should confront him. You can't deal with another senator this way."

"But you agreed."

"I was wrong."

"What if he's coming here to threaten me? Or worse?"

"Get out of it. Call him up and cancel. Baxter's too important to have you put him in a bad light."

"Bad light? He's a cheat and a liar. You of all people should know how this kind of double-dealing politics has to stop."

"I think you're being very naive. Look, this country is confused these days. Not many people know how to keep it on course. We've lost all our fundamental faiths. Respect for government. For the flag." Stewart shook his head sadly, as if he were talking about a death in the family. "Some people try to keep the country on course. Try to do the right thing. One of those people is Baxter, and I don't think you should try to destroy him because of a couple of checks from people in Florida."

"But I have to find out."

"No you don't. Just back off."

"No way. I'm not backing off anything. I don't know about Jake Browning. And I don't know if there is any connection between his death and the person who killed Amy Walker. But I do know that Amy was involved in finding out about YANKS. And that I told her to do it. And now she's dead."

"Amy could just be an assault," Stewart insisted. "Or our Viet vet friend Bob—well, who knows what somebody with his background is really into? Counter-intelligence. Hand-to-hand combat. Hey, Uncle Sam taught his boys to be killers. I feel bad saying it, but some of the returned vets came back a lot different from the boys that went away."

I sat listening, playing with the mail in front of me. My silence somehow encouraged Stewart to keep talking.

"There's certainly a lot of evidence that Bob knew a lot of stuff that the average GI just didn't know. Real spook stuff. Not simple intelligence-gathering, but antiterrorist, undercover, kill-the-bad-guys stuff. Like it's spook stuff to shoot somebody full of insulin."

"That was something, wasn't it?" I asked offhandedly.

I needed time. I needed to keep the conversation going. And I needed to figure out if Stewart meant what he had just said.

"It's quick. Insulin's as easy to get as aspirin, especially from outside the U.S. And with highly concentrated doses, it's fast and fatal. No traces."

"And how does it work, exactly?"

"Jesus, Norie, I don't know the details. I know that it was something spooks did in Vietnam."

"Stewart," I asked, trying to smile and having a hard time doing so, "this is crazy. But speaking of outside the country, it was so wonderful to have you at the memorial service. We've never talked about it, but did you know Jack? In Vietnam?"

"I met him at the officers' club. Once. Didn't know him well. And I was just a desk jockey. He was out fighting the war. But I remembered him. He was something else. Unforgettable."

"Do you have a good memory, Stewart?"

"One of the best. Never forget a face. Or a fact."

"Then tell me who told you Jake was killed by a dose of insulin."

He didn't miss a beat.

"You, I guess."

"Nope. Not me." I shook my head vehemently. "I said 'injection.' But Carver told me not to tell anyone what Jake was injected with—so I didn't. Think. Who told you?"

"God, I don't know. Maybe Milton. Maybe Amy."

"I didn't know you talked to Amy, Stewart."

"Sure. Nice kid."

I got up and went to get more coffee.

"Stewart, nobody, but nobody, knew about Jake and the insulin. I didn't tell anybody. And Carver told only me. And how do you know so much about Bob and what he did in Vietnam, anyway? I never talked to you about him."

"Of course you did. You're just mixed up."

"No. I'm not." Stewart looked angry, and I was suddenly truly afraid. "I'm just tired. I want you to leave. I want to think about all of this."

"Norie, I'm your friend. I'm trying to help you."

"I know. You're always trying to help me. You helped me with that information on the Norwegian sighting I used the first day of the select committee hearings. And look, here's the very same stuff, right here, in the YANKS newsletter."

Stewart only glanced at the papers. He looked sad, not angry, but disappointed.

"That's just a coincidence. All this information, all these sightings, they circulate through these groups."

"I need some time to think, Stewart. I'm going to send you home." I wanted him gone now, right now.

"And leave you to face Baxter alone? No way." Stewart reached across the table and took my hand.

"You need a friend. And I've been behind you ever since you got appointed, ever since the day you got sworn in."

I was standing by the refrigerator. My eyes instinctively swung to the side, where my mother had put several newspaper clippings, attaching them with magnets shaped like cats. There it was, in front of me every day, every time I went to get a cold drink. Big as life, and I kept looking right past it. I took my anger at Baxter's attitude toward me—and I let it blind me to seeing what was as clear as a picture in the newspaper.

"Sure you've been my friend. Here we are, together, in the picture from the swearing-in. With me. With the Viet vets. With Baxter. The picture that poor old Jake had a copy of, crumpled in his hand as he fell dead off the subway platform."

"Don't be silly. You're getting upset about nothing."

"No." I held the coffeepot tighter. I wondered if I could hit Stewart with it, could bang it so hard against his head that he would fall down, that he wouldn't be able to hurt me. "It's you. You're the one who Jake was upset about. I don't know why. But I do know that it's you. And you were talking to Amy that night. When she was killed."

"The night Amy was killed? Norie, I was with you. We had dinner. At the Monocle."

"No." One piece of the puzzle allowed all the others to fit. "We weren't together all the time. You went on ahead. I got called back for a vote."

"Lieutenant Carver checked it all out. I was seated,

waiting for you at the Monocle, for a full fifteen minutes before you got there. And we stayed there for at least an hour after Amy was killed."

I didn't listen to his explanations. I just kept on talking, laying it all out, more to myself than to him. He already knew what I was going to say. Every word made me more and more his enemy, but I was compelled to take it to the final conclusion.

"My beeper went off. I had to go back and vote. You would have had time to phone Amy. On that little cellular phone. One of your special little gadgets. You could talk and walk. Tell her you were sending somebody to meet her on her way home. To meet her right outside, near the parking lot. Tell her that you were sending her some information. She trusted you. After all, it was me, her very own senator, who had brought you into the office."

Stewart glanced at his watch, then locked my eyes with his, freezing me with his cold, vacant look.

"Norie, you're upset. You're mixed up."

"No, I'm clear-headed. You could have set it up. Right there. And then, my God, Stewart, we sat over dinner and talked and laughed. Answer me. Am I right? Did you have her killed?"

His answer was a quick, jerky movement that let him pull the phone out of the wall with one hand and grab the coffeepot from me with his other.

"I'm just going to remove any chance of an interruption, Senator. I don't want us to be bothered. I'm going to need a little time to get out of here."

"Are you going to kill me, Stewart? Are you going to kill me, too?"

"Norie, I never killed anybody. Never. Some people, people I work with, felt the need to do that. But not me. Never."

"And who are these people, Stewart? Patriots? Members of some weirdo militia? Freedom fighters?"

He put his hands around my throat and told me to quiet down.

"Who, Stewart?" I asked in a softer voice.

"Norie, sit down. I'm going to tie you up. I'm not going to hurt you. I'm just going to tie you up."

"But who are these guys, Stewart?" I screamed. "Your friends? What are they protecting that they'd have to kill people?"

"Let's say that my friends, my business associates, are running their own foreign policy. In Southeast Asia. It's the standard stuff. Guns in and drugs out. Hurrah for private enterprise. In some ways, it's no different from what Uncle Sam did for years. We're just lending support to a corrupt regime here and there, all for a good cause. Only this time, the cause is us."

"And us is what—YANKS?"

"Hell, no. Wiggins was just a convenient conduit. Right under his nose. We did what we wanted. Just used the planes carrying supplies in to ship our stuff. He thought he was subcontracting for consumer goods—telephones and batteries and stuff like that. Black-market stuff. 'We' are just guys trying to make a buck, Norie. Guys like me, who learned a lot about

Vietnam and Laos and Cambodia when we happened to wind up there. And guys interested in trade. Simple, really. Guns in, and drugs out. It would have been good to keep it up. Just for another couple months."

"And you used me at the hearings? You used me with your Norwegian sightings?"

"It was important to Wiggins, to keep his contributors convinced that they were backing a winner, that there were still lots of POWs out there to get rescued and rehabilitated. They were losing faith. I figured giving you information was good for both of us. It would make a splash for you, and give Wiggins a new hook for fund-raising. I never thought you'd figure out YANKS. Never thought you'd have someone in the office start to investigate the complaints from the folks back home. Hell, I never thought anybody in any Senate office read any of the mail, paid any attention to some fleeced citizen writing complaining letters."

As he was talking, Stewart pushed me into a kitchen chair, pulled my hands behind my back, tied them there with the phone cord. It hurt as soon as he looped it around my wrists, and when he pulled it tighter to make a knot, I cried out in pain. Stewart took a dish-towel and stuffed it deep into my mouth. It gagged me. I pushed with my tongue, but the thick cloth stayed firm. I was silenced.

"I'm sorry I told you these things, Senator, but I have to do something with you anyway. I need the time. Just a couple hours. And I'm sorry. I really am. I liked you, Norie. That part was for real. I really liked you."

Stewart took a few steps back and took out what looked like a fancy pocket calculator. With a flick of his wrist, a needle snapped out of one end.

"Nice, huh? Developed by the British. They were always a clever lot, but then they had James Bond to copy. We only had Dirty Harry."

He looked down at me and then at the refrigerator, where the other photographs from the swearing-in ceremony still dangled from their magnets.

"Bad luck, really. Browning knew me from Vietnam. Funny. I didn't remember him that day he showed up in my office. He knew me. Said I was 'scum.' I just didn't remember him. Been around D.C. too long. You run into people you don't want to. Jake had some personal grudge, I guess, over some black-market deals I had in Saigon. Bad luck, that's what it was. He came to my office that morning, the day after the swearing-in. He threatened me. Said I was a traitor. Said I had to 'own up' or he was heading off to the Hill, to tell you. . . ."

I listened, but I was trying to figure out what Stewart was going to shoot into me, how long I would have to try to get to the phone in the other room. Could I even move after he shot me full of whatever was in that needle? Was he going to kill me? Or just knock me out or something—and give himself a little time?

Then the roof fell in.

The glass from the skylight crashed down around

our heads, giant pieces and slender shards. One massive needle skimmed Stewart's forehead and blood poured down his cheek, a giant crimson teardrop. A man in a ski mask and turtleneck came crashing through the skylight to the floor between us.

His leap overturned my chair, and I found myself, still tied tightly, leaning against the kitchen counter. The impact had almost knocked me out, and I had trouble clearing my head.

Stewart and the intruder circled each other. Stewart grabbed a knife from the side of the sink, lunging and parrying. The intruder had no weapon, but he was quick.

Stewart parried and the intruder dodged.

Around and around, until a knock at the door froze both of them.

"Norie, Garrett Baxter here. Your phone is out of order. I didn't buzz. Just came up in the elevator with Senator Ballston. He lives on the floor below you. Didn't mean to startle you, but I thought it was okay to just come up."

Stewart, after a moment's hesitation, opened the door. He kept his knife pointed toward the guy in the mask.

"Thank God you're here. This guy tried to kill Norie. You've come just in time," Stewart managed. He was holding the knife out, holding Bob like a dog at bay. I knew by then it had to be Bob.

Bob managed some guttural noise, but he was stopped from advancing toward me by Stewart waving his knife.

"What the hell is happening?" Baxter almost shouted. He started toward me himself. My head swayed slightly, and the chair barely held its precarious leaning position against the cabinets.

Stewart handed the knife to Baxter.

"He pulled the phone out and cut my arm pretty bad. I'm not sure I can hold him off. If you think you can manage him, I'll go next door and call 911."

I couldn't scream. The dishtowel was still gagging me. I threw my head, side to side, and banged my feet on the floor.

Stewart started for the door. He was almost through it when Bob began to shout, in a terrible, primeval voice, rusty from lack of use: "Liar. Liar. Liar. Traitor. Traitor. Traitor. Traitor. Traitor. Traitor."

Stewart was edging past my tilting body.

My head must have finally cleared. I shot my leg up and inserted one violent kick between the legs of one Stewart Conover.

He doubled over with pain, and Bob smashed him over the head.

As Baxter fumbled with the knife, still unsure who was the real assailant, Carver ran through the door, gun drawn.

The policeman looked at the shambles around him.

I was still tied to the chair. Stewart was doubled over in pain. Bob once again was held at bay, this time not so much by Baxter with the knife, but by Carver's gun.

"Terrific, Senator," Carver announced. "Now my only question is whether or not the good guys won."

☆☆☆ **44** ☆☆☆

"I STILL AM TRYING TO PUT TOGETHER ALL THE PIECES."

I had joined Garrett Baxter for a drink in his hideaway and was pleasantly surprised to find Lieutenant Carver there, a tall drink already in his hand.

"You're lucky, Senator Gorzack," Carver offered, "that we're not having to put the pieces of your head together. I thought you and I had a deal that you were going to call me with any suspicions. Then I'd have had the chance to act like a policeman."

"I did call you. I called the switchboard. And I felt like a fool for suspecting . . ." I took a deep sip of my vodka tonic.

"Suspecting me? Why not? When I looked at that list, I thought I might be guilty myself." Baxter nodded approvingly at his own words. "I was coming to tell you that you were right. And that in the morning, I was going to track down the name of the person who had bundled that money."

"And it was Stewart?" I couldn't believe my own good luck in sitting here discussing the details, all of us intact. Thinking about it made me both sad and furious. "I should have caught on even earlier, I now realized, when Stewart mentioned that the contributors were 'from Florida.' "

"Stewart knew an awful lot of stuff. It was hard to keep it straight," Carver offered.

"I was introduced to him as one of the good guys here. Marco Solari didn't know him that well, only that he could raise money. He was clever—even showed up at a small dinner at Galileo as though I had invited him. And I thought Marco or George had."

"Stewart was a well-liked guy all over town. He'd given money to candidates in both parties, didn't ask for much, and was a genial fellow," Baxter said. "Stewart had a sweet thing going. He was a lobbyist, making a decent living of more than two hundred and fifty thousand a year."

Carver said, "I'd say that's a decent living."

"Yes. But it was puny compared to Stewart's real income—millions, from what's been going on in Southeast Asia."

"Well, he was a Washington rep for other people, too, Senator," Carver interjected. "One of my friends in the agency calls Stewart's buddies 'the graduates.' Kind of a ragtag group of what we used to call 'formers'—former military guys, former spooks, even a former journalist."

"And that's how Bob knew him?" I asked.

"No, Jake Browning was the person who knew Stewart. Recognized him as someone he knew in Vietnam, a guy who operated as a black marketeer. Browning was obsessed by people who he thought had done wrong in Vietnam. He'd researched the whereabouts of many people he hated for their activities there. Kind of his own personal war crimes tribunal. So he saw Stewart's picture with you. Confronted him. Warned Stewart off you, then went off to his own death."

"From what Bob's told me," I said, "Browning told him that Stewart had been involved in bad stuff in Vietnam and was probably just as crooked back here, in the States. Certainly not the kind of person to be hanging around me. That's what Jake Browning was coming to warn me about, before Stewart sent his 'associate' after poor Jake."

"Bob couldn't tell us anything. First, because he was afraid he wouldn't be believed even if he could talk," Carver said.

"And typing out an accusation of murder on a computer screen doesn't really cut it," I added.

"And, second, he had no real proof. Just what Jake Browning had told him."

"How is Bob?" Baxter asked.

"He's going to be in the hospital for a couple weeks. Out at Bethesda Naval. We've got some people who think they can help him. It's some story," Carver said. "The voice thing is apparently totally psychological. It's very much what the guys at the Vietnam Memorial had put together. Bob went into North Vietnam with a Special Forces group. But their information was wrong—or the Cong had simply decided to beef up their troops at this one location. The rescuers got cut off about a hundred yards from where the POWs were held. Then the Cong drove them back. When the helicopters took off, Bob kept yelling to the prisoners, telling them they'd be back to rescue them. It was the last thing he said until he confronted Stewart in Norie's apartment. I mean Senator Gorzack's."

"I think we've been through enough that we're all on a first-name basis," I said.

"And what will Stewart Conover's punishment be, Lieutenant?" Baxter asked. "He's been involved with the deaths of two people, not to say the deaths of who knows how many more, with the gun trafficking and dope smuggling."

"Stewart's probably going to get immunity by turning himself into a federal witness." Both Baxter and I groaned. "I know. But I don't make the laws. And we're still not going to know very much, since I'm sure old Stewart kept himself purposefully ignorant."

"But my God, man, what about the murders?" Baxter asked.

"Stewart's claiming that he killed neither Amy nor Jake. He simply fingered them, or, as he so gently put it, 'moved on them.' He said he assumed that Amy was just going to be knocked over the head and her report stolen," Carver said.

"Wiggins is still on the radio," I added. "Now he says that he will prove that every cent is going to help

'Asian-American children. The tragic legacy that our GIs left behind.' In fact the good reverend is just about claiming credit for tracking down the bad guys and bringing peace and justice to the nation's capital."

Baxter got up and refilled all our glasses, then sat down shaking his head.

"I feel like a fool," Baxter announced. "It was Stewart Conover who put together the checks from Florida contributors. I never dealt with him. I'd never even met him. He just offered the help to my fund-raiser—who took the help, took the checks, and never asked any questions."

"I've got a question, Senator Baxter," I countered. "We didn't nail them, did we? We didn't get the bad guys."

"We nailed them some," Baxter said. "We stopped them from doing what they had been doing. Running arms and drugs through Wiggins." He paused. "But maybe they're off doing it somewhere else, or through someone else. Probably are."

"Not very encouraging, Senator," Carver said.

"It's okay, Lieutenant. That's what we basically do up here, on this white shining Hill. We shore up one piece of the wall, the wall that holds back the barbarians. As soon as we get one piece done, another cracks. But time and again, we do mend the wall and we do stave off the barbarians."

We sat and sipped our drinks and gazed down the Mall at the sunset over the Washington Monument.

Finally I spoke.

"I still might be ambivalent about some of what's

connected to politics. But there are a lot of good people, up here on this Hill, who are busy building up the wall."

Baxter colored under my praise.

"There's a lot more to being a senator than I ever realized." It took a minute for me to figure out just why Baxter and Carver were laughing so hard, but then I decided to join them. "Anyway, I didn't know you had to be a detective, too."

SPECIAL TO *HARRISBURG PATRIOT*

HARRISBURG—Sen. Eleanor Gorzack, whose few months in public office have turned her into a national figure, announced today that she will run for election.

Don't Miss
Senator Norie Gorzack's next
suspenseful mystery

Capitol Venture

by Barbara Mikulski
and Marylouise Oates

Coming Soon in
A Dutton Hardcover